CORSAIRS: ADIRON

CORSAIR BROTHERS BOOK 1

RUBY DIXON

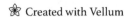

For everyone that struggled in 2020.
(I'm pretty sure that's all of us.)

CORSAIRS: ADIRON

It's not easy being a space pirate...

Actually, wait.

Yes it is. It's keffing awesome.

The three va Sithai brothers — that's us — cruise the universe looking for abandoned ships, treasure, and other pirate ships to rob. Right now, we're on the hunt for the Buoyant Star, an abandoned cruiser rumored to have a massive treasure inside. The ship's been found at the edge of an ice field at the far reaches of space.

That treasure? About to be all ours.

But the ship's not all that abandoned. The Star is crewed by a few lonely, attractive human females who are thoroughly grateful at being rescued...

Actually, wait.

They're not grateful at all.

They've set us a trap, and their leader, a beautiful human female named Jade, gives me a smile just before she captures me.

It's official. I'm in love.

1

ADIRON

*I*t's so noisy in the V'tarr cantina that I can barely hear myself think. Not that there's a lot going on between my ears regularly, but there's a reedy instrument wailing just over my shoulder that's making it hard for me to concentrate. I kind of want to reach over and shove it down the musician's throat. I mean, my brother Mathiras wants us to create a diversion, but I'm not sure attacking an innocent musician will do anything other than make me look like a keffing ass.

A music-hating ass, to boot. And there's a lot of things you can be in the universe, but if you hate music, people look at you funny.

I scan the busy cantina for my other brother, Kaspar. He's still at the bar, leaning against it, trying to look oh-so-casual as he nurses a beer. He looks pissed, too, and I suspect that's my fault. We're not sitting together because we're trying to blend in with the locals on V'tarr Station. That's proving a little tricky considering we're the only two mesakkah in the entire damn cantina...

Our eyes meet and he gives me an impatient look.

Right. Diversion. We're supposed to create a scene without drawing attention to ourselves. Cause a little chaos in the cantina so the authorities will show up here and Mathiras can do some light-fingered work on the local records in search of mentions of the *Buoyant Star*, the long-lost ship we've been chasing these last two months. V'tarr's the biggest port in this far-flung system, and the most convenient re-fuel spot. If the V'tarrians haven't seen that particular ship, it means our search area is narrowed down by quite a bit. We'll find our ship through process of elimination if nothing else.

Mathiras has the hard job—hacking into the V'tarrian systems and extracting the records without being noticed. Me, I just have to sit here and make a scene.

It's something I should be pretty good at. I'm not the brightest out of us three, but I'm pretty good with my fists. So, as I sit in my booth, I look for something to hit. Someone ugly. Doesn't matter the species. My fists are equal opportunity. I look around the place. It's dark, a little smoky, and crowded. The booths are spaced a good distance apart, allowing people to walk freely between them, and the bar curving along the far wall is shoulder to shoulder with males of every species...with one blatant exception. My brother, the mesakkah. Among them, Kaspar stands out like a sore thumb, and that's going to make it difficult for us to quietly make a scene and slip out.

"Hello there, handsome," a female voice trills.

Uh oh. I look up, and one of the cantina girls is smiling at me. She's one of the locals—the bird people with delicate yellow down covering their skin and legs that bend backward. Got a nice rack, though, and I smile at her. "Well hello to you."

Out of the corner of my eye, I see Kaspar make a face and turn back toward the bar, no doubt thinking I'm distracted again. He should know me better, though. Females are nice to flirt with, but I'm not buying company. If I wanted to purchase the affection of a female, I'd be with Shaalyn at this moment.

The avian female beams at me, sliding into the booth to sit at my side. A friend sits across from her—another cantina girl, judging by the filmy outfit that leaves nothing to the imagination.

"You look like a male with a lot of credits," the avian female trills, brushing one of her breasts against my arm. Her hand touches mine, where I'm holding my drink, and it takes everything I have to keep smiling.

"Looks can be deceiving," I say easily, picking up my drink and shaking off her hand. I do a mock-toast to the ladies. "Mine is an empty wallet."

"Mmm, I don't think so." She leans over me, her breath smelling like ooli brew. Her tits are definitely pushing against my arm, no matter how much room I try to give her. On the other side, the female scoots around the circular booth and moves in my direction.

Trapped.

"A mesakkah on this end of the universe? You're not broke." Her friend giggles and touches my other arm while I shift uncomfortably. "You're a pirate, aren't you?"

I scoff. "Me?"

"Mmmhmm." They both eye me. "And pirates are never broke. You can buy a round." The one on my right taps the table, bringing up the drink request system.

I guess I can. I let them order, sipping my drink. Maybe I can find some interesting stuff out from them. Maybe they know something about some of the ships that come in. I glance over at Kaspar, who's still glaring in my direction, and I get a different idea, one for a diversion. "So, do you ladies entertain or do you just drink up a male's credits?"

They both giggle, the sound a bit more like shrill cawing

than I'd prefer. "You interested in entertainment?"

"No, but I know someone that might be." I wonder what Kaspar will think if he suddenly gets two avian females all over him when he's trying to pick a fight at the bar. He'll probably kill me later.

I bet it's still worth it. I pull out a few credits and slide them across the table. "See that blue male at the bar? I bet he'd like company."

The first female leans over my shoulder, giving me a sultry look. "But we want to stay with you." She taps a long, spindly finger on my cheek. "You seem like fun."

"I really am," I agree. I'm definitely the fun one. Also the dumb one, but who cares about smarts when you're having a great time? And right now, I'm starting to enjoy myself. I could send these two over to Kaspar, get him all riled up, and when he's distracted, I can start a fight. There's a fat merchant with a few bodyguards in the corner—and a few more of the avian females at his booth—that looks like he'd be ripe pickings for a fight. I do know that I can't really start anything with two females hanging off my arm. I don't fight with females.

Well, unless it's Zoey. But she's my sister, so it doesn't count.

I gesture over at Kaspar. "They say you can get to know a man by the company he keeps," I say.

"And what does that say about your friend, who is alone?"

"It says I have to pay pretty females to talk to him." I give them a grin and throw another credit on the table. "Will you go and make his day better?"

"Eventually," the one on my left says, and clings to my arm. "Maybe we like the view here at the moment."

Flattery is always nice, and I've got a few minutes. "I admit, I am pretty good to look at."

"And soooo modest." They giggle. The handsy one on my left clings to my bicep. "So what brings you to V'tarrian space? We don't see your kind much around here."

"Oh..." I don't have a good excuse, so I stare at my beer and try to think something up. I lift my drink, trying to play this off all casual. "This and that? Wrecked ships and uh...other stuff."

"Do you know Lord Straik, then?"

I spit my beer all over the table. Uh. Do I know Lord Straik? That's an absolutely random name for a female to bring up. "Like...Lord Straik sa'Rin? From Homeworld? Why do you ask?"

She shrugs and drags a finger down my cheek, and I wonder if she'd be offended if I asked her to use plas-film? I don't know where her fingers have been, after all, and this cantina isn't exactly clean. "He's been buying weapons around here."

I shoot a worried look over at Kaspar, coughing loudly to try and get his attention. My brother, meanwhile, is arguing with the male seated next to him, no doubt looking to start a fight and get that distraction going. We have bigger problems, though, if Lord Straik is in this region. He's a mesakkah with deep pockets, an army of clones at his disposal, and a massive chip on his shoulder. If he's hanging out in V'tarrian space, he's not doing anything good. "What's he buying weapons for?"

The clingy one pouts, holding her hand out.

With a sigh, I put a credit in her hand.

She pockets it, her smile returning. "I heard he's buying weapons for his private army...because they're going to take over a ship."

"Take over a ship?"

"Find a ship," the other one corrects. "They're looking for some lost ship. Came in here and asked a thousand questions about shipping lanes and such." She rolls her eyes and drinks the last of her ooli brew, then eyes the ordering system. "Can you buy us another round, friend?"

"I think I have to go," I say, and get to my feet.

The females pull me down again, just as Kaspar grabs his barstool and slams it over his neighbor's head.

2

ADIRON

"*I* can't believe you two keffing idiots," Mathiras rages as we race onto the bridge of the *Little Sister*, several V'tarrian guards hot on our heels. "What happened to 'create a diversion to peel off the guards and sneak out'?"

"How are we supposed to sneak when we're the only mesakkah in the entire V'tarrian system?"

"You could have tried a little harder." He pauses to shove Kaspar up the ramp, since our brother seems determined not to leave without finishing the fight.

I automatically grab at Kaspar's shirt and shove him through the *Sister's* door, something we've gotten down to a science. Most battles end like this—us knowing when to pull out and Kaspar too stubborn to do so. So between Mathiras and myself, we've become experts at hauling Kaspar's ass out of danger.

And they say *I* am the dumb one.

"We're not done here," Kaspar complains, trying to aim his gun around my horns. "We can take them—"

"You're our navigator now," Mathiras reminds him, easing up the ramp with his back to me as I hover in the doorway. He keeps his eyes on the V'tarrians who are no longer racing for us but for a control panel—no doubt to trap us before we can take off. "Go and keffing navigate! We've got to get out of this place!"

Kaspar growls, then turns and races for the nav panel. Mathiras continues to back up, shooting. The enemy is pinned down behind a crate, but I see someone race ahead and I know it's just a matter of time. In his way, Mathiras is just as bad as Kaspar in never wanting to leave a fight. So I grab him by the collar and haul him backward onto the ship, then slam my hand on the hatch release, the door zooming shut.

Mathiras glares at me, putting his blaster away. "I was coming," he mutters.

"Sure, sure." We both head for the bridge.

"Why do you smell like ooli brew?" Mathiras asks, glancing over at me. "And why are you all wet?"

I just grin. "You said you wanted a distraction. I jumped into the bar fight that Kaspar started. And I might have made the bartender angry."

He sighs.

"And a few barmaids." I pause, considering. "And some cantina girls. And a patron or two."

"I told you to blend," he complains as we move onto the bridge and slide into our seats. "Fighting with everyone in the cantina isn't blending."

"Neither is being blue, but we didn't realize that was a problem until we got there," I point out. "We stood out no matter what." I flip switches at my seat, running checks on the landing gear and initiating the ship's protective shields as the engine fires up, whining as we begin to lift off. "Weapons systems?" I ask, my hand hovering over the next panel.

Mathiras shakes his head, concentrating on his controls. "They're trying to detain, not destroy. I don't think they realized that I hacked their records. It's probably just about the bar fight."

"Then we did good." I grin broadly...and then sniff my clothes. Whew. I do smell bad. Like I rolled around in an ooli's armpit.

Kaspar glances over at the two of us as the *Sister* lifts off, heading for the rapidly closing gates on the station. "Did you get what we needed, then?"

"Yes and no." Mathiras shakes his head. "I got in, but I couldn't find records of the *Buoyant Star*. If she came through this system, she never made it here. It narrows things down... but not by much."

I grunt, scratching at my damp, itchy tunic. "So what now?"

Mathiras shoots me a look, as if I'm an idiot for asking. I'm used to that sort of look, though, so it doesn't offend me. "We worry about getting away from the authorities, first. Then we figure out our next steps."

"Nag, nag," I tease, but I double our shields as we zip narrowly out of the gates. Just in case.

A short time later, I'm in the shower, washing off the stink of sour ooli brew and thinking about the *Buoyant Star*. And Zoey. And Sophie.

Sophie's gonna be so pissed that it's been weeks and weeks since we left her with my buddy Jerrok, and we're still no closer to finding the *Buoyant Star* and all its fabled riches. She seemed forlorn and unhappy when we left her behind, and after a month of being in Jerrok's company, I can only imagine how mad she is. Jerrok's a trustworthy sort, but he's not exactly friendly. Or clean. Or pleasant. If Sophie doesn't give us a verbal lashing that scours years off our lives, I'll be surprised. I should send her a comm, but I can't exactly give away our position in space. We're currently hiding the *Little Sister* on the dark side of one of V'tarr's far-flung moons. Once the coast is clear, we'll head out again, moving in a different direction as we send out a tracing signal for the *Buoyant Star*. It's pure luck that we found the records—and the private frequency ID—that the *Buoyant Star* was using before it disappeared. That means we're the only ones that will be able to pick up a distress signal, no matter how old. And if she's active (for whatever reason) we can just say hello. With the frequency ID, it's like looking for a needle in a haystack, as Zoey would say. Without the frequency ID, it'd be like looking for a needle in an entire field of haystacks. At least we can narrow it down, bit by bit.

The payoff will be worth it...I hope. Because once Zoey finds out we're in the off-limits Slatra system on a treasure hunt, she'll blister our ears with her choice words. She hates it when we risk our necks. Doesn't matter that they're our necks to risk —as our younger sister, Zoey, feels obligated to look out for us, and to tell us when we're being keffing idiots.

Myself, I know hunting for a fabled ship like the *Buoyant Star* is likely going to end up in failure. The stories passed around cantinas could be all wrong. Maybe it's not filled with riches. Maybe it wasn't abandoned on the edges of space. Maybe it wasn't called the *Buoyant Star* at all, and it was just a merchant vessel that showed up on station on time, offloaded her cargo, and the stories just grew because people get bored in deep space.

But...it's something to do. I've struggled ever since Zoey left our crew to go mate with Sentorr of the *Jabberwock*. I know she's ridiculously keffing happy and I want that for her, but...I miss having my mouthy little sister around. Feels like there's a hole in the crew and it's sucked all the joy in piracy right out of my system. I suspect it's the same for Kaspar and Mathiras.

We're all looking for something to excite us again. *The Buoyant Star*—for all that it could be a wild chase leading nowhere—is our distraction for now.

I sigh, looking over at the mirror above the sink. If Zo were here, I'd write a stupid message in the mirror for her to find when she takes a shower. Usually I'd leave something like "Your feet smell" or "I stole your snacks" just to make her laugh. There's no one to write a message for anymore, and I feel stupidly empty. It's not the same without Zoey on board.

I miss her. I'm almost as miserable as I was back when I discovered the truth about the female I thought I loved. Shaalyn. I hope her new mate gave her a communicable disease. I hope they're both riddled with sores. Great, big, gross ones.

And then I check my junk, just to make sure the universe isn't going to punish me for wishing something like that on someone else. All's clear, though. I give my cock one last jiggle under the water and then turn the shower off.

The moment I start to towel off, the bridge clicks on over the comm. "Uh, hey...Mathiras?" It's Kaspar.

Mathiras chimes back from the engine room. "What?"

"Did you run into anyone we should know about back on V'tarr Station?"

A pause. "No, why?"

Kaspar sounds tense. "Because we're being approached by another corsair vessel...and I'm pretty sure this one is from Homeworld."

"Homeworld?!" Mathiras sounds puzzled. "What the kef are they doing out here in the Slatra system?"

"Great question. You should also be asking why they're hailing us and demanding we surrender."

"Surrender? I'm coming to the bridge."

Uh oh. I haul the towel around my hips and hit the intercom. "Hey...so uh, you guys will never guess what I heard back on the cantina."

"What?"

I'm not sure which brother it is, but I'm pretty sure it doesn't matter. I click over again. "I might know who that ship belongs to..."

"Get your ass in here, Adiron," Mathiras snaps. "Bridge. Now."

"On my way," I say cheerfully. I mean, if we die, I should go out with a smile. I'd make an ugly corpse with my face all snarled up. I tie the towel around my waist even tighter, then run a comb through my hair. Again, an ugly corpse is not how I want to be remembered. Zoey would be totally pissed to see me looking like shit at my own funeral.

Zoey.

I stare at the fogged mirror, think for a moment, and then soap up the tip of my finger and use it to write a message.

Lord Straik sa'Rin.

There. Even if we don't make it back to mesakkah-space and the *Little Sister* does, Zoey will know whose ass to kick.

3

ADIRON

"You...forgot." Mathiras's voice is flat. He scowls at me, his hands behind his head as we march through the ship-to-ship hatch over to the enemy vessel. "Are you keffing serious, Adiron?"

I shrug—not an easy task given that my hands are behind my head, too. "There was a lot going on."

"You forgot," he echoes, disgust in his voice. "Well that's just great."

It's not like I've had a moment to think straight since we left the cantina. First there was the bar fight, and then I had to pull Kaspar off of a particularly ugly szzt fellow who looked as if he wanted to remove Kaspar's head from his body. Which...I've been there. Anyone that's met Kaspar has wanted to choke him at least once or twice. But Kaspar's my brother and I've always got his back, so I waded into the fight instead of slipping away and got doused with a dozen drinks. I'm pretty sure I soaked up some of the alcohol through my skin, because by the time we raced back to the *Little Sister*, I was feeling good and loose. And then we had to race the ship out of V'tarrian airspace, and then there was my shower and then we got hailed by Lord Straik sa'Rin. Since they'd caught us by surprise, there was no time to escape.

Or put on pants.

It was either go in fighting or try diplomacy. Kaspar wanted to go in fighting, of course, but Mathiras wanted diplomacy. As the tiebreaker, I chose diplomacy. Much as I love a good fight, I remember what the females at the cantina said about the lord and his army of a'ani clones. We can take out a small crew easily. An army of clones is an entirely different matter—and sa'Rin's ship is three times larger than ours.

Unfortunately, we didn't even get the chance to try diplomacy. Once the larger ship locked onto the *Little Sister*, they sent a pulse through our ship, knocking us to the floor and freezing us in place. I don't know what kind of weapon that is— some kind of shock-collar for an entire ship—but I know we've gotta get one for ourselves.

Now we're here, aboard Lord Straik's massive ship, and captive. Not our finest moment. At least I left Zoey the message I did. Maybe she'll find it someday.

We keep our hands on our heads as the clone bodyguards lead us through the ship. I glance over at Kaspar, but he's not looking at me. He's looking around at anything and everything, clearly spoiling for a fight and just waiting for the right moment. Picking a fight with at least ten guards around us—all of them armed and us not—would be the height of stupidity, but Kaspar loves stupid odds. Even I know this isn't smart. Using my tail, I smack him on the ass to get his attention.

Kaspar turns and glares at me. "What?"

"Let's just see why we're here before we try staging a break-out, huh?"

One of the guards nudges me in the shoulders, a silent command to shut up.

"Isn't it obvious?" Kaspar hisses. "We're being robbed. Considering that we rob people for a living, you think you'd recognize the signs."

I scoff. "Look at this keffing ship, you noodle-brain. You think this guy needs our little ship? Think again."

"Will you two be quiet?" Mathiras snarls. "I can't think when you're arguing."

This time, the guard walking behind me gives me a shove, and Kaspar gets the same. "All of you keffing shut up or you get shock collars."

I shut up. Kaspar glares at me, but his gaze wanders to our surroundings, and I suspect what I told him is sinking in.

It's obvious to me that whatever Lord Straik wants, it isn't our "riches." The *Little Sister's* a decent ship thanks to our constant work on her, but to the rest of the universe, she looks like a piece of junk. She's also a Class IV freighter, which is usually a passenger ship. No one's going to think we're hiding a ton of snazzy cargo somewhere on board. As far as robberies go, we'd be a shitty target. And this ship we've been dragged aboard is of a much finer make than ours.

Lord Straik's ship is cutting edge technology. The metal walls of the corridor are cool and pristine, without old scorch marks from blaster fights or dents from, say, getting into a noogie-fight with your brother. The endless hallways we've been dragged down are large and airy and well lit, the temperature comfortable, and to me, that says more than anything else that this is run by a male that doesn't care about credits. If he knew how much it'd cost to change out the air filters on a ship like this, he'd run something smaller. The *Little Sister*, for example, has tight, short hallways because the less living space that has to be climate-controlled, the better.

He's definitely not after us for our credits. Especially not a corsair that can afford to feed an entire score of a'ani body-guards as well as a crew. So then...what does he want?

We're led down another hall, and at the far end of this one, double doors are flanked by uniformed, red-skinned clones. One nods at our guards and taps the door panel, then steps aside. We're then brought into a large chamber, and I stare at my surroundings in utter surprise. I expected a war room and this...looks more like a keffing fancy retreat. There's art on the walls, old paintings of important-looking nobles, tapestries from distant colonies, and a few golden-looking weapons that are clearly for show and not actual defense. In the corners of the room, expensive flowering plants curl around wrought trellises, and I swear I can hear the tinkling of a fountain somewhere. On one wall, there are several large star maps pulled up on-screen, and across from the screens there's an enormous window that looks out on deep space. Right now it's full of the V'tarrian moon's dark side, but I imagine it's a nice view most times. There are vases and books on elegant shelves, which is kind of ridiculous in a spaceship that can lose gravity control in a solar storm, and I spend a happy moment imagining those expensive vases flying through the air and landing on our captor's head. At the far end of the room, near the wall of vid-maps and star charts, is a huge desk made of impractical wood and covered in ornate carvings. It looks very heavy, very expensive, and completely ridiculous. There's a marble bust of a mesakkah lord on the desk, and it only adds to the realization that stupid amounts of credits have been spent on this male's room, a room that would be completely destroyed in a single battle.

Something tells me this lord never actually gets into fights. He just shows up and browbeats his opponents with his superior ship and masses of troops at his disposal.

Lord Straik sa'Rin stands with his back to us, gazing at one of the star charts, hands clasped just above his tail. His hair is long, which isn't surprising as most mesakkah society lords prefer that sort of thing. He turns and I'm surprised to see that he's young. Certainly younger than me, and I'm the youngest of my brothers. He looks a bit sulky, this lord, dressed entirely in black clothing with dozens of fasteners and a shoulder cape. His horns are extremely ornate, the metal tooled with intricate patterns, and he's got piercings all up one ear. His collar is high so it's impossible to tell if he has any tattoos or scars, but I suspect not. I'll eat my trou if he's seen a sniff of war.

Guess it doesn't matter if he has or not, because we're his captives now.

4

ADIRON

"*S*o it's true that there are other mesakkah in the Slatra system." He sounds bored as he addresses us, striding forward, his hands still clasped behind his back. "You know you're not supposed to be here."

"And you are?" Mathiras shoots back, glaring at the lord.

Lord Straik scowls at my brother, his expression one of extreme distaste. I imagine his nose crinkling up like Zoey's when she smells Kaspar's boots, and smirk. "I have reason to be here," the mesakkah lord eventually states. "And your presence is affecting my business." He pauses and looks at me. "Why is this one naked?"

"That's *my* business," I quip.

Mathiras smacks me with his tail. Lord Straik just looks at me as if I'm a bug. He turns to one of his clone soldiers, and in the next moment, one of the males steps forward and wraps a towel around my hips. Guess my junk was a little offensive to high and mighty Lord Straik.

Mathiras glances over at me and Kaspar. I'm watching him and the lordling, and I don't look over at Kaspar on my other side, because I know he's shifting and flexing his wrists, trying to loosen his cuffs. I'm not too worried about our situation. This isn't the first time we've been outnumbered or taken captive, and as long as we keep our wits about us, I'm sure we'll be fine. Wits aren't my strong suit, but Mathiras is smart. He'll figure something out.

And until then, I'm kinda interested in hearing what this lordling has to say.

Mathiras eventually speaks again, drawing the attention back on himself. I flex my wrists in my cuffs, too, but all I get is shooting pain going up my arms. Ow. "I don't see how our presence affects you at all," he says. "We're not here for trading or anything of the like. We're just...pleasure cruising. Exploring."

"You started a bar fight on V'tarr Station," Lord Straik snaps back. "My invitation from the Voo Rees has been rescinded thanks to you. Another mesakkah showing up would put too much of a target on their dealings, and so I've been told to leave the system."

"Well now, that is a pickle," Mathiras says easily. "The Voo Rees, did you say?"

He doesn't look over at me, but I know what my brother's thinking. The Voo Rees is an infamous cartel that operates on the fringes of known space. I've never dealt with them, and they're just a legend to most of the universe, because they control far-flung systems that the mesakkah empire doesn't touch...places like the Slatra system.

Also, the Voo Rees are connected to the *Buoyant Star*, our legendary lost ship. It's rumored that there was supposed to be an utter fortune-making cargo on the *Buoyant Star*, heading right for the Voo Rees cartel headquarters on V'tarr, but it never made it there. What that cargo was, no one knows. But it wouldn't keep making stories circulate if it wasn't something impressive. Even if it's not, the *Buoyant Star* itself was a sleek, well-made vessel. If we find her, we can scrap her for parts and at least break even.

That's the theory, anyhow. Me, I'm holding out for a big payoff. If nothing else, I want an adventure out of things...and right now, it's paying off.

Lord Straik looks irritated. "It's none of your business what my connections are."

"Is that why you're here in the Slatra system? You doing their dirty work?" Mathiras is clearly trying to get under his skin, insult him. "Playing pirate?"

Straik narrows his eyes at Mathiras. "I could shove you out my airlock right now, you know. No one would be the wiser."

"Or you could turn us in to the cartel," I add helpfully.

Mathiras kicks me.

I give him a glare, because I'm helping, damn it. "What? I'm just saying." At least if he turns us in to the cartel, we're still alive. "I'd rather be cartel bait than bouncing off an asteroid."

"Or..." Mathiras drawls, glancing over at Straik. "We could tell him what we know about the *Buoyant Star* as collateral."

Oh. Or we could do that. "Probably a better option," I mumble.

Lord Straik stalks over to us, his black robes swirling around his legs. That's another impractical thing for space. I know the mesakkah lords prefer flowing materials and ornate robes for clothing to show how rich they are or something, but in space, clothing is best when it fits tightly. I imagine Lord Straik floating through his room of vases, his skirts above his head because his ship lost gravity, and fight back a snicker.

Everyone looks at me like I'm crazy.

Straik glares at me, then at Kaspar, who's utterly silent, and then moves to Mathiras. "Did you say the *Buoyant Star*?"

"Maybe. What's it to you?"

"That is my family's ship," Straik bites out. "It's precisely the reason I'm here and working with the Voo Rees. Tell me what you know."

Mathiras lifts his chin. "Why, so you can space us and pretend we never met? No thanks."

The lord stalks back and forth, robes swirling, and I snort-chuckle again, still stuck on that mental image of floating skirts. It's hard for me to take a male seriously when he's dressed in something so keffing impractical. "What's your family name?" Lord Straik demands.

"Va Sithai," my brother Mathiras says proudly. "I believe you've heard of us."

That makes Lord Straik pause. "I do know the va Sithai family," he murmurs, rubbing his chin. "It's a very old family, much like mine."

"Which means if you space us, you'll be blacklisted from every decent society function for the rest of your life if they find out you're our murderer." Mathiras is calm and cool. "And we all know how terrible that would be for your family."

Lord Straik snorts. "Not much of a threat there. I'm already blacklisted. And it's not as if anyone would find out where you went. Your ship will be found, eventually, drifting through V'tarrian space, and no one will be the wiser as to what's happened to you."

It's Mathiras's turn to glare. At my other side, Kaspar shifts, and I know he's still hard at work on his cuffs.

I glance around the room, because our next option is to fight our way out. There's the two a'ani by the door, but the others left us alone with Straik. Either he's bluffing or...well, I'm not sure what else. But I'm pretty sure he's bluffing. "I might have already sent a message," I casually mention. "If you kill us, it's just a matter of time before you're rounded up. I've already alerted our sister Vanora back on Homeworld that your ship approached ours."

Lord Straik freezes. "Is that so?" He turns to his men. "Find that communication and stop it."

"It's not a vid comm," I blurt out, and Mathiras looks at me like I'm crazy. "It's...a secret comm."

And it's on a mirror. On our ship. Which...in hindsight is probably not the best way to send a message, but I guess he doesn't have to know that. And it's not going to Vanora, either. It'll go to Zoey, if she ever figures out that I've sent it.

Lord Straik sa'Rin takes a deep breath and then begins to pace. He clasps his hands behind his back and shakes his head at the guards, indicating they should remain where they are. He paces back and forth slowly, glancing over at us. "So. You've ruined my plans with the Voo Rees and yet I can't kill you. What options are left?"

"We can work together," Mathiras says boldly. He gestures at his cuffs. "Take these off and we'll work with you. We've got intel on the *Buoyant Star* that no one else does. You need us if you want to find it, and we can split the treasure four ways."

"Why do I need you?"

"Because you're not very good at playing pirate," Mathiras says bluntly. "And you have a crew that takes orders and won't think beyond obedience."

"Buuuurrrrn," I whisper, using one of Zoey's favorite human sayings. "Super burn, brother."

"Shut up, Adiron," Mathiras fires back.

"Yes, do shut up," Lord Straik says. He focuses on Mathiras. "If we work together, the split will be fifty-fifty—half for your household, half for mine. It's only fair since the ship does belong to my family."

"Yeah, but it's salvage," Mathiras counters. "And if it's been abandoned for three years, it falls under salvage law, which means anyone can claim it. So that doesn't hold. And you need us. We have the frequency they used and star charts downloaded from their navigation systems."

The lord tenses, eyes widening just a bit. "How did you get that?"

"We stole it from other pirates—" I begin, but Mathiras kicks me.

"Doesn't matter," Mathiras overrides, giving Lord Straik his most arrogant grin. "All that matters is that you need us more than we need you. Seventy-five, twenty-five."

"Absolutely not," Straik retorts, pausing in his pacing to glare at all of us. "If we're taking my ship and using my troops, I'm taking on the bulk of the responsibility. Fifty-fifty."

I shake my cuffs at them, because they're starting to hurt my wrists. Plus, I have to take a piss. "Can we figure out the financials later? Some of us are tired of being treated like prisoners."

The lord smiles thinly. "Very well." He nods at his guards, who approach. "I guess you're my guests, then."

"Well, kef me," Kaspar says, and flings aside the cuffs he's managed to pull off and throws them at Lord Straik's feet. He sounds disappointed. "Guess I don't need to bother with that anymore."

5

ADIRON

*I*t takes a week of arguing before Mathiras and Straik settle on a sixty-forty split. In that time, we eat Straik's amazing food, use his fuel, and play Sticks with his crew constantly. So...I guess sixty-forty works, since the sixty is in the va Sithai favor. None of it matters if we don't find the *Buoyant Star*. I let Mathiras and Kaspar squabble over star charts with Lord Straik and do my best getting to know the crew. After all, if we're in a pinch, I'd much rather rely on the crew than Straik to save my ass.

Plus, they know a lot about their employer.

So I play Sticks and eat in the cantina with the clones. I get to know them and play up being the dumb, easy-going brother. It's not a hard role for me to take on. I *am* the dumb brother. But I'm not so dumb that I can't learn a little, and so I do my best to befriend our clone friends. I make sure everyone's drinks are full, I lose more credits than I win, and I listen to a lot of gossip.

Seems that Lord Straik is not the most colorful member of the sa'Rin family. Lord va'Rin—the head of the household—married a human, which I'd heard, and pushed Straik down a rung, inheritance-wise, when the human Lady va'Rin gave birth. I knew that much, but I didn't know that sa'Rin threw a temper tantrum after the birth of the youngest va'Rin and refused to mate the female he'd been arranged to be joined to since birth. The family was shamed by his actions and he was cast out of the good graces of society.

Which might explain why he's out here in the middle of nowhere, but doesn't explain why he's so eager to partner up with us. I know something about being the black sheep of a household. After all, me and my brothers come from a good family, but our reputation as corsairs has put a bit of tarnish on things and our sister Vanora won't speak to us any longer. Family tends to frown upon credits made by piracy, no matter how badly the family might need those credits. If Lord Straik thinks he's going to return to his family's good graces by robbing and pillaging through the galaxy, he's got a few things to learn.

And they say *I'm* the stupid one.

To my surprise, the a'ani army actually likes the lordling. They speak proudly of serving him, and when I inquire about them being slaves, I'm told that he's purchased all of them and freed them, and they earn a wage serving as his crew. That isn't what I expected to hear from a sulky brat of a lord like Straik, but it makes me like him a bit more. They also say he's brave and isn't afraid of a fight.

He does wear black all the time though. "I'd bet my entire pot that even his underclothes are black," the a'ani captain of the guard states. His name is Dopekh and he's become a good friend. Plus, he's a decent partner in Sticks. I'm sitting across from him with nothing but two credit chips left to my name, the rest of the pile on Dopekh's side of the table. The a'ani shakes his head, grinning. "He's a good leader, but he does have a certain look about him."

"Your entire pot?" I pretend to consider the credit pile in front of him. I don't need the credits and I suspect that Dopekh does, but I do love a challenge. "You're on. Where's his laundry chute?"

Dopekh's brows go up. "You're serious?"

I throw my sticks down. I was losing anyhow, and this sounds like more fun. "Of course I'm serious. Let's see if these underclothes of his are as severe and ridiculous as everything else he wears."

Dopekh hesitates, then a grin spreads across his face. "You think they'd have a cape?"

Underclothes with a cape? I snicker at the thought, because Lord Straik does love himself a cape. "A small one for his tail."

The a'ani laughs and then gets up from his seat, and I do, too. Then we race down the hall, heading for Lord Straik's personal quarters.

Lord Straik sa'Rin's enormous ship is called *The Darkened Eye*, and I'm not sure if that's supposed to mean something or if he just thinks it sounds impressive. I'm told that the ship has two eyes painted on the front of the hull, which seems pretentious to me given that we can't see the hull, but Lord Straik is a man who loves nothing more than appearances, so I guess I'm not surprised. As Straik's guests, our quarters are between his and the a'ani, and while ours aren't large or posh like his, they're decent quarters. I suspect we all share a laundry bot, though, and when I get to the hall that houses our rooms, I pause, waiting for Dopekh to catch up.

Now that we're in front of Straik's double doors, my companion looks as if he's having second thoughts. I'm not going to let him walk away from his bet, though. Dopekh hesitates, gesturing at the ornate doors. "Those will be locked."

"We don't need the door," I tell him, moving to the closest

wall panel and running my fingers along it. I've learned a few things from my years as a corsair—namely that wall panels on a ship can hide anything and everything. Since the laundry bot in my quarters picks up my clothing and disappears into the wall, I suspect it does the same for his rooms. The first panel I pry off reveals nothing but pipes and wiring, but the second one I pull off has the bot I'm looking for.

With a grin at Dopekh, I haul it out of its dock and pull it into the hallway. "This thing weighs as much as your mother," I grunt as I haul it forward.

Dopekh just snorts. "Your insult is useless. I have no mother. And Lord Straik likes clean clothes, I guess." He grins at me again. "You ready to be proven wrong?"

"Absolutely." Though I forget which one of us bet that his underclothes would be black. Don't suppose it matters. I pry the lid off the bot and pull out a few pieces of wet clothing. I don't find what I'm looking for at first, but then at the bottom... sure enough.

I yank the wet black underclothes out of the bot's belly and hold them triumphantly into the air. "I had black!"

"No, you idiot," Dopekh tells me, laughing. "I had black! You took my bet. That means you thought they were another color!"

I twirl the piece of clothing on my finger, just out of his reach when he tries to grab it. "Does it matter? The point is that his ass is just as pretentious as the rest of him."

"What the kef are you doing?" calls an angry voice.

Whoops. Busted.

6

ADIRON

aspar stares at me with an expression of confused disgust, his hands on his hips. In this moment, he looks just like Mathiras, disapproving and disappointed in me.

I lower the wet underclothes and toss them back into the bot. "This isn't what it looks like."

Kaspar turns slowly and eyes the large chunk of wall that I've pried the panels off of, then at the wet clothing strewn in the hallway. At the embarrassed clone at my side. "I'm not entirely sure what this looks like," he admits. "But can you not piss off our host? For five keffing minutes?"

"Maybe," I say grumpily and nudge the bot aside with my foot. "We were just having fun."

"I've been pinging your personal comm for ten minutes," Kaspar says, his exasperation giving way to that look of pure excitement on his face. "We've picked up a distress call on the frequency."

My eyes widen and I go still. "On THE frequency?"

Kaspar nods. "That very one. If you're done playing around with Lord sa'Rin's laundry, can you join us in his war room?"

"Right. Sure." I wipe my damp hands on my trou, hoping they don't smell too much like soap, and give Dopekh a sheepish look. "Uh, I've gotta go, buddy."

The clone just rolls his eyes. "I'll put everything back together. But if anyone asks, I'm blaming you."

I just laugh, because he might as well blame me. When you're the stupid one, you also get to get away with a lot more. "I guess you get to keep your credits for now," I tell him, reaching over to ruffle his hair like I would Zoey. He looks a bit like her, given that he doesn't have horns or mesakkah plating. Sure, he's bright red, and male, and a lot taller, but...he could be an overfed human. In a way, it makes me miss Zo because she was always up for my bone-headed schemes. "I'll catch up with you later," I tell Dopekh and jog down the hall to meet Kaspar.

My brother is already leaving, heading back the way he came, his tail swishing with impatience. I'm used to running after Kaspar, though, so I catch up easily and nudge him with my shoulder. "So, a distress signal?"

"Yes. Which you'd know if you spent more time on the bridge with the rest of us."

I make a face. "You really don't want me there." I'm not good with star maps. One quadrant looks much like another in my eyes, and I'm bad at charting fuel-efficient courses. The last time they let me navigate, I burned through all of our fuel because I wanted to get a good look at a double-ringed planet. I mean, if you can't enjoy the view, what's the point?

Kaspar doesn't answer, mostly because we both know I'm right. "The distress signal has to be from the *Buoyant Star*. It's the only thing we've picked up on this particular frequency. And it's in this quadrant, too. We're really close." He lifts his hands and cracks his knuckles, like he always does when he's antsy.

"I'm surprised anyone's still on board after three years. What're they saying?"

"Nothing. It's just the signal. There's no voices at all, which I thought was weird." Kaspar shrugs. "It might be that there's no one alive to turn off the signal."

The small hairs on the back of my neck stand up. "So it's haunted."

"It's not haunted."

"It might be. You said it's in this quadrant, right?" I gesture at one of the windows we pass by as we head for Straik's quarters. "Look around you, brother. This quadrant is utterly abandoned. You said yourself the only thing in this particular system is a couple of Class C planets." Class C means low resources and not eligible for colonization at this time.

He nods. "And the only one that supports life is an ice planet with poison air. No one's visiting this system at all. It's totally deserted...which is why it makes sense that the *Buoyant Star* is out here. Who's gonna look for her near a shitty little binary star on the fringes of a forbidden system? No one, that's who." His eyes light up with enthusiasm. "Except us."

"Still say it's haunted," I grumble, but I leave it at that.

We enter Lord Straik's apartments, and my brother Mathiras is standing next to Lord Straik, both of them regarding the star map up on screen with intent faces. Over the last few weeks, while I've been befriending the crew, Mathiras has had his head down with Lord Straik, insisting on going over every star chart of the Slatra system. He seems to be handling the loss of the *Little Sister* better than myself and Kaspar, who's still bitter about the fact that our ship was abandoned. "We'll get her back," Mathiras has told us a half-dozen times. "Let's focus on getting the *Star* and making our fortune, and then we can retrieve the *Sister* at a later date. No one's going to find her this far out off the beaten path."

I'm not so sure about that. I suspect Zoey is gonna come looking for us after not hearing from us for a while, and she's gonna be super pissed if all she finds is an empty ship. But Mathiras is the smart one, so I don't point this out. Personally, I think he likes working with Straik. They both seem to be cut from the same plas-film. They both take things way too seriously, spend all their time planning for everything, and basically don't enjoy life much at all.

"I'm here," I announce as I approach them. "Let the fun begin."

Both Straik and Mathiras shoot me disgusted looks.

"About time," Straik says.

"Why do I smell soap?" Mathiras asks.

"You don't want to know," Kaspar replies.

I rub my hands, doing my best to look as excited as the others. "So. Where's this distress signal? Can I hear it?"

Lord Straik turns back to the star map and touches a small section of it. The screen sharpens, zooming in on the area he touched. "It's coming from the vicinity of this particular binary star, right at the edge of the ice belt." He touches the screen again, zooming ever closer. "In fact, it might be too close. Perhaps that's why it was never heard from again."

"It iced over?" I ask. "What's an ice cloud doing out here?"

"Sometimes a planet disintegrates," Mathiras tells me as if I'm a child who's never cracked open a vid-lesson. "With the pull of the sun—in this case, twin suns—being too great for it to handle, it falls apart and creates a debris belt. In this case, it's ice." He gestures at the screen. "Nothing but pure ice as far as the eye can see."

"Sounds like Kaspar's last date," I joke, nudging Mathiras.

Both of my brothers—and Straik—glare at me.

"Oh come on. That was a good one."

"Can you be serious for a moment? Just one?" Mathiras puts a hand on the console and taps it. A noise comes out, the particular unique, ear-screeching klaxon used for all distress signals, followed by the ship's registry number and name, read aloud by the ship computers. Normally, though, a distress signal is followed by a statement from the distressed ship, but there's nothing but silence from the *Buoyant Star*. Mathiras turns to me. "Well?"

"Ghosts," I say again. "Definitely ghosts."

Kaspar lets out a pained sigh.

"It's not ghosts, you noodle-brained idiot," Straik snaps. "Ghosts don't exist. Someone's on board that ship or it's been abandoned. Either way, I need to get there and recover her. That is my family's legacy."

"Why do you care so much about your family's legacy if they kicked you out?"

Straik glares. "No one kicked me out. We had a disagreement or two. That's all."

Kaspar coughs into his hand. "Not what I heard."

Mathiras glares at both of us.

Why does he care so much about his family's legacy? It hits me and I laugh. "You want to buy your way back into their good graces, don't you? That's what this is. You don't give a keffing flip about what's on that ship, you just want to show Mommy and Daddy that you're a good son and you can be invited back to Homeworld again."

"Someone shut him up." Straik rubs a hand over his face. "His constant nattering is giving me a headache." He gestures at the screen. "Besides, it could be a trap."

I snort. "Are you kidding? It's most LIKELY a trap." Glancing between my two brothers, I continue. "How many times have we chased a distress signal only to find that it's more pirates waiting on the other end?"

"Dozens," Kaspar admits. "But that just means more people to rob. More credits for all of us."

Mathiras gives him a dirty look. "Here's the thing. I know it seems too good to be true. After weeks of searching every nook and cranny of this keffing end of the universe, it doesn't make sense to find her just sitting so quietly out here. It sounds like a trap for sure." He glances at the map and then touches a portion of it again. "Here's the thing, though. It could very well be a distress signal. Look at how close it is to the ice belt. Now, compare this map to one that's ten years old." He flicks through a few images on the screen and then lines the two up next to one another. "The ice belt is moving in rotation, no doubt being pushed along by the force of the other planets." He gestures at a point on the map. "The distress signal is coming from here."

"Right in the path of the ice belt."

He nods, a thoughtful look on his face. "If they get swallowed up, it's going to be a constant barrage of comets and asteroids hitting the craft. It'd tear anything stationary to shreds in a short matter of time. That could be why they're sending out a distress signal instead of just leaving the area. Maybe they can't. Maybe their engines died and they're just floating and waiting for rescue." He pauses. "Or...it's a trap."

"I know which one I think it is," Kaspar says, grinning. He cracks his knuckles again. "But if it's a trap, there'll be more than just one ship. And that means more for us to take home."

"We can definitely make our fortunes," Mathiras admits, and he's got a smile on his face. At Straik's scowl, he adds, "Or at least sixty percent of a fortune."

"The *Buoyant Star* was the largest cargo ship of the va'Rin fleet," Lord Straik says, crossing his arms. "Whatever cargo it has on it, it should belong to my family."

"Except the laws of salvage declare that whoever finds it at this point gets to keep it," I point out. Even I know that. "You get forty percent. Not more."

The mesakkah lord turns and glares at the screen, a pensive look on his face. "We'll see."

7

JADE

I'm fast asleep in my room when Alice wakes me up, shaking my shoulder. There's a look of worry in her big eyes, and her heart-shaped face is lit up with a mixture of excitement and fear.

I know that look, and I sit up the moment I see it. "A ship?"

"A ship," she agrees. "A big one."

"I'll get dressed. Get the others and have them come to the bridge?"

"I'm on it, cap," Alice says in a jaunty voice, racing away again before I can chide her for the "cap" crack. She always calls me that and it drives me crazy. I'm the oldest of our small group, so I'm unofficially in charge. But just like Alice, I was a slave brought on ship. And just like Alice, I was a slave left behind when the others abandoned us. That doesn't make me captain of anything.

I shove my legs into a pair of pants and throw on a wrap-shirt that Ruth made out of discarded uniforms, and then I race toward the bridge to meet the others. My hair's a mess, but it can wait a little. I need to see what the situation is first. I race down the silent, empty halls of the *Buoyant Star*, my bare feet slapping as they hit the ground. When we were first left behind, I found the ship creepy. It was so deserted and empty it felt like a tomb. But after three years of this, it no longer bugs me.

It's home. As much as we have one anymore.

The doors whistle open as I head onto the bridge. The *Buoyant Star's* bridge is enormous, every bit as big as a spaceship this size deserves—at least to my unknowledgeable eyes. It's got enough seating for twenty, each with different control panels and button set-ups. There's a captain's chair in the center of the room (complete with its own set of controls) and one massive wall is a view out into space. Most of the time, we see nothing but stars. I can see Alice is there with the others. Ruth's slouched in her favorite chair, her long legs stretched out in front of her, black hair falling in front of her sulky face. Helen sits across from her, legs delicately folded, and there's a look of such excitement on her perfect features that it sends a surge of adrenaline through me.

"A ship, Jade! Are we excited?" She gives me a bright smile, waiting on a verdict.

"I don't know yet, honey," I say. "Let's see what we've got, first." I move toward the window, gazing out. The ship's the size of a lemon on the massive screen, but as I watch, it's getting closer and closer. "How long do you think we have, about an hour?"

"I think that's about right," Alice says, coming to my side. She crosses her arms under her breasts and regards the sight with me. "They've been hailing us, so they absolutely are coming for us."

I stare thoughtfully at the approaching ship. I don't ask Alice if she hailed them back. I know the answer to that—we don't know how. We only know how to use a handful of the buttons on the wealth of controls on the bridge. We've been floating, stranded in space, for years now and we still can't speak or read a lick of the language. No one's here to teach us, and the computer won't acknowledge us in the learning programs because we're cargo.

I study the ship, trying to compare it to the others we've run into. Most of those ships have been smaller. I don't know much about spaceships, so I always compare things to fishing, since it feels like we're stranded out in the biggest ocean ever. The *Buoyant Star* is like a whale, floating alone on this edge of the universe and in a class of its own. We've run into a few ships of different shapes and sizes, the biggest being the size of, say, a dolphin in comparison. Impressive on its own, but nothing to the "whale" we're currently in. Most are the size of regular fish, small little cruisers that the pirates like to run. The cruisers are easy to strip and launch back out into space, their control system not nearly as complicated as that of the *Star*. I was hoping we'd have another one of those middling fish, just the right size for us to steal supplies and turn out.

But as the ship steadily approaches, I feel a ping of worry. This isn't a regular fish we've caught with our bait.

This might be a shark. It's not quite as big as our whale, but it's pretty big, and I'm growing more concerned by the moment about the size of the crew she'll have on board. We can handle two or three pirates. We've handled five once, though that involved a lot of trickery.

We're gonna need a fuckton of trickery if that approaching ship is full of pirates.

I take a deep breath, thinking, and then turn back to "my" crew. "We've got a live one, girls."

"Yay!" Helen says, clapping her hands with excitement.

"Not yay," Ruth hisses. "I'm so tired of this slave girl shit. I don't want to be bait this time." She sits up in her chair, pushing her dark hair away from her pale face. "We need a better plan."

"This one works," I tell her. "Unless you've got something up your sleeve, we're going with what works."

"Ugh," she groans, dropping back into her chair again like a sulky teenager. "I hate aliens. They're such fucking hornballs. The moment they see human tits, they just lose their damn minds."

"That's exactly what we're counting on," I say tightly, glancing over at Alice. "Anyone else object to the plan?"

"Nope," Alice tells me, shaking her head. "I'm good with the slave girl plan."

"All right, then."

Helen clasps her hands in front of her chest. "Who's who today?"

I glance at my team. Even though we've done this at least three times before, I get a nervous feeling in the pit of my stomach each time. We've been stuck here together for three years and we've come to think of each other like family. More than family, even. I cried when I was taken from Earth and everyone I loved, but that's nothing compared to the devastation I'd feel if I lost Alice, Ruth or Helen. It'd be like missing a limb.

Alice is my can-do girl. Even though she's small in stature, she's up for anything and everything. She jokingly refers to herself as my sidekick, the Robin to my Batman. Her two blonde topknots atop her head make her look younger than she is, but she's got a pretty face and an elfin build that the aliens seem to like. I think they're attracted to her diminutive stature.

Ruth, on the other hand...Ruth is beautiful, but she's also quick to declare that she hates aliens. And space. And lying. And...whatever else she can think of. With her long black hair and pale skin, she reminds me of an old-school goth. She's the crankiest of our small group, but she's smart and good with her hands. She's also tall, with long legs, and if our aliens are the frog guys, they won't like that she's tall and intimidating. First impressions are so important for our plan to work.

And Helen is...well, she's Helen. She came out of her stasis tube fully grown and absolutely new to the world. She's a fully adult woman, but everything is new to her. Literally everything. She's innocent as hell and it terrifies me to put her into any sort of dangerous situation but...she's perfect bait. Helen is some sort of strange species that's utterly, completely breathtakingly beautiful. She's mostly human-looking, but she's got bright red skin and long, silky lavender hair. Her catlike eyes have the longest lashes I've ever seen and they're an equally stunning shade of purple. Her figure is perfect, and her mouth is full and pouty. She's even got pretty iridescent fins on the backs of her arms and legs, and a bit of webbing between her fingers. I don't know what she is, but she's so overwhelmingly beautiful that we started calling her Helen after Helen of Troy.

So yeah, Helen needs to be bait. The male aliens lose their minds every time they see her.

As to my role, it depends. I'm not as young as the others. I'm thirty-three, and I'm pretty sure that Alice and Ruth are both mid-twenties. Helen is apparently a fully grown three, since we're counting the years that she's been out of the stasis tube (since Helen has no memories prior to that). Alice has blonde hair, Helen purple, and Ruth's hair is long and silky. Mine's kinky and coily, and even though I've been growing it out, it puffs around my head, wild and untamed. My skin is a rich shade of golden brown, which the aliens seem to find exciting, but I'm not as slender and busty as the others. I'm solid. More than solid. Whatever. I'm plus sized, and there's nobody out here in space to impress, so I don't care.

Normally I'd opt out of dressing up as a slave girl because I feel a little awkward standing next to the others (especially Helen) but Ruth's in a mood, and the last thing we need is her scowling at the aliens as they board. "Alice and I will greet them. Helen, you know your role, right?"

She nods, giving me a thumbs up. "I lay down in my stasis pod and pretend like I'm just waking up. And I look pretty and helpless."

"Bingo. Ruth, that means you're going to be in charge of doors. It looks like they're coming in from the right-hand side of us, so you'll need to get those doors. Can you handle that?"

"Yup." She pops the "p" sound at the end of the word and gets to her feet. "I'm on it."

I glance back at the window, and the incoming ship looks enormous. Bigger than a shark, I decide, upping it. Whale shark. That's worrisome. "Go ahead and change into your costume too, Ruth. Just in case we need backup."

"Ah, fuck me," Ruth grumbles, but she'll do it.

I take a deep, steadying breath, smile at them, and put my hands on my breasts. "Five minutes, ladies. Change clothes, fluff your tits, and get ready to wow some aliens."

8

ADIRON

*B*oth Kaspar and I watch from the staging room as the hatch-to-hatch connection extends out to the *Buoyant Star*. I'm not entirely surprised to see it hook on to the other ship, though it does fill me with a creepy feeling. There's no green light to show we've been approved to board. There's no response from the other ship at all, actually. No shields, no response to our hailings, no nothing.

I look over at my brother as I ready my blaster. "Ghosts."

He snorts. "It's not ghosts, you idiot. Mathiras said his readouts show that she's venting carbon dioxide from time to time, so the life support systems are on and working. Someone's in there. If it was all ghosts they wouldn't need life support."

"You don't know that," I shoot back. "You've never met a ghost."

"Will you two shut the kef up?" Lord Straik snarls from behind us. "You're getting on my last nerve."

I make a face at the door and then lean over to Kaspar. "Ghosts," I whisper, just to have the last word.

He looks thoughtful, then crooks a finger, indicating I should come closer.

I do.

He licks his finger and shoves it in my ear.

With an outraged sound, I stumble away, glaring at him. "You monster."

"You left yourself open for it," he says with a shrug.

Damn it. I totally did.

"I'm about to shoot both of you in the back and declare to your brother that it was an accident," Lord Straik says from behind us. "How has he not killed the both of you yet?"

I grin. Kaspar does, too. We're always a little antsy when we're about to board an enemy ship. I mean, sure this one's full of ghosts, but that doesn't mean it's not the enemy. We don't know what's over there, so we'll treat it like the bad guys, and this is part of our ritual to pump ourselves up. We joke around, we're obnoxious, and we try not to take things too seriously.

I wonder for a moment if I'd be able to lick my finger and stick it in Straik's ear before he notices. Probably not.

The ship chimes a warning, indicating that the staging room is about to be sealed off from the main part of the ship. It's designed that way so if the ship-to-ship connection gets torn away by accident, the rest of the crew inside the vessel doesn't get killed. Usually, it's also a signal that shit's about to get real and to pay keffing attention. I glance at the ship-to-ship connection, but it hasn't been refused. The *Buoyant Star* connects with *The Darkened Eye* as if she has a crew on the other side, manning the controls.

"You think that's automated?" Kaspar asks, clearly on the same page as me.

"You know what I think."

"Right. Ghosts." He smirks and plays with his blaster,

pulling it out of the holster at his hip. "Ten credits if you let me go first."

I snort. Ten credits won't even buy a pack of carcinogels. "Keep your credits. I don't want to go first anyhow." I mean, if there ARE ghosts...

"Shut up. Both of you." Lord Straik sounds like an angry parent. "Or I'll leave you both behind."

Kaspar steps in front of me and I grunt acknowledgment. Go first. See if I care.

The portal clicks, then chimes a confirmation as it locks on to the *Buoyant Star*. Air rushes into the expanding tunnel walkway between the two ships, and I feel a rush of adrenaline. For better or for worse, we're about to get to the end of this crazy chase. We've lost our ship—temporarily—and we've teamed up with the enemy, but it'll all be worth it if there's something good on the other side. I imagine enough riches to buy a planet...not that I want one. I'm not entirely sure what I'd buy if I grew obscenely wealthy. I like spending time with my brothers on our ship. I don't care about the credits. I just don't want to be alone with my thoughts.

There's a positive, chirpy little chime from our ship, indicating that it's now safe to move forward. I turn to look behind me, and Lord Straik is wearing his cloak and dark clothing, because of course he is. He's flanked by six of his a'ani retinue, all of them armed and in body armor. They're ready to take on whatever we find on the ship, most likely by force.

Straik nods at me.

I turn forward and nudge Kaspar. "Let's go in."

My excitement builds as my brother takes the lead with me a step behind him. As we cross through the tunnel, I look out the window and see the enormous hull of the ship. The *Buoyant Star* is a cargo ship, like many that take to the outer lanes of the known galaxy, and so most of her hull is cargo space. The ship's sleek on top, not much bigger than *The Dark-*

ened Eye, but latched on behind her, connected with cables and pulleys and a few strategic walkways, is an enormous cargo hold. It reminds me a bit of an iceberg, with a small tip and the bulky, dangerous underside.

I lean close to Kaspar as I walk. "Look at the size of that cargo hull. What do you think they were shipping?"

"Dunno," Kaspar murmurs back. "Better hope for our sake it's not livestock."

I make a face at that thought. I can just imagine going all this way to hunt down some lofty treasure...and finding nothing but a hold full of long-dead meat-stock. That'd be some luck. "Maybe it's weapons," I whisper back to Kaspar. "Isn't that what Mathiras thought it might be?"

He grunts, and I suspect we're both thinking of our brother, still on the bridge as the rest of us check out the mysterious ship. It has to be eating at Mathiras that he doesn't get to go on board with the rest of us. We talked everything over the night before, though, and it was agreed that if someone needed to step in and take control of things, it'd be Mathiras. Everyone likes and respects him.

They're a little terrified of me being in charge of anything. Same with Kaspar.

So Mathiras is on the bridge of *The Darkened Eye* and Lord Straik is at our back. A new idea occurs to me, and I lean forward to whisper to Kaspar again. "Do you trust him?"

"Who, Straik?" At my agreement, he snorts. "Of course not."

"Then why are we going in first?"

"What other choice do we have?" He grins over his shoulder at me. "Besides, you want to see what's on here as badly as I do."

He's not wrong. Curiosity is killing me.

We get to the end of the tunnel and into the staging room on the other side. We're now officially on the *Buoyant Star*, even if we're still breathing *The Darkened Eye's* oxygen. I peer around me curiously as the others file in behind us. Doesn't feel haunted so far. I glance over at Kaspar, but he's stationed himself at the door of the *Star*, waiting for the signal.

Lord Straik has his weapons put aside for the moment and his data pad is out. He holds it up to the door and then frowns as an error message flashes across the screen. "I can't synch up with the ship."

"You thought you could?" I look at him in surprise. "Even I'm not that dumb."

He gives me a withering look. "It's one of my family's ships. Of course I should be able to connect with the system. I have access to everything. Or I should." He frowns down at his data pad. "Someone's been tampering with things."

"Let's go tamper back," Kaspar says eagerly. He nods at the door. "Say the word."

"Er, before we race in...do we know how many crew were on this ship when she last left port?" I ask Straik, curious. The bigger the crew is, the more likely the odds for a mutiny.

"Seven," he says. "All very loyal sa'Rin males."

"Huh," is all I say. "Seven crew to operate this enormous ship?"

Kaspar shrugs. "So it's not livestock, then."

I guess not.

Straik turns to Kaspar and nods. He slides his data pad back into its holster and pulls his fancy-looking blaster back out. I admire it for a moment. I need to steal me one of those. Before I can ask where he got it, Kaspar hits the panel on the ship.

The doors glide open in a silent welcome.

The hairs on the back of my neck stand up again. We didn't have to hack that at all. "Ghosts," I whisper again.

9

ADIRON

$\mathcal{I}$ follow close behind Kaspar, my weapon at the ready as we walk down the hall of the eerily quiet ship. The lights are on, and the floors surprisingly dust-free. That doesn't mean anything, of course. The cleaning bots could be going through their regular cycles, not realizing that there's no one on board. The hall itself is long and unadorned, the walls the same treated metal that most ships are made from. There's no damage to the gray paint coating them, either. No scratches or blaster scorch marks, and best of all, no blood. That's a good sign.

Kaspar lifts his head and sniffs the air. "You smell that?"

I look around and sniff. I don't smell anything. Well, no, I take that back. I smell dust and the air is sour and musty, but nothing else. "I don't smell anything but your socks," I joke.

"The air smells, but it's not as bad as it should be," Kaspar points out. "I thought it'd smell like your sac when we came in here, but nothing smells that bad."

I snicker, because that's a pretty good one.

"But no dead things, and the air's not too bad." Kaspar gets a thoughtful look on his face, his blaster raised at the ready as he looks around. "Someone's here."

"Hmm." I turn to look behind me and I can't help but notice that Straik and his men are waiting near the door, watching Kaspar and me wander in. I guess we're bait as much as anything else. Lovely.

I turn back to the front, taking a few steps ahead of Kaspar as he pauses. The hall branches in three different directions, all of them leading to new long corridors and myriad closed doors. There's a lot of places for someone to hide.

Kaspar turns back to Straik. "You have a schematic, right? Which way to the bridge?"

As my brother speaks, a pale face peers around the corner.

My heart skips a beat in my chest. Keffing ghosts. I was *right*. Before I can scream like a child, though, the pale thing steps forward and I realize it's not a ghost.

It's a pale human.

I fire up my blaster, the cartridge whining as it comes to life, and instantly, Kaspar is on alert. He turns at my side, his blaster pointing in the same direction as mine.

"Don't shoot," the human calls out, raising her hands in the air. For a moment, her voice sounds so much like my sister Zoey's that my skin prickles. This female doesn't look much like Zoey, though. They're about the same age, but this one's got pale yellow hair falling around a small, heart-shaped face and bright green eyes. Her expression is one of pleasure as she takes a few cautious steps forward, and I can't help but notice that she's small. Where Zoey was short but sturdy, this one is slender and delicate.

She's also wearing next to nothing.

Her clothes are rags, her small feet bare. What once might have been a standard issue jumper (worn by ship crews and maintenance) is shredded. It hangs at her hips in pieces, a skirt that shows far too much pale, peachy-white skin underneath and slender legs. Her top is little more than a few pieces of fabric harnessed together to cover her tits, and the fabric is doing a terrible job. They're practically bulging out of the skimpy little top, and it looks like the fabric itself will give way at a single touch.

The female takes another wary step toward us, and as Kaspar lowers his weapon, she lets out a tiny sob and rushes forward, flinging herself into his arms. "We're saved!" she cries, weeping.

My brother looks over at me with pure bewilderment as he strokes the human's hair. She clings to his chest, sobbing, and the sight would be utterly comical if it wasn't so damned confusing.

"What's a human doing on board my family's ship?" Lord Straik calls out from behind us, marching up to my side. His clones remain a few paces behind, their weapons ready.

The female just burrows closer to Kaspar, as if he's the only thing keeping her safe. I've never seen my brother look so helpless. Kaspar's always got a plan, a way to figure things out, even if it's an utterly foolhardy, reckless plan. This is the first time I've seen him utterly stymied. Hate to say it, but I'm kinda enjoying the stunned look on his face as the human just snuggles closer to him.

"Wait a moment," I ask as something else occurs to me. "We? What do you mean, we?"

"There's three of us," the tearful human says, lifting her face. "Me and Jade and Helen."

"Where are they?" Kaspar asks, still stroking the human's silky yellow hair. I've never seen him look so instantly protective. Uh oh. That's not a good sign.

"Jade's guarding Helen." She hesitates, biting her lip. "Helen's...sick. We don't know how to take care of her."

"What do you mean, she's sick? How did she get sick?" Kaspar asks.

The human retreats a step and tugs on his hand. "It's something in the air. Please, come with me. I'll show you. You can help us."

Kaspar glances over at me and puts his blaster back into his belt, letting the human tug him down one of the halls. I glance over at Straik, who seems more annoyed than anything. Probably still pissed that humans are polluting the halls of the ship. Let him be pissed. I like humans. I think of Zoey, who's one of the best people in the universe. She's a human, one we adopted as our youngest sister after we rescued her from a slaving ship. She's smarter than all of us put together, and I miss her every keffing day. She's happy, though, acting as navigator on the *Jabberwock*, another pirate ship, and is mated to a stiff-necked but decent mesakkah male who treats her like she hung the stars.

Seeing this small human makes me realize how much I miss my sister, though. Corsairing through the stars isn't the same without the runt to crack jokes with.

The little female leads us down the hall, and we march after her. "What are you doing here?" Straik asks, his voice full of irritation. "Where's the crew?"

"They left us here," she says, glancing back, and her eyes fill with tears again. "They got in a pod thing and left us behind. They said there wasn't room for pleasure slaves."

"My crew wouldn't do that," Straik protests.

"But they did," the human says, her eyes big and sorrowful.

"Your men sound like dicks," I mock-whisper to Straik.

He glares at me and then shakes his head. "I don't understand. They never made it to port anywhere. Never contacted anyone. Why would they abandon a human and then just disappear?"

I shrug. I don't have the answers for him.

The human tugs on Kaspar's hand, leading him on. "This way. In this room." She pauses and gestures us all forward. "Jade's in here."

We step into the ship's med-lab. One of the beds has been replaced with a stasis pod, which is odd, and it's in the center of the room. Standing next to it is another human, and as she turns, my tongue glues itself to the roof of my mouth.

This new human is more like it.

She's older than the yellow-haired one, for one. The other reminds me too much of my sister for me to be attracted to her, but my trou feel painfully tight at the sight of this new female. She's probably Mathiras's age, early thirties for a human, and her skin is a rich, golden-brown shade. Her hair is a dark, frizzy puff that floats around her head like a nimbus, and her hips and breasts are extremely generous. She's spilling out of her ragged clothing in every which way, and I can't decide if I love that or hate it.

This new female looks over at us, and I'm not surprised to see she's got the most gorgeous, expressive eyes I've ever seen. They're more gold than brown, and stand out in her lovely face. She seems worried, her gaze flicking between all of us. "Are they friends, Alice?"

Kef me, even her voice is sultry. I'd gladly be stuck here if it meant being left with this sort of company. Those males that abandoned her here were fools. "I'm your friend," I volunteer, grinning.

She gazes at me as if seeing me for the first time, and her full lips curve in a little smile. "I'm Jade."

And I'm smitten.

10

JADE

*T*his is not going as I hoped.

I keep up the act, my expression one of a soft, terrified female relieved at being rescued. Alice is in full gear, clinging to the one at the front, her tears wetting the front of his tunic. She's such an incredible actress that even I believe her. The poor alien keeps patting her hair and looking like he has no clue what to do. These are blue aliens—mesakkah—like the ones that brought us on this ship.

They're still the enemy, though.

So I bite my lip and pretend to shiver, doing my best to look helpless in my slave girl outfit.

"Here," says the grinning one, the one who said he'd be my "friend." He taps the fastener at his throat and it slithers down the front of his tunic. His clothing opens up, showing an expanse of blue muscled chest and tattoos, and my heart lodges in my throat. Am I about to be raped? I—

I breathe again as he takes the tunic and drapes it around my shoulders.

I don't have to fake my trembling this time. "Thanks." In a way, that was a good thing. It reminds me that no matter how pleasant someone might seem, they're still the enemy, and they enslave humans. We're better off just robbing them and sending them on their way.

Except...in the past, each time we've been visited by pirates lured in by our distress call, it's been a small crew. With a little maneuvering, we have no problems outwitting and taking over a crew of three to four aliens. Right now, though, I'm counting six red-hued aliens (red like Helen, I can't help but notice), a blue-skinned important-looking guy in black clothing with ornate horns, the pirate that Alice is crying on and distracting, and my new shirtless buddy at my side. That's nine. And if they're a smart crew, they'll have left someone on board that great big ship in case of trouble.

Which means things are getting hairier by the moment.

I'm always cautious. Ruth sometimes chides me that I'm too cautious. She'd look at this as a great opportunity—a big ship has lots of supplies. But I prefer to be safe, because there's more than just my life at stake. There's a lot to consider, and sometimes it feels utterly overwhelming. I don't want to be in charge.

But there's no one else to do it, and so I force myself to focus on the task at hand.

The shirtless one leans in closer to me. "Are you all right? Your friend said you were sick."

He's got kind eyes and a roguish smile, and I'm probably going to feel a little guilt when we rob this one. But I force a tremulous smile to my face, my eyes wide and hopefully damsel-in-distress-like. "I'm okay now that you're here." I touch the pod, which we've covered with a strategic towel over the faceplate. "And I'm not sick. Helen is."

"You guys can help us?" Alice's voice rises, ever theatrical. "You're here to save us?"

"I told you we are," the one Alice is clinging to says, and he sounds a little exasperated at her tears. She needs to dial it back a little.

A voice chirps in out of nowhere. "What about the bridge?" calls another voice. The language is alien, but thanks to the translator implant, I pick it all up. Ten, I mentally count. Ten men, one separated from the rest. Okay. We can still handle this.

"I'll go to the bridge," the shirtless one says, trying to put an arm around my shoulder. I cringe away, sliding out from under his grasp, and I hope I don't hurt his feelings. Hell, I'd let him grope me if it'd sell things a bit more, but if he's holding onto me, that ruins the plan.

"You have to help Helen," I say, making my voice sound urgent as Alice detangles herself from the male she's been clutching at. She moves a few steps away, sniffing, and out of the corner of my eye, I watch her creep, one step at a time, toward the door. That's my signal. I give a sad look to the men, leaning over Helen's stasis pod so my tits fall out of the front of my tiny top. Sure enough, that distracts all eyes. "Please. She's been inside this thing so long."

The one dressed in black—the important one, the grumpy one—gives us an irritable look. "What's wrong with her?"

"I don't know," I say dramatically. "She won't wake up." And as Alice creeps another step toward the door, stepping back, I pull the cloth off the front of the stasis pod, where Helen is lying down, her lovely pale lavender hair fanned out around her head, her eyes closed as if she's asleep like an intergalactic Sleeping Beauty.

The moment I do the big reveal, I take a step back. Instead of looking at the stasis pod, though, Shirtless continues to watch me, that hint of a smile playing on his mouth. He's supposed to be interested in the pod, not me, and my smile falters a little, which only makes his grow wider.

"Kef me, is that a qura'aki?" says one man.

That draws everyone's attention. The men all move forward now, eager to peer at Helen. Someone whistles. Another man curses under his breath, and I hear someone else suck in. The sight of Helen never fails to make everyone flip their lids, and it's the perfect distraction. I take a few hasty steps backward, moving to join Alice by the door as they all gape at the sleeping woman.

"Two human slaves and a qura'aki? What exactly were your men up to, Straik?" says Shirtless.

"I don't know," says the one called Straik, and he sounds pissed. "Why are there slaves on a sa'Rin ship?"

Boy, he really doesn't know the half of it, does he? Alice waves me forward, urgency in her eyes, and I bolt for the door. We both rush through it just as one of the men leans over the stasis pod and taps on the glass.

Then, Alice slaps a hand on the door release and they slide shut, lickety split.

"Ruth?" I call, breathing hard.

"On it," Ruth's voice pipes over the system. "Nighty night, boys."

The room we just vacated fills with sleeping gas.

I stare through the window and notice that while the others are grabbing at their weapons and looking around in anger, realizing they've been betrayed, Shirtless is just watching me through that window.

And grinning. Like he's proud.

11

ADIRON

*W*hat a magnificent female. She's set us a trap.

The room springs into wild action, men calling out in alarm as gas pours in from the ceiling.

Jade. I test her name on my tongue, repeating it over and over so I won't forget it. Jade. It's an interesting sound for an interesting female. I can't stop grinning as one of the females peeks through the window in the door, looking back at us as the room fills with gas. It's Jade, and her gaze moves over us in a worried sort of way, until it lands on me. I just grin wider, and she immediately breaks eye contact, flustered.

Interesting. She likes me and doesn't want to. I can't think of another reason why she'd be so unnerved about looking at me. She feels guilty that she betrayed me.

And that just makes me all kinds of happy.

Kaspar socks me in the shoulder. "Told you it was a trap."

"I figured," I say, a little lightheaded as the room gets smokey with gas. I don't think she'll kill us. Not my Jade. She's too soft. The guilt in her eyes tells me everything I need to know about that. I mean, I might wake up in chains, but it wouldn't be the first time and it probably won't be the last.

I push my face into the crook of my elbow, but I don't have a sleeve to help my breathing. I gave her my jacket. Looks like I'm going down, but at least I'll go down happily. I look over at Kaspar, but he's scanning the room, looking for a way out. The clones are trying to pry the doors open, and Lord Straik is staring at the pod as if he's seen a ghost of some kind.

I look back at Jade, but she moves away from the door. A female on the comm is laughing, which just makes Kaspar scowl and bang his fist against the wall.

I stagger over to the pod, peering down at it. Might as well take a look at what we've been trapped with.

It's a qura'aki, all right. I've never seen one in the flesh, just on a vid. She was a clone of this one, I think, or a sister to it. This female has bright red skin—indicative of her cloned nature—and pointed ears and the lilac hair indicative of her race. She's also sticking her tongue out and making faces at us from underneath the safety of her pod's glass.

"We've been outsmarted," I tell Lord Straik, and I can't help but feel a mixture of amusement with my dismay. It sucks, sure, but it was also pretty clever of Jade, and I want to tell her that. I hope I get the opportunity. Something tells me that Jade's the one in charge here. It was the way the little yellow-haired one looked to her, the way she had a subtle hint of authority in her voice as she spoke.

I liked it. I like her. Not since Shaalyn have I been interested in another female. Maybe my cock only stands up for females that betray me. Heh. Wouldn't surprise me one bit if that was the truth.

"Why is there a qura'aki on my family's ship?" Straik demands, then coughs again. "What the kef is going on?"

"You tell me," I say, and I have to lean on the pod to hold

myself up. My legs aren't working, and there's a terrible taste in my mouth. I know this gas, I realize. It's one that some of the shadier cantinas use on bar fights...or in Sticks games. It knocks you out and makes you forget everything for the last day or so.

The realization is sharply disappointing. I don't want to forget Jade. I look down at the qura'aki female, even as my vision blurs and fades. They're supposed to be the most beautiful creatures in the galaxy, the most perfect. She definitely is beautiful, but I can't help but think that I'd rather have Jade.

Everything fades out.

JADE

I pace in the hall, waiting for the gas to take effect. I don't like how things are turning out, but I'm not sure what else to do.

"Quit worrying, Jade," Alice tells me as she adjusts her boobs in her tiny top. "They're all going down like lights, just as we planned." She bounds toward the window and peers in. "I see six...oh, no, seven down. Two more to go."

"And how many more are on the ship?" I worry, chewing on my lip as I pace. "We're not out of the woods yet." There's a lot to do and still so much that could go wrong. The gas is effective, sure, but does it wipe their memories enough that they won't be able to remember the *Star*? We'll turn off our distress signal for a few weeks, of course, to give them nothing to hang onto, but it's still dicey.

Once they're all down, we have to raid the other ship. That'll be make or break. By this time, they'll know we're up to no good and they'll be preparing for it. They'll come weapons blazing, and it won't matter that we're cute, helpless-looking human women. If we lose the upper hand, we're fucked.

"How many are down?" Ruth calls out over the ship's intercom.

"Nine," Alice yells. "Last one just went down." She knocks on the window and I move to her side, but no one's stirring in the room. They're all collapsed where they stood, though the red-skinned troops are all clustered at the door as if they tried to open it. Shirtless is passed out next to Helen's stasis pod, no doubt drawn in by her beauty. I try not to think about the fact that he took his shirt off and gave it to me. It's easy to be chivalrous when you think your dick's about to get wet, and most of the alien men we run into are nice enough...

Well, no, now I'm just making excuses. Most treat us like simpletons or fucktoys. I've had my tits grabbed a dozen times. I had one stick his finger in my mouth and demanded for me to suck on it. I've had my ass pinched, my face slapped, and I've been groped...but no one's ever given me the shirt off their back so I could cover up.

"Airing out the room," Ruth calls. "Give me a minute and then you guys can go in."

I shake my head. "Those men can wait. They're out for now, so they don't pose a problem. We need to figure out who's still left on that ship and how we handle them." Once we know we're safe, we'll tie up the drugged men and send them away on an escape pod that's programmed to find the nearest station... which is weeks away, or so I'm told. It's our way of getting rid of the men without killing anyone. I don't know if they remember us at all, but no one ever comes back for seconds, so I'm confident our plan works.

But we've never had nine men to tie up, plus more on the other ship. I don't know how they're all going to fit on one of the *Star's* escape pods, which hold six. Two pods, perhaps? It's twice the work, though. I think about this, and I pace a bit more. And more.

"Slave girl schtick or guns?" Alice asks, all business as the doors to the trap-room open up. Helen hits the release on her pod and sits up, a grin on her face as the blonde moves through the room, pulling weapons off the men.

I do the same, heading for Shirtless. Not because he was nice to me and I want to check his pulse, but because he had a big honking weapon strapped to his belt. I brush my fingers over his neck anyhow and find that his pulse is strong, if slow. Good. I pull out his blaster...and it's a different make than I'm used to. I have no idea how to operate it. I set it aside and turn to look at the next man. "How are you on guns, Alice?"

She picks one up and arms it, the pistol-like weapon whining as it comes online. "I think I'm good. I—"

"Guys?" Ruth's voice is urgent. "I'm getting a weird reading from the other ship."

"Are they firing on us?" I yell up at her, a cold prickle of fear moving through my system.

"I don't know what it is. I've never seen it before. It's a charge of some kind—"

That's the last thing I hear before an electrical rush courses through the *Star*, hitting me like static electricity and knocking me flat. My hair sticks straight up, and the wind is knocked out of me.

And I can't move a muscle.

Fuck.

12

ADIRON

I wake up with a slap to the cheek. My head pounds, and I've got an awful taste in my mouth. Blearily, I peer up at my oldest brother, Mathiras. "Why'd you hit me?"

"I need you to roll over." He pulls out a nasty-looking syringe. "You need a shot to counteract the gas you inhaled."

"I inhaled gas?" My memory's a blur, but I roll over. A moment later, I frown at him as my ass cheek stings. "I think you had too much fun doing that."

"I think you're right. You deserve it," Mathiras says, a disgusted note in his voice.

I do? I rub my ass once he walks away, noticing that Kaspar's laid out on a nearby med-bay bed, probably in the same situation as me. Heat burns through my veins, and I wonder what happened. I sit up, noticing that I'm without my tunic...and then memories creep in, filling in the fuzzy blanks in my mind.

A qura'aki. A trap. Jade.

I hop up from the med-bay table, and I can't help but notice that we're back on *The Darkened Eye*, not the *Buoyant Star*. Mathiras and his crew must have retrieved us from the other ship and brought us to med-bay. I look around and Dopekh and a few of the other clones are rubbing their faces, wearing bleary expressions. I count heads. Everyone's here, even Lord Straik, who rubs his red eyes and looks as if he wants to murder someone.

Probably does. That means I have to get to Jade first.

I storm out of the med-bay, ignoring Mathiras's sound of protest and the curious clones still in uniform who look up when I bust out of the room. I head down the hall, my skin still tingling from a reaction to the shot. I scratch at my chest and look around the *Eye*, trying to figure out where prisoners would be taken.

Ten credits says that Straik has a brig. He's pompous enough.

I turn to the a'ani at the end of the hall—Kaje, I think his name is—and try to sound authoritative. "Where's the brig?"

He tilts his head. "Head to the right and go down a floor."

Knew it.

I race down the floor, slapping the elevator's controls. I want to get there before Mathiras can stop me. Not that I think he will, it's just...I want to talk to Jade. Say hello to her. Let her know that she doesn't have to be afraid, because I'm not going to let anything happen to her. That no matter what happens, I'll make sure she's all right. All of the humans will be, I mentally tell myself, because Zoey and Sophie would want that. Kaspar and Mathiras will probably be on the same page as me when it comes to the humans, but I don't know Straik well enough to guess. And Mathiras is gonna be in a bad mood because we were tricked. He's going to stomp his feet for a while and wear his "disappointed brother" look and tell me that I shouldn't give my tunic to the enemy or get myself shut into a room because I gawked at a qura'aki. I know all these things. Everyone does. We just got distracted by a few pretty faces.

Which, I suspect, is exactly what Jade and her friends were hoping. Show off the qura'aki, jiggle their tits, and when the males are good and distracted, take 'em out. I mean, we fell for it, so it's not like it's an ineffective plan. The rare qura'aki is what clinches it. Even someone as scowly and dismal as Straik fell for that one. I wonder how many ships they've robbed along the way. Ten? Twenty? A distress signal is one of the oldest tricks in the book, of course, but they've added a fine twist.

Oh man, Zoey is going to laugh so hard when she hears this.

Then I sober, because I think Zoey might like Jade. That's important to me, because I plan on keeping Jade. Not as a slave, of course. As my female. My mate. Jade doesn't know it yet, but she's stuck with the dumbest keffer in this system...which doesn't say much, because this system is pretty deserted.

I make my way to the elevator and down a floor. Sure enough, the moment I step off the elevator, I see another a'ani guarding one set of doors. He's wearing a breather, too, the shiny nose-clip preventing him from the same situation we were in. Smart.

I saunter up like I know what the kef I'm doing, and scratch at my chest again. Everything itches. It's miserable. I glance down and notice that I'm breaking out in welts. I might be allergic to something. Ah well. It'll go away soon enough. I scratch at my skin again and nod at the big double doors at the far end of the hall, the ones that aren't guarded. "What's down there, Basch? Janitorial?"

He frowns at me with those mobile eyebrows, just like the humans have. Like my sister Zoey, he's able to pull off the "Are you keffing stupid?" look with ease. "It's the cargo bay."

"Right." I gesture at the doors in front of him. "And in here are the prisoners?"

The a'ani nods.

"Great. I need to go in and talk to them. Don't shoot me, all right?" I grin at him and head in like Straik and Mathiras totally sent me down here.

I'm not entirely surprised when the a'ani steps aside and nods at me. That's one reason clones make great subordinates. They don't ask a lot of questions. I stand in place and put my hand on the pad, and the doors open up a moment later. Huh. I'm not locked out. Well, that makes things easy. I thought for sure Straik would revoke some of my clearances after the laundry stunt, but I guess not.

With more than just a little swagger, I saunter into the prisoner hold.

13

ADIRON

*L*ord Straik sa'Rin's prisoner hold isn't much like the cells I've been held in in the past. There's not a corsair in the universe that hasn't spent at least one night in jail, and most of mine involved being elbow-to-elbow with some grungy ooli or praxiian, jostling for space on a hard bench, and trying to catch a few hours of sleep on a filthy floor. Everyone would be wearing shock collars, and if you were lucky, there'd be a lavatory of some kind. You'd be manacled to your fellow prisoners by your feet and there'd usually be a dead guy somewhere in the room, just because some idiot was bound to pick a fight he couldn't win.

Oh, and the entire place would smell like sweaty balls. There's no smell quite like a jail smell...except for sweaty balls, I guess.

This room smells like flowers.

I wrinkle my nose as I walk in, because why the kef does a prisoner hold smell like flowers? I study the too-clean, pristine walls with nary a dent, and sure enough, there's a scent dispenser located near the ceiling. Well, that's just dumb. Some enterprising prisoner could climb up and disable it, and use the scented oil to blind or poison someone...provided they weren't cuffed, though. Cuffs are easy enough to get out of, if you know how. It's just more evidence that sa'Rin doesn't have the killer instinct that makes for a good corsair. He's far too pampered.

This cell is the height of luxury, prison cell-wise. It's temperate and comfortable, and I'm almost surprised there isn't soft music being piped in along with the flower scent.

In the harder jail cells, prisoners are given magnetic cuffs on their wrists (or legs) and then those cuffs are attached to a bar on the wall. There, the prisoners usually have their hands above their heads on the magnetic bar, their feet stuck to the second magnetic bar near the floor. It ensures that the prisoners won't try anything. In this pleasant room, the four females are seated in individual chairs, lined up neatly, and even though their hands are cuffed, they're comfortable.

Looks more like a tea party than a keffing holding cell.

"Did I miss snack time?" I joke as I saunter in. I scan all four females in front of me, saving the best for last. I'm pleased to see that no one looks hurt, at least. I don't like the thought of females—no matter how devious—getting abused by us. Humans are fragile—the qura'aki, doubly so. There's a tall, lean female with long black hair and a wide face. She's got a murderous scowl on her face and I'm guessing she's the one that was so delighted to gas us. Next to her sits the delicate qura'aki, who's very clearly awake. She jerks her hands in her cuffs, frowning as she tries to work her hands free. The little yellow-haired one that sobbed all over Kaspar is still wearing her skimpy outfit, and she lifts her chin defiantly when I look in her direction.

And then I look at Jade. Jade, who I'm thrilled that I haven't forgotten, thanks to the antidote shot in my ass. Jade, who's still wearing my tunic. Jade, whose fluffy hair encircles her head like a dark nimbus, and who blinks those fascinating golden eyes at me. She's unafraid and utterly magnificent, her cuffed hands calmly in her lap.

"If you're expecting an apology, you're not going to get one," Jade says calmly.

"No, seriously," I tease. "I'm here for snacks. Did I miss the cheese tray?" I glance around and pretend to look disappointed as I scratch at my skin. "This is the nicest holding cell I've ever seen. You want me to ask if you guys can watch a vid? I bet we can arrange that."

"Tell them to let us go," the dark-haired one says, defiant. She sits up straight in her chair, glaring at me like Zoey does when I take the last chski pickle. "We won't come along easily."

I scratch at my head, pretending to be confused. "Didn't you guys just try to kill us?"

This time, Jade gives me a look of exasperation. "No one's killing anyone. We were just trying to protect ourselves from invaders on our ship."

The qura'aki looks confused. "I thought we were robbing them—"

The dark-haired one kicks at the qura'aki's chair, and the lilac-haired one goes silent.

I grin, deliberately letting my smile spread wide across my face because the females look infuriated. "I can guess which one of you is gonna be interrogated first, then."

Jade lifts her chin, looking regal and beautiful. "Is that why you're here? To suss out which one of us you're going to rape and torture into telling you everything?"

"Uh, no. Rape and torture?" I shake my head. "I can reassure you that we're not those kinds of pirates. And look around you." I gesture at the holding cell. "Shit, these quarters are better than mine. I might bunk down here with you guys instead of my brother. This is pretty nice." There's a bench along the wall and

I sit down on it, stretching out and putting my hands behind my head. "I just came to say hello."

The females shift, and as I pretend to be my lazy, indolent self, I watch as they all glance over at Jade. She's definitely the leader. I like that. She's got a quiet sort of authority to her, a calm presence that indicates she's smart and won't take any shit. Here I always thought I'd fall for someone more like my sister Zoey—a scrappy sort of female that gives as good as she can get.

Instead, I'm obsessed with rounded human curves, defiant amber eyes, and a calm demeanor of control, even as a prisoner. Makes my cock hard as kef, but I don't point that out. Human females are skittish, and these four are probably terrified they're going to be murdered.

Jade studies me with those calm, calculating eyes. I wait for her to address me, to offer a deal of some kind. To bargain. Not that I have the authority to make bargains with prisoners. I'm just along for the ride. But I recognize the look on her face— she's not about to give up, even though she's in chains. She watches me for a moment more and then shifts, sitting up.

Here it comes. The bargain. I lean forward, eager to hear it.

"What happened to your face?" she asks.

"My face?"

"You look like you fought a swarm of bees and lost," says the yellow-haired one.

"Did you get into a fight with someone?" Jade asks. "You're swollen."

I reach up and touch my face. Sure enough, around the nose ridges and brow ridges, my face is puffy and hot. I absently scratch at my skin. "I think I'm allergic to whatever gas you gave us."

A flash of regret crosses Jade's face, and it fills me with glee. I knew she wasn't trying to hurt us. Knew it. But she settles back in her chair. "That's too bad. It was necessary, though."

I shrug. "In the future, you'd be better off taking hostages and negotiating."

She blinks at me. "What?"

"You know, force us to come off the other ship and to you. Get everyone in one place. You had to know that we were going to leave someone on the other ship. That's just piracy basics." I gesture at them. "Next time, take someone hostage, demand that everyone else hand over their weapons and no one gets hurt, or something along those lines. I'd suggest Lord Straik next time. He's the one in the black clothes."

Jade processes this, her expression thoughtful. "You can't negotiate with a ship-wide taser. That's something we'll need to consider in the future."

I don't know what a taser is, but guessing how the humans have their hair floating around their heads like they were shot up with electricity, I can guess. Mathiras used Straik's weapon on the females. That's how they ended up here and captive. I don't know if I'm impressed that my brother pulled out the shock system immediately...or if I'm irked? Because that thing hurts like a son of a bitch, and I don't like the thought of Jade being hurt. I'm already strangely protective of her.

She's just so...alone. She's in charge, but it's clear to me that other than the three equally fragile females, no one's looking out for her in the universe.

That's gonna be my job from now on, I decide. "I'm sorry he did that to you. I've experienced that shock, and it sucks."

Jade just gives me a suspicious look. "Why are you in here talking to us? Being nice to us?"

I shrug. "Because I like you, and I'm curious what would make a human so desperate she'd take on an entire ship full of a'ani."

"What's a'ani?" the yellow-haired one asks.

"A clone," I say, scratching at my arm. "You know, the red skin."

The qura'aki gasps. "I'm a CLONE?"

Er... "You didn't know that?"

She looks over at Jade, her purple eyes wide and terrified. "Is that bad?" Her lower lip trembles. "Am I the enemy?"

"It's fine, honey," Jade soothes. "You're perfect. You are absolutely not the enemy. He's just talking out his ass." And she glares at me as if I'm the problem.

These females make no sense. The clone doesn't know she's a clone, they don't know how to operate a ship, and they're terrible at being pirates. "You wanna tell me what's going on?" I offer. "Maybe I can help."

14

JADE

*M*y head feels like it's splitting, but what feels worse is the failure. I couldn't keep us safe. I gambled on a plan, and I lost. Now Ruth, Helen and Alice are going to suffer for it, and I want to just curl up into a ball and cry.

I can't, though. I have to pretend like I'm strong and in control. The other women are shooting me worried looks, and I know they're scared. I have to be strong for their sakes.

"What do you think is going on?" I answer coolly.

The big guy grins at me. He paces around the room, but there's no urgency in his steps. He's not doing it because he's agitated. It's like he's doing it just because he's not the type to calmly have a seat. His tail swishes back and forth in a calm manner, and I've learned enough about the mesakkah race over the last few years that I recognize that he's not angry, or seething with rage. His smile must be legit, because his body language just enforces his easy nature.

Body language is something I've had to lean into over the last few years. Even with a translator chip unceremoniously implanted behind my ear so I can understand alien languages, things don't always line up. Aliens have different sayings, different customs. This particular race might get offended at a bared teeth smile. This one might not look you in the eye. With all that going on, I've learned to look for subtle cues instead. To see how someone holds themselves, the set of their shoulders, if their knuckles are tight, or if they stand too close. If a tail flicks in agitation. All these things can tell me a lot without saying a word, and I trust them far more than any platitudes spewing out of alien mouths.

As aliens go, though, I'm glad that whoever this guy is, he's the blue-horned race. Mesakkah. Out of the alien races I've seen so far, the mesakkah are the most appealing to human sensibilities. They're blue skinned with armored plating on the brows, arms, chest, and a few other spots. They've got enormous, curling horns that arch back from that plated brow and crown impossibly thick black hair. Their facial features are somewhat angular and oversized, but it all comes together to be strikingly attractive. They're around seven feet tall and have three fingers and a thumb, fangs, and a tail. It's a mixture of elements that are just enough to be familiar and appealing... and different enough to be alien.

The one standing in front of me, grinning like a loon, is attractive enough. Okay, fine, he's cute. He's got a roguish grin that promises naughtiness and bright eyes. He's built like a pro-wrestler, and his somewhat messy hair tickles at his brow and the curve of his ear instead of staying in place. If I was back on Earth, I'd say this man looks like someone that knows how to have fun.

But since we're in space, he's the enemy.

I wait for him to answer me, irked by the playful smile that remains on his face as he paces. He pretends to study all of us, but his gaze keeps straying back to me. "I think you were going to rob us and dump us. Steal our ship and enjoy a tidy little profit. And I'm also guessing it's not the first time you've pulled this sort of maneuver."

He looks impressed instead of angry, and I don't know how to handle that. "We weren't going to kill you," I point out. "Just send you back into space on your ship."

"If it makes you feel any better, it wouldn't have worked. We deliberately came to this sector looking for the *Buoyant Star*. We would have turned right back around and headed in your direction again, memory-altering gas or not."

I'm not completely stupid. "We'd turn off the distress signal so you wouldn't be able to find us."

His lips tilt into a smile. "And you'd move the ship?"

I remain silent. I can't point out that we don't know how to do more than tap a few buttons on the ship. That most of what we've learned how to do has been through punching one button and waiting for the results, good or bad. That the only way we know how to turn on the gas in the one room was because Ruth was scrubbing air filters and hit the wrong button and knocked herself out for a day. It's been a lot of guess work, and since we have nothing else but free time, we've taught ourselves some rudimentary defenses.

I don't regret that our plan failed. At least we had a plan. At least we tried. It's been clear to me from the get-go that no one looks out for humans except humans, so Ruth, Alice, Helen and I have done what we had to do to survive. If this one wants an apology, he's going to be waiting for a while.

I lift my chin, defiant. "Does it matter if we move the ship or not?"

He shrugs. "I mean, I'd move it. At this rate, the ice field's going to swallow you up in a few weeks. Maybe a month or two. Unless that's part of your plan...?" He crosses his arms over his chest, tilting his head at me.

I try not to let my shock show. Ice field? What ice field? We've noticed that the ship has had to work a little harder to maintain a regulated temperature, but we didn't know what was causing it, just that the meters were showing an increase in output of some kind. But if we're slowly drifting toward an ice field...what does that mean? And what happens to us then? I want to look over at the others, but I don't dare give away how much or how little we know.

I just shrug. What else can I do?

The door behind him opens, and three other big aliens walk in. I glance at my "friend" and a hint of irritation crosses his face, quickly masked. Interesting. Is he annoyed that they're here to torture us before he could get information out of us? Or is it something else?

"I just want you all to know that I bite," Ruth snarls as the aliens glare at us. "I will absolutely tear a chunk off of any appendage that comes into range."

"And I have a disease," Alice announces. "If you touch me, you'll catch it."

I glance over at my ladies, and they're wearing looks of defiance. Except Helen. She looks depressed. "I want a disease," she whispers.

Alice shakes her head at her.

The friendly one joins the others, looping his arms around the shoulders of two of the men. They look alike, now that he moves in between them, I realize. Cousins? Brothers? They're all handsome in that alien way, but they're still the enemy. The one in black robes glares at us, his tail flicking back and forth under his skirts.

Now THAT one is agitated. He doesn't have to say a word for him to make me uneasy.

"Well, boys," my "friend" announces, grinning. "How do we punish? I vote spanking."

15

JADE

*S*panking? Is that man serious?

Actually, I know the answer to that, somehow. No, he's not serious. Judging from the wide grin on his face, the man is rarely ever serious. It's even more evident when his friends roll their eyes at him.

"Be serious, Adiron," says the tallest of the three.

Adiron. All right. I memorize that name because I have a feeling I'm going to need it in the future. Adiron. Adiron. I study the aliens and it looks like they're all irritated at the spanking suggestion. A prickle of relief moves over me because if they're not into that idea, we're probably not getting raped. Thank god for that. I shift in my cuffs, trying to free my hands.

"Do you wanna tell us what that was about?" One shrugs off Adiron's arm and marches forward. His gaze is locked on a defiant Alice, and he's glaring at her like she's betrayed him. That's the one she cried against, I realize. Guess his feelings are a little hurt at being deceived. Too bad for him. Alice keeps her expression bland, her gaze locked on the floor, and she remains silent.

"Anyone?" calls the black-robed one. "Speak now and we'll be merciful."

I can feel Adiron's gaze on me, but I say nothing. I calmly stare ahead at nothing and tug at my cuffs again. No one else speaks. I know they won't. We all know we're in this together, and we're not going to screw the others over by blabbing our guts out. Not that it's a big secret, but the way this one demands makes my hackles go up.

"Well?" snarls the one in black. "Are you going to explain how human slaves got a hold of my family's ship? Did you steal it? What did you do with the crew? Where are they?"

No one talks.

In fact, no one talks for the next half-hour or so while they continue to pepper us with questions. Why did we attack them? How many ships have we lured? What's our goal? How did we acquire the *Buoyant Star*? Where's the crew? What's in the hold? As the minutes pass and the men get more agitated, I can't help but notice that Adiron—the spanking enthusiast —takes a seat across from us and crosses his arms over his chest. His legs are sprawled out and he looks bored, his tail calm.

I'm choosing to take that as a good sign. The other three are worked up as they ask us more questions we don't answer, but I'm starting to feel comfortable that no one's going to torture information out of us. Whoever these aliens are, I don't think they arrived onto the ship with malicious intent. I don't know how we're going to break free, but right now, I'm taking it one problem at a time. I'll watch and observe, and eventually the right opportunity will present itself.

Adiron might be the key, in fact. I glance through my lashes over at him, and he's watching me. He seems fascinated with me for some reason, and I can use that to my advantage if I have to. I can distract him in some way, or convince him to let us go, or...

As I subversively regard him, Adiron jumps to his feet. "We're not getting anywhere with this," he announces. "I have a better idea."

"Oh, here we go," mutters the black-robed one.

I lift my head and watch, uneasy, as Adiron grabs the three men and pulls them in for a football huddle. They whisper, too low for my translator to pick up, and now my worry spikes again.

They turn to look at us with calculating gazes, and my neck prickles with alarm. "Leave the others alone," I volunteer suddenly. "They can't tell you anything."

"Jade," Alice hisses.

I ignore her. If I have to sacrifice myself to save the others, I'll gladly do so. Those girls are my family. "You don't want them," I boldly claim. "You want me."

"Big words for someone that's said nothing in the past half hour," says the tallest of the group, and then he nods at Adiron. "We'll try your suggestion. Grab one."

The men surge forward and I bite back a scream of terror. Ruth growls, Alice tries to shove her chair backward, and Helen whimpers in distress. This is it now. This is the end of the "nice guys" act. I lift my chin, trying to look far more defiant than I feel as Adiron stalks toward me. Of course he's coming for me. He's been fascinated with me since the moment our eyes met.

Well, if he expects me to go down without a fight, he's going to be in for a surprise.

Except...I'm the one surprised when he moves behind my chair and activates a mechanism. It surges forward and he steers me toward the door. With a worried glance backward at the others, my captor steers my chair into the hall. I hear commotion in the room behind me and a called out "Get her to stop kicking!" rings in the hall.

That'd be Ruth, I wager. I hope she kicks a few of them in the blue gonads.

Meanwhile, Adiron keeps rolling me down the hall. We zoom past a few of the red-skinned guards who look at us with curiosity, and I try to add them to my mental tally. It's hard, though—they all have the same faces. I don't know if these are the same guards as before or different ones. Clones, someone said. Right. Well, shit. How many clones are on this ship with us? My heart sinks, because the more people we run across, the worse our chances are.

A group of four smart, canny, prepared women can absolutely take down a handful of enemies. But fifteen? Twenty? I don't like those odds and my stomach tightens with distress.

Behind me, Adiron whistles as he guides my chair forward. At the far end of the hall, a door opens and reveals an elevator. He steers me onto it, and my anxiety just increases. I twist at my cuffs again, desperate. "If you think you can rape some answers out of me," I warn, "you are sorely mistaken."

"Rape you?" He sounds disgusted and more than a little shocked. "Why would you think that?"

"Because you're separating me from the others? Because you want answers?" I pause for a moment, then add, "Because I've seen the way you keep looking at me?"

He moves to the side of my chair and taps a command into the elevator. The doors close, and as they slowly shut, I see the dark-robed one coming down the hall with a kicking, writhing Ruth flung over his shoulder. A knot forms in my throat. Is this it? Is this the end? Are we being separated to be interrogated and executed? If an alien man doesn't want a human woman for sex, what the hell does he want, then?

I don't have the answers, and I don't like it.

The doors close, and then I'm alone with my captor. I close my eyes, trying to calm myself, and feel his weight press down on both arms of my chair. When I open my eyes, he's looming over me, his face inches from mine.

"I *have* been looking at you," Adiron confesses. "That's what you wanted, wasn't it? Distract us with your bodies in those outfits? Well, it worked. I'm plenty distracted." And he gives me another crooked, disarming grin. "But I'm also not an asshole. I'm not touching you unless you ask for it."

"Don't hold your breath," I retort.

"Oh, I won't." With another naughty grin, he straightens. "But you're right. We're separating you in the hopes that someone will crack and give us answers."

"No one will," I bluff. Except...will they? We're a tight group, but we have our flaws. Ruth has a temper. I'm overprotective of the others. Helen...well, Helen's a fully grown adult but she's also incredibly innocent. It'd be easy to trick her. I know Alice is solid. The others, I'm not so sure about, including myself.

Adiron just shrugs, looking unperturbed at my declaration. "If you don't break, at least I get to spend some time in your company." The elevator stops, a gentle lifting motion the indication we've reached our destination. The doors open, and Adiron wheels me down another hall and then stops.

"Where are we going?" I ask, unable to remain silent.

"I thought you might be hungry," my captor says. "We're heading to the mess to see what kind of fancy food Lord Straik has on tap. And we're gonna eat it."

16

ADIRON

I guide Jade's chair into the mess hall, and I'm glad to see that it's empty. The a'ani tend to take their meals on a fairly rigid schedule, so it's deserted around here between meal times. That's perfect for my needs. I'm not hungry, but I keep thinking about Jade and that little falling-apart outfit she's wearing. I think about how long the *Buoyant Star* has been missing in deep space. If what the humans mentioned is true—that they were left behind—then I wonder at their food supplies. If it's a lie and just part of the story designed to trap us, she won't bat an eye at Straik's food supplies.

So I settle her chair in front of one of the tables, consider her, and then deactivate the cuffs.

She rubs her delicate wrists and looks over at me. "Are you sure that's wise?" She arches a brow in my direction. "Shouldn't you lock down the big bad humans?"

I just shrug. "You aren't going anywhere without your

friends. And we can't exactly get to know each other with you trussed up, can we?"

Jade rubs her wrists again and shrugs. "There's nothing to tell you."

I doubt that very much. I head to the series of dispensers above the countertop and study them. There's a variety of foods of all kinds—from comfort foods like askri noodles to more exotic things, like a variety of fruits, or spicy cheeses from one of Homeworld's moons. I pretend to study all of it and turn to her, all casual. "What do you feel like eating?"

"Whatever," she says quietly, her watchful gaze on me.

So she's determined not to give away anything either. Her expression is impassive, and if I wasn't already besotted with this female, I would be now. She's a challenge, this one, and I'm dying to know her story. She doesn't kick and scream like the long-haired one, or glower mutinously like the yellow-haired one. Her rebellions are subtle, and I get the impression that she's watching me closely so she can use whatever information I give her, just like I'm doing to her.

I cross my arms and pretend to consider the menus available. "Are you in the mood for noodles? Fruit? Some sort of sweet?"

"What part of 'whatever' don't you understand?" she retorts, her voice tart. I hear her get up and when I glance over, she joins me at my side. Not running, not attacking. Assessing. Waiting.

Kef me, what a female.

I lean over toward her, enjoying this immensely. I don't even care that she got me all drugged up on something that's making me itch, still. I scratch at my chest as I speak. "You said 'whatever,' but if I pulled out a bowl of kelp soup, would you be happy with it? Lord Straik has tons of credits and feeds his soldiers well. We might as well take advantage of his largesse."

She looks over at me and chews on her full lower lip. "It's been a while since I've had fruit," she admits in a small voice.

For a moment, I think this is a trick. That she's throwing me a tidbit to make me curious. Maybe so...and I love that I can't read her. I punch in the request, and soon, a few pieces of fruit tumble into a serving bowl, and a plas-film napkin shoots out after it. I grab them and gesture that she should join me at the nearest table.

She does, and her gaze is on the fruit. I can practically see her mouth watering, and that tells me plenty. She might not want to tell me anything about how they got on the *Star*, but if her excitement over fruit is this obvious, then she truly hasn't had any in a while. I mean, who gets excited over jirri or gomaii stone fruit? No one in the universe, that's who.

I hold a piece out to her, and she takes it from my hand with eagerness and then turns it, curious. "How do you eat it?"

"Jirri?" I take it from her, making sure to brush her fingertips with mine just because I'm that keffing guy, and pull one of the spiky petals off of it. "You unwrap it like this, and the rind falls away. Then you can eat the soft insides."

Jade gives me a grateful smile, practically snatching the fruit back from me. I watch her fumble with it for a moment as I pull out my knife and split my stone fruit in half, discarding the stone in the center. I pretend to be focused on my food, but I'm watching her as she puts the first bite into her mouth. Her eyes close and she bites back a sound of pleasure that makes my skin prickle with awareness and my cock jump in my trou. It takes everything I have to remain still as she licks a bit of juice from her thumb, because I want her to lick parts of me like that.

I'm such a keffing idiot. Why did I go with fruit? I should have gone with noodles. No one eats noodles sexy...but I bet Jade would. I think I'm keffed any way I look at it.

"Good?" I ask, scratching at my arm as she devours the fruit.

Jade beams at me, not pausing in her chewing, and nods. "Amazing."

I offer her half of my stone fruit and then snap my fingers. "I know something else you'll like," I say all casual. "It's a fruit juice made from a plant that grows on Homeworld. Very sweet and tart."

"Should you get that looked at?"

I glance over at her as the juice pours into a tumbler. She gestures at my face. "It looks uncomfortable."

Not half as uncomfortable as the swelling in my trou. But I shrug and pay it no mind. "If it becomes problematic, there's a med-bay on the ship."

"A working one?" Her tone is slightly wistful. "Ours hasn't worked in over two years."

She's letting her guard down. Opening up. I hide my excitement and bring the juice to her side. It's the part of my master plan that I'm proudest of, and it's been incredibly easy to bring it into the conversation. "Here you go," I pronounce grandly. "We call it sweetjuice back home. I think you'll like it."

If she knows what sweetjuice is, she makes no indication of it. Jade sniffs the tumbler and then gives me a shy smile that makes my heart stutter in my chest. "Thank you."

And she takes a sip. Smiles. Takes another.

I lean back in my chair, grinning at her, waiting for the effects to kick in. I remember when Zoey was a tiny little runt, no more than arms and legs, running around our ship. She tried sweetjuice for the first time after we brought back a carafe from a station cantina and then drunkenly wandered around the *Little Sister* for hours, talking to her shoe. It made her drunk beyond any alcohol, and after that hilarious incident, we kept sweetjuice off the ship.

But Lord Straik has it on his. The alcoholic properties only truly affect humans. To me, it's just juice.

I'm hoping it gets Jade to open up a little, though. And if she talks to her shoe for a few hours, okay, that will be fun, too. She'll probably be mad at me when she sobers up, but as I watch her drain the cup of juice, I figure it's just payback for drugging me, and I scratch at my chest again.

"That's delicious," she tells me, setting down her drained cup. "Can I have another?"

"Hell yeah." I nudge my fruit toward her. "You can eat that, too."

She does, tearing into my stone fruit before I even get up to snag her refill. There's truth in her actions, from what I can tell. She hasn't been around enough mesakkah to know sweetjuice will knock her on her ass. She doesn't know how to eat common fruits, which tells me that the food system on the *Star* is either cleaned out or supplied with cheap stuff.

And for all her initial skepticism, Jade is trusting. She's eaten and drunk what I've placed in front of her with a trusting eagerness that makes my chest ache. For all that they tried to rob us, these humans aren't hardened criminals.

I can't wait to get some answers. I put the refill of sweetjuice in front of Jade and wink at her. "Bottoms up."

17

JADE

*I*t takes a few minutes for me to realize that this juice has a hell of a punch.

It takes a few more before I realize I'm completely drunk. Oh fuck.

I stare down at the empty tumbler in my hands. It's the second one I've sucked down, and I should have realized there was a catch. It's just...Adiron was so casual about the fruit, and it's been so long since I've had anything but protein bars or those goddamned noodles that I got excited. Juice sounded like manna from the heavens. Juice is so benign, too. It's just...juice.

Apparently not.

I blink up at my captor, and he's grinning at me. "Did you drug me?" I ask, and my words come out wobbly. Silly words.

"No. That particular juice just packs a real punch for humans. My sister's human, you know."

I just blink at him. He's really pretty. Real pretty. Those eyes are playful and kind, both. And he fed me. I like a man that knows to feed a woman, even if he is the enemy.

Oh, right. He's the enemy. I consider that for a moment and then lick the rim of my glass, because I really want more juice even though I know I shouldn't.

"Still thirsty?"

I push my glass toward him. It nearly skids off the table, but he catches it. "Fill 'er up, bartender."

Adiron chuckles. He gets up and heads to the food and drink dispenser, and as he does, I look around the room. Ooh, there's a door. I should find the others. Tell them not to drink the juice, no matter what. It's delicious but it makes your head wobbly. So wobbly. I stand up and stagger toward the door. My legs don't work quite right—it's like they're made of noodles—and I run into a table. And a chair. And then another table.

I giggle, because how do all these tables keep getting in front of the door? It's like there's an obstacle course in here and at the other end are my friends. Well, I've watched TV shows. I know how you handle an obstacle course.

So I start climbing on the table in front of me, crawling over the top.

"Hang on, now," Adiron says, and he sounds amused. Big arms haul me off the table and carry me back to my original seat. I try to get up again, and Adiron grabs me by the waist, this time dragging me toward him.

Fine, if he wants me to sit, I'll sit right on him. I drop down on his leg. "Boom."

Instead of grimacing at my weight, he just chuckles again, and his arms tighten around my waist. "If you want to sit on me, I'll allow that."

"Hmph." I wiggle, trying to get comfortable, but his thigh has plating on it underneath his clothes. After a few moments of shifting, I find a decent spot and lean against his chest. He's big and actually pretty comfortable to lean against, and I sigh. "I'm tired."

"I bet." He strokes my back, and gosh, that feels good. "You've had a big day."

"I need to tell the others not to drink the juice," I mumble. "It's tricky."

He keeps rubbing my back. "I'll tell them."

That sounds like a good idea. I'm too out of it to walk around. I feel all light and drifty, like I'm going to lift right off of his lap. I put his hands tighter on my waist. "Hold me down. So I don't float away."

"I will," he promises, and grips the waistband of my skirt underneath my borrowed shirt. "Better?"

I nod, curling up against him. "Don't wanna fall."

"I'd never let you fall, Jade," he murmurs. "You feeling all right?"

"You got me drunk," I point out, feeling loose and kinda awesome despite the fact that I know I should be angry. How long has it been since I've been drunk? Too long. I've been stuck on a boring ship for forever. Being drunk is kinda...fun. I glance up at him and poke his nose. "You look funny."

"You mean sexy," he corrects. "I look sexy. In fact, it blows your mind how sexy I am."

I snort. "I'm not that drunk."

His chest shakes and I realize he's laughing. I cling to him so I don't fall off of his lap—or the world—and wonder where my friends are. Are they being snuggled? Because being snuggled is pretty nice. I burrow in close to him again, pressing my face against his neck. His neck smells nice. His skin is soft, too. Like a kitten. "A great big kitten," I announce. "Meow for me, kitty."

"What?" He sounds confused.

I stroke his neck. "Maybe purr instead? Prrrrr." I roll my tongue. "Prrrrrr, kitty."

"You're a cuddly drunk, aren't you?"

"Mmm, I feel good." I press my nose against his neck. "And you're warm."

"It's because you're not wearing more than a few scraps." He tugs his tunic over my breasts, making sure everything is covered. "Is that all you really have to wear or is that just part of your plan?"

I sniff him again, trying to figure out what he smells like. Sunshine, maybe. Does sunshine have a smell? He smells happy, I decide. Kinda musky and warm and just a hint of fruit. "Can I lick you?" I ask, reaching up to touch his face.

"No licking, Jade," Adiron tells me in a firm, parental voice. "You don't get to do anything you'll regret once this wears off."

I whine in my throat and then go back to snuggling against his chest. "Meanie."

He pokes my side. I push his hand away. He pokes me again. I slap at him. "Stop it."

"Are you gonna answer me?"

I try to think, but my mind is fuzzy. "Did you ask me something?"

"Yeah. Do you really not have any other clothes?"

Oh. I yawn and smack my lips, wondering if I can get more fruit out of him. Or another cup of juice. I'm already drunk, right? What's the harm in a little more? "Aliens like human titties. Might as well use 'em as a distraction." I grab one of my tits and jiggle it. "So we can rob 'em."

"That's what I thought. And...you were gonna rob us?"

"Yeah." I sigh heavily, thinking about all that new food we aren't going to get. "Running low on noodles. Fucking noodles."

"Fucking noodles," he agrees, sounding amused.

"And we need air filters. Can't drive the ship, so we steal from people that show up to rob us."

"And you kill them?"

"No. We don't kill anyone. We drug 'em and tie 'em up. Put

them back on their ship and push it away from ours and we turn off the distress signal so they can't find us again. We go quiet. Real, real quiet." I put my finger to his lips. "Shhh."

"That's good to know—"

"Shhh," I say again, pressing harder on his lips. "I said quiet." Instead of being quiet, he licks my finger.

I squeal, pulling my hand away, and he grins like the naughty boy he is.

"So you rob everyone. Have you robbed a lot?" he asks.

"Four," I say, wiping my finger on my borrowed shirt. "But they all were gross. They tried to touch us. No one wants to be our friends. They just want to touch our titties."

"If they tried to touch your titties, they weren't your friends," he says solemnly.

"Exactly!" I smack my lips. "Can I have more juice?"

"Mmmm, I'm not sure that's a good idea. Maybe if you're real good and answer my questions?"

I'm pretty sure I'm not supposed to, but my mouth is so, so dry and it's hard to think straight. I cling to his new shirt— because he found a new one somewhere, it seems—and poke his puffy face. "I'll kiss you if you get me more juice. Even when you're all ugly and bloated."

"As opposed to ugly and unbloated?"

"You're not ugly," I reassure him. I even stroke his cheek a little, just to make him feel better. "You're just alien. I'm sure you're very handsome for a battle-smurf."

His mouth twitches. "Why don't you tell me more about your plan? You were going to steal our food?"

"And your filters," I point out. "And then we'd push you back into space." I make a whooshing movement with my hand. "And then you'd go away and we'd stay on our ship, forever and ever, eating noodles and waiting and guarding."

"Guarding?" He asks. "Guarding what?"

I lean in close. "The others," I whisper conspiratorially.

"What others?"

"The humans that were left behind, of course." I roll my eyes at him. "Can I have my juice now?"

He stiffens under me. "What other humans? How many?"

"One hundred and thirty-two," I tell him, turning in his lap. I pick up my cup and since he's not filling it, I lick the edges again. So sweet and cool. I definitely want more.

"One hundred and thirty-two what, Jade?" Adiron steers me back onto his lap, turning me so I have to look at him.

Is he drunk, too? How is he not understanding what I'm saying? I sigh in frustration and talk slowly so he gets it. "One hundred and thirty-two others in pods," I tell him. "I counted them all."

He stares at me and then rubs his jaw. "Kef me."

I push the tumbler against his mouth, squishing his lips. "Not until I get more juice."

18

ADIRON

"**B**oys, we've got a problem," I announce as I rejoin the others in Lord Straik's private chambers.

Kaspar is sprawled in a chair in front of Straik's desk, the lord himself is behind it, and Mathiras paces near the maps. They all look up as I enter in dramatic fashion, being me. Mathiras immediately looks behind me, a hint of a frown on his face. "Before you get started, did you take your prisoner back to the cell?"

"Nah," I say. "She's in my bed."

Lord Straik jumps to his feet, shocked. "WHAT?"

"Calm yourself." I move to the chair next to Kaspar and flop down, tired. Man, it has been a DAY. "She's drunk as hell and kinda grabby, so I'm letting her sleep things off."

"You got her drunk?" Straik looks disgruntled. "This is highly inappropriate—"

"No, it really wasn't," I point out. It could have been. Oh man, could it have been. I gave Jade another cup of sweetjuice after she opened up and two-cup Jade is a clingy little thing. Three-cup Jade is an absolute horndog, as Zoey would say. I kept having to pull her hands off of me, because I know all about drunken regrets, and that's the last thing I want Jade to have. "I got her drunk so she'd open up, and now she's sleeping it off."

And I scratch at my chest.

Straik stares at me with a puzzled look. "Are you allergic to humans?"

Kaspar snorts. "He's allergic to doing what he's told."

"Meds reaction," Mathiras points out. He leans on the desk, arms crossed, tail swishing. "So she opened up while she was drunk?"

"Oh yeah." I pause, scratching. "You guys didn't get yours drunk?" I look over at the three of them. "Maybe you should tell me your news before I tell you mine."

Straik settles back in his chair, looking as sulky as ever. "I have no news. The black-haired one screamed and kicked the entire time. I did learn a few new curse words, but nothing of use. She wouldn't tell me anything."

Kaspar leans forward. "I'm useless, too. The yellow-haired one? Alice? She talked, all right. She talked my ear off. But I'm pretty sure she lied about everything. She's a good storyteller but I absolutely can't buy a thing she said. It's clear she was saying whatever she thought I wanted to hear." He sounds utterly disgruntled.

Mathiras runs a hand down his face. "That's better than what I got. Mine cried the entire time."

"The qura'aki?" Straik asks.

Mathiras nods. "I got some information out of her, but she made me feel like an absolute monster the entire time."

"But you did get information out of her?" I prompt. "What'd she say?" I'm suddenly very curious how much it lines up with what Jade told me. Maybe two-cup Jade is a liar as well as a clinger. It's a possibility I didn't consider.

"I got some. Helen isn't good with names, though. Everyone she talked about had names like 'the Angry Face one' or 'the Smelly Breath one.'" He grimaces. "They woke up the three humans after the first mutiny, from what I understand."

"A mutiny?" Straik jumps to his feet again.

"The first one," Mathiras emphasizes. "It gets messier." When Straik sits down again, he continues. "From what I can make out, Helen was told by the others that the girls were pulled out of stasis so they could amuse the crew."

I suddenly find it hard to breathe for all the rage flaring through my system. I clench the arms of the chair, all casualness gone from my body. I know what happens to human slaves. I know what they're kidnapped for. It makes me sick—and furious—to think that Jade, MY Jade, has been abused by someone. I want to snap necks. I want to tear out throats. I want to punch faces. A lot of keffing faces.

"Barbaric," Straik mutters. "I can't believe that happened on my ship."

"Why did your ship have slaves in the first place?" Kaspar retorts, and Straik is silent. Something tells me he doesn't know the answer to that, either.

"According to Helen," Mathiras continues, "Stinkfoot was in charge of the mutiny. He had her taken out of stasis because he was curious about a slave like her, but he didn't tell her she was a clone. Just mentioning that sends her off into fresh tears." His nostrils flare and his tail flicks, agitated. My big brother is very protective, and I can tell it bothers him that Helen cries...or that Helen was abused. Probably both. "But from what I can gather, they didn't touch her because she's worth more on the slave market whole."

"You mean a virgin," Kaspar says grimly.

"Yeah." Mathiras pauses, and I know we're all thinking of

our little sister, Zoey. Zoey, who we protected like crazy, because a pretty human virgin goes for a shit ton of credits on the black market. Her new mate better be watching over her, or he's going to have us to answer to.

"So they abused the three and left the qura'aki untouched," Straik prompts. "That doesn't tell us what happened to the crew. Did the humans kill them?"

"From what I understand from Helen, there was a big argument and a lot of screaming. Stinkfoot was killed, and the crew was divided. One group snuck out in the middle of the night with about twenty stasis pods—"

"Twenty more keffing pods?" Straik interrupts. "How many keffing slaves did my keffing family ship have on it?"

Oh boy. His day is about to get SO much worse. I sit up, a little excited for my turn to share.

"Yeah, well, the crew that was left ended up being two males. From what I understand, they were nice enough to the females but skittish that the others would return. They took a pod and left the females behind because they didn't want to be caught dealing slaves."

I make an angry noise in my throat. "So they just left them behind?"

"It would seem so. That was three years ago and no one's ever returned for them, mutineers or otherwise." Mathiras shakes his head. "Three years, stranded in space on a ship you don't know how to run. I can't imagine."

"They don't know how to run the ship?" Kaspar asks, surprised. "They sure were quick to gas us."

"They did have three years to figure this shit out," I point out. "So basically, Straik's crew was shit, they played with their toys, fought with each other, and left them behind. Do I have it summed up?"

Straik makes an angry noise in his throat.

Mathiras raises a hand. "I don't think they were Straik's

crew. The only men Helen remembers seeing were 'ugly' and 'skinned like a tarsi fruit'."

"Szzt," I say, thinking of the bright orange, rubbery-rinded fruit. It's a pretty good comparison. I also wonder if Jade likes tarsi fruit. She must have had them at' some point for the qura'aki to know what they are. I make a mental note to bring her some when she wakes up, just so I can see her reaction.

"I would never hire szzt," Lord Straik says in his most indignant, stuffy voice. "They are absolutely not trustworthy."

"So your ship was probably stolen long before the girls got woken up," Kaspar concludes.

Mathiras nods. "I think so. I'm no longer angry at them for trying to kill you idiots. They're just doing what they have to do to survive. I'm actually surprised they managed to last this long."

I'm sadder that they're not around for me to kick the shit out of. Bunch of slaving szzt...or just pirating szzt. It's entirely possible that Straik's crew hired some szzt for shady work on the down-low—like, say, helping move slaves—and the hired crew turned on them to steal the profit. It happens a lot. "Well it's obvious we can't leave them behind," I say to my brothers. "They're our responsibility now."

Kaspar nods.

Mathiras has a grim look of displeasure on his face, but he nods, too. "We can't leave them. No one knows how long that ship's air filters are going to keep working without proper maintenance. And Helen said they'd eaten all their food except for a little bit of noodles. If we leave them, we're condemning them to certain death. We have to take them—and the *Star*—back with us." Mathiras continues to flick his tail, thoughtful. "And I hate to say it, but we probably need to approach the authorities."

"What?" This time, Straik speaks up. "We're not taking four

human slaves back on my ship. Slavery is utterly repugnant and I won't have it."

"Uh, you have a ship full of clones already, buddy," Kaspar points out.

I lean over. "He freed them."

Kaspar frowns. "Oh."

Straik gets out from behind his desk and begins pacing. "This looks bad enough as it is. I can't show up on Homeworld with a long-missing ship piloted by human slaves. It will be a blemish my family name will never recover from."

And that means he'll never get into their good graces ever again.

Oh boy. I am about to make his day so much worse. I lean forward, rubbing my hands together. "Is now a good time to tell you guys what the cargo is?"

"It's silks, right?" Straik leans forward on his desk, his hands splayed atop it. There's a desperate look on his face. "Tell me that it's silks."

"Wrong," I tell him gleefully. "It's more keffing humans. A shit ton more. A hundred and thirty-two more."

Straik's bellow of anger echoes down the halls.

19

JADE

I wake up in a strange, soft bed, with a hangover and no idea how I got here. Oh fuck. This is karma, coming back to kick my ass.

Alarmed, I sit bolt upright, my eyes wide as I look around. The large room is totally unfamiliar to me. I'm in space, clearly, but I don't know this ship. I don't know why I'm in a double bed in a very messy room, or why the sheets smell like a masculine sort of soap. I sniff the blankets, curious. What's the last thing I remember? I try to recall. My mouth tastes like something sweet. I squint at the bright lights around me, pushing my hair back out of my face. All around me on the floor and the bed are wrappers to protein bars, the kind we have in our ship.

For a dreadful moment, I worry someone's eaten all of our supplies and we'll starve to death on the edge of space.

But then I remember...the man. The one with the allergic reaction and bright blue skin and the silly, roguish smile.

Adiron. I sigh, because something tells me this is his place. I swing my legs over the side of the bed—

—and immediately tumble to the floor, woozy with a hangover. My stomach churns and I lie still for a long moment amidst the wrappers and dirty clothes, waiting for my queasiness to pass. He got me drunk, I realize. Just sat there and smiled and gave me some sort of juice cocktail that knocked me on my ass. With a groan, I vaguely remember other things, too. Like trying to unbutton his shirt, and trying to lick his neck, and grabbing his dick.

Not a good look, Jade, I tell myself. Not a good look at all.

Slowly, I ease back off the floor and rub my eyes. There's a familiar-looking indention in the wall, and I move to it and slap at buttons on the wall panel until it activates. A door folds back, revealing a small lavatory with a shower, a bath tub, sink and toilet. The sink is cluttered with various things—does this man not know how to put ANYTHING back in its place?—but the tub and shower are clean, at least. I eye them wistfully. We've been very conscious of our water supply back on the *Star* and we've been sparing with bathing as a result. I'm tempted to get in and use up all his water, but with my luck, he'd show up while I'm buck-ass naked and offer to scrub me down.

So, yeah, no.

I rinse my mouth out with a few handfuls of water from the sink and splash my face. At least I'm still dressed. That's a plus. I eye my slave girl outfit and it looks as intact as ever. I touch the crotch of my panties and it's dry, so thank god for that. I knot the oversized borrowed shirt—his shirt, which I'm still wearing—at my waist and then return to the main quarters.

No sooner do I sit down on the bed than my captor, Adiron, saunters in. He grins at me, looking thoroughly pleased. "Jade. You're awake."

"You're no longer swollen," I return as a greeting. I should scream at him, demand to know where the others are, but he's in a good mood and I need to play into that.

"Yeah, Kaspar said my ugliness was making him lose his appetite, so I got a few histamine shots from med-bay. I'm back to being only somewhat dashingly handsome." He mock-rubs his jaw, preening. "Do you like?"

"Am I going to get thrown into the brig if I say no?"

He shoots a finger-gun at me. "I'll change your mind. Give me time." Whistling, he kicks aside a pile of laundry on the floor and heads toward the bathroom I just came out of. The door tries to automatically shut behind him, but a discarded tunic gets in the way and the thing doesn't close. I watch in consternation as he strips off his pants and climbs into the shower, naked. This is...super awkward.

This is also a good time to escape.

I tiptoe toward the door as he steps under the spray, making as little noise as possible. The door doesn't open when I approach, but when I tap the panel, it opens. I peer out...

...and see three of the soldiers at the end of a long, bare hall.

Okay, so much for that. I glance back toward the bathroom and consider my options. I can make a break for it, but I won't get far. I can try to find the others—again, won't get far. Or I can stay here with Adiron and try to get some information out of him. Maybe he's got a gun lying around somewhere in this mess. With that thought in my mind, I pick up a pair of pants and squeeze the material, looking for something that might be left in a pocket somewhere. "So, uh," I call out. "Why am I in your room?"

"You fell asleep," he calls out from the shower. "I thought you might be more comfortable in a bed." Adiron laughs. "You're a terrible drunk, by the way."

"You shouldn't have gotten me drunk," I retort. "That is an absolute dick move."

"Yeah, I know." He doesn't sound all that concerned. "It worked, though."

I tiptoe toward the bathroom door, imagining all sorts of horrible things. What exactly did I say when I was three sheets to the wind? I try to remember but all that goes through my mind is that I cuddled on the man's lap. Ugh. "What worked? What did you do? And where are my friends?"

The shower shuts off, and a moment later, a big, naked alien comes sauntering out of the bathroom, the tiniest of towels over his groin. I let out a yelp of alarm, backing up to the wall and flattening myself against it. Adiron moves right past me, bends over, and starts digging through some of the laundry on the floor. "Gimme a sec. I figure we can have a better conversation if I'm not in the shower."

I stare in horror at his perfect ass. I mean, he's the enemy. He should not be built like a marble statue. I should not be noticing round, juicy buns underneath his tail. That is so wrong on so many levels. "Find some damn pants!"

"That's what I'm doing," Adiron says easily. He picks up a piece of clothing, sniffs it, and then tosses it down again. Then he finally moves toward a wall panel opposite me, touches it, and a closet unfolds from the wall. He yanks out a long piece of clothing, swipes his teeny tiny towel over his chest, and begins to dress.

I close my eyes so I don't see more than any captive should. I don't want to get used to his nudity. I don't want him to think it's okay to change in front of me. I'm not going to be casual about his sexuality, because that's a slippery slope. With this guy, it might start with just buns, but it cannot end up with me in his bed. So I keep my eyes squeezed shut and wait. "Tell me when you're decent."

"I'm never decent," he jokes. "But I have trou on now, if that's what you're asking."

I open one eye cautiously, just in time to see him adjust his clothed junk. He slides his arms into the top part of what must be a uniform or a jumper, and then runs a hand along the auto-fastener, fitting the fabric to his body. With a grin, Adiron regards me. "You're skittish."

"You would be too, if you were in my place."

"That's fair." He tilts his head, wet hair dripping in front of his eyes. "And your friends are fine. They're with the others. We've decided that you're our guests now."

Wait, what? "Hold on a moment. What are you talking about?"

Adiron turns and picks up a boot, then looks around the floor, obviously searching for its mate. "You told me that you guys were left behind by the crew of the ship. That you're low on food supplies and air filters. Your ship is also heading toward an ice field the size of a small galaxy, and if you get caught up in it, you're never going to be found again. So you're going to stay with us. You're our guests."

"I-I don't want to be your guest." Especially if it means waking up in his bed. I can only imagine what being a "guest" means. I'm sure they'll be nice at first, and then it'll turn into us needing to "earn" our keep somehow. That we're using up precious food, water, and oxygen, and we'll need to pay them back somehow. We'll be powerless and at the mercy of aliens once more. Not that we aren't in that situation already, but this is against my will. If I run headlong into danger, then I'm just as responsible for whatever happens to me. "I want to go back to the *Buoyant Star*. Take me and my friends there."

"No, you don't," he says, kicking aside a pile of laundry. "Have you seen my boot?"

"Yes, I do."

"Where?" He looks up at me.

I clench my jaw. "I want to go back to MY ship," I enunciate.

"Oh." He pauses. "No, you don't."

"Yes, I do."

"No, you don't."

"Yes, I do."

"No, you don't."

I resist the urge to pinch the bridge of my nose in frustration. "Are we really doing this?"

"You wanna do something else?" He gives me an utterly roguish smile.

"You mean like push you off a bridge?" I retort.

Adiron laughs as if I've said the funniest thing ever. He shakes his head, grinning at me. "You wouldn't do that. Not when I'm about to take you back to your friends."

I pause at that. "Are you really?"

"Of course. You're not a prisoner." He digs out his boot with a look of triumph. "Let me finish putting these on and I'll show you around."

20

JADE

*A*s we walk through the ship, Adiron talks. And talks. And talks. If he's trying to keep anything secret, he's doing a poor job of it, because he fills me in on everything that's been going on while I was asleep. I'm not surprised to learn that Ruth and Alice didn't break, and that Helen did. She's never been apart from us, and I'm guessing she panicked. Adiron says she cried the entire time and his brother feels guilty, and all I can think is that I'm glad. I hope he feels guilty as shit for bullying her.

I also learn I didn't blab as much as I thought, but I did talk about the human cargo—the others waiting in the huge bay of stasis pods. Adiron says that Straik freaked out and wants to see the "cargo" for himself, but he can't get access. Someone's changed something in the *Buoyant Star's* computer systems and it won't allow him in. That's a surprise to me, because we've been able to come and go as we please...but in a way, it makes sense. The *Star* thinks we're cargo, too.

So this "Lord Straik" and the brothers need us to get their hands on the other humans. That buys at least one of us some safety, possibly all of us if we play our cards right. I tuck this away mentally. I need to talk to the others so we can come up with a plan, make sure we're all on the same page. I don't want these corsairs killing three of us in order to force the fourth one to act. Unfortunately, I also think this means we can't tell Helen anything. She's too innocent and she'd share our plans in a heartbeat if someone even looked our way threateningly.

Meanwhile, Adiron just keeps talking. I'm only half listening—I need the information he's spilling, but I also need to figure out a plan, and my head throbs and I'm also trying to simultaneously map out our surroundings in my mind. It's a lot to take in. "Mathiras is my oldest brother," he's saying as we turn down another hall. "I guess if we have a leader, it's him, though Kaspar and I don't listen to him all that well." He shoots me another cocky grin. "Kaspar's my other brother. I'm the youngest and the most charming."

I absently snort at that, noticing that a couple of the dark-uniformed troops are heading down the hall in our direction. I stiffen, holding my breath, but they only stroll past us, shooting me a curious glance. Whew. I exhale and then glance over at Adiron. He's got a thoughtful look on his face that's edging toward a frown. "What's wrong?" I ask.

"They were looking at your legs. I don't like that." The frown deepens as he studies my clothing. I'm still in my slave girl rags, with his shirt covering me. It's not like I've been offered a change of clothing.

I cross my arms over my chest, a little worried. "Am I in danger from them?" A horrible thought occurs to me—I've been dealing with Adiron but...what if he and his brothers aren't interested in claiming us for themselves and hand us over to the crew? What if we have to service all twenty-odd alien men on this ship? That's a nightmare.

"From a'ani? No. Not at all." Adiron continues to look thoughtful. "I just didn't like it. We should get you some clothes."

"Is that what they're called? A'ani? Is that what Helen is?"

"No, she's a qura'aki," Adiron points out. He turns and steers me down a different hall, apparently changing his mind. "She is a clone of an old race that no longer exists. Every now and then, a female clone turns up on the pleasure markets and is sold for an obscene number of credits. A'ani are another cloned race, but they are quite common." At my blank look, he adds, "They are marked with the red-hued skin so all may know they are cloned."

"Lovely," I say in a flat voice. Skin color bullshit, even in space. And poor, poor Helen. "So Helen is someone's pleasure doll."

"Unfortunately, yes." He doesn't look pleased at the thought, which makes me feel a little better. He leans in close to me. "This universe is not kind to humans, I'm afraid. Or qura'aki. But don't worry. You have me."

"That somehow doesn't make me feel much better."

"It will. Give me time to win your trust." He shoots me another cheerful smile and then gestures at another door. "Here. I bet we can find a uniform of some kind for you to wear. I just need to do some digging." Adiron tugs me in after him, and when I see the messy clothes on the floor, I think for a moment that this entire ship is full of slobs.

Then I realize we're back in his room. I cross my arms again, my brows going up. "I'm not wearing your dirty clothes."

"I know. But there's not exactly a clothing boutique around here. You'll have to wear our castoffs until we get better for you." He pulls open his closet again and considers.

"I have clothes back on the *Star*," I offer, my voice sweet. If I can get us back to my ship, that's half the battle. I just need the upper hand in some way.

Adiron glances over at me, a smirk on his face. "Nice try, but no."

I breathe out a long sigh. "So you're no better than anyone else we've run into. You're just using us."

He actually looks wounded at my accusation. "Not at all. You're safe with us. My sister, Zoey—she's human, too. We saved her from a slave ship when she was little more than a tiny runt." He has the softest smile on his face, and it's clear that he adores his sister. "She's on another ship with her mate right now, but if she were here she'd smack me as hard as she could and tell me to take care of you guys." He pulls out a jumper that looks suspiciously like his. "Here. Try this one on."

I take it from him, cautious. "You have a human sister?"

"Yeah. She's pretty much an irritating little shit. She's also the greatest." His look gets a tiny bit wistful. "I miss her now that she's off and mated, but she's happy so I guess I can't be selfish."

I wonder if this is true. "So...we're like sisters to you? Us humans?"

Adiron leans against the wall, giving me a heavy-lidded look. "Oh, make no mistake, Jade. I'm sure your friends are nice and all, but as for you? I am not interested in you in a brotherly way. At all." His smile is slow and confident. "But I'm pretty sure you guessed that already."

21

ADIRON

*J*ade is quiet as I dig through my clothes, looking for a uniform of some kind small enough for her. I don't have one of course, so at this point I'm just going to settle for one that's clean. The clones are far more human-sized and I'm sure Dopekh or one of the others would loan me something, but...the thought of Jade wearing another male's clothing eats at my gut. I want her to wear mine.

Kef me, I'm already getting wildly possessive and I've only known the female a few hours. I can't imagine how bad I'll have it in a week from now. Even when I was infatuated with Shaalyn, I was never this bad.

I find my favorite work uniform, a single-piece jumper that has seen me through a lot. I smell it to make sure that it's clean even though it's hanging up, and then I hold it out to her. "You can wear this."

She crosses her arms under her magnificent chest, and it

takes everything I have not to drop my gaze. "If I do, will you take me to my friends?"

"Of course."

Jade gives me a look as if she doesn't quite believe me and then heads into the bathroom to change. I hear a bit of rustling and then the sound of a panel being plucked out of its place. I grin to myself. No doubt she's raiding my toiletries, looking for something she can use as a weapon. All she's going to find is some personal deodorizer and plas-film that came with the room, since this isn't our ship but Straik's. My old lavatory had a compartment with blasters and knives, because you never know when you'll need a weapon, but I don't have that here. I lean close to the door and offer, "If you're looking for something to use as a weapon, you're better off looking under my mattress. There's nothing in there."

She comes out a moment later, glaring at me. The jumpsuit is bunched up at her ankles and her hands are buried in material, the crotch of the outfit somewhere around her knees. Instead of it being sexy, she looks...ridiculous. I snicker.

Jade runs her fingers through her wild hair, pushing it back, and ignores my laughter. "Got a belt, you giant?"

I turn to the closet and dig around, looking for a spare. I hear her movements—humans really are loud in everything they do—and I know she's heading for the mattress, looking for a blaster. She can take it if it makes her feel less worried. I'm not afraid of her shooting me. It'd probably just make me fall more head over heels for her.

I do love a difficult female.

When I close the closet, I see her adjusting the front of her borrowed clothing, puffing it out, no doubt to hide my blaster that she's got stuffed in there. "I'd use the belt," I point out as I hold it out to her. "I have a holster for that blaster. Don't tuck it into your underclothes or you'll shoot a hole in places that shouldn't be shot."

She looks at me with that too calm gaze, her eyes narrowed. "Why are you giving me a weapon?"

"Because you're my guest?"

"I've heard that line before. It didn't involve me being anyone's guest."

I can just imagine, and my blood boils at how she's probably been mistreated. "I figure if you were going to kill me, you'd have done so already, back on your ship. If it makes you feel better, carry my weapon. Just try not to shoot the a'ani. They really are decent males."

She reluctantly digs into the front of her clothing and then pulls out my blaster. "And your brothers?"

"Not all that decent, but I promise on my balls that they won't harm you."

"And the one in black? Straik?"

I grin. "Him, you can shoot."

She grins back, a genuine grin, and I'm utterly dazzled. This female is so keffing beautiful. Her smile fades as she catches me watching her, and she tilts her head, then considers the blaster in her hand. "I wonder if I should shoot you? Considering you got me drunk so you could wring secrets out of me."

"It wouldn't be the first time an angry female shot me the morning after a drunken bender," I joke. It actually would be, but it sounds good.

Jade just shakes her head at me. "Are you ever serious?"

"Not if I can help it. That's Mathiras's job."

"One of your brothers?"

"Tallest one," I agree. "Looks constipated."

"Probably because he's dealing with your shit," she quips.

Aaaaand I'm in love all over again.

I give her another lovesick grin, and she just rolls her eyes at me, putting the blaster in her belt. "Quit looking at me like that. Anyone ever tell you that you have a rotten poker face?"

"My sister Zoey. Like, a dozen times." I follow her back out of my room and put a hand to the small of her back to guide her. Jade jerks in surprise, watching me, but relaxes when I don't touch her more than that. "She also says I can clear a room with a belch, but that's a lie. Kaspar is much, much worse with that sort of thing."

"Charming."

I actually do wish I was more charming in this moment. Kaspar can be pretty suave when he wants to be, and Mathiras is good with ladies. Me, I just grin like a fool...kind of like I am right now. Not that I've ever really cared about getting a lady-friend, but now that I do, my goofy smile isn't doing me any favors. Jade's shooting me wary looks, like she expects me to pounce on her. I guess I can't blame her...I did get her drunk and trick her. "Can I ask you something?"

The expression on her face has "uh oh" written all over it. "What?"

"How do you and I become friends?"

Her mouth flattens for the barest of moments. "You're very direct, aren't you?"

"I don't know another way to be." I shrug. "I'm not a good pirate for my smarts. I'm good because I'm loyal and I like to run into danger. Mathiras and Kaspar are the smart ones."

"Mmmmhmm."

"So...how? Because I want to be your friend."

Jade keeps walking, her gaze on the hall in front of us, but she gives her head the tiniest, rueful shake. "That cat might be out of the bag. I don't know if I can trust you."

"So..." I continue, not willing to give up. "How do I put that cat back in the bag? Also, what's a cat?"

Her lips twitch, and a hint of a smile curves her lush mouth. All right. If we can't be friends right off the bat, then maybe I can win her over with jokes. Maybe what Jade has needed all her life is a big goofy idiot like myself who doesn't take anything too seriously and loves a good time. Maybe she needs someone like me so she can have a good time, too. So she can relax a little bit because she knows I've got her back.

Yep. I think I'm exactly what this female needs. Now to make her realize it.

22

JADE

*E*ven though I don't trust him as far as I can throw him, Adiron is a perfect gentleman as he escorts me through the halls of the ship. *The Darkened Eye*, I repeat to myself, in case I need the name of it later. Lord Straik. Mathiras, his brother. Adiron. And...Gaspard? Close enough. And clones. I can't forget the clones. It's all information, and information can be currency when you've got nothing else. So I make note of people and faces, and doors, and I try to pay attention to everything as we walk through the large ship.

Adiron pauses in front of a large double door, and I touch the blaster strapped to my waist. I feel much better with it at my side. Just knowing I have a weapon in a ship full of strangers means that I can't be overpowered and attacked. I can at least protect myself. I think. I forgot to ask him to show me that the gun works. I just took it on his word.

God, I really am bad at being a badass.

My companion notices my frown as I touch the gun again. He puts his hand on the pad to open the doors. "What?"

"How do I know this weapon works?" I gesture at my waist. "How do I know this isn't another one of your tricks?"

Reaching over, Adiron takes the weapon from the holster with practiced ease, flicks a switch that makes the thing hum like it's powering up, and then turns and points it at the nearest wall. He fires, and a concentrated beam of light flies toward the wall, the sound so flaringly loud that my ears pop. Sparks fly and a massive scorch-mark appears on the pristine wall, and an alarm goes off overhead.

The door opens to a meeting room, where the other corsairs and my friends sit.

"What the kef are you doing to my ship?" the one in black bellows. Lord Straik. "You keffing idiot! You could get us all killed!"

At my side, Adiron shrugs, handing the weapon back to me. "Jade wanted to make sure it worked."

"Can we not fire weapons inside an environmentally controlled ship?" Mathiras asks, his expression weary, as if he's seen this shit a dozen times before. "I'm a big fan of breathing."

The other brother—Kaspar, I remember now—just looks over at me and the weapon at my waist. "Should have picked a double-barrel Kith model," he says to Adiron. "Less of a kick for human hands."

Adiron gestures at him. "Excellent point. I'll get her one later."

"You," Mathiras says, pointing at Kaspar, "are not helping."

"Hello," Alice calls out in her sweet, musical voice. She snaps her fingers twice, getting everyone's attention. "Can we please focus here?"

"It's like being on the Good Ship Attention Deficit," Ruth adds sullenly. She's slouched low in her seat, which tells me she's still wearing her "brat" persona like a protective cloak. I don't blame her. The less these strangers know about our real personalities, the better. Ruth lifts her chin in my direction. "So where's my gun?"

"You don't get one," Lord Straik snaps at her. "I don't even know if that keffing idiot should have one."

"Probably not," Adiron says cheerily. He steers me around the long table and pulls out a chair for me, just like we're on a weird date of some kind. "I can't be trusted around weapons...or laundry."

"Oddly specific," I murmur as I sit down. I note everyone's appearance, making sure that the girls are all right. Alice's hair is a little mussed, but she looks good, even if she's still wearing her slave girl outfit. Ruth sits to one side of her, and she's dressed similarly to me, but her cuffs aren't rolled up nearly as much. I notice that they're flanked on either side. Ruth is close to Lord Straik—probably so he can choke her if she doesn't shut up—and Alice is next to Kaspar, who she's doing her best to ignore. Between Kaspar and Mathiras is Helen, who has on one of the clone military uniforms, a bright smile of excitement on her face. She looks like she's having a blast. She probably is —this is undoubtedly the most excitement she's had in her short life.

I also notice that her chair is close to Mathiras's and his arm rests on the table, but Helen is within reach of him, and I do my best not to glare. Every male alien we've ever run across is possessive of Helen, and I'm not going to let her fall into anyone's clutches. I'll have to warn her when we get a moment alone. For now, I relax in my seat between Mathiras and Adiron, who drops into his chair beside me as if we're on a date and I'm his girlfriend. He even puts his arm on the back of my chair.

I try not to roll my eyes.

"I am glad we are all here now," Straik says in a stiff voice. His accent sounds different from the others, even through the translator, and I wonder if he's speaking a different dialect than the others. Different country? Planet? I wish I knew. "We need to discuss the matter of the discovery of the *Buoyant Star* and its...ahem, cargo."

"We also need to discuss the weapons we'll be receiving, since we're now part of this crew," Alice says boldly. "If Jade has a weapon, I want one, too."

"I am not arming you," Straik continues. "Now, can we discuss—"

I watch as Kaspar leans toward her. "I will," he mock-whispers. "After this." And he winks.

Alice fights the smile that curves her mouth, but she looks pleased, and a new thought occurs to me...we set a seduction trap for these men. What if they're playing the same game with us? Feed us, clothe us, seduce us with weapons and promises of safety...and then what?

I wish I could trust someone. Anyone.

I look over at Adiron as Straik continues speaking, and I notice he's not paying attention to the others. He's watching me, and there's that weird mixture of pride and affection in his eyes as he regards me. I don't know what to make of him...but I wonder if he's the one I can trust.

After all, he DOES have a terrible poker face.

23

JADE

"*L*et us discuss the *Buoyant Star* now," Lord Straik demands in a pompous voice. "We've wasted enough time as it is."

Suddenly, I'm tired of this. I'm tired of being bossed around by men all the time. I'm tired of being afraid and not being respected. I feel like a ping-pong ball that's been bounced back and forth between parties ever since I woke up to find myself in deep space instead of on Earth. First, it was the crew of the *Star*...or at least, *a* crew. Then they fractured and split, and we were left with two grope-happy idiots, and when we made it clear we were not submitting as simpering bed slaves just because they had the keys to the ship, they left us behind.

Now these blue guys think they can run roughshod over us, and I'm tired of all of it. I'm tired of being pushed around this universe just because I don't have a penis.

And it ends now.

I lift a hand into the air before Straik can say anything else. "I need to know a few things before we go on." And I wait, calmly.

Straik makes a blustering noise, but Mathiras watches me with sharp eyes. Maybe he senses I've been pushed to the edge of my limits. "What is it?"

I clear my throat, feigning a serenity I don't quite feel. "Before we discuss anything, I need to know if my ladies are all right. If they are still cuffed or they've been harmed in any way, then none of this..."—I gesture at the table we're seated around, as if we're holding a very civilized sort of meeting—"...matters."

Straik opens his mouth to speak.

I lift a finger, silencing him. "I didn't ask you." I point at Alice and Ruth, then at Helen. "I asked them."

At my side, I hear Adiron huff in what has to be laughter, and I discreetly kick him under the table. Now is not the time.

For a moment, Straik looks as if he's going to burst a blood vessel in his eye, and I suspect no one talks to him like I just did. I don't care, though. I'm tired of people bargaining for me or around me. I have nothing left to lose, and so I'm going to bet it all. I'm not a warrior. I don't win my battles with a gun or elite skills. I've got jiggly thighs and a fear of heights, so I have to win my wars with smarts. And I know right now that if I let these men make plans around me, I'm never going to be on equal ground with any of them.

If they don't like it, they can just send me back to the other ship. It's probably safer there for us anyhow.

"Alice?" Kaspar asks, and for a moment, he looks just like Adiron, because he's doing his best to hide a laughing smirk behind a hand...and doing it poorly.

Alice licks her lips and gives me a proud smile that tells me she's thrilled I've taken charge. "I have been treated well enough," she says. "No torture, no rape, and while I would like some clothes, I'm content to wait a little longer." She lifts her hands to display her wrists. "No cuffs, either."

"Ruth?" I ask.

"Fine," is all she says.

I turn to Helen. "Are you all right?"

Her smile is broad and sweet. "I'm wonderful, thank you for asking."

"No one tortured you or hurt you? Did they touch you inappropriately?" I have to push it, to make sure Helen grasps what I'm referring to.

"Mathiras didn't sex me, no," she says cheerily. "I asked him to tongue kiss me, but he declined. But if I feel a sexual urge, I'll probably ask him to service me."

Now Mathiras is the one making strangled noises. He shifts in his seat, looking distinctly uncomfortable. "Uh. I would never touch her without her permission. Let's just set that on the table."

"Well shit, I didn't ask for tongue kisses," Adiron chimes in. "I should have asked."

"You wouldn't have received," I say tartly and turn back to Helen. "You and me will chat later, all right?" It's natural for Helen to be sexually interested in the first halfway decent men we've run across in our adventures, but I need to remind her that she needs to be careful. I eye each of the women again. "Is anyone hungry? Do we need to eat something before we have our meeting?"

"I'm good," Alice says.

Ruth just shrugs, turning to give a smug look at Straik.

Helen lights up with excitement. "Jade, you should have seen it! They have a thing in their dispenser that makes cake! I had a cake! With whipped stuff on top of it! And Mathiras said I could have as much as I want!"

That makes Ruth sit up. "Well, now I want cake."

"Oh my stars, Ruth, it was SO good," Helen enthuses.

Straik just sighs, rubbing his face. "I'll put in an order for cake. While we wait, can we please continue?"

"Yes," I say, stepping in again. I straighten in my chair. "We women need to know what our position on this ship will be before we agree to anything. Are we cargo? Are we crew? What rights do we have?"

At my side, Adiron shoots me an admiring look, as if he approves of my ballsiness. "You'd be crew, of course."

"If we're crew, we get weapons, then? Our own quarters? Bodily autonomy?"

"Access to the ship and her workings?" Ruth asks in an innocent voice and then ruins it with a slow smile.

"All the cake we want?" Helen adds.

"And someone to show us how to use everything on the ship, I assume," Alice chimes in, ever practical. "We'd need lessons on how to do the remedial stuff. Access to language lessons, too."

"This is my ship," Straik begins, and I can tell he doesn't like the way the bargaining is going. "I'm in charge here—"

"And Jade is in charge of us," Helen interjects quickly. "That's why we trust her to talk for us." She pauses for a moment, and then adds, "Not you."

I'm proud of her. She's not been completely distracted by cake—or trying to kiss Mathiras—after all.

"I cannot believe this." Lord Straik makes an indignant noise. "We're trying to rescue you, you ungrateful humans."

"You're crew," Adiron reassures me. "We'll figure it out. You're in control of your body. That's not even a question."

There's so much I want to address in this moment. Lord Straik's calling us ungrateful, Adiron and the others ignoring him, the whole body thing—but I need to stay focused. "Let's talk about rescue, then. What does that entail, exactly? Are you bringing us back to Earth?"

Adiron hesitates for the first time and looks at his brothers. I get a sour, sad feeling in my stomach.

Something tells me that no matter how this goes down, it's going to make me unhappy.

24

ADIRON

I hate that I don't have the answer Jade needs. I hate that I can see disappointment in her amber eyes. She wants to go back to Earth. There's two problems with that. One—Earth is supposed to be off-limits to everyone, not that slavers pay much attention to that.

And two—there's not much Earth left to go back to. A few years ago, the stupid Earth people caused a temporal rift to open up in their planet's atmosphere and everything got all keffed up. There's no "Earth" to return to...at least, not how she thinks it is. The planet's still there...just the people aren't. The cities have fallen, the humans have more or less disappeared, and rumor has it that a few misplaced drakoni just run around burning everything.

"You can't go back to Earth," Mathiras says, but his tone is odd. "Long story, but it's not on the table. I'm sorry."

There's a long, aching pause, and I remember all the times my little sister begged to be taken back to Earth, "just for a visit." I remember how devastated she was when the news about the rift back on Earth made its way to us. It's one thing to choose to stay in space. It's another to realize you can never go home again, because your home has been destroyed.

"So that's it, then?" The yellow-haired one—Alice—says. She crosses her arms over her chest, looking mutinous. "You just decide we can't go home, but we're not slaves. So what are we, then?"

Everyone looks over at Straik, but he's silent. He's got a strange look on his face, as if he's just now realizing the magnitude of what we've found. For a male that seems to hate slavery, he sure does find himself with a lot of slaves.

"Guests," Mathiras says. "You're guests."

"Crew," I volunteer. If no one else wants to arm the humans, I will. I'll give 'em whatever they need to feel safe and secure. And at some point, when that suspicious, haunted look leaves Jade's face, I'll even tell her about Earth. Not right now, though. No one needs that sort of bomb dropped on them when everything else in their life is so uncertain. It can wait.

"So we're your guests," Jade continues. "Until when? And where are you going to take us, if not to Earth? Another space station where we'll be sold off once more?"

"Rather just go back to OUR ship and take our chances," Ruth adds, shooting an angry look my way, as if I'm the one to blame.

"You can't do that," Mathiras says. "Let's for a moment forget the one hundred and some odd slaves in stasis—"

Straik makes a strangled noise. Something tells me he's not about to forget.

"—you won't be safe there. You don't have the supplies, and your ship is heading toward an ice field in deep space. In another month or two, you could be lost forever. If you go into that field, you won't be coming out, and no one will be able to come after you."

"Provided it doesn't completely destroy your ship with debris," Kaspar adds helpfully.

"You say there's an ice field. How do we trust you?"

Mathiras gestures at the computer on the wall. "We can show you on the screens!"

"And how do we know it's not another trick? You're still not answering my question. If we leave our ship, where do we go that's safe?"

"There's a farm planet," I begin. "It's called Risda III, and it's friendly to humans."

"Why does that man have his head in his hands?" Helen asks, interrupting.

We all turn to look at Straik. Sure enough, he's shaking his head, his hands over his face. I try to bite back a smile. I can just imagine how he feels about that. The scandalous uncle his family has been trying so hard to make everyone forget will be front and center, and Straik will be tied to him if he dumps dozens of humans in his lap. This has to be his worst nightmare.

Which makes me kinda amused. Straik's decent enough—the way he treats the clones tells me that—but man, he does not have a sense of humor at all.

"A farm planet sounds like a load of bullshit," Ruth says. "How do we know the moment we agree to this you don't drive us straight to a brothel?"

Mathiras seems unbothered by her skepticism. "We're different than the others you've run across."

"You mean you're not pirates?" Jade asks.

"Well...no, we're pirates."

"But you're different," Jade says, her voice flat.

I turn toward her. I get fear. How long did it take before Zoey started to trust us? I know she's backed into a corner and she's trying to bargain for the best position for her friends and herself. But she has to trust us. If they don't come with us, it's a death sentence. "You can trust me. You know you can."

Her eyes soften as she looks at me, and I see the fear and hope in her gaze. She wants to trust. She does. Jade licks her lips, thinking, and then looks over at the girls across the table, and I realize she's not deciding for herself, but for all of them... and that's going to change her answer. "Look at it from our perspective," Jade says in a soft voice. "Ever since we woke up, we've been abused and enslaved and told that what we want doesn't matter. We've met round after round of pirates who all wanted the same thing. And now you show up—"

"Still pirates, I might add," Alice interjects.

"—and you say you're different," Jade continues. "But you used a stun gun on us—"

—after you attacked us first," Kaspar points out.

"—and then you cuffed us, separated us, interrogated us, but NOW we're supposed to trust you." Jade tilts her head, watching me. "How do we know that you're not going to just put us in chains and enslave us the moment we agree to head off with you guys? How do we know we're not condemning a hundred and thirty-two people to the same fate? Because right now, those people are safe in those pods. They're dreaming, and they're safe, and they're not aware that when they wake up, they're going to be slaves. But if I agree to go with you guys and you betray us, I'm fucking all of them over. Not just me, not just Alice or Ruth or Helen, but everyone."

No wonder she's so stressed. That's a lot of responsibility, and Jade's taken it all on her shoulders, I can tell.

It's a good thing she has someone like me. I'll make sure she never takes things too seriously. I'll make sure she smiles. And I can massage the stress out of her shoulders every night.

Kef me, I think I just gave myself a boner.

I shift in my seat, uncomfortable. Now's not the time. "So how do we get you to trust us? You either believe us or you don't. Whatever we show you, you'll just find an argument against it."

Jade looks over at the others, and no one speaks. She thinks for a minute and then turns back to me. "We're going back to our ship tonight, so we can talk in private. We'll let you know our decision in the morning."

"First of all, that is my family's ship," Straik says in a tired voice.

"Actually the laws of salvage mean it's theirs," Kaspar points out.

"And it's full of slaves," I add helpfully. "I definitely wouldn't keep bragging about the whole 'family' thing if I were you."

He ignores all of us. "Second of all, I don't trust you to go back to that ship and not try to leave."

Ruth just snorts as if he's being ridiculous (which he is). "Where exactly do you think we're going to go?"

"Sabotage, then."

"So send a bodyguard with us," Jade says quickly.

"You mean a hostage?" Lord Straik asks.

Jade's expression tightens. "He's only a hostage if someone's a hostile party."

Spending all night with Jade? In her natural environment? Sounds like a slice of "Yes" to me. Before another argument can break out, I gesture at myself. "I volunteer."

25

JADE

I should have known that Adiron would volunteer. He seems to be fascinated with me. He also seems to not be bothered by anything at all, so I guess he's a good choice. I'm just glad it's not Straik, though it might have been easier for me if it was one of the other two brothers. Adiron just...watches me all the time. And smiles. Like...he's having a blast just being around me.

I don't know what to make of it.

We wait near the ship-to-ship walkway as Adiron grabs a change of clothes. The other brothers don't seem concerned at all, which makes me think that they're exactly who they say they are—not slavers, just brothers looking for an easy score and found us instead. That they will absolutely take us some-place safe and not abuse us. Lord Straik, I'm not too sure about. He watches us with an expression that Alice sums up perfectly. "He looks like he just found out his fancy house has a roach infestation," she whispers to us.

She's right. And humans are the roaches. Straik's family ship IS infested with them.

Adiron finally returns, a bulging bag in his arms. "I'm ready."

Alice and I exchange a look. "You're not supposed to bring weapons," I point out. "This is you being a go-between and guest on our ship while we figure things out."

"It's a change of pants and some fruit," Adiron says, opening the plas-film bag to display its contents. "I knew Jade really liked it and it sounds like you guys are low on everything, so I thought I'd share." He leans in and mock-whispers, "Straik has plenty."

I hand the bag to Helen. "Check this, please?"

Ruth and Alice move forward to pat Adiron down while I train my blaster on him, just in case this is all a trap after all and I'm a bad judge of character.

Adiron is all smiles as his arms and legs are patted down. "Careful, ladies, I'm ticklish."

Ruth jabs a finger into his kidneys, making him wince.

"He's clean," Alice says, turning back to me.

I nod and glance over at Helen. Her arms are full of fruit and she shoots me a guilty look. "Nothing but underpants in his bag. And these."

I turn back to Adiron, who flutters his lashes as if he's oh-so-innocent. "Come on, you," I say, and do my best not to smile. "You're MY guest tonight."

RETURNING to the stale air and quiet halls of the *Star* feels like slipping into a comfortable pair of shoes. Straik's ship might be state of the art for aliens, but after three years of haunting these halls, I feel at home here. Even the musty smell of the air filters makes me feel safer. I take a deep breath and then look at the others. "Why don't you guys go split up the fruit in the kitchen? I'll show Adiron where he's going to be sleeping."

"You can't wait to be alone with me again," he says, delighted. "I accept." And he holds the crook of his arm out like we're going to go for a promenade. "I'd love to take a stroll."

I want to roll my eyes at him but I'm slowly becoming charmed by his irreverent attitude. He doesn't take himself seriously, that much is clear, and he brought fruit for the girls after seeing how much I enjoyed it. I raise an eyebrow at him. "There better not be the fruit that makes you drunk in that bag."

"Sweetfruit?" He shakes his head. "Nah. No one eats it plain. We just juice it. And I wouldn't bring that. I don't need to interrogate you again. We're friendly now."

As if that solves everything. I glance over at the others, but they're heading toward the kitchens. I want to sit down with them and find out what they think, but I also want to pick Adiron's brain. I want to know the reason he was so quick to volunteer, and if he's got an ulterior motive.

I also want to do that without scaring the others—especially Helen—so I'm going to peel him off from the group and see what I can find out.

Ruth clears her throat behind me, and I glance backward. She makes a quick gesture of typing, and I realize she's going to watch me on the monitors—one of the few things we know how to operate. I nod at her. She's got my back. Then, I turn to Adiron and gesture that he should walk at my side.

The big guy looks a little disappointed that I won't link arms with him, but he shrugs and follows me. "Where are we headed?"

"I'll show you."

We head down one of the halls of the *Star*, and I keep a careful distance between us. Adiron just watches me instead of looking around, so if he's a spy, he's a shitty one.

I open the door to one of the empty rooms, where the crew used to stay. We've ransacked it for useful stuff, but there's still a clean, made bed and privacy. "You'll be staying right here," I say to Adiron.

"Is this your room?"

"Why would I let you stay in my room?"

"Because I let you stay in mine?"

There's a boyish eagerness to his expression that turns my irritation into laugher. It's hard to get mad at a man who approaches the world with such puppyish enthusiasm. "Nice try, but no."

"Can't blame me for trying." He shrugs, still grinning. "I like hearing you laugh, by the way."

I just shake my head at him. I wish I knew how to read him better. I find it hard to believe that someone like him—a pirate —is so lighthearted and chipper. That solving the problems of the universe is as simple as he makes it sound. "I wish I had more reason to laugh."

"You will," Adiron promises me. "You're with me now."

"You assume we're going to decide to go with you," I point out. "That we're not going to stay here and take our chances."

His expression falls. "I know you don't trust me, but it really isn't safe. Your best bet at any sort of life is to come with us. I promise you, no matter what happens, you're safe with me."

"I want to believe you, but I don't know if I can." I spread my hands. "Whatever decision the four of us make changes the lives of a hundred and thirty-two people. That's a heavy weight to carry."

"I understand." He pauses for a moment and then the impish grin returns. "So can I see your room anyhow?"

How can I resist? I move down the hall, heading for my door. "There's not much to see. All I have is what I've scavenged from what our captors left behind." I open my door and gesture that he can walk inside. He does, and I know my room is neat and tidy compared to his. There's a pretty glass bowl that I found in someone's room that I snagged, just because it made me happy, and a small potted plant. Other than that, I have a few pillows and multiple blankets on my bed, because I like cocooning when I sleep.

Adiron heads in, opening my closet and the attached bathroom, and then gives me a curious look. "This was someone else's room first, right?"

I nod. "When we...woke up, we weren't given rooms of our own. After they left us, we took what we wanted, because fuck them."

His jaw clenches, and I suspect he likes hearing about that time in my life about as much as I enjoy thinking about it. It's in the past, though, and I'm determined not to let it haunt my future. Adiron rubs his hands, looking around my room again, and then gestures at the wall panel. "What do you want me to show you? I can probably get you going on the basics."

"Even if I'm not listed as crew but cargo?"

When he pauses, I know it's a dead end. "Yeah, that's a problem." He turns back to me. "But you can get to the pods? In the cargo bay?"

I shrug. "So far, yeah. Again, I guess it's because we're listed as cargo. We can't operate much, but we can get into the bay."

Adiron nods. "Can I see them?"

There goes my easy mood. I stiffen, wondering if this is a trap of some kind. He was so sly in getting me to drink that juice that I wonder if I won't see another trap coming. "You can see them from afar. There's a window in one of the halls that allows you to see the pods."

I half-expect him to argue, but he only nods. "That's fair." His lips quirk as he looks over at me. "Still don't trust me yet?"

"It's not just my life I'm playing with here."

"And would you trust me with your life, then?" he presses.

"After knowing you for a day? No," I say bluntly. "I trust Helen and Ruth and Alice with mine, because we've been stuck together for the last three years. We're like family. You're..."

"If you say 'family,' I'm going to be very sad."

"...like a really pesky neighbor."

"I'll take that. You can get romantic with a neighbor." And he winks at me.

"Are you ever serious? Ever?" Even though he's making me crazy with his assumptions and jokes, there's also something completely charming about him. Like he's as deep as a puddle and he's aware of it, and that's part of his charm. Like despite his job, he's got a ray of sunshine in his soul, and I can appreciate that. He makes me smile, even when I want to throw my hands up in frustration at another one of his cracks.

"Very rarely serious," he reassures me, grinning widely. "But I am definitely serious about a few things."

I snort. "Name them."

Adiron's expression just becomes more and more delighted. "You. I'm very serious about you, Jade. It may not seem like it, but I take your safety—and your need for control over the situation—very seriously. That's why I'm here."

"You *volunteered*."

"Well, yeah. Because I know I can keep you safe." He gives me a look as if to say the answer is obvious.

"And you think your brothers can't?"

Adiron looks positively wicked in the next moment. "Oh, I imagine they can, but this way, I get to be around you all night long. There's no way I'd give up this opportunity for one of those chuckleheads."

"So this is about me?"

He blinks. "Of course it is. I thought I made that pretty clear."

I purse my lips, studying him. "Is this a trick?"

"Is what a trick?"

I gesture at him, standing in the middle of my room. "You acting like you're half in love with me after we just met."

Adiron beams at me. "Glad you noticed. And I'm not acting."

26

JADE

"*J*'m sad," Alice says. "We skipped out before we got cake."

"We can have cake when the world isn't burning around us," Ruth points out. "We need to figure out how to outsmart these guys and get our freedom."

Helen just watches as Ruth paces, her head resting on her arms as she leans on the table. She's been oddly quiet, and I get the weird sensation that she's not happy to be back on the *Star*. That Helen wanted to stay on the other ship. And why wouldn't she? It has new people to talk to, new experiences, new foods, and a guy that Helen apparently wants to try "sexing" with. I worry we're going to lose her if we decide to stay behind, just because Helen's ready to start living her life.

And I can't blame her for that.

Since Ruth is pacing, I'll let her be the source of all nervous energy in the ship and I do my best to stay calm and collected.

Or I try to, anyhow. I'm chewing my lip a mile a minute and doing my best not to look over at Adiron.

After my disconcerting conversation with him in my room, I steered us back towards the others. Truth be told, I don't know what to think about what he keeps declaring. That he likes me. That he's in love with me. We just met this morning. But there's something about Adiron that makes me think that he falls in love as completely and enthusiastically as he seems to view everything...and he's sincere. And good lord, I just don't know what to think. We've been betrayed and used at every turn for the last few years, and so it's hard for me to believe in "good guys" anymore.

But if I did, I think Adiron would be one. I step closer to the table and pretend to examine one of the pieces of fruit, but I'm really watching Adiron. Adiron, who knew we needed to talk in private and set himself up in the rec room as far as possible from us. Right now he's got a wall panel disassembled, pieces of metal everywhere, as he tries to bypass the system and hardwire the vid screen so we can watch something. He's whistling, lost in his own little world, but I know, I just know, that he's doing all that deliberately so we won't feel like he's listening in.

And I know it's all for my benefit. He wants me to trust him.

I'm both grateful and confused by his actions. It's been so long since I've trusted a man. I've felt utterly responsible for everything and everyone here, because I'm the oldest and the most experienced. They look to me to solve problems. Adiron has made it clear that whatever I choose, he's going to support it and me.

I'm trying not to like that idea too much, in case it doesn't turn out to be reality.

I pick up a small piece of fruit, shine it on the oversized tunic I'm still wearing, and consider. Ruth wants to outsmart. To get the upper hand. "So you don't think we should trust them?" I ask Ruth. "You don't like the idea of going back to their ship?"

She looks at me as if I've grown another head. "You really want to be part of their crew?"

"I don't know if we have a choice," I admit. "There's a fine line between being cautious and being so hardheaded that we get ourselves killed."

Ruth just shakes her head. "I think we figure out how to rob them, replenish our supplies, and send them on their way." She speaks in a low voice, glancing over at Adiron, but he's oblivious. "I don't trust them. How can we believe that the first four rounds of pirates were awful creatures but somehow these guys are all right? That they just happened to find us and want to rescue us because they like humans but don't want to fuck us? It sounds like bunk to me."

At the table, Alice takes a bite of fruit, then shrugs. "What about the ice field thing? Do you believe that?"

"They could be lying to us about drifting," Ruth says. "Trying to force us to go with them."

Alice thinks for a moment, then nods. "They might be."

"What are our choices?" I ask. "Even if they are lying, are we any less vulnerable with them than we are here? We're low on air filters. We're low on food. We can't operate a good deal of the ship's controls. If we stay, I worry that we're making a bad decision." I sigh, considering. "Then again, if we go, I'm worried about the same."

Helen is quiet. She sits up and wears a sad expression on her face. "I wish we knew if they were lying. That would make this all so much easier."

"That's the problem," Alice says. "We don't know if they're lying or not. Everything they've told us sounds believable...but they've also been so kind and quick to volunteer to help us that it makes me suspicious."

Ruth gets an intense expression on her face. She slides into her seat and leans in. "I can sneak on board their ship when everyone's sleeping," she whispers. "Climb into the ductwork and spy on them. Listen to some conversations. Then we can find out if it's the truth or not."

"No," I protest. "That's dangerous and a bad idea."

"Are you kidding? It's a great idea."

Alice looks worried. "If we spy on them and get caught, we could piss them off. And if what they're telling us is true, we might need them."

"No spying," I say again with a shake of my head. "We could always try and get that one drunk and see what he confesses."

"But won't he know what we're doing?" Helen asks. "Then he could just tell us whatever and pretend to be drunk."

She has a point. After he got me drunk, he'd be foolish to think I wouldn't try to retaliate at some point. "Doesn't really matter," I say. "I don't think we have enough alcohol left on the ship. Unless he can get drunk on noodles, that plan won't work."

Ruth grabs another piece of fruit, frowning. "I'm so sick of noodles."

"But you want to stay?" Alice asks her.

"I'm not sick of living," Ruth replies. "Just noodles."

"So your vote is to stay?" I repeat, needing clarification.

"Unless you let me go spy on them to learn otherwise, yes, my vote is to stay and take our chances," Ruth says.

"Helen?" I turn to her.

Helen's beautiful face is troubled. She glances between all of us for a moment and then says, "I want to go." Her answer is strong and sure, and surprises me. Helen's never one to disagree, especially not with strong-willed Ruth. That must mean she's more excited about the other ship than she's let on.

The other ship...and probably Mathiras. If we go with them, I'm definitely going to have to have a talk with him. "You, Alice?" I ask. "What do you think?"

"I'm going to go with whatever you think, boss."

"That's not an answer," Ruth protests.

"Jade hasn't led us astray so far," Alice counters. "I trust her to make the right decision."

Ruth glares at her. "Still a bullshit answer."

"I don't care if it is or not. I feel things are shit all around, and the only person I trust right now is Jade. So...Jade?" Alice prompts. "We're tied. Do we stay or do we go?"

I look at their expectant faces. I think about the people in the stasis pods, waiting to be woken up.

And even though I shouldn't, I glance over and look at Adiron.

Stay or go?

27

ADIRON

I can't get the vid-screen working. Or rather, I can, but we're so far out and there's so much interference from the nearby ice field that it can't link up to anything. I'm selfishly glad, because I don't want to give them a reason to decide to stay behind. I don't sabotage the vid-screen...but I would if it made a difference. I'd just pretend to be real stupid and accidentally put one of my tools through it or something. Kaspar or Mathiras would see through me right away, because they know me, but maybe these females wouldn't.

Doesn't matter, though. They don't tell me what's decided. No matter how much I hint that I'm curious, they just shake their heads, exchange meaningful looks, and talk discreetly about other things. They eat all the fruit and then one by one, head to bed.

Jade waits by the door, indicating that it's time for me to go to sleep, too.

I gesture at the room. "Maybe I'll stay here and clean up."

I'm too wired to go to sleep. My entire life has changed in the space of a day. This morning, I woke up excited to go treasure hunting, and tonight, I'm going to sleep worried that my female —because Jade is definitely mine—is going to be stubborn and demand to stay behind. If she does, I'm going to have to kidnap her and her friends, because I'm not going to let her get stuck out here. Walking away from her is not an option, no matter how much she might think it is.

She's mine now. She just doesn't realize it yet.

By the door, Jade arches an eyebrow and gives me an amused look. "You forget I've seen your living quarters. I don't think you know how to clean anything."

Busted. I laugh. "I'm just not all that tired."

"Well, I am, and I'll feel more comfortable if I know you're in your quarters instead of poking around on the ship. Can you please just do this for me?" Her tone is weary, her smile tired.

Damn it. She knows just how to get to me. I can spar with a teasing Jade all night long, but weary Jade just makes me want to take care of her. "Of course."

She's quiet as we head through the silent, echoing halls of the *Buoyant Star*. The sour smell of the filters tickles my nose, but I can live with it for a day. The rest of the ship seems clean, at least, and I wonder if they know how to run the bots or if they just clean it all by hand out of sheer boredom. I can't imagine what their life is like on this ship, and if they can survive three years of being trapped, I guess I can live through one night of going to sleep early.

Even so, I have to be me. When we get to my door, I turn to Jade. "Don't suppose you'll let me tuck you in?"

She snorts, but her lips curl in a smile. She puts a hand on my chest, gently pushing me into my room. "Go sleep. There'll be plenty of time to harass me in the morning."

That sounds promising. "Because you'll be coming back with us?"

"I didn't say that," Jade replies quickly.

"Yeah, you did."

She gives my chest another, far-less-subtle nudge. "Just go to sleep already, okay?"

I grin at her. "My sister Zoey always wanted a kiss good-night. Can I interest you—"

This time she shoves me, but I deserve it. I laugh to myself as the door slides shut and I'm alone in my quarters. You never know unless you ask, and I'm a big fan of asking.

Hours later, I still can't sleep. I lie on the bunk, scratching at the base of my horns, and stare at the ceiling. There's just too much to think about. My head is full of Jade and her smiles, Jade and her wariness, Jade and her need to protect those around her. She's so smart and responsible. I like that in a female. I like that she cares about others. I think of Shaalyn, who only liked people she could use. The difference between them is night and day...or human and mesakkah, I suppose.

I don't like thinking about Shaalyn, though, because that's long past. So I get to my feet and head out of my room, deciding to go for a nighttime walk. I know if Jade catches me, she'll think I'm spying, but I just need to get some of this restless energy out. I'm not going to touch anything she doesn't want me to touch. I head out of my room, the floors cold under my bare feet, and rub my arms. It's definitely cold on this ship, and I wonder if they're deliberately keeping the temperature down to conserve fuel? Or if it's just another thing they don't know how to fix?

Either way, I can solve that.

I pause by Jade's room, listening, but when I don't hear noise or movement, I conclude she must be asleep. I won't wake her, then, to tell her what I'm doing. The protective feeling in me surges once more, and I want her to get a good night's sleep. I want her to get her rest. She deserves it.

My stomach growls, and for a moment, I consider heading to the mess hall on the ship and seeing what they have in their dispensers for a snack...but I remember how much Jade delighted over their food. How she said they had nothing left but noodles. I don't want to eat away at their stash of supplies, so I just pat my angry stomach. "Some other time, buddy."

I head for the control room, checking out the systems. Everything is neat and clean here, and there's a few of the buttons with tiny labels stuck to them, strange, blocky letters written next to arrows. This must be the humans making notes for themselves on how to run things. They're smart, and I wonder how much they had to figure out on their own.

I think of Jade and the others, pushing strange buttons and hoping that this one doesn't make the ship explode, or space them, and I can't imagine. They're so keffing brave. I think of the males that woke them up just to abuse them, and my fists clench. Part of me wishes those males were here so I could strangle them with my bare hands...but then that means Jade would have been abused that much longer. So I guess it's good that they're gone. Maybe after we get the *Little Sister* back we can hunt them down and make them pay.

I brighten at that thought and get to work on the control panel.

A couple of hours later, I have to acknowledge that I'm not getting anywhere. Whatever system is set up here, it's locked down tight. I can't override anything without taking it all apart, and I can't risk doing that in case something breaks. The systems haven't been serviced in three years and there's a bit of rust here and there, and dust clogging things. If it's working, best to just leave it alone.

At least I'm tired now, though. With a yawn, I head back down one of the halls, heading for my room. As I turn down another shadowy hallway, something appears out of the corner of my eye. I could have sworn I saw a figure moving, disappearing the moment I came around the corner.

Ghosts?

Kef me. I knew this place was haunted.

28

ADIRON

*G*hosts. I hate that this ship has ghosts. That should be against the rules, shouldn't it? If a ship already has bad luck, adding ghosts on top of things is just adding insult to injury.

I hesitate in the dark halls of the *Star*. Do I wake up Jade and tell her that her ship is haunted? Or do I try to hunt down the ghost and protect my female? Not that I know how to stop a ghost, but I could at least try to scare it off. I war with myself for a moment, then decide I have to check it out. Damn it. I jog in place for a moment, trying to work myself up, and then race after the ghost, heading down the lonely halls in search of it.

Two turns down the corridors later, I'm relieved to find it's not a ghost at all. It's Lord Straik, of all people.

"You scared the kef out of me," I blurt out as I jog over to his side. "I thought you were a ghost."

"Of course you did." His tone is thoughtful, distracted. He leans against a railing that curves along the hallway, and stares out the large window in front of him. I'm not entirely surprised to see he's gazing out at the cargo bay. Jade showed me this window earlier. She didn't take me in to look at the cargo closer, instead just showing me from here. Instead of a view out to space, this window faces the cargo hold and from here, I suppose whoever was in charge of the ship watched the crew working on the cargo. There's no crew now, and all of the work stations are empty.

The cargo hold is not, though. It's filled with dozens upon dozens of pods that anyone familiar with the slave trade recognizes. They're stasis pods, stacked high and deep, and I'm just guessing, but I suspect the entire hold is full.

And I also suspect it's weighing heavily on Lord Straik's mind. For all that he likes to pretend he's a badass pirate, something tells me he's not as familiar with the seedier underbelly of the universe as he thinks.

"Couldn't sleep?" I ask, moving to stand next to him. I pretend to stare out at the pods, but all I can think of is Jade. She was in one of these, at some point, and some keffing loser saw her sleeping and decided to wake her up to entertain himself.

If I ever find out who that male—or female—is, I'm going to destroy them.

"Sleep?" Straik shakes his head. "No. I'm not sleeping. There's too much to think about."

"So you came over here to think?" I look around. "Do the girls know you're here?"

He shakes his head. "I needed to see for myself. No need to wake them."

I'm pretty sure Jade isn't going to be thrilled that Straik's hanging out on what she considers "her" ship, but the male just seems so depressed that I don't have the heart to go and wake her just yet. "You all right?"

Straik stares out that window so hard that I'm surprised his eyes don't burn holes through the glass. "Ask me that question again tomorrow."

I get it. He wants to mope tonight. I cross my arms over my chest and stare out the glass myself. That...really is a lot of stasis pods. "I was kinda hoping that the big cargo would be dark-matter cores or untraceable credits. I mean, this definitely counts as a big score, but...it's slaves. I guess we're lucky that we found them instead of someone else who'd actually sell them."

"Slaves," Straik repeats, and he sounds utterly melancholy. "I don't know how they got here."

I frown at that. "You mean how they loaded the pods onto the ship? There's bots for that sort of thing—"

He turns and glares at me. "My family is not in the business of running slaves! We are a proud lineage! The house of Rin is an old, respected name. We are a proud family!" He gestures angrily at the window. "This is not what we do!"

"How do you know that? 'Cause it kinda looks like it is what you do."

Straik looks as if he wants to rip my face off. His response comes out in an angry hiss. "We do not need the credits—"

"Now," I point out. "You don't need the credits now. Where did the credits you have come from if not this?"

His face falls. He turns back toward the window again. "We made our fortune in trade. I was told it was silks." He stares out at the stasis pods as if he's a man betrayed. "These...are not silks."

"You think they lied to you, then?" It's entirely possible that someone took over the ship, dumped all the silks into deep space and loaded the humans on but...that seems awfully stupid. It'd be far easier to just sell the silks somewhere, and with this big of a cargo hold, someone would have had word of a massive shipment of illegal silks sold somewhere. Either the silks were dumped, or they never existed in the first place.

"I don't know." Straik puts his hands on his hips, staring out the window. "It bothers me that I don't know. Here all this time, I thought I was the one in the family that broke the rules, the one that was shaming our good name. Now I see this..." He gestures at the window. "I don't know what to think."

"Hey, cheer up. Your uncle was a rebel before you were, right? The one that married a human and gave away a bunch of the family lands to them on Risda? You probably look pretty good compared to him."

Straik blinks. "Yes. You're right."

"I am?"

"I need to talk to my uncle." His look of melancholy disappears, replaced by one of determination. "He will know the truth of things. He will tell me if everything the Rin house stands for is a lie."

"Okay, uh...great?" I'm not sure when he thinks we'll be going. We're in the Slatra system, and there's no way we can get a comm out to Risda III, which is all the way on the other side of the galaxy. "I suppose we can all head that way after we bring in the *Star*, since we'll need to figure out a place for all these humans. I guess we can't wake them up yet. And I guess someone's going to have to stay on the *Star* here and fly it, since there's no crew."

"Yes," Straik says thoughtfully. "There are a lot of moving pieces that need to be considered."

"It's a pain in the keffing ass," I admit. "Might have been easier for everyone if this ship was never found."

"Mmm." Straik stares out the window. "Indeed."

Of course, that would mean I never met Jade, so I'm personally glad we found the *Star*. I can see how it bothers Straik, though. For all his pretentious black clothing and lofty way of speaking, he's got a good streak and tries to do the right thing, even as a pirate. There's no faking how horrified he is about the flesh trade we've discovered. I don't envy him trying to make sense of things.

I'm too tired to think about any of that anyhow. I yawn, ready to head back to bed. Now that I'm actually tired, I'd like to just rub one out while thinking of Jade and her delightful amber eyes, and then sink into sleep (also hopefully filled with Jade). "What's done is done," I say with a shrug. "I'm heading to bed. You going to sneak back out or do I need to tell Jade and the others that you're here?"

"No need to wake anyone," Straik says. "I'll be gone before anyone wakes up. I promise."

Perfect.

29

ADIRON

I'm a keffing moron.

I stare at the unconscious forms of my two brothers, dumped unceremoniously in the hall where the ship-to-ship connection used to be.

Used to be.

The Darkened Eye is gone. She left while we slept, and took Straik and his a'ani soldiers far away.

When Straik said he'd be gone when everyone woke up, I didn't realize he meant GONE gone. I didn't think he'd abandon us here...and I hate that I'm the one that gave him that idea.

Shit. Everyone is going to be so keffing mad at me.

I jog over to Kaspar's side. He's passed out cold, sprawled on the floor. Their bags of clothing and possessions are strewn at the end of the hall, along with mine, as if they were just tossed in carelessly. I see our blasters, holstered and waiting, mixed in with the mess. At least we have weapons. I guess Straik doesn't want to leave us completely helpless. Then again, Kaspar's in nothing but his underclothes, his ass and tail sticking out when I turn him over. He snores, and when I tap him on the cheek, he doesn't wake up. I move over to Mathiras, who's in the same condition, and when neither one rouses, I conclude that they're both drugged.

This...is not good.

I gaze down at my sleeping brothers, wondering if I should try to wake them or go let Jade know the bad news first. Ugh. I rub my scalp, frustrated, because I can't stop thinking about how upset Straik seemed last night. How defeated. I thought he was just bummed. I didn't realize he'd do...this.

Not good. Not good at all.

I nudge my brothers one more time, but when neither one wakes up, I take a steeling breath and decide to try Jade, instead. I jog (okay, I run) toward her quarters and rap on the door. "Hey, Jade? Wake up. Wake up, please."

My knocking is urgent, and on the other side of the door, I hear a crash. I picture Jade falling out of bed, racing toward me, and in the next moment, the door to her room slides open. Sure enough, Jade looks disheveled and utterly terrified. Her soft-looking, kinky hair floats around her head like a cloud and she clutches a thin plas-film blanket to her body. It hides practically nothing, outlining her rather magnificent breasts and the abundant curves of her hips.

"Adiron? What is it?" When I continue to dumbly stare at her chest, she reaches up and lightly taps at my jaw. "What is it?"

"Oh." I shake myself, forcing my brain to stop picturing me peeling that too-flimsy blanket off her delicious body. "We have a problem."

"What kind of problem?" She gathers the blanket around her body, hiding her cleavage from me, and pushes past me, heading down the hall. "Are the others all right?"

"They're not the problem," I say. "It's the other ship."

Jade turns back to me, her eyes confused. "What about the other ship?"

I wince. "It's...gone."

Her chin lowers and she stares at me. "Gone?"

"Left during the night." My tail is flicking, all restless energy. "See, ah...I think Straik abandoned us."

She blinks. Twice. Then she's racing down the hall, toward the distant portal where the ship-to-ship connection once was. I follow after her, my gut clenching in dismay. Jade is going to be so keffing mad at me when she learns it's my fault. That I was the one that gave Straik the idea to abandon us. But how was I supposed to know that if I said "Gee, it might have been easier if the ship was never found" that he'd decide that was a good idea and leave us all behind?

When I catch up with Jade, she's crouched next to my brothers, pressing two fingers on Mathiras's neck. She glances back at me as she straightens. "Why did he dump your brothers here? Aren't you with him?"

"Well...yes and no."

Jade gives me an impatient look. "Which is it? Adiron, we don't have time for these games."

"We were looking for the *Buoyant Star* ourselves," I say, and decide the best way to explain is to blurt it all out. No secrets, because they just confuse matters. "We were fishing around for information on a station and Straik got wind of us. He didn't like what we were doing so he captured us and made us abandon our ship. But because we're awesome, we smooth-talked our way into working together with him. Except, I guess we're not that awesome because he dumped us all here. With you."

She looks at my brothers one last time and then gets to her feet, like a regal princess in costly silks instead of a bare-foot human in a thin pals-blanket. Jade approaches me, a look of worry on her face. "Is it possible that he didn't do this?"

"Uh...no, because I talked to him last night." I put on my brightest smile. "I might have also put the idea in his head to leave us behind. By accident."

"Oh, Adiron. You didn't." Her tone is full of disappointment.

"I can explain." And I do, rushing through all of it. Of last night's run-in with Straik and how he eyeballed the stasis pods like they were the enemy. How he seemed so melancholy at the realization that his family was slave trading. His realization that he needed to talk to his uncle, and my stupid joke about how it would have been better if we never found the ship. "And then he said he'd be gone before anyone woke up."

Jade puts a hand to her forehead and moans.

"I know. You're disappointed in me. I am, too." Mostly I'm just crushed that I've ruined a good thing for Jade. "I've keffed it all up, like usual, but I'll figure something out. Just...don't hate me."

She shakes her head, then moves forward to pat my chest. "I don't hate you, Adiron. How did you know he was going to do something so ruthless and shitty? Don't beat yourself up, all right?" She sighs and looks down the hall at my brothers. "I guess I should be glad he didn't space us all while we slept, but it's not exactly rebuilding my confidence in there being good space pirates out there."

"If it makes you feel any better, I'm starting to think me and my brothers are the only ones." I cock my head, thinking about Zoey's new crew. "Well, with one exception, I guess."

Jade gazes at the portal, now empty of ship-to-ship passage, and her shoulders slump. I can see the realization hitting her, that she's been abandoned once more. I hate the sight of it. More than anything, I want to fix this for her. I'm going to get her off this keffing ship and somewhere safe if it's the last thing I do, I vow silently.

"I'm going to go wake the others," Jade says in a soft voice. "They need to know that our plan isn't going forward."

Now I just feel worse, because if I'd kept my big mouth shut, Jade and her friends would be safe on Lord Straik's ship. Instead, Straik's turned tail and abandoned us, no doubt rushing off to Risda III to go talk to his uncle. "I'll wait here in case my brothers wake up. They're gonna be pissed." I think about the gas they were probably given and add, "And hungover."

Jade nods, padding silently back down the hall. I watch her go, fascinated by the sway of her hips. I need to focus, but somehow her movements are distracting all of my parts, especially the ones below the belt. There'll be time to stroke one out later, I tell my cock. If we're truly stuck here, there's gonna be a whole keffing lot of time.

I move toward my brothers, nudging Mathiras with my toe as he sleeps, just to see if he's ready to rouse. I notice there's a small crate by the doors, one I didn't pay much attention to before. I move toward it and brush Kaspar's belt off of the crate.

More noodles. Man. Jade is gonna shit herself. I guess I should be glad that Straik doesn't want us to starve, but damn. He could have thrown in some fruit.

"Adiron! Adiron!"

That's Jade. Alarm shoots through me and I stumble over my sleeping brothers in my haste to get to her. I plummet down the hall and turn the corner to see her racing back toward me, a look of sheer panic on her face. "What is it?" I ask. "What's wrong?"

Panting, she skids to a stop in front of me, the blanket about to fall off her gorgeous brown body. The look in her eyes is sheer terror, though. "Ruth. She's not in her room. I think she's gone, too."

"Where?"

"With Straik."

30

JADE

*M*y head is spinning with everything going on this morning. I thought we'd wake up, agree to work with the men to rescue the *Buoyant Star*, and become part of the crew. We'd hitch the *Star's* systems to that of *The Darkened Eye* and let our home of the last three years be towed back to "civilized" space and take our chances. We're relatively safe out here, but we've known we were living on borrowed time.

Now, though, everything has changed.

Straik and *The Darkened Eye* are gone. Mathiras and Kaspar have been dumped here.

And Ruth—stubborn, pigheaded Ruth—is somewhere on *The Darkened Eye*.

"You know she went to go spy on him," Alice says, wiping angry tears from her eyes. "You know that's what she did. She thought her plan was better than ours."

"I know." My voice is soft, my eyes dry. I'm too numb for tears. I've done my best to protect and lead my friends over the last few years and the thought of Ruth in danger and me unable to help her is like a knife in the gut. I know she's an adult and made her own decision, but I still feel responsible. I should have checked in on her again last night, made sure that we were all on the same page. Instead, I was distracted by thoughts of Adiron just across the hall, and what our future might mean if we joined forces with the men.

Well, in a way, I suppose we ARE joining forces. Just...not the way anyone intended.

"There's no sense in beating yourself up," Helen says, dishing up bowls of noodles. She's sprung into action this morning, pressing a kiss of sympathy on my brow and Alice's before deciding to feed us. Everyone's always happier with a full belly, she reasons, and she's determined to stuff ours. "You know how Ruth is. Ruth is always right in Ruth's eyes."

Alice snorts, wiping a fresh round of tears from her eyes. "You think he's going to hurt her? When he finds her?"

"I don't know," I say softly. I imagine Ruth, hiding in the ductwork somewhere on *The Darkened Eye*, and wonder if she's feeling panicked. If she feels alone and lost, and I just feel even worse.

"He won't hurt her," Helen says, patting my shoulder. "He doesn't want to hurt anyone. Now eat." She bustles toward the control panel and holds down the button we've marked with a smiley face so Helen knows it's the system comm, and calls out in a chirpy voice. "Breakfast is ready, come and eat, male crew members!"

"How do you know he won't hurt her?" Alice asks, curious.

Helen shrugs, happily setting bowls along the table for the three brothers. "He brought Kaspar and Mathiras here instead of tossing them into space. He was on the ship last night and didn't hurt us. He didn't touch the sleepy people." She smiles at us. "He's just sad because he doesn't know what to do so he ran away."

"Like a little bitch," Alice mutters.

"Helen's got a point," I admit, stirring the noodles in my bowl. I'm not the slightest bit hungry. "He hasn't hurt anyone and I guess he could have if he was ruthless."

"He can't get to the stasis pods," Alice says, taking a big bite of food. She can always eat, no matter the news, and I have no idea where it goes considering she's a tiny thing. Me, I sniff the noodles and gain ten pounds on my butt.

"He says it's his ship," Helen says. "That means he can work it, right?" She thumps down next to me, a curious look on her face. "So he can get to the sleepy people."

Also true. We're listed as cargo and so our options are limited, but I imagine Straik had a way to figure out how to run everything. Hearing Helen's simple reasoning makes me feel better. I picture Ruth's sour reaction when she realizes she's stuck with Straik...and his. "She's really going to make him regret leaving us behind," I say with a chuckle. "Can you imagine?"

"I think he will be very mad," Helen says, giggling. "And make lots of very mad noises."

The door opens and the three brothers file in.

Our laughter dies, and Helen's the only one in a cheerful mood this morning. She pats the table, indicating that the men should sit. "You come sit next to me, Mathiras," she says happily.

The tallest brother shoots us a chagrined look, but does as he's told. When Helen tries to scoot closer to him, he carefully scoots an equal distance away, as if letting us know he's not encouraging her. He doesn't have to. Helen's been sheltered. This is the longest relationship she's had with a man, ever.

And right now we've got bigger problems than Helen's crush.

I study the other two brothers. Kaspar eats in silence, a grim look on his face. To my surprise, big, happy, blustery Adiron just stares down at his bowl. He's hollow-eyed and his shoulders are slumped with defeat. He blames himself, I know. He said as much over and over again as his brothers woke up and realized what happened.

"Well?" I ask, once we're all at the table. "How is the bridge?" Once the brothers woke up, they immediately went to the bridge to see what they could access on the ship.

"Locked down tight," Kaspar says between bites. "Won't recognize anything we do."

"You're pirates, though. Aren't you used to this sort of thing?" Alice frowns at them. "Isn't this what you do?"

"We're limited without our equipment, which I'm sure was part of Straik's plan," Mathiras says darkly. "He's leaving us here to guard the shipment until he figures out what he wants to do."

"Or he's abandoned us entirely and hopes if we sink into the ice field that will hide his family's crimes," Kaspar retorts.

Adiron is silent. It's very unlike him, and I'm a little worried.

"So," I say, taking a deep breath. "What are our options?"

Mathiras appears to consider things. "Our ship is still in this system—hopefully. If we can connect with it, I'm hoping we can override some of the systems here remotely and slave them to the *Little Sister*...but it's a long shot."

"Slave?" Helen asks, a worried expression on her face.

"Tying in electronics," I explain gently. "Not a real slave."

She nods, biting her lip. "Ships don't have feelings, right?"

"That's right, they don't."

"Just making sure." She glances over at Mathiras again and then takes another bite of her food.

I poke my noodles. "So do you think you'll be able to do that? Hook the controls of this ship up to yours?"

Mathiras hesitates. "It's a long shot."

"A really, really long shot," Kaspar adds. "Probably have to force a reboot on this ship's systems, which might not be a good thing. That means shutting everything down and starting it back up again...and hoping it all comes back up."

"I'm not a big fan of that idea," Alice says, her eyes wide. "What's plan B?"

Kaspar eyes her. "There is no plan B."

I'm not sure I'm a fan of that, either. I glance down the table at Adiron again. He's still wearing that hangdog expression on his face, and my heart squeezes with sympathy. This isn't his fault, even if he thinks it is. If Straik was going to betray everyone, he was going to do it anyhow, I reason. Better here where we have a safe place versus somewhere worse. "Adiron?" I ask. "What do you think?"

He seems to brighten visibly as I mention his name, and I feel warm when he straightens. "I have an idea, but I don't know if it's a good one."

"All ideas are good ideas right now," I point out. "We don't have many options other than just floating along and waiting for the next round of pirates...or hoping that Straik comes back."

Adiron looks right at me. "There's always escape pods."

31

JADE

"*E*scape pods." I taste the words in my mouth, weighing them. It's not a bad idea. The *Buoyant Star* still has four of them left, each one capable of holding two people comfortably. There's more than enough for the six of us at this table to get away...but only us. It's a flawed plan because it involves sacrificing those sleeping, or abandoning them to their fates.

"Escape pods?" Mathiras asks. "You guys have escape pods and you've stayed here for the last three years?"

"Where would we go?" Alice retorts. "You think if someone picks up a pod full of women, they'll be all, 'Oh, cool, let me take you to the closest embassy'?" She snorts. "Yeah right."

I reach over and squeeze her hand, because she looks ready to punch someone. "It's something we've considered, but we're safe and comfortable here, and so we stuck with the devil we know." I gesture at them. "You're welcome to stay here as long as you like, too. There's room for everyone."

"But not supplies," Kaspar says. "The amount of food you've got left is going to run pretty low very fast if you're feeding six people."

"And you're still heading for that ice field," Mathiras points out. "You're safe for another month or two...and then what? We're all dead. The ship systems will go into overdrive trying to regulate the temperature to support life, you'll burn through all your fuel, and then you're dead."

Helen says nothing, watching us talk, her expression grave as she absorbs it all.

Adiron finally speaks again. "I think the escape pods are a good idea...if we split up."

"Split up?" Kaspar asks. "How so?" He gestures at himself and Mathiras. "Like send us out to get help and leave the females here? I don't like that idea."

"I'm not a fan of it either," Alice retorts. "And what about Ruth?"

Kaspar grins over at her. "When we find Straik again to kick his ass, we'll get her back. If she hasn't already kicked his ass, that is."

I squeeze her fingers. "Ruth will be fine. She's a survivor." I keep thinking about what Helen said—how Straik didn't want to kill anyone. I think she's right. I think he's left us here until he can figure out what to do with us. He'll be back...eventually. I hope.

"When I said we should use the escape pods, I meant we should pair up." Adiron gestures at me. "One female, one male. So we can protect you."

My face flushes and I can just imagine who Adiron wants to pair up with.

"Are you still thinking with your cock?" Kaspar asks him with a roll of his eyes.

"No, I think he's right," Mathiras says. "The females are recognized by the ship so they would need to be split up between pods. And if something goes wrong, we're there to protect them or to try to override the system. It's really the best choice we have."

"So where are we going, then?" Alice asks. "Where exactly can we escape to? Or are we going to try and meet up with Straik and just hope he lets our pods on board?" Her brow wrinkles. "Because I'm pretty sure he doesn't want to be infested with human cooties."

I wonder if he's found Ruth yet...and I wonder how much hell she's giving him. I hope it's a lot. A whole fuckton of hell. It's the only thing that makes me feel better about knowing that she's gone...that she's going to make him absolutely, utterly miserable.

Mathiras speaks. "We'd head for our ship, of course. The *Little Sister's* still out there. A bit farther out, so it'd be a bit of a journey, but an escape pod can absolutely make it. It'll take what, two or three weeks, I think, but—"

"Two or three weeks," Alice protests. "In an escape pod? Are you out of your mind?"

"You have a better solution?" Kaspar asks. "This is enemy territory. We should be glad it'll only take two or three weeks to get to a safe ship. Then once we get to the *Sister*, we can come back. It'll take maybe a week with the stronger, faster engine. Then we can slave the *Star* to the *Sister* and find a safe port... and figure out what to do next."

Now, Helen speaks. She looks over at me, worried. "What about the sleepy people? Where do they go if we use escape pods?"

"There's not enough pods," I say softly. "We'd have to abandon them, or someone would have to stay behind to watch over things."

"No one's staying behind," Alice replies quickly, a note of worry in her voice. "Don't be ridiculous."

"Actually." I give her fingers another squeeze, because she's not going to like my answer. "I'm going to stay. No matter what."

Both Helen and Alice turn to look at me.

"Someone's got to stay and look after the stasis pods. I wouldn't be able to live with myself if we all left and they ended up dying." I shake my head. "I can stay here and keep things running on the *Star*. I can send out a message if Straik has a change of heart and comes back. I can protect them if another pirate heads in this direction. If no one's here to guard them, they're sitting ducks."

"So wake someone up," Alice cries, upset. "You have to go with us, Jade. I'm not leaving you behind."

"Me either." Helen sounds dangerously close to tears. "We all stay together. The men can go."

I shake my head. "Someone has to go with them on the pods, remember? So the system will recognize them."

"So, what, you're just going to stay here alone?" Alice looks horrified. "On this big empty ship?"

But Helen's frowning at me. She's already figured it out. "If you stay back, that means only two pods can launch. We'd have to leave one of the men behind."

I glance down the table at Adiron.

He just grins. "You already know me so well, Jade. There's no way I'd leave you alone on this big derelict ship by yourself. The way I look at it, my brothers are going to come back, and I get a month of bonding time with my new ladylove." He leans back in his chair, hands behind his head, and beams at me as if this has been his plan ever since he mentioned the escape pods. Maybe it has been. There's one thing I'm learning about Adiron. He plays stupid, but he's absolutely not.

Alice's lip curls in disgust as she looks over at Adiron. "You are seriously gross. This is not a date! Jade's being selfless—"

He gives her a wounded look. "So am I."

"Alice, come on, now," I say. I'm trying not to blush, but...I did know Adiron was going to stay the moment I said I would.

Oddly enough, I trust him, and it fills me with a comfortable sort of sensation to know that I wouldn't be here all alone. That of course he'd stay with me. "It makes me feel better to know you and Helen are going to have someone with you that knows how this universe works. They have a plan. They know what they want to do. More importantly, they know how to operate a ship." I give her a rueful smile and turn to Helen. "The best chance for us to succeed and save everyone is if we split up. Two pods—two pairs—head out for the other ship, one pair stays behind. This way, even if they're betraying us, there's a reason for them to come back. And we all regroup a month from now and we find homes for everyone. Stasis people and all."

Alice and Helen exchange a look. Alice thinks for a moment, then reaches for my hand. She gives me a falsely bright smile. "Just so you know, I hate all of this."

I chuckle, because it's not my favorite either. We've lost Ruth, and now we're splitting up even further. This might be the last time I ever see Alice and Helen again. But I keep my expression calm, because I can lose my shit later. "It's just a month. We can survive a month of bullshit. We have before, and we'll do it again."

Helen takes my other hand and clings tightly to it. I can feel how tense she is, and I imagine this is both frightening and exciting to her. "When should we go?"

I turn to Adiron. "Any chance that Straik is going to have a change of heart and turn around?"

His mouth twists in a wry smile. "Doubtful. But even if he does, his ship can just scoop up the pods mid-flight. There's no reason to delay for that."

"Well," I say, and pull my hands from Alice and Helen's grips before they realize that they're getting clammy with sweat. I'm nervous and terrified and determined and resigned and just a little bit defeated. "Let's get this show on the road, then."

32

ADIRON

*J*ade is a good leader, I realize, as I watch her take care of the others. Alice and Helen both cry, their small packed bags on their shoulders as they say their goodbyes to Jade. She's utterly calm and downright motherly at times, wiping away their tears and giving them gentle pep talks. She hugs both of them for a long, long time, and then waves as Alice steps into the pod with Kaspar, her smile bright. She gives her a thumbs up and I just nod at my brother. He'll be good. It'll take a lot more than a piss-poor corsair like Straik to take us down. I'm not worried. "See you in a month."

Then the pod closes, and activates, and it's Helen and Mathiras's turn.

The qura'aki is practically bouncing with a mixture of excitement and tentative sadness—like she wants to be excited but thinks she should be sad. Jade whispers in her ear, gives her a squeeze, and then smiles at Mathiras.

My brother looks at me. "You sure you're going to be okay here on this ship?"

"I'm going to have an amazing time," I reassure him. In a way, I'm kind of looking forward to it. Now I have Jade's undivided attention for an entire month. Surely that's enough time for her to fall in love with me. "You got everything you need?"

He nods. "We'll be in touch." Mathiras looks over at Jade. "And Helen will be in good hands. I promise you that I'll keep her safe and treat her like my own sister."

"Wait, what?" Helen says as she steps into the pod. There's a hint of a frown on her face.

"I'll see you soon," Jade calls, blowing kisses to a confused Helen as Mathiras steps into the hatch. The escape pod—a room-sized bubble tricked out with all the life support that a pair will need for months—hisses as the door shuts and panels light up. I see Mathiras get to work, strapping Helen into her seat and then moving into his own. Jade keeps waving, remaining in place, and Helen offers her a timid wave before the pod windows go black and then the pod itself detaches from the wall and heads down the chute to eject into space.

The moment the second pod is out of sight, Jade sags, like all the strength has left her body. It's quiet in the ship, and I can only imagine how she feels. First Ruth, now Helen and Alice. I put a hand on her shoulder and rub. Maybe she could use a snack. I like to eat when I'm depressed, because it always makes me feel better. "Do you want to..."

My words die in my throat as she turns and buries her face against my chest. A low sob escapes her, and her arms go around my waist.

Oh.

I hold her tight as she cries into my uniform, rubbing her back and murmuring positive-sounding stuff to her. Things like "you made the right decision" and "everything's going to be fine" when who the kef knows what's going to happen now.

Danger and taking risks is just a part of my life, but I guess it hasn't been a part of Jade's.

It makes me want to protect her even more.

"Hey now," I murmur, resisting the urge to bury my face in her fluffy hair and just drink in her scent. "Are you crying because you're stuck with me for the next month? I promise I'll be a good roommate. I might even pick up after myself."

She sob-laughs. "Liar. I saw your quarters. You're a pig."

"That's an earth animal, right? Are they handsome?"

Jade gives another teary laugh, sniffing. "Oh, the handsomest." She pulls back—much to my dismay—and gives me a faint smile. "You're trying to distract me, aren't you?"

"Me?" I pretend to be shocked. "I would never."

She rolls her eyes, but the smile plays at her lips. Jade swipes at her nose, staring glumly at the empty chambers where the two pods were. "Remind me that this is for the best?"

"It's absolutely for the best," I tell her. I move back to her side and put a hand on her shoulder. I want her to get used to me touching her, because I absolutely intend on touching her in the next while...as long as she lets me, that is. And when she covers my hand with her own, I fight the urge to grab her and kiss the kef out of her like they do in the human vids that Zoey loved. Most mesakkah are horrified by mouth-on-mouth stuff, but I think it'd be keffing grand. I'm certainly ready to tangle tongues with Jade and see what it's like. "If you're worried about Kaspar or Mathiras, I can assure you that they really are good guys. Neither one will touch the girls."

She crosses her arms over her chest, hugging herself, and I notice that her clothing is a modified jumper like my own, except the stitches have been pulled out and awkwardly re-done up the sides. It reminds me that everything she has, everything she wears, she's had to fight for and reclaim. Jade is so keffing strong. I'm in awe of her. The human female stares at the spots where the escape pods left just a short time ago, and she seems to be lost in her thoughts. "I've always had them, you know? No matter how scary or wild things got, we had each other. And now we're all separated. I guess I'm scared for me as much as I am for them."

I gesture at one of the remaining pods. "We can go, too, if you want. You know I'll follow you anywhere."

Her smile is faint as she looks back at me. "I can't do that. Those people sleeping in those pods, I have an obligation to them. I'm going to keep them safe and watch over them, because it's what I'd want someone to do for me."

Even though no one did it for her.

"Well, luckily you have me to entertain you in the next month," I tell her with a grand sweep of my arm. "And I am quite the entertaining male, or so I have been told." I grin at her, determined to keep my spirits light in the hopes that I can buoy hers. "I never did get a proper tour of this place. You want to show me the ship?"

She bites her lip, then shakes her head. "If it's all the same to you, I think...I want to be alone for a little bit. I need to process. I'll be fine, I just need to work through a few things."

"Sure. Right. I'll go hang out in my room. Maybe take a nap...maybe rearrange the furniture. Dunno. I'll figure something out." I give her a brash smile. "I can amuse myself. Don't you worry." With what, I don't know, but if Jade needs time to sort through her feelings, I'll give her as much as she needs.

Jade smiles sweetly at me, moving forward to touch my chest. "Thank you, Adiron."

33

JADE

I can't sleep.

I'm tired—exhausted, really—but as time crawls past, my brain won't turn off. I keep thinking about Ruth, and if she's all right or in danger. I think about Alice, her eyes filled with tears as she left in the pod with Kaspar. I think about Helen, who's even now probably trying to get a reluctant Mathiras to kiss her, just so she can experience it. I should probably be the most worried about Helen, because she's innocent, but strangely, I'm not. She'll have so many new experiences she won't have time to be sad or worried. This is all a new adventure to her; it's the others that I stress over.

And I think about the people in the stasis pods, of course. What if no one comes back for us? What if we drift into that ice field? What if it's a mistake to leave them sleeping? Would I want to drift into death in my sleep or would I want to be awake to try to do something about it? I can't wake them up of course

—there's not enough food for so many people—but I can still have guilt about it.

In the end, I toss and turn, and when I can't stand it any longer, I get up. I shrug on my robe—some larger creature's modified tunic—and tuck it around me before I go to pace the empty halls of the ship. I head toward the kitchen, past the rec room, and wander toward the bridge. It all feels so empty now. Even before, when it was just the four of us on here, it didn't have that abandoned feeling like it does now. Like I'm the only one left on this end of the universe, all by choice.

Depressing. I know I've done the right thing, but it's still hard.

The bridge is empty, of course, the large windows full of nothing but open space. There's a distant, colorful nebula in one corner, and I know that even though it looks large in the view, it's probably bajillions of miles away from here. No sign of an ice field, though, which makes me wonder if that really was all a lie. It's conveniently "behind" the ship, which means we can't see it, but they swear it's there. I curl my bare toes on the metal floors, wondering if they seem cooler than usual or if it's just my imagination. I stare out the window, sigh, and then turn to leave.

As I do, I see a pair of legs sticking out from under one of the stations. Legs, and a blue tail that twitches ever so slightly.

"Um, Adiron?"

I can hear him sigh from under the desk. "I was hoping you wouldn't notice I was here."

I pad over to him, curious. "It's late. What are you doing? Shouldn't you be asleep?"

He slides out from under the station, his uniform rumpled, the collar open and loose. He gives me a boyish grin. "Shouldn't YOU be asleep?"

"I asked first." I nod at the station, because I can see a bunch of wires hanging down. "And I want to know what you're doing. Don't change the subject."

"I couldn't sleep." Adiron sits up, shrugging. "I was worried about you. You seemed real sad that the others are gone and I wanted to fix that."

I move to the chair the next station over. It's mounted to the floor, just like each station's "desk" and covered with a million controls I know nothing about. Everything's covered in a fine layer of dust because we don't know how to use most of the switches. I cross my legs, and as Adiron's gaze goes there, I can't help but feel a little...vulnerable. I'm wearing a knee-length tunic, but no panties and no bra. I wasn't exactly expecting to see anyone tonight, and seeing Adiron's focus makes me feel... strange. Uncrossing my legs would be awfully obvious, so I pretend not to notice. "So you decided to, what, play hide-and-seek?"

He laughs, a look of sheer delight on his face. "Did you play that, too? That was my sister's favorite when she was just a little runt. Man, she crawled into everything." With a smile, he shakes his head. "Nah, I was trying to override some of the systems, maybe get a vid-comm working for you."

That's kind of sweet. "Were you going to surprise me? Is that why you didn't want me to ask?"

"Uh, not exactly. I figured you might not approve of my methods."

"Your methods?"

To answer me, Adiron reaches up to one of the wires, yanks it from its home, and cocks his head, waiting. Then he puts it back into the socket and taps on a button.

I can't help it; I laugh. "Is this your equivalent of 'Have you tried turning it off and turning it on again?'"

"Huh?"

"Just a tech support thing on Earth." I chuckle. "So what happens if you unplug a wire and it breaks something?"

"That's why I thought I'd do it while you were sleeping." He grins. "Hide the evidence before you woke up."

I should probably be mad, but I'm just amused. It's not like I'm doing anything with most of these controls anyhow. "I appreciate the thought, but I'm not sure if I'm in the mood to watch anything even if you get the vid-comm working."

"I know. I like being able to help you, though. Makes me feel less like a useless piece of keffing shit." He sighs and yanks on another wire, staring morosely at it. "I don't want you to be angry at me forever, so maybe if I do a few small things to make this next month better, it'll help."

"I'm not angry at you," I tell him, surprised he'd think that. "None of what's happened is your fault."

Adiron shrugs. "But I could have done more. I ran into him on the ship last night. I should have asked what he had planned, or stopped him, or something."

"You didn't know," I say gently. "None of us did. If we had, I'm pretty sure Ruth wouldn't have gone over there to spy. Now she's stuck with him...or he's stuck with her."

A reluctant smile curls the corner of his mouth. "They're both probably making each other miserable...or falling into bed together."

"I am very certain THAT is not going to happen."

He tilts his head, regarding me. "You don't think so? Some males like a fiery female. They like someone that fights them at every turn."

"Do they?" I arch a brow at him. "Do you?"

Adiron is quiet for a long moment, and I want to kick myself for asking it. Why do I care if he likes a "fiery female"? I'm not one. I'm definitely more on the calm end of the spectrum. But Adiron gives me a thoughtful look and shakes his head. "I'm into other stuff."

"Like what?" The words come out before I can stop them.

Why am I encouraging this? He's made it clear that he likes me. Why do I need to hear it again?

He grins. "Small brown feet, for starters." And his big hand curls around my bare ankle.

I suck in a breath, fascinated at the pulse of attraction that zings through me. It's just a touch. Nothing more. It's a gentle one, though, and it feels good. I'm reminded of how he held me and comforted me when I cried.

And then I remind myself that it's only been two days. It hasn't been enough time for me to see who Adiron truly is. He could be pretending to be this big, lovable goof with a protective streak. The real Adiron will come out in a few days, when the sheer monotony of being trapped on the *Star* sets in.

So I tug at my ankle, indicating he should free me. "If that hand goes any higher, I'm going to kick you in the face."

"Might be worth it," he teases, but he lets me go.

I don't know why I'm disappointed that he does.

34

ADIRON

This ship is boring. Keffing boring. The first day alone with Jade fades into the second. I putter around the ship, trying to override systems and get access to things, but I'm locked out at every turn, and eventually, I give up. For all I know, Straik put in a program that locked shit down before he left us here, and I'm just hitting my head against a wall.

Jade's in a funk, too. She hasn't been without the others in a long, long time, and now that she doesn't have them to fuss over, I don't think she knows what to do with herself. I get it. For so many years, we were ultra-protective of our sister Zoey. We avoided certain stations, had complicated contingency plans if she was discovered, refueled on remote, questionable satellites, and basically re-routed our lives to make things easier for her. When she left with her mate, it left a big hole in our lives. We suddenly didn't have to take back routes to refuel. We didn't have to avoid ship inspectors or hide out from patrols. It kinda felt like we weren't even trying anymore.

I know it depressed me. Being on jobs with my brothers helped, though, and we've kept ourselves so busy that we've made enough credits to take a nice, long vacation—and take Zoey and her new mate with us. We also took on wild chases, I admit to myself. Chases like the *Buoyant Star*, with very little chance of a reward, just to give us something to look forward to.

Jade needs that, I realize. She needs something to look forward to. Right now she's sleeping a lot, and listless when she's awake. So I need to be there for her. I need to show her there's still a lot of fun to be had on this ship with me as her company. And I think I know the perfect way to do that.

On day three, I decide to make breakfast. Jade doesn't wake up early, so I go and knock on her door. "Good morning, sunshine," I call out, like Zoey always did to me. "Time to get up."

I hear a groan from inside her room, and then Jade pads to the door on the other side. After a few moments, it opens a crack. "Are we really doing this?" she asks in a sleepy voice.

"I made you breakfast," I say. "We can't waste food, so you'd better come eat it."

"Right," she says softly. "I'll be there in five."

Pleased, I head back to the mess hall and put her food in the warmer. I lean against the counter, rubbing my hands and thinking about my plans. I need everything to be perfect for this. I think about the human vids Zoey was so fond of, and ideas flood into my head. Yeah, this'll be perfect. Hastily, I grab a few of the noodles, spread the plas-film napkin on the table, and arrange the long, chewy noodles into a sentence, using the food to form the lettering. I place it directly in front of her spot at the table so there will be no way she can avoid seeing it.

And for some keffing stupid reason, I start to sweat with nervousness.

Jade arrives a few minutes later, her hair tamed back with a strip of fabric. She wears one of the modified uniforms and there's a listlessness to her step that tells me she wants to go back to bed, but she manages a smile for me. She sits down at the table across from me, and it takes her a moment to notice the message I've spelled out on her plas-film napkin.

She blinks at it, then at me. "Did you spill something?"

"No. That's for you." I nudge it toward her, waiting.

"Am I...supposed to eat it?"

"It's a message. Spelled out in noodles."

Her lips twitch. "Adiron, I can't read your language, remember?"

Oh. Right. I'm used to Zoey. Man, I really am the dumb one. I read it for her, instead. "It says, 'will you please be my date tonight for a special dinner so we can get to know each other better?'" Actually it says something more like "Date Night" and a question mark, but since she can't read it, I figure I'll embell-ish. It's keffing hard to spell things with noodles.

And since we're not wasting food, I pluck one of the noodles and eat it.

Jade's brows draw together. "It says all that?"

"Yup," I lie. "So...will you say yes?"

"But we eat together every day," she protests. "What about the date makes it different?"

"Humans go on dates in the vids I've seen," I tell her, picking another cold noodle off the napkin and eating it. "We dress up in our finest clothing, speak romantic words to one another, and share a romantic meal. Then afterwards, I walk you to your door and there's the potential for some kissing."

She laughs. "It always goes back to kissing with you, doesn't it?"

"I'm a male with a plan, what can I say?" I like that she's laughing, though. I like that the sparkle is returning to her eyes. "So is that a yes?"

Amusement brims in her eyes. "We're eating a meal you made right now. Why not have the date now?"

I shake my head. "Because it's going to be a *special* meal." Somehow. "And I'm going to make it special for you. We'll have mood lighting and music and everything, just like they do in the human vids. And if we do it later, it gives us both something to look forward to at the end of the day." This way, she gets a full day of distraction instead of just an hour or so.

Her smile remains and she stirs her noodles with one of her utensils. "I don't have anything fancy to wear."

"I don't either. We'll improvise. You could always wear your slave girl outfit..."

"Nice try." She chuckles. "That outfit has one specific job— to distract."

"It's effective. I still get distracted thinking about it." A lot. Like...a lot. "But if you're not comfortable in it, wear something else. Surprise me. I just want you to have a good time."

Her smile remains, but it fades a little. "You don't have to."

"I know. But we're here for the next month. We might as well get to know each other. Become friends. Really, really good friends."

She arches a brow at me. "Or is this the world's slowest seduction?"

Man, I hope it's not the slowest. I'm kinda hoping she'll just fall into my arms after a few weeks of flirting, but if it takes longer, I guess I can wait it out. "I'm not going to lie to you— part of this is so I can spend time with you. Romance you. Show you that you're the one for me." I shrug, trying to be sly. "Maybe sneak a kiss or two in there."

Her jaw drops, and she shakes her head, but she's laughing. "Damn, you do not beat around the bush, do you?"

"Being coy about what I want isn't going to get me anywhere," I point out bluntly. "I'm not smart enough for mind games. I like you. I want you. We're here together alone. Why not make the best of it? I'll shut up now if you want me to leave you alone, but I'm letting you know what I want out of this so you can plan accordingly."

Jade watches me for so long that I suspect she's going to tell me to kef off, that she's not interested. And if she isn't, well, I'll stop all the flirting. I know she's stuck here with me and pushing my wants on her would make her damn uncomfortable. She just needs to tell me what she wants and I'll play the role accordingly. But...I hope she wants me, just a little. She looks down at her breakfast noodles, stirring them slowly. "If I tell you to stop hitting on me, you will?"

Oh no. I hide my disappointment behind a wide, easy smile. "Well, yeah. If you're not interested, I'd just be a keffing monster if I pushed myself on you. My sister Zoey would beat the shit out of me with her puny fists the next time she saw me if I pulled anything. And just between you and me, she's a dirty fighter. Goes right for the balls."

She laughs again. If nothing else, I can make her laugh. I can brighten her day a little.

Jade picks up her bowl, not giving me an answer. She heads for the door and then pauses. "What time tonight?"

Hot damn. "Twenty-two hundred hours."

A little smile curves her mouth. "Wear something sexy for me."

Me? I laugh, amazed and delighted again by this female.

35

JADE

a date. It is absolutely the silliest idea...and yet it's exactly what I need. Adiron's smart. He knows I could use a distraction. Something to look forward to—even something as corny as a date in deep space when we're literally the only two around for thousands of miles—is perfect. I spend the afternoon picking through my admittedly small wardrobe, hand-sewing a few changes in my uniform with my makeshift needle created from an old chip that's been filed down to nothing, and thread that is made from thin strips of fabric. I bathe, then tease my hair, letting my natural curls fluff around my face. If I had makeup, I'd put some on, but I don't. That's the only thing that doesn't make this feel like a real date. There's no makeup, no perfume, no nails to paint.

I wonder how much Adiron knows about human dates.

I wonder if he knows that a lot of them end with a kiss on the doorstep.

Then, I wonder if I'll allow it if he tries. Adiron's made it very clear that he likes me, that he finds me attractive despite the fact that we're two completely different alien races. He's also made it very obvious that he'd be interested in getting to know me in very explicit ways, but he's done so in a way that doesn't make me feel trapped or cornered. I don't feel like I have to have sex with Adiron to ensure my safety. I feel like for the first time since arriving in space, I'm in control of the relationship. If I want to cut things off and end them, I will. I think Adiron would be disappointed, but he wouldn't attack me or harm me.

That realization is surprisingly freeing. Knowing that whatever I decide, I'm going to be okay. That I don't have to suck an alien's dick just to ensure a few more days in space, or that I'll get fed. The only way his dick gets sucked is if I feel like sucking it.

And because I have that control, it allows me to look at Adiron differently than the men that abused us in the past. I can look at him as a potential partner, if I want, even though the timing is awful. After all, we're here alone for the next few weeks. A little flirtation can't hurt things. And Adiron has been...kind. Sweet. Goofy, in his own way. He's been obvious in his interest, but also hasn't acted on it. He's just letting me know where he stands so I can decide if I want to pursue things with him or leave them as they are.

So I dress to let him know just how I plan to go about things. I put on my slave girl costume—or at least the top half. The bra of it makes my tits jiggle and pop out of the tiny strips of fabric that hold them in place, like the world's worst bikini. I've added a bit more material this afternoon, so it's slightly less scandalous and my breasts are covered more, and I've hand-sewn a long length of fabric from one of the pale gray bedsheets into a skirt. As I put it on, it flows over my body like a busty sundress with spaghetti straps, the skirt swishing just above the knees. All of my shoes are ugly, functional boots that are far too big for human feet, so I leave them off. I take a bit of fabric from the sheet and use braided strips to make gray bracelets for each hand.

I feel pretty, I realize, as I look in the mirror. I don't feel the heavy weight of responsibility or the need to be the "mom" of my small group. I'm pretty and sexy and ready to have a flirty evening with a big alien corsair who looks at me as if he wants to eat me with a spoon.

I might never get off this ship ever again. I might meet my death in a month from an ice field, or I might be stuck in deep space for years and years on end, waiting for a rescue that will never come. Either way, I deserve to do something a little reckless with a fun-loving, handsome alien that makes me smile.

So I check the time, recognizing the slashes on the doorpad as alien numerals, and I head back to the kitchen for my date. It's a little chilly as I pad through the silent halls of the ship, and I wonder if I should have worn something warmer. Too late now. I spent all afternoon making this awful-looking dress, and I'm going to wear it, damn it.

As I step into the kitchen-slash-dining area of the ship, Adiron is already there. He's dressed up for our date, too, in clothing I haven't seen him in before. It's a one-piece ship uniform, like I've seen so many aliens in, but this one is deep blue in color, so dark it's almost black. The front has a few decorative zips trailing along the legs and up the chest, flashes of silver in the unrelenting dark fabric of the uniform. He's got a patch on his shoulder with some alien words written on it, and a belt slung over his hips in that sexy angle that makes me think all kinds of filthy things that have nothing to do with guns or weapons. His uniform is...surprisingly tight, too. It's tight across the pectorals, showing off his muscles, and his biceps bulge against the fabric of his sleeves. His, ah, package is extremely outlined as well, made all the more obvious by the decorative zippers that bulge on either side, as if straining to let a trouser-beast out.

I might stare at that bulge a little.

Okay, a lot.

"You look beautiful," Adiron says, a big smile creasing his blue face. Even his horns look buffed, the silver shiny, and I wonder if he spent all afternoon getting ready to impress me.

"You're...impressive." My cheeks feel hot just saying that.

As if he knows what I'm thinking, he grabs his junk. "Looks good in this, right? I figure I have one chance to impress you, so I might as well go all out. And you DID say to wear something sexy."

The absurdity of the situation gives me the giggles, and I put a hand to my mouth, trying to stifle them. It doesn't work, though, and I just keep on giggling. He just grabbed his junk. Right in front of me.

Adiron grins. "I know, right? But sometimes it pays to play the handsome pirate, so I bring out this uniform for those occasions." He mock-adjusts the tiny silver buttons at his wrists. "Learned that one from Kivian."

"Who?"

"Captain of the ship my sister's on now." Adiron winks at me. "If you look like a hot piece of tail, you can distract people into thinking you're little more than that. It gets you a lot further than you'd think." He moves toward me and puts a hand out. "Speaking of, did I mention how magnificent you look?"

"I'm open to hearing it again," I tell him in a light voice and put my hand in his.

He takes my fingers and lifts them to his lips, kissing them, and I admit it, my silly heart flutters like wild. He gives me a rakish grin, too. "Saw that in one of your human vids."

"It's...a good move," I agree, breathless.

"There are a lot of human vids about courtship, which I find fascinating. Most of ours are either gladiator battles or just go right to the keffing." He shrugs and then takes my hand and leads me toward the table, which he's covered with a tablecloth...another bedsheet from the extra linens we have stored. I recognize the faint gray pattern on it. "May I pull out your chair for you?"

"Of course," I say, charmed and more than a little amused. "You must have watched a lot of vids."

"My sister Zoey was obsessed with them. I think I spent months of pay just getting her bootleg human vids instead of actually doing anything productive with my credits." He chuckles as he pulls my seat out and, once I'm seated, pushes it back in.

"You must love your sister very much."

"She's one of the five best things in my life," Adiron admits.

"Five?" I ask. "Your brothers, your sister...that's three?"

"Our ship," he says, ticking a finger off as he sits down across from me. "That's four."

"And five?" I ask.

"You can't guess?" His grin is positively devilish.

"Me?" My voice is squeaky with surprise. "I'm on that list? After only a few days?"

"I didn't say where on the list," he points out, impish.

And I have to laugh.

36

ADIRON

I'm sweating. I hope Jade doesn't notice that I'm sweating, but...keff me, she's beautiful.

She's beautiful, and I'm so keffing nervous.

I wipe my hands on my legs, my palms sweaty. Sure, I've been pretty blatant in my affection for her, but to think that she's actually halfway interested in a rock-head like me is hard to believe. I'm going to kef this up, I know it. I'll say something stupid and then all that interest in her face will die away. I'd give anything to be half as smooth as Kaspar, and he's not all that smooth.

Jade smiles at me as if she senses my nervousness. She cocks her head slightly and gestures at the room. "Well? You promised me fine dining and music if I showed up. I can't wait to see how you manage that."

Right. Music. Food. Romance. I can do this. The trick is to keep her laughing. If she's having a good time, she won't be disappointed in what an idiot I am. So I make sure she's settled in her chair and then pull out the covered tray I've prepared. "Music first, then dining." I set the tray on the table and unveil what's underneath—a few standard containers, all of them bottoms-up. I immediately start to drum out a beat, using my hands. I lift my head and let out a ululating wail, starting into an old Sakh rhyme that we're taught back in our boyhood days. It's a combination that never failed to make Zoey erupt into fits of laughter when she was young, because it sounds so outlandish to human ears. I figure Jade will get a kick out of it, too.

So I beat the drums. Close my eyes and wail some more. Drum. Wail. Drum. Wail.

And as I finish the wailing first verse of the rhyme, I notice that Jade isn't laughing. She's utterly silent. I squeeze one eye open and she's frozen across from me, a tumbler of water half-raised to her lips. Her eyes are wide and startled.

I immediately stop drumming. "You didn't like it."

Her eyes go even wider, which I didn't think was possible. She puts her glass down and leans over to touch my hand. "No, no, not at all, Adiron! That was lovely! It was just...wow..." She pauses, blinking. "It was..."

"A joke," I cut in. "It was a joke."

Realization dawns on her and she slaps my arm. "You son of a bitch! I thought that was real!"

I laugh.

She buries her face in her hands, her shoulders shaking with silent amusement. "I hate you," she eventually wheezes, and her tone makes it very clear that she does not, in fact, hate me.

"If it makes you feel any better, it's a really old song from where I come from, and it always made my sister Zoey crack up." I love her reaction, how her face lights up with amusement, and how she laughs so hard that her eyes get wet. Kef me, I love a woman that knows how to laugh. Jade does it magnificently, too. Her tits jiggle in that low neckline of hers, enticing me with that dusky brown cleavage that's just begging to be caressed. She's seated now, but earlier I got a great glimpse of curvy, dainty legs and her ample backside outlined in that dress she's wearing. It makes me want to flip that hem up and touch her.

I wonder if it'd be too forward of me to ask her to sit on my plate and be my dinner? Probably.

Jade's mirth fades, and she leans back, laughing and breathless, her hand on her stomach. "I haven't laughed so hard in forever."

"Well, this evening is just getting started," I tell her, encouraged. "Now that the entertainment portion is over, shall we commence with the food?"

"I can hardly wait," she teases, her smile bright.

I'm absolutely dazzled by that smile. I want to just bask in the warmth of it, but it's my duty to entertain (and hopefully woo) her. I head over to the two bowls I've prepared, the contents covered by a warming lid. I pretend to be one of the snotty waiters that were always in Zoey's vids, and hold the tray out to Jade. "The finest military-grade noodles for you, female," I say in a severe voice, bowing over the food.

Jade erupts into new laughter, clapping her hands. "You're such a liar! I thought you were going to give me something new to eat!"

"Well, it's a bit of new and old." I take the lid off the bowl and set it before her. The noodles are bright red, which makes her give me a look of mild alarm. "It's the same old noodles, but a special recipe." I set my own bowl down in front of my seat. "Let's just say that it's a couple of ingredients, that when mixed together, cause a flavor combination that was much beloved by my human sister." I'm personally not a fan of it, but I'd chew on a boot all night long if it meant I could stare at Jade while doing so.

She twirls a noodle onto her eating sticks and takes a hesitant bite. After a moment, her expression changes to one of wonder. "Cheese pizza. It tastes like cheese pizza."

I grin. "Yeah."

"That's amazing," Jade cries, and takes a larger bite, leaning over her bowl to slurp up the noodles. "How did you do this? Can we have this every night?"

"Like I said, it's a couple of spices that, ah, aren't normally combined together. And no, you can't have it often, I'm afraid." I grimace. "In fact, I don't even think you should have seconds. It's a spice that my people put in mixed drinks, but it's known to cause a bit of...gastric distress amongst humans."

Jade pauses, mid chew. She puts a napkin to her mouth, her actions fascinatingly dainty, and asks, "Gastric distress?"

I nod solemnly. "We found out the hard way that it's rough on human systems. You've never seen three pirates move faster than when their little sister is making distressed sounds in the lavatory."

Her shoulders shake with laughter again. "I'm going to finish eating—if it's safe—and then you're going to tell me that story."

"It's safe, I promise you. The last thing I want is to poison you." I take a big bite of the oddly flavored food. "And we found out the hard way. Zoey was addicted to flavoring her noodles like that and we couldn't figure out why she—"

"After," Jade warns me again. "Tell me after!"

We eat, and I'm pleased to see that Jade doesn't pick at her food. She eats with hearty enthusiasm, just like me, and when we're done, I clear the dishes and offer her a hot cup of tea. I tell her my Zoey stories as we sip our after-dinner drinks, and she laughs so hard at my coarse tales that more tears stream from her eyes. Zo would probably kill me if she ever knew I was telling these stories, but I'll take that chance later. For now, I'm just happy that Jade's having a good time.

"After that," I finish, "Mathiras made sure that Zoey ate new foods in small amounts. Very small amounts."

Her smile is wide. "Mathiras sounds very caring and conscientious."

"He has to be. He's stuck with a bunch of idiots." I grin, fully acknowledging that I am one of those idiots.

Jade's expression grows thoughtful. She stares down at her tea, and I can tell her mood changes. Her smile dims and the sadness creeps back in. "Have we had any word from anyone? Anything from Helen or Alice? Or even Ruth?"

I doubt we'll hear from Ruth any time soon. She's probably even now scratching her way out of Straik's keffing posh (scented!) holding cells and vowing revenge on him. Helen or Alice, though... "We might not hear anything from them for a while," I tell her. "The pods are dialed in to our ship here, but the farther away they get, the better the odds are that someone else can intercept a message. It's best to not let anyone know that we're here alone, or we're just inviting trouble to our doorstep."

"Of course." I can see the acceptance on her face. "I just... miss them. And I worry."

"Well, yeah. Of course you worry. They're stuck with my brothers, after all," I tease, but her smile is gone. I think for a moment and then offer an alternative. "You know...we can always go check. Maybe something came in while we were here."

"I'd love to check," Jade says in a soft voice. She reaches across the table and brushes her fingertips over mine. "I know there's nothing there, but I'd still like to check anyhow."

"I figured."

"Thank you, Adiron."

As long as she keeps touching me, I'll give her anything she keffing wants. Anything at all.

37

JADE

I'm having fun.

A teeny, tiny part of me feels guilty that I'm enjoying myself when the world's going to shit, when the others are stuck in escape pods, when Ruth is missing...but I push that thought aside. I'm allowed to have a little fun. Life can't just be one big unending shitstorm, right? There have to be pleasant moments to look forward to.

This is definitely one of those pleasant moments.

I loop my arm through Adiron's as we stroll toward the bridge. Tonight, the lonely, sterile halls of the *Buoyant Star* don't seem quite so desolate. I've got Adiron for company, and even if he's not the most serious of types, he's exactly what I need to distract me. He finishes another story about his sister Zoey— it's clear he adores her—and turns to me with a smile. "After that, she joined her mate and the crew of the *Jabberwock*. They navigate together, which, I gotta be honest, I'm not entirely sure how it works. Probably a lot of fighting over the controls. Zoey's a tyrant when it comes to setting flight paths and running fuel estimates." He shrugs. "Sentorr's a decent male, though. A little more stiff in the collar than I'd expect my sister to fall for, but he adores her."

"She sounds easy to love," I say as we head down the hall. I can't resist putting my other hand on his arm, touching the enormous bicep that bulges against his ridiculous uniform. The man is absolutely a mouthwatering snack, and I can't stop thinking about the times I saw him naked. I really should have paid more attention to what I was looking at. I remember broad shoulders and narrow hips that led down to a fascinatingly tight butt. I remember a flicking tail and strong thighs.

I absolutely do not remember if I saw his cock, and that makes me sad. It has to be as magnificently built as the rest of him, right? Surely fate wouldn't be so cruel as to make him this mouthwatering and then give him a sad little sausage.

Not that I intend to do anything with him, but it's not a sin to look.

"You got quiet," Adiron says, nudging me. "What are you thinking about?"

Oooh. I come up with an answer on the fly. "Just wondering about you. You have a sister that got married, but you and your brothers, none of you are married? Is that not a thing in your culture?"

Adiron makes a sound of assent in his throat. "Mathiras is devoted to life on a ship. Kaspar doesn't like to be tied down. And we come from a family with an old name, which means there are a lot of expectations. Unfortunately, we've all more or less shamed the family by going into a life of piracy. My sister Vanora—my real sister—is still on Homeworld. She mated well, increasing the family fortune and name. The rest of us aren't mentioned in polite circles." He shrugs. "It's fine."

"You mentioned why Mathiras and Kaspar never settled down, but I noticed you avoided yourself," I point out.

"I almost mated a female," he says after a moment, his expression thoughtful. "It was right after the war. I'd just started spending time on the ship with my brothers, and I met an exciting mesakkah female on a station. Her name was Shaalyn and she was the most beautiful creature I'd ever seen—bold and alluring and very, very sexual."

"You don't have to keep sharing," I tell him. For some reason, I don't want to hear more about the "sexual" Shaalyn. "I was just being nosy."

"It's all right." Adiron thinks for a moment and then goes on. "I was obsessed with Shaalyn for months. I'm sure some of it was because I'd just gotten out of the military and that was its own kind of hell. I was looking for something or someone to latch onto, and she was beautiful and loving and everything I thought I wanted. I was madly in love with her. I think she's the only female I've ever fallen in love with before now, of course."

"Of course." I decide not to stew on that. Everyone has a past.

"Turns out that Shaalyn's sweetness was an act," Adiron says. "She robbed me and my brothers and nearly got us killed. Took our ship, too. That was my fault. I gave her a system-access pass one night so she could sneak on board." He sighs heavily. "Mathiras was so keffing mad at me, too. We had to pay a large ransom for the *Little Sister* and I just felt stupid. Really stupid."

And hurt, I imagine. I squeeze his arm. Poor Adiron. "And after that, you stopped trusting people?" I ask quietly.

He looks over at me and grins. "No, of course not. One bad seed doesn't ruin the entire orchard."

What a remarkably positive outlook. It's one I can't share, not after being enslaved, abused, and abandoned. "Says a man who's never had anything truly bad happen to him," I reply, a hint of acidity in my tone. Adiron's a happy type because he's from a wealthy family and the worst thing that's ever happened to him was that he was hoodwinked by a woman. We should all be so lucky.

"Mmm." He looks over at me. "I was in the war for three years. Front lines, because I was a third son. I lost everyone in my first regiment. Got reassigned. I had friends die in my arms while I tried to stop the bleeding. My best friend went home in pieces, a broken shell of himself. He's living alone on an abandoned base on an asteroid right now because he can't function around people." He thinks for a moment. "Well, he's no longer alone, but whatever. And when Shaalyn robbed us, she stabbed me three times and left me for dead, all while I pleaded with her not to do it because I loved her. But maybe you're right. Maybe I'm just lucky."

My throat goes dry.

There's no judgment in his tone, but...I feel like an asshole. I stop, turning to look at him. "Adiron, I'm sorry. I shouldn't have said that. I didn't realize."

Adiron's smile is effortlessly bright and easy. He takes my hand in his and lifts it to his mouth, kissing my knuckles again. "You didn't know. I don't share, most times. And bad shit happens to everyone. I just prefer to live my life with pleasure instead of dealing with the pain. I can let the bad things swamp me or I can learn from my mistakes."

I smile. It's a beautiful way of looking at things. I'm envious of how easy he makes it sound. Just ignore the ugly bits and the dark spots. Focus on the light and the happy. My fingers tingle where he brushes his lips over my skin, and I'm disappointed when he lowers my hand. I'd almost prefer that he start making out with my hand than return it to me, which is a little ridiculous. "So, have you? Learned from your mistakes?"

"Uh...it's a process." He grins, tucking my hand into his arm again.

I can't help it—I laugh. That's such an Adiron response. I love it. "You'll get there."

The door to the bridge is at the end of the hall, and Adiron steers me toward it. They open automatically as we approach, revealing the large, lonely bridge and the view of deep space. "The good things outweigh the bad in my life," Adiron says finally. "So those are the ones I focus on."

"Like Zoey and your brothers."

"And you." He gazes down at me.

Instantly, I'm breathless. "You just met me."

"Yeah, but some things you just know about." He smiles and leans in, and I wonder for a moment if he's going to kiss me. "Does this count as walking you home, by the way? Because I've seen the human vids. I know what happens at the end of a date."

Seems like we're on the same wavelength. I tilt my head, regarding him. "You've just got a one-track mind, don't you?"

"Two tracks, actually. But they're both going in the same direction." He shrugs. "And we've got this big, empty, cold ship. Who better to warm you up than me?"

I pretend to consider his offer. In reality, there's not much to consider. What's a little bit of harmless sex? I like him, I need a distraction, and he's just the man for the job. "Can we check for messages first?"

His eyes flash with a look that's pure excitement. "Kef yeah we can."

38

ADIRON

*T*here are no messages.

I hate the clear disappointment on Jade's face, and hate even more that she tries to hide it. "I knew there wouldn't be any," she says with a brave smile. "I just was kind of hoping." She turns to regard the ship's empty bridge with a sigh. "And we can't send anything out, right?"

"Not unless you want to take the risk of someone tracing down the signal and heading in this direction."

"Of course not."

She keeps smiling, but it doesn't reach her eyes, and I feel like I failed her. I don't want our date to end on a down note, so I grab her hand and haul her after me. "Come on. I have an idea."

Jade's expression brightens, and she lets me drag her down the halls of the ship, her bare feet making the cutest little smacks against the metal flooring. I lead her into the main lavatory on the ship, the one just down the hall from the bridge. A ship this big has small, private lavatories in the personal quarters, but there's also two larger ones to accommodate crew needs. This one will suit me just fine. I pull Jade inside after me and immediately head toward the shower heads, turning them all on.

"What are you doing?" she asks. "We can't waste water."

"We're not wasting it," I tell her. "It'll just go right back into the system and be recycled. But we need the steam."

She tugs her hand from mine and gives me a suspicious look. "What is it we're doing in here?"

I take her by the shoulders and turn her so that she faces the large mirror over the row of sinks. Kef me, but she looks good in front of me. Her full, bouncy hair puffs up and brushes against my chin, and she's so curvy and dainty against my chest that it makes me want to crush her against me and never let her go. Seeing her like this—with me—does strange things to my heart. But she watches me in the mirror with expectant eyes and I force myself to focus. Right. I can moon over how beautiful she is later.

"The mirrors get steamy," I tell her. "I saw a human vid once where they left each other messages in the steam. They wrote on the mirror. I used to make it a thing with Zoey. I'd leave her a message, and then she'd leave me one. I left her a message on our ship for her, but I figured you could leave one here? That way if—uh, when—you see the others again, you can share it with them."

Her pleasure fades at my little slipup. But she smiles anyhow, and nods. "Leave secret messages. I like it. Does it matter if I write in English? I don't know your language."

"Sure, that should be fine. In fact, if you want to write something out, I can walk you through it." I beam innocently at her.

Jade thinks for a moment. "Can you write 'Please send food'?"

"Of course." I move toward the mirror, soap my finger with

some of the cleaner on the sink, and then begin to write in my language's blocky, formal letters. I leave a short, silly message instead. "There."

Jade watches with her head slightly tilted. She taps the mirror and one of the symbols. "How do you say this character?" I pronounce it for her, then deliberately pick one in the middle of the stream, and teach her that one, too. We go over the sounds, Jade's lips moving as she tries to memorize them. I'm impressed by her cleverness. She never takes a moment to stop learning. Everything is a weapon and she wants to be prepared.

"Sa-zhed-li-is-ka-mro-da-sha-nal-vru-ta-li," she says slowly. She repeats it, faster, and it still doesn't sound quite like my language, but enough that I can tell when her translator picks it up. "Sa zhedli iska mroda shanal vru tali? I am naughty girl, spank me?"

I can't help it, I chortle. "If you're asking, I'll gladly spank you."

"Adiron!" Her expression is utterly exasperated. "Are you ever serious?"

"Never," I admit. "What's the point? If you want to write sad things in the mirror, go for it. But you're better off smiling and spending your time in pleasant ways."

She glares up at me, but her glare softens ever so slightly when I move closer and put a hand to her waist. "It should have said 'naughty boy' instead of girl," she chides me, but her expression is no longer irked. She looks thoughtful. Distracted. And she's gazing at my mouth.

"But then I wouldn't have the opportunity to spank you," I point out. I pick her up, lifting her onto the counter so we're close to the same height. She doesn't complain, just watches me with those fascinating amber-colored eyes. "I guess we can skip the spanking if you want to move right along to the end-of-the-date kiss."

"Who says you deserve a kiss anymore after that stunt?" She arches a delicate brow at me.

"Me." I grin at her and lean in. "Come on. You know you want to kiss me. How can you resist?"

She snorts.

I sidle a little closer, until my hips are pressed against the countertop and her legs are on either side of me. I take her hand and put it on my shoulder, and her lips twitch with amusement. Oh yeah, she wants to kiss me, I think. She just doesn't want to admit it. I lean in, moving ever closer, and ask, "Is your mouth off limits? Or should I kiss other things first and save the best for last?"

"I thought aliens didn't kiss," Jade points out. "It's unhygienic, remember?" But her hand slides to the base of my neck and her other arm lifts to go around me, her face tilted up toward mine. Her eyes are soft as she gazes up at me, her pretty mouth parted as if she's just waiting for me, and my cock hardens in my pants at the sight.

Beautiful. Absolutely beautiful.

"Some don't. There's all kinds of hygiene laws on Homeworld, but last I checked, we weren't on Homeworld." I grin down at her, moving close enough that I can rub the tip of my nose against hers and feel her warm breath. "And I've watched so many human vids that make it look enticing. I'm sure I can wing it."

"Lord help me," she mutters.

"Here, I'll warm up first," I offer. Instead of kissing her inviting mouth, I lean in and kiss her cheek. "How was that?"

"Very sweet." Her smile widens, and this time, she tilts her mouth toward me in a silent request.

I ignore it, though. I'm a stubborn fool like that. I kiss her cheek again, then continue to kiss that warm brown skin over to her ear. I kiss it, too, and then I can't resist taking that small earlobe between my teeth just because it looks so keffing enticing.

Jade's breath catches. Her hands clench tighter on my neck, and my cock jerks in reaction. Now we're getting somewhere. "Better?" I whisper, nipping at that delicious little ear again. "Or do you think I need more practice?"

Her only response is a soft whimper.

"You're right," I tease. "More practice." I move down to her neck, burying my face against her soft skin and breathing in her scent.

Jade moans. One hand goes to my hair and she digs her nails against my scalp. Kef me, that feels incredible. Now I'm the one that wants to moan. I love the feel of her pressed up against me, and I hold her just a little tighter, until those glorious breasts of hers are against my chest. I kiss the side of her neck, enjoying how she trembles in my arms. I graze my teeth over her soft skin and I'm rewarded with a delicious little whimper.

"Better?" I ask, my voice husky.

"Adiron." One hand goes to my horns and she grabs one, steering me away from her neck. "You big tease. Just kiss me already."

I don't need to be asked twice.

39

JADE

*I*t occurs to me that I have a hard time letting go.

After years of being on guard, on alert, of feeling like everything in the universe is against four small humans, I can't seem to relax. I can't just close my eyes and enjoy a wild evening without being full of doubts. I itch to turn off the water that's steaming up the mirrors. I feel an obsessive compulsion to check the messages again. Or to go over how much we have left, food-wise. I twitch with the need to check on all the stasis pods and make sure they're functioning properly. I know the micromanagement issues are me desperately trying to have some sort of control over my situation.

I don't enjoy it, though.

I gaze up at Adiron as he leans in, ready to kiss my mouth. My hand is on one of his horns, ready to steer him to my lips, but he's paused, and now all the crazy thoughts come flooding back in. Control. Control. Always control. Never let my guard down. Never relax.

I'm suddenly so fucking tired of it. I deserve a night off. I deserve to have fun and be a little reckless.

So I grab Adiron by the collar instead and push my lips against his.

He makes a sound of surprise as I tug him forward. He doesn't know the war going in my head. There's no war in his. He chooses to be happy, and I need to learn how to do that. I want him to teach me. I want him to rub off on me. I want to enjoy life, even if I might only have a month left. I'm going to take this opportunity and knock his socks off.

Adiron's mouth is firm underneath mine for a hot minute, as if he doesn't quite know how to react to my boldness. I flick my tongue against his lips, and he softens, then groans. He holds me against him and his mouth slants over mine, hot and eager and enthusiastic.

And it feels...amazing.

I bury my hands in his short hair and lose myself in the kiss. He tastes a bit like noodles, but more than that, he tastes like himself. It's impossible to put a finger on, just that his mouth is enticing and oddly sweet, and when he licks into mine, he does so with all the enthusiasm of someone that's utterly new to kissing, and I find it endearing rather than off-putting. I take control of the kiss for a moment, keeping my movements slow and steady, flicking my tongue against his in lazy grazes so he doesn't jackhammer into my mouth. He's a quick learner, and when we pause for air, he takes my bottom lip between his teeth and tugs on it, sending heat skittering through my body.

"You taste keffing amazing, Jade," he tells me, panting. His hands slide to the sides of my face. "I love your little tongue." And he licks me again, boldly, across my lips.

It should feel weird and awkward, but I find it oddly erotic. He wants me so much he can't stop licking my face long enough to go back to kissing, and it makes me smile. "Is...do you have ridges on your tongue?"

Adiron grins and sticks his tongue out, showing me the ripple of ridges that go right down the middle. He leans down and licks my jaw again, and this time, that delicate little hitch that comes with his tongue moving across my skin visualizes— it's the ridges of his tongue catching, just a little, as he licks.

It makes my pussy clench tight around nothing at all.

"Is that bad?" he asks, not lifting his head as he tongues and licks his way across my jaw. "Do I need to stop?"

In response, I grab his belt and tug him forward. I wind my legs around his hips and lock my ankles behind him, and lift my mouth so he can kiss me again.

"Kef me," he breathes, and then he kisses me on the lips again. This time, I can feel it, the slide of those ridges against my tongue, and my skin gets covered in goosebumps with each drag of his tongue. I imagine it on other parts of my body, even as he conquers my mouth, and I shiver with excitement. Adiron pulls back and nips at my mouth in slow, unhurried motions, his nose brushing against mine. "Can we..." He nips me again. "Just kiss..." Nip. "...for the next month until they come back?"

"You don't want to do more than kiss?" I whisper, raking my nails over his scalp and tilting my head back as he makes his way back down to my neck again.

"Oh, kef me, I really do." His hands slide down my waist and then move to my hips, and he grips them tight. "I want to grab you and flip you over onto this counter and pound into your tight cunt until you cream." His lips slide over my skin, his mouth hot on my neck. "I want to bury myself so deep inside you that you take every bit of my cock and beg for more. I want to tongue that pretty cunt of yours—because I know it'd be pretty—and have you drench my face with your honey."

I gasp, heat flooding my veins. "Adiron."

He kisses me fiercely. "Sorry, do I need to shut the kef up? No dirty talk? Do humans not like that?"

Do I want him to stop? Is he crazy? "No, it's good," I promise him between frantic kisses. "I'm just surprised."

"But...not turned on?" His gaze searches mine.

"Very turned on," I admit.

He gives me another slow, wicked smile. "All right. I guess I should ask what humans do. I know mesakkah have hygiene laws, so I guess I should ask you what humans are comfortable with—"

Tonight, I'm not all that interested in thinking about boundaries. Boundaries are something that rule my life already. Tonight? I just kind of want to cut loose. I gently bite down on his lower lip and release it slowly, even as I reach between our pressed bodies and brush my hand over the hard length of his cock. "What do humans do? Everything, sweet man. Everything."

40

JADE

*A*diron groans, pressing his strange forehead to mine. "I'm the luckiest male in the universe."

That makes me laugh, because there's nothing lucky about our situation. "Or just the easiest to please." I slide my hands over his shirt. "Are all these muscles real? Because they feel amazing."

"You've seen me naked." His hands clench my ass tight. "You tell me."

"I wasn't looking," I admit. "I mean, I peeked a little, but I tried not to pay attention. It didn't seem right."

"Well I keffing stared hard at those magnificent breasts of yours," he tells me boldly. "You're welcome to stare down my cock. I can pull it out right now if you want a good look."

Even though I've vowed to be bold, his blatant statement makes me pause. In the length of time that I do, he gives me another mischievous smile. "Too much too soon?" He leans in and kisses my jaw again, then moves back down to my neck. "It's fine, I'm good with a bit of a chase. Might prefer it, actually."

"It's not that I don't want this," I stammer, feeling flustered.

"Don't apologize," he says, kissing my collarbone in a way that makes me feel utterly weak with need. "Not your fault I have all the finesse of a stampeding vuulax."

I don't know what that is, but anything stampeding...yeah, that sounds like Adiron. "I swear I'm not trying to be a party pooper. I want you." I rake my hands down over his hard, incredible arms. "God, how I want you."

He chuckles. "It isn't a contest. We can both want each other equal amounts." He kisses lower, his tongue skating between the cleft of my breasts. "Ah, kef me, you're so soft here."

I whimper, clinging to his head. My hands go to his horns—horns, of all things—and I clutch at them, leaving fingerprints all over the metal as he nuzzles at my cleavage.

"You tell me how far you want to go tonight, Jade. If you just want a kiss, I'll end right here. If you want to sit on my nose and grind until you come, I'll get on the floor right now." He tugs at the hem of my top. "And if you want everything, I just need to ask—your bed or mine?"

Oh god. Are we talking about beds already? It feels like too much, but he also feels so good that I don't want to stop. "You pick."

Adiron pulls back and flashes me a handsome, cocky grin, and then scoops me into his arms. "I have a better idea, actually."

"Oh hell," I mutter, my arms going around his neck, and I love his bark of laughter. With a smile, I bury my face against him. Even if I'm a bit of a stick in the mud compared to him, I can make him laugh. That counts for something, I hope.

Adiron moves to the shower and turns the water off with

the tap of a button, giving me a knowing grin. "Can't have my sexy female worrying about the water while I've got my face buried in her cunt."

I whimper at that. Adiron is utterly forthright about what he wants, that's for damn sure. "T-thank you?"

He casts a hungry look down at me, his lips curving into a faint, naughty smile that's pure Adiron. "Oh, Jade, you are so keffing welcome. Now come on. I know just the place to make you squeal."

"I don't squeal," I say primly as he carries me out of the lavatory.

"Not yet," he agrees. "But give me a few minutes."

"My, you're confident." I like his confidence, though. I like everything about him, really. Even if he's an alien. It's a little strange to me that I was kidnapped and abused by aliens, but in the arms of this one, all that stuff seems very far away. Adiron's funny and sweet and kind and just a little crazy, and I love that combination.

He's going to make the next month so damn fun. My toes curl just thinking about it.

To my surprise, he heads down the hall toward the bridge. "Are we checking for messages again?" I ask, confused.

"Nope." Adiron grins down at me. "Do you want to know my plan, or do you want to be surprised?"

I squirm a little. I don't think I'm that much of a rebel just yet. "Go ahead and tell me. I'm not a big fan of surprises."

"Well," he says as the doors open and he enters the bridge. "I'm going to sit in the captain's chair, and I'm going to lay you down on the control panel in front of me. I'm going to hike those skirts up, and I'm going to lick that pussy into the next galaxy. Because you deserve something far more exciting than just a simple bed. I figure what's more exciting than the captain's chair?"

Oh dear, sweet lord. What indeed.

He carries me over to the captain's chair, just like he promised, and there's a hungry look in his eyes. "You tell me at any time if you want me to stop," Adiron says. "I know I'm about as subtle as a supernova, but if I do something you don't like, you gotta tell me."

I bite my lip. "Are you really going to lick my pussy into the next galaxy?"

He nods, his smile wide and confident. "Kef yeah I am."

"Then you're allowed to be unsubtle." I'm blushing as I state it, because I'm totally not this person. But today? In this situation? I am absolutely going to be this person. I'm going to take the pleasure that's offered and have no second thoughts. "You can be as unsubtle as you want tonight."

"Good." Adiron places me atop the control panel and sits down in the captain's chair. He lounges back, studying me, and I fight the urge to squirm. The station I'm sitting on is covered in buttons and controls, and curves around like a low-walled cubicle. My butt is plastered across a touchscreen monitor and I suppose it's a good thing that we're entirely locked out of the system, or it'd probably be overloading right now.

Adiron remains sprawled where he is, utterly gorgeous and practically popping out of that tight uniform that shows all his muscles. One of his horns is covered in my fingerprints, the shine of it slightly dull, and his hair is tousled. He looks ready to fuck, except...he's not moving. Instead, my "date" watches me with that same hungry look in his gaze, as if he's deciding the best way to approach the situation.

Or...is he waiting for me to take charge?

Or...does he expect me to back down?

Well, I'm a lot of things, but I'm not a coward. I lift one foot and extend it until it presses against the middle of his chest. "Well?" I say confidently. "This pussy isn't going to lick itself, Adiron."

His face lights up, as if I've said just the thing to get him in motion. "If it did, I'd want to watch." He releases a control on the chair and it moves forward about a foot, and then his big chest is between my thighs. Adiron gives me the most devilish grin ever, and I bite back a whimper as he tugs my hips forward, to the edge of the control station.

41

ADIRON

Whatever god or celestial being that runs the universe is clearly looking down on me with favor right now. I must have done something right at some point, because I truly am the luckiest of males. I pull Jade against the edge of the control panel, her soft thighs brushing against my arms.

She looked so confident a moment ago, placing that small foot on my chest. Now, though, as I scoot in, some of her confidence wavers. I can see it in her gorgeous eyes, and I half expect her to call my bluff. To tell me she's decided to wait until we get to know each other better. I take one of her feet and place it on the armrest of my chair, then put the other there, too. Her knees are hiked because I've pulled in so close, the skirt of her dress tented.

And I can smell her arousal. Kef me, but there is nothing sweeter than that scent. It makes my mouth water, and I raise a hand to wipe at my lips, just in case I'm drooling on myself and that's a turn-off. She's utterly gorgeous, her eyes bright with anticipation, her lips slightly swollen from our earlier kisses, and her chest heaving with each panting breath.

I lean in and press a kiss to the inside of her knee. "I have to admit, I'm new to kissing, but you don't have to worry about the rest. I can lick the paint off a starship."

She lets out a high-pitched, tense little giggle, and her hands grip the edge of the control panel. "It's been a while for me."

"Me too," I admit, rubbing my mouth against the soft skin of her inner thigh. "You might not believe this, but I haven't been interested in a female since Shaalyn, and that was years and years ago."

"You?" she teases, but there's a little wobble in her voice, as if she's on unsteady ground. "Mr. Subtlety-of-a-freight-train? I do find that hard to believe."

She smells amazing. I close my eyes, breathing in the scent of her skin. "It's true. I thought that part of me was just dead, but then I took one look at you and realized it was just waiting for the right female to come along."

Jade makes a skeptical sound. "And I'm the right one?"

"Oh, kef yeah, you are." She might not believe me yet, but that's all right. Not everyone has to fall in love instantly. I'll allow her to slowly fall for my charms, as long as I get to touch her in the interim. So I kiss my way down the inside of her thigh and reach for the hem of her skirt. "Can I pull this up?"

"Kinda hard to lick my pussy with it down, don't you think?" She sounds utterly breathless.

I chuckle. I love when she teases me back. I can tell she's nervous, but that's all right. I plan on making this really damn good for her. It's not about me tonight. It's about making Jade fall in love with me. And if that means showing off my fantastic licking skills, I am more than ready. I've been dreaming of doing this to her since the moment I saw her. "Tell me to stop if you need a moment," I tell her, and then lift her skirts and shove them up past her hips.

And I drink her in. Kef me, she's gorgeous. Just endless warm skin, soft thighs, and then between her thighs, a tight cluster of curls. Below those curls, I see the cleft of her cunt, and her skin gleams with slickness. I groan, dragging her forward a little more. "I'm the luckiest male ever," I breathe again. "The keffing luckiest."

She makes a sound in her throat that might be assent. Jade's trembling, though. She's nervous, and she doesn't need to be. I'm going to be so keffing good to her. I tug her forward a little more, until that plump, gorgeous ass is practically hanging off the edge and she's forced to go back on her elbows to hold herself up. I slide one of her legs over my shoulder, bend over, and lick her, long and slow.

Jade moans.

Kef, I practically do, too. Her taste is incredible, and she's already so keffing wet for me. She's soft here, too, softer than I ever dreamed, and in this moment, I completely understand every bastard that's ever stolen a human...and I want to kill them for doing so. This female deserves only good things in her life. She deserves to be dressed in the finest clothes, eat the finest foods, and deserves the finest tongue on this sweet, soaked cunt.

Luckily I can give her the latter.

I slick a finger up and down in her folds, teasing them apart, and I love that her head falls back, her eyes closed. She trembles against my hand as I tease my fingertip back and forth, but I don't stop. She'll tell me to stop if I do something she doesn't like. I've made it quite clear that I'm at her disposal, not the other way around.

"You have the prettiest cunt I've ever seen," I breathe, dragging my finger through her wetness. My hand looks so big against her delicate folds. I'm fascinated by how sleek and plump they are, and there's a tiny little bump at the apex of her cunt, which I've never seen before. "What's this?"

She sits up a little, frowning. I touch it to show her, dragging my finger underneath, and her head drops back again. "Adiron," she pants. "You don't know what a clit is?"

"It's not something mesakkah women have. Is this like your spur?"

"My what?"

"Your spur?" I'm tempted to take my trou off and show her mine. She still looks confused, her hand sliding down to cover herself and I push it aside. "Don't cover up, I want to look at you."

"It's a clit," Jade tells me, panting. "Lord help me. I fell for your lies and you don't even know what a clit is. What happened to you licking the paint off a starship?" She tilts her head, a rueful smile on her face.

"I didn't say I wouldn't lick it. I just need to know if it's sensitive." I circle a finger around the dusky little bud, and watch as Jade's mouth trembles and her head falls back again with a low cry. Her entire body shivers in response. "I'm gonna take that as a yes."

"Very..." she pants, "...sensitive."

"Good to know." I lean down and lick her again, keeping her cunt spread with one fingertip. She quivers against me, and then one of her hands steals to the top of my head. Her fingers knot in my hair as I drag my tongue over her. I lick from her opening all the way up to that little bead of her clit. I tongue Jade with long, slow drags, reveling in the taste. She's sweet and musky all at once, wet and warm and so keffing good I want to just leave my face buried between her thighs for forever. Each time I move my tongue over her, there's fresh wetness to lap up, and Jade makes soft, delicious little cries each time I do so.

I take my time with her. I'm going to enjoy every moment of this. I lick her over and over again, slow and steady, and as I do,

I watch her responses. I pay attention to which things make her quiver, which touches make her inhale sharply, and which ones get no response at all. When I drag the tip of my tongue in leisurely circles around her clit and she clenches a fistful of my hair, I know I've hit on something she likes. It's such an enticing little bud, that clit, and I keep teasing it and playing with it, loving her reactions. Jade moans and arches against me, her hips moving in slow thrusts, and I imagine her under me, my cock buried deep into this soft, wet cunt.

I groan. Right now it's trapped in my too-tight trou, and it's hard to resist the urge to free my cock and start stroking it even as I pleasure her. Slow, I remind myself. Go slow. You don't want to scare her off. Not when she's so willing in your arms right now.

I apologize inwardly to my cock, because it's just going to have to wait its turn.

Jade whimpers and rocks against my mouth when I give her another long, slow taste. She pushes up against me, and I go down to the entrance of her core, teasing into it with my tongue. She moans louder, and I push into her tight, wet warmth with it, burying my face between her thighs. Will she let me use my tongue to make her come, I wonder? Or should I play it safe and use my fingers instead?

If my data-pad ever connects to any outside source ever again, I'm going to look up everything I can on human anatomy and find out the best way to make her squirm. For now, I just have to guess.

I tongue her sweet entrance a little longer, until she's wriggling up against me and panting my name, and then I go back to her clit. I tease her with light presses of my tongue, over and over, and I want to tell her all the filthy things I've dreamed about doing to her, but my mouth is occupied. I'll have to save the words for some other time. For now, her clit needs some more licking. She's rubbing up against me like a xushen in heat, and I'm going to lose control if she doesn't come soon. Just blast right through the front of my trou and spray seed all over the keffing bridge.

No, I need to make her come. Hard. And fast.

I redouble my efforts between her soft thighs, my tongue focused on her clit. With my fingers, I work two of them up and down her wet slit, rubbing, and I love the keening little cry she makes.

"Oh, please, Adiron," she pants. "Please. Please."

I push into her with my fingers, and she sucks in a breath, hard. Maybe that was too much all at once, but I work on her clit, tonguing it, and she calls my name out again, her hand fisted in my hair. I fight back my own groan and pump her cunt with my fingers as I lick her clit. She's so keffing wet and tight. I've never felt anything better, and I'm dying to tear my trou off and shove deep inside her.

She makes this high-pitched little whine, and her back arches as I thrust my fingers deep, and then she's coming, a fresh wave of fluid soaking my fingers. Her entire body tightens and I nuzzle her cunt, unwilling to let her go just yet. I want to watch her do that again, and again, and—

The lights flicker overhead. Then they go out.

All is quiet. I look up, waiting, but nothing turns back on again.

"Um...please tell me I just blacked out," Jade pants.

42

ADIRON

"**I** think the power just died," I tell her, and reluctantly slide my fingers from her body. Kef me, that is the worst timing. I lick them clean of her taste, because I am absolutely not about to let that juicy cunt go to waste, and then I get to my feet, adjusting the too-tight front of my trou. "We...might have a problem."

Jade looks wonderfully disheveled as she sits up, tugging the hem of her strange dress down. Her hair floats about her face and her cheeks are flushed, her eyes glassy. There's the barest hint of lighting on the dark bridge due to a few emergency lights that offer a blue glow, just enough to make the darkness not quite so overwhelming. "The power?" Jade asks. "Did we do something wrong? Is it because of where I'm sitting?"

I wish. Because then I'd just take her into my lap and grind my cock against that sweet heat of hers and— Focus, Adiron, I tell myself. "No, the control panel won't respond no matter what we do. It doesn't recognize any users on board, so we could hit every button and it'd never react. I think it—"

Before I can finish, the power flickers on again, something whines, and then it flickers back off once more.

Jade sucks in a terrified breath.

"—I think it's a busted connection somewhere," I tell her.

"What about life support?" she asks, and there's so much fright on her face. "What about the stasis pods?"

"They'll be fine," I reassure her. I put a hand on the back of her neck, just because the animal side of me wants to grunt and beat my chest and pull her against me. I rub her skin with my thumb instead. "The stasis pods aren't hooked to the ship itself. They're going to remain in stasis until each individual pod is activated."

She lets out a little breath of relief, leaning closer to me.

"And as for us, the life support for the ship will be fine for hours and hours, but it won't matter because the back-up systems should kick on at any moment." I stroke her neck, trying not to think of my cock. "We just need to wait it out."

"You're sure?" Her arms go around my waist, and she presses her cheek to my chest.

Kef me, she's a cuddler. I'm such a goner. The only thing I love more than licking cunt is cuddling. Okay, I also love getting my rocks off, but I'm also happy to put that third on the list, like any good male should when it comes to his female. I press her against my chest, wrapping my arms around her, and I love that she leans into my touch. I bet she's clingy when she sleeps, too, and I love the thought of that. "Oh yeah, all these ships have a back-up system. It'll kick on, I promise."

So we wait.

And wait.

And I'm pretty sure that the system should have kicked on. I frown as I look around and my breath fogs in the air. Jade moves a little closer to me, shifting her weight, and she must be freezing in that tiny scrap of clothing she's wearing. I'm gonna need to warm her up...

But first thing's first. "Okay, so maybe the back-up is dead, too. I think we're going to have to go see for ourselves. I'm sure we can get it up and running again."

Jade clutches the front of my uniform. "Adiron, I don't know how to do anything on this ship. We manually clean the air filters, but...that's it. We're fucked if—"

"Shhh, hey, it's all right." She sounds far more panicky than I'd like, and my protective instincts come rushing to the forefront. "I know just what to do in this situation," I lie. "We just need to head down to the control room, pop off a few panels, and take a look at the wiring. This sort of thing happens all the time."

She lets out a shuddering breath. "It does?"

"It does," I reassure her. "You seem awfully panicked. What, are you scared of the dark?" I add a teasing note to my voice, because I don't like to see Jade so terrified. I much prefer her when she's full of sass and confidence. "You afraid of ghosts?"

"No. I'm afraid of dying because we run out of air!"

Oh. We're far more likely to freeze to death before that happens, but I don't say that out loud. "It's all under control," I tell her. And it will be. I'm reasonably confident I can figure things out. It can't be that hard. I know how the *Little Sister* runs like I know the back of my hand. Sure, this ship is three times the size, but I bet it's all the same when you come down to it. "Come on. Do you have tools you keep anywhere?"

"Tools?" she asks, her voice vague and a little panicky.

"Yes, love, tools." I find her hand in the shadowy darkness and take it in mine. She clutches at mine tightly; her palm is clammy with sweat. Kinda gross to hold onto, but Jade can't help it, and I'm not about to let her go. "Let's go find your tools, all right? Did they leave any behind when they left you here?" I prompt, heading down from the captain's station and across the bridge. "You girls scavenged whatever you could find, yes? Did you find tools of some kind?"

"Tools," she echoes, her hand tightening on mine. "Yes, I think so."

"Excellent. Where did you put them?" I'm sure there's bound to be more than one set of tools around here, but the less I have to go hunting for, the better.

"Ruth..." Jade murmurs. "Ruth keeps them in her room. She likes to do the maintenance."

"All right. We'll go to Ruth's room," I say easily. "Lead the way."

She sucks in a deep, steeling breath and then takes the lead. Her hand firmly clutching mine, Jade leads me back down the halls of the ship, past our personal quarters and toward more of the doors to additional rooms. She touches one panel and a door slides open, revealing what must be Ruth's private quarters. They're neat as a pin, completely austere, and her bedding is entirely in black. Oh man. Keffing Straik is gonna shit when he realizes he's stuck with the human female version of himself. I wish I could be there to watch when he finds out she's hiding on his ship.

Jade releases my hand for a moment and then heads to the closet. Inside the neat stacks, there's a small hardshell case of tools. Not many, but I'll work with it.

"Perfect," I tell Jade as she holds it out to me. "Let's trade."

"Trade?" she asks, confused.

I pull the heavy plas-blanket off the bed and wrap it around her. "You're gonna get cold, and much as I'd love to warm you up, my hands are gonna be busy with other things."

"Oh. Thank you, Adiron." She still sounds a little dazed and scared.

I take the tools from her and hold my hand out again. "Come on. Let's go beat that control panel into submission."

"I'm sorry," she says as we head out of Ruth's rooms. "I need to get ahold of myself. I just...this is my biggest fear."

"Then it's good you've got me along," I tell her smugly. "Because I'm going to take care of you." And I mean it, too. Jade's never going to be forced to rely on herself solely again. She's got me now, and I'm going to look out for her. If I have to take on the universe to protect her, I will. She's mine now. And she'll realize that soon enough.

43

JADE

*T*he fact that the ship gets so cold so quickly makes me a little panicky. I clutch the blanket tightly to my body as Adiron guides me through the dark halls. He walks with confidence, as if he has the ship memorized already. Maybe all alien spaceships have the same layout, and that's how he knows exactly where to go. He doesn't seem worried, though, and that helps ease my frazzled nerves a little.

To think, just a short time ago, I was feeling better than I have in years, drowsy and delicious from a hard orgasm and the best oral sex I've ever had...and poof. Gone in the blink of an eye. The ship breaking down is my worst nightmare. It's the one that haunts me in my dreams and makes me break out into a cold sweat. I like control, and I don't have any with this ship. I don't know how to make much of it work, and if it's anything like cars back home, it'll need maintenance at some point. The smallest thing could go wrong and then we're without oxygen, or food, or water...

Or, as I'm noticing rather quickly, heat.

The temperature drops rather fast, which is a little alarming to me. Maybe it's because I'm not wearing a lot of clothing, but the floor feels colder against my feet within minutes. I think of the ice field Adiron claims we're on the edge of and wonder if we're slipping over into it. If we're going to turn into human (and alien) popsicles before the power comes back on. "Adiron," I whisper, worried. "How long do we have before the ship freezes over?"

He squeezes my hand. "Don't you worry. There's plenty of time to get things up and running again. I won't let you freeze."

His confidence makes me feel better. "It's really damn dark."

"I know. I've got you, though."

"Should we get a light of some kind?"

"Don't need it. We're almost there. Look." He points the tool case at a door at the far end of the hall. It's dimly lit thanks to the tiny blue emergency lights that are along the floor of the ship. I'm not all that familiar with this particular hall. There's a lot of doors and rooms in this ship that I don't know all that well, simply because they house technology that I don't know how to use. But Adiron seems to know what he's doing. He releases my hand and puts his on the panel to open the door. When it doesn't open, he chuckles. "Right. Power's off." He drops to his knees and presses a tiny button in the wall, and a panel pops out. "There we go. There's always a manual override."

He flicks a tiny switch and the doors make a clicking sound. Adiron stands and pushes them open and then steps inside.

I follow behind him closely. "What happens if we don't get it running?"

"We will."

"But if we don't?" Gosh, he's stubborn and frustrating some-times. I don't want an answer meant to soothe me, I want a real answer.

It's even darker in here, so I can't make out his face. His legs are lit up, just a little, though, and I see his tail do a little shimmy that makes me think he shrugs. "Then we get cozy in an escape pod and figure things out from there."

"Oh...but we can't leave..." I protest.

"We also can't save anyone if we're dead," Adiron reasons. "I promise you, though, it won't be necessary. We're going to get this old girl working." He heads toward a large, smooth black structure with a few dead screens on it. It takes up most of the room, has a few cords curling around it leading off into the ship, and is bigger than my last car. I have no idea what the thing is, but Adiron seems to recognize it. He runs a hand along the surface. "We just need to get inside and check the wiring. There's a switch here somewhere." He touches something, and then I hear a snap. A moment later, Adiron holds up a piece of metal and chuckles. "Well, that ain't good."

I feel like I'm going to hyperventilate. "Oh my god. What do we do?"

"Don't worry. There's another way to get in," he reassures me.

"There is?"

"Oh yeah." He hands me the case of tools. "Hold this for me." As I do, he opens it and considers the contents. He pulls out an object that looks a lot like a pointy screwdriver and holds it up. His white teeth flash in the darkness, showing me a hint of fang. "Observe."

"You're going to use that to pry it open?"

"Kind of." He slams the tool into the metal casing of the black monstrosity and punches through the casing.

"Adiron!" I hiss. "What the fuck?"

"It's okay," he reassures me. "It's already dead, right? It can't hurt us."

"What if you just broke something?"

"We'll find out soon enough." He bends over, running his

hand along the metal structure once more. Then he punches the tool through again. I bite back an angry sound that rises in my throat, because he's worked on ships before. I haven't. I have to reassure myself that he knows what he's doing.

When he jams the tool into the thing a third time and pries off a large section of metal, though, I start to have my doubts.

"There's a manual override in here," Adiron says, as if I've voiced my worries aloud. "It's hidden away so you can't accidentally hit it, and locked down. It's a manual switch because if the computers go down, you're keffed." He pauses and grins up at me. "Kinda like now."

I squat down next to him, trying not to block his light. "Show me? I want to see." In case I need to know for the future.

He runs a big hand along the panel and then grunts. "Found it. Okay. Here." He finds my hand, then takes it and guides it toward the switches. "It's the big one that feels like a knob. Run your fingers over it."

There's a large, smooth thing under my grip. "Okay."

"Got it?"

"Yeah."

"Okay, now...put your fingers around it...and pump."

"Pump?" It feels like a thick knob. How am I supposed to pump it? "I don't understand."

"Squeeze the base, too. Tell it how big and thick it is, and how wet it makes you—"

I reach out and smack Adiron on the arm. "You dick! That's not funny!"

He chuckles, batting away my hands. "Oh, come on. It's a little funny. Can I help it if I'm still thinking with my cock?"

"YES." I smack him one more time, just because.

Adiron grabs my hands and kisses my knuckles. "All right, my humor is misguided. You're right." He releases me and puts a hand back on the knob. "It's a process, this thing. You have to pull it out of the housing, turn the shaft, move it across to the secondary housing, and then lock it into place. Like I said, it's so you don't accidentally reboot the ship at a critical moment." He snaps the lever into place, and I hear the "clink" of things locking in.

There's a low beep, and then silence.

I lick dry lips, tugging Ruth's blanket closer around my body. "What now?"

Adiron sits on the floor and reaches for my hand again. He pulls me down into his lap, and then slides his arms around me. "Now, we wait."

Waiting. Well, I'm pretty good at that. I've had a lot of practice.

44

ADIRON

*J*ade smells so keffing good. She's warm and soft in my arms, and even though she's tense and worried, I can't get over how amazing today has been. We had a date. She let me lick her gorgeous pussy until she came. Even now, she goes into my arms without protest.

A male could die happy like this.

I can still taste her on my lips.

I just hate that she's so keffing scared. I stroke Jade's back in the darkness, murmuring soothing sounds to her as we wait for the ship to hum back to life again. The manual override is chirping along, running through its paces, and I have no doubt that eventually everything will be back online again. Ships are complicated beasts, sure, but they're also meant to be running. The lights and the air will pop back up soon, and then Jade can relax.

Heck, even if it doesn't, it's not like we don't have options. There's an escape pod with our name on it, and we could easily manually launch it from the ship. It would mean leaving the people in stasis behind, but it doesn't have to be forever. I'm more interested in keeping Jade safe than anything else.

Well...almost anything else.

Because my cock is still hard and aching from earlier. Jade's curled up against me, her face buried against my neck, the blanket wrapped around both of us. It's hard not to think about pushing her onto her back and licking her pussy again, but something tells me she's probably not in the mood, what with being terrified and all.

"You want to play a game?" I ask her in the darkness, my breath freezing in the air.

"A game?" Her voice wobbles, but she manages a laugh. "No."

"Come on," I say, nudging her. "Ask me something, and if I can't answer it, I'll..." I cast around for an idea. "I'll lick your pussy again."

Jade sits up, and she pinches my nose in the darkness. "Is this an excuse for you to go down on me again?"

"Do I need an excuse?" I joke. "Because I'd be more than happy to have you sit on my face right now—"

Her hand covers my mouth to stop my words, but I get a low chuckle out of her. I'll take that. "How about every question you don't answer, you have to tell me an embarrassing story about yourself instead."

I'm glad to see pussy is back on the table, so to speak. "I can do that. And you'll do the same?"

"Sure." Her hand slides to my chest, and then she puts her head on my shoulder, her fluffy hair tickling my chin. "You go first."

I think for a moment. I think I'll start with something funny, ease her into things. "Did I lick your pussy better than anyone else?"

"Is this whole conversation gonna be about pussy?" she asks, but there's an amused teasing in her voice.

"It's been on my mind...and it could be on my face if—" I laugh as she covers my mouth again, and speak through her fingers. "Come on, that was a good one!"

"You are outrageous!"

"Of course I am." I press a kiss to her fingers. "There's no one here but us. It's just me and the female I'm utterly crazy about here alone on this ship. We're on the edge of the universe, and with a ton of uninterrupted time. I can think of no better way than to spend every last minute trying to kef you sideways. I mean, unless you had something else planned for the next month?" I press more small kisses to her fingers. She doesn't pull away, so I figure that's a good sign. If she listens to me telling her how much I like her, maybe at some point it'll start to sink in.

"So you just want to, what, make out until dawn?"

"Dawn, and dusk, and then to dawn again, and..." This time, when her hand moves over my mouth, I capture it and press a kiss to her palm. "So I guess you don't want to play our game?"

"We're playing games right now, aren't we?"

That we are. I'm not entirely sure if I'm winning or losing, though. I open my mouth to speak when something electronic whines, and then the lights flicker overhead.

A moment later, they come on.

Jade stares up at the ceiling with a look of sheer relief on her face. "You fixed it!"

"More or less." I'll have to give it a thorough once-over later, but there'll be time enough for that when Jade's not in my lap. Right now, I am far, far too distracted to be playing with the delicate components of ship technology.

Jade's relief is intense, though. She turns to me, gives me an incredulous laugh, and then flings her arms around my neck, peppering kisses onto my face. "You're a miracle worker!"

I should tell her the "miracle" was knowing which switch to flip, but I get it. I've been in her place, where you feel out of your depth and when the world rights itself again, the relief you feel is utterly intense. She's showing me that intense relief right now as she kisses my cheeks, her weight pressing up against me.

And because I'm shameless, I take advantage of the situation. I roll backward, my arms around her waist. Then, suddenly, she's on top of me, and our faces press together, her lips skating against the corner of mine.

She draws back in surprise, clearly not expecting that. I just grin up at her. I'm half-expecting another light smack to the shoulder or a verbal jab. I'd deserve it, too. Instead, she just eyes me thoughtfully. Her gaze flicks to my mouth, and my cock gets harder than ever. Kef me, she's staring at my lips. I never thought looking at someone could be so keffing sexy.

"Do you always get what you want?" Jade murmurs, brushing a lock of my hair back from my face.

"Very rarely, actually. My sister calls me a try-hard."

"You definitely are." Her thumb skates over my lower lip and my balls feel as if they can't get any tighter or they'll just migrate completely into my body. "It's cute, though," she says softly.

"Is it?"

"To me it is." Her mouth teases up into a smile. "You make me laugh."

"What every male wants to hear when a female's on top of him," I quip.

Her gaze slides to my mouth again, and then she leans closer. "Well, we can't have me harming your ego, can we?" Her lips brush over mine. "Still want to play that game?"

Game? I want her to rip my trou off and ride my cock. I want to bury my face between her legs again until she's begging for mercy. I want to lick every bit of that gorgeous soft skin of hers. But...I guess I can play a game. "Sure."

"I have a rule change, though." Jade tilts her head at me, grinning. "We ask each other questions, and if the other person can't answer honestly, they lose an article of clothing. Deal?"

"That works." It more than works, because Jade's only wearing that little dress. I know, because my head was under the skirt of it. "But if you want to see me naked again, all you have to do is ask."

"It's more fun like this," she tells me with a teasing look. "Or are you not into games?"

"All right, but I still like my version, where I licked your pussy every time I didn't answer. I mean, in that one, we're both winners."

Jade laughs, getting to her feet. She tugs the blanket around her body, cocooning her smaller form. "Play your cards right and maybe you can do both."

Now we're talking.

45

JADE

*T*onight has been very instructive. A bit too adventurous for my taste, but instructive.

Tonight, I learned that our safety here on this big ship is not guaranteed. I learned how fully helpless I truly am if something goes wrong. I don't have the means or knowledge to fix anything. Tonight, I learned that, and I learned that Adiron is protective and caring and kind, even when things are going to shit around us. I learned he's a good kisser, and a giving lover.

I'm also learning that I don't want to be alone tonight. Not after the fright I've just had. I feel fragile and uncertain, but I also feel that I'm less frightened than I would be because Adiron is at my side.

He's the person I didn't know I needed in my life—coarse, unabashed, and utterly, completely endearing.

Even right now, as we walk back to the living quarters in the ship, I'm filled with affection for him. Adiron tucks the blanket around my shoulders as we head down the hall, as if he needs to make sure that I'm warm enough. He stays close to my side and makes funny little jokes about the state of the ship—that maybe the ship's hard reboot will improve the smell coming from the air filters, that because it's so cold I shouldn't hold a little shrinkage against him—all designed to take my mind off the scare we've had.

It's like I'm the only thing that matters to him, and it's so damn sweet.

We pause outside of my quarters. Adiron brushes a twisted lock of my hair back into place, but it only springs forward again. "We'll save our game for the morning," he says. "You look tired."

I am absolutely tired, but I also know I don't want to be alone. So I grab his hand and tip my chin, indicating he should come in. "Don't chicken out on me now."

His eyes light up and then gleam with amusement. "You want company?"

"I sure don't want to sleep alone tonight. Doesn't make sense to me on this big, empty ship that we sleep a few doors apart." I shrug, trying to add lightness to my words. "Sometimes when one of the girls would get scared—usually Helen—we'd all pile in bed together and have a sleepover."

Adiron gives me an impressed look. "Now I'm getting all kinds of sexy images—"

I smack him lightly before he can continue that line of thought. "Just to enjoy each other's company. Just to feel not so alone."

He steps inside of my room, but his gaze is completely on me. "Is that what you want right now? Just to not feel alone?"

I'm not entirely sure what I want. All I know is I'm not ready for him to leave my side just yet. "Maybe? Do I have to have a reason?"

"You want your pussy licked again, don't you?" He leans over to me as if sharing a secret. "Jade, love, all you have to do is ask—"

I smack him again. "Are you going to keep bringing that up?"

"Absolutely. I love that you're blushing, despite the fact that we are the only. two. people. on. this. ship." He taps the tip of my nose lightly with each word. "I could lick your pussy on every surface in this ship and no one would know but the two of us, and yet you blush and look shy."

He's right, of course. It doesn't mean I'm going to stop blushing at the thought. Adiron's just so damn forward with what he wants. I like it, but it makes me feel shy anyhow. "I don't know," I say, moving to the edge of my bed and sitting down. I adjust Ruth's blanket around my shoulders and lift my chin, looking over at him. "All this pussy-licking talk could be a distraction to hide from the fact that you've got no game downstairs."

Adiron rubs his hands together, a gleeful smile on his face. His tail flicks wildly behind him. "A challenge? You want me to show you just how much game I have?"

I raise a hand into the air, stopping him before he can just whip his pants off. "We were going to play a game, remember?"

"Haven't forgotten." He grabs a chair from the corner of my room, flips it around, and straddles it, parking it directly across from the bed. "Game of truths—the person that can't answer has to remove an item of clothing. I remember, and I'm more than ready to play." The big alien gestures at me. "You start."

I settle in on the bed, crossing my legs and adjusting the blanket around me as I think. He's all eagerness, this guy, his eyes bright and his tail swishing. My gaze settles on his shiny metal-covered horns, and I can still see my handprints all over the one. Mentally, I'm back on that control panel, his mouth going to town between my legs, making noises of sheer delight as he licks every inch of me.

Oh man. It is suddenly very warm in the room. I let the blanket slide off my shoulders a little so I don't have to fan my face. A question. A question. Hmm. I could ask him about his brothers, or the ship, or what his favorite foods are, but those all feel like total softballs and I think Adiron would call me out on it. So I decide to start personal. "How many women have you slept with?"

"One. Shaalyn." He nods. "Okay, my turn—"

"Wait," I blurt out. "You only ever slept with one woman?"

He shrugs his big shoulders. "Why is that surprising? I'm a romantic. It's easy to flirt, but I wanted something that I thought was real. I wanted a deeper connection between myself and my partner. I thought I had it with her, and it took me a long time to get over her betrayal."

"Oh." I don't know what to make of that. Someone as playful-seeming and carefree as Adiron should have a laundry list of lovers. The fact that he's only had her—and now wants me— should make me run for the hills. That he's a man who makes bad choices.

Instead, I find it sweet. It makes me ache. It makes me feel...special.

Adiron leans forward on his chair. "You do realize that was two questions, right? So now I get to ask you two."

So it was. "That's fair," I say with a smile. "Ask away."

"If I could touch you anywhere right now, where would you want to be touched?"

My brows furrow. Is this another blatant seduction? As I look at a grinning Adiron, I realize the answer is probably "yes." My body flushes with heat, and I consider what he's asking. "Well, your mouth was amazing on my pussy...maybe just to try something new I'd say 'breasts.'"

"So they're sensitive?" he asks, voice husky. "I bet they are. Those little hard tips perk up every time I touch you. I bet you'd like those nibbled on."

I shiver, my body clenching with arousal. "They are sensitive," I say. "And that's two questions."

He blinks. "Shit. I got all distracted thinking about your breasts."

I shake a finger at him. "And now it's my turn." Or at least it will be, the moment I think of something to ask him. It needs to be a good question, not something that feels like a cop-out. I think for a minute and then go with the question that keeps popping up in my head. "Do humans look odd to you? Be honest."

Adiron considers. "Yes and no. Some parts of you do. Your wiggly little toes weird me out. Zoey had these long toes that looked practically prehensile." He lifts a hand and waves his fingers. "But I like your smooth brows and your round hips, and I really, really like those breasts of yours."

And I blush again. This man's always making me blush.

"My turn," Adiron murmurs, and the heat in my belly turns up a notch.

46

ADIRON

*T*his game is an absolute cock-tease and I love it. It's just drawing out the hunger I feel for Jade, and treating me to a lot of her blushes and squirming, which only makes me harder.

It's my duty as a lust-addled male to come up with a question that she won't answer, simply because I need her to strip. And then we can continue to play the game, and when she squirms, I'll get to watch her naked breasts jiggle with her movements. Just thinking about that makes me shift in my chair, my cock rock hard and aching.

It's my turn to ask a question, and this one's easy. "When I licked your cunt—what part did you like the best?"

I love that she blushes—as if anyone else is around! As if I haven't been tongue-deep in that glorious cunt of hers! "You're terrible."

"I play to win." Actually I wouldn't mind losing, but I want to see some skin first.

She wriggles under that blanket, embarrassment stamped across her face. "Um."

"If you don't want to answer—"

"I'm answering!" Jade straightens and gives me her most haughty look. "Give me a moment. I'm thinking."

"Do you need a reminder? I'm happy to demonstrate."

The look she gives me would wither plants on some worlds. I love it. With as much dignity as she can muster, Jade lifts her chin. "I liked your tongue against my clit."

I file that information away. "That it? Or was there more?"

"That's a second question!"

Tricky, tricky. I approve. I gesture for her to take her turn. "You go, then."

Her cheeks are stained with deep color as she watches me. "This isn't a fair fight. If I ask you something sexual, you'll just eat it up. There's nothing you won't answer, and here I am, exposing all my private thoughts."

I grin, because she's not wrong. "Then ask me something non-sexual."

"Do you think we're going to die out here?"

Her vulnerable question takes me by surprise. I hate the look of sheer uncertainty on her face, so my answer is automatic. "No, I don't."

"You're not lying to me, are you, Adiron?" Jade's gaze searches mine.

"That's not how this game is played," I joke.

"I don't want to play a game," she whispers, her eyes heartbreaking. "Just tell me the truth, please. I can handle it. I just need to be prepared."

My poor Jade. She looks so stressed and worried. I want to reassure her. More than that, I want to grab her and drag her into my arms and just squeeze all the strain off her face until she smiles again. "You and I are not going to die," I promise. "Even if things get a little dangerous here on this ship—and I don't think they will—we have an escape route. We can always take an escape pod somewhere safer and regroup." I know how she thinks, so I choose my wording wisely. Jade won't abandon the stasis pods, so I need her to know that if we left, it would be temporary only. I know how much it means to her to do the right thing, and we will...but I'm not going to risk her life for it. "I'll keep you safe. And I'll get you back to your friends."

She considers my response for a moment and then nods. "Your turn," she says with a shaky laugh. "Ask me something completely appalling."

"Would you like my tongue on your clit right now?"

Jade sucks in a breath. "No."

I grin widely. "Now I know that was a lie. Time for you to lose a layer."

Knowing Jade, I expect her to protest and chide me about how I'm trying to push her into stripping her clothing off. To my surprise, though, she just gives her head a little shake and tosses the blanket aside.

And kef me, need roars through my system. I bite back a groan, and gripping the chair tight is the only thing keeping me from stroking my cock right here and right now. Seems like our game just got even more interesting. "Your question," I say, voice hoarse. "Ask away."

She nibbles on her lip, thinking, and I want to grab her and drag her back onto the bed and kiss that full mouth of hers. I want to graze my teeth against her soft neck and feel her shudder underneath me. I'm done with this game. I just want to get back to touching her. Finally, she speaks. "Have you ever regretted being a pirate?"

That's the lame-ass question she's going to ask? When I'm aching for her? When I want her to ask me what her skin tastes like or how long I can hold my breath or anything along those lines...she's going to ask me about piracy? Heaving a sigh, I decide to take matters into my own hands. I get to my feet, kick the chair aside, and start to unbuckle my pants.

"You're not going to answer?" Her voice takes on a surprised note. "Really?"

"I don't believe in second-guessing myself," I tell her, and kick off my boots. In the next moment, I undo the fastener on the trou of my jumpsuit, and the fabric parts at the waist, then slithers down my legs.

Jade squeals, her gaze moving to my underclothes. "What are you doing? I thought it was one piece of clothing?"

"You didn't say which one, so I figured I'd pick these, since they're cutting off my circulation." I tug the low-banded under-clothes down my bare legs and then kick them to the side. As I do, I let out a sigh, giving my now-freed cock a quick rub. It feels so much better this way. Still hard and aching, but at least my blood flow doesn't feel as if it's been cut off.

I give my cock another absent rub and notice that Jade's staring at it. The look on her face makes me groan, even as a fresh bead of pre-cum slides down the crown. Her lips are parted, the look on her face slightly stunned. Unable to stop myself, I drag my hand slowly over my shaft, watching her expression as I do so.

"Do you like what you see?" I ask, voice husky.

She bites back a little moan, collecting herself and looking back up at me. "You...was it your question or mine?"

"Does it matter?" I know I'm pressing my luck, but kef it. I'm an idiot that likes to take chances. I take a step forward, my hand still on my shaft. "You keep looking at my cock, Jade. You just want to look the whole time, or do you want to touch?"

It's so quiet in the room I can hear her breath catch. She looks up at me, amber eyes full of heat, and then she gets to her feet. Disappointment crashes through me, because I'm positive this is where it ends. She doesn't want to touch me. She just wants to leave things as they are. I'm moving too fast for her and she's letting me know her boundaries.

Instead, Jade takes the hem of her dress and pulls it over her head, baring her body. "I...guess I lose," she breathes, looking up at me with those hot eyes. "I'm out of clothing. Game over."

Brave, gorgeous female. "One last question," I tell her, and reach out to run my knuckles along the line of her jaw. "Can I touch you?"

"Please," she whispers.

47

JADE

*W*hen Adiron took his pants off, I expected his dick to be magnificent in size.

I didn't expect it to be pierced. That's...new.

I had to blink twice to make sure I wasn't imagining the twin silver studs crowning the head of his cock, right next to each other. They're positioned in just a way that I can imagine what it rubs against inside me, and everything in my body tightens in anticipation. That, combined with the ridges running along his shaft and whatever the hell that finger-like protrusion above his cock is, and I suspect he's been designed to be a party in bed.

Perhaps this is the universe's way of apologizing to me for all the bad shit that's happened. I imagine some celestial deity pushing Adiron my way. *Here*, it says. *Have this. It'll make you happy.*

I look up at him, at his intense eyes as he watches me. He

moves forward, cupping my face and skimming his fingers over my cheeks. "Am I pushing you too hard?" he asks, a rueful little smile on his face.

I shake my head. "I think I like being pushed. It doesn't give me time to overthink things."

"Then it's a good thing you're with me. I won't give you a chance to think through anything." Adiron grins, and before I can reply, he scoops me up into his arms and carries me the short distance back onto the bed. I make a small noise of protest, but it's a very small one. His body is warm despite the fact that he's still wearing his long-sleeved, high-collared shirt. I'm completely naked, my tits mashed against his chest. His cock brushes against my backside, leaving a wet trail as he sets me back down on the bed.

He grins down at me, then rips his shirt off over his head. Good god, but he's beautiful. His shoulders are so broad they do that inverted triangle thing, tapering down to his lean waist, and his pectorals look as if they could crack a nut between them. He's gorgeous, right down to those slim hips and thick thighs.

And thick cock, too. It's larger than I expected—much larger—but somehow that just fills me with an excited heat instead of dread. This is Adiron. He's going to make sure I'm good and slippery before he tries to push that monster inside me, and when he does, it's going to feel so damned good, I just know it.

The big alien thumps down on the other side of the bed and immediately pulls me into his arms, drawing me down against him. He lays on his back, snuggling me against his side, and pulls me in for a kiss. It starts out soft and sweet, a gentle exploration of mouths, but quickly turns fierce. I can't get enough of him, of his tongue, teasing against mine. I can't get enough of the way he holds me, as if he never wants to let me go. Hot arousal floods through me, and by the time we pull apart, gasping for breath between each kiss, I'm rubbing up against him, needing more.

"Jade," he groans. "Beautiful, sweet Jade. You're going to let me touch you all over, aren't you?"

Am I ever. I let out a little moan and nod.

His arm goes around my waist, tugging me against him, and his other hand moves to my breast. It's full and heavy, the nipple dark and tight and aching to be touched. "You said you wanted me to play with these, didn't you?" he whispers, his voice hot and delicious in my ear. His thumb brushes over the tip, and it feels like lightning crashing through my body. "You're so soft here. Almost as soft as that tasty cunt of yours."

I love that he palms my breast, his hand moving over it as he watches my reaction. I love that he hasn't pointed out that my breasts overflow even his big hands, or that they're not perky. Gravity isn't kind to big boobs, but Adiron doesn't care. He's fascinated with them—and me—regardless, and I feel sexy when I look at his awed expression.

He teases my nipple, rubbing his thumb in circles over it until I'm rocking against him, making soft little noises of need. "What would you do if I took one of these little nipples and put it in my mouth?" he asks, watching my face with hooded, sexy eyes. "Nipped and licked at it like I did your clit?"

I rock my hips against his side, even as I brush my fingers over his face. Breathless, I tell him, "I'd say...it's about time."

He laughs. I love that even in this moment, Adiron is full of sunshine and joy. The big alien grins up at me and then rolls forward. His arms are around my waist and he tips me onto my back, changing our positions. Then, he studies my body, his expression utterly fascinated. He captures one of my breasts again, squeezing it with his fingers and then feeding the tip into his mouth.

It's the most erotic thing I've ever seen.

The breath hisses from my throat and I whimper as he nuzzles at the tip, his teeth scraping over sensitive skin. He licks and teases my nipple, and every time he moves his head, I swear, his big, curling horns threaten to get in my face. I don't care, though. I don't want him to stop, ever. It feels far too good.

"You're such a keffing mouthful, Jade. Look at this bounty." He looms over me, entranced, gripping my other breast even as he teases the first with his mouth. "I could feast for days here," he murmurs between teasing little nips. "Soft and pretty and so full. I love watching these jiggle when you walk. It makes me want to bury my face between them."

And then he does just that, licking the deep valley between my breasts.

He groans as if he's in heaven, and I squeeze my arm to my side, trying to subtly prop up the girls and make them seem perkier. I've never been a fan of my overly abundant cleavage until now. It's just been a body part that's a little too "much" in a world full of slim and elegant. A little too jiggly, as he likes to say. But Adiron loves my jiggles. His every action and word convinces me that he adores my curves. "You're a goddess," he murmurs. "My goddess."

I sigh, gazing up at him with wonder. If anyone's perfect, it's him. There's never been a man—alien or otherwise—so very fine to look at.

"My goddess," Adiron tells me again, and kisses his way down my rounded belly. "Now let me worship at your altar again."

And he goes between my thighs once more.

I make a little sound of protest, because he was between my thighs just a short time ago. "Again? Are you...sure?"

He grins up at me, all wickedness. "I'm going to make you fall in love with me."

That's exactly what I'm afraid of...that I'm going to lose my heart to Adiron and his cheerful, blustery nature. That I'm going to fall hard and there will be no one there to catch me.

I don't stop him, though. Because if a big, gorgeous alien wants to go down on me repeatedly, who am I to complain?

48

ADIRON

*K*ef me, I love licking Jade's cunt.

I'm there for what feels like hours, and I love every moment of it. My new favorite flavor is Jade. My new favorite dessert? Jade. I would happily feast between her legs for three meals a day, tasting her sweetness and letting her coat my tongue. With every flick of my tongue, she writhes and makes little noises of pleasure that make my balls tighten. Her plump thighs threaten to trap my head between them every time her body clenches, and there's no better feeling.

She could squeeze me in a headlock for hours with those legs and I'd be giddy.

I drag my tongue over her clit, teasing the little bud even as her thighs squeeze my face again. Jade's close to her release. I can feel it in the quivering of her body. Her hands are frantic as she tugs on my hair, and she works her cunt against my face, trying desperately to increase friction. I'd love nothing more than to sink into her and kef the daylights out of her small, curvy body, but I also know I move fast. I need to know what she wants...because that's what I want, too. If she wants to wait, I'll happily wait.

I give her cunt one last slow taste and then lift my head. "Jade, love—"

She whimpers and tries to drag me back down, panting. "Please, Adiron. I'm so close. So close."

"I know." I press a kiss to the top of her mound, right on the little tuft of hair she's got there. It's so cute, just like the rest of her. "Tell me how you want this to go, love. Do you want me to use my fingers and make you come right now? Or do you want everything? Because I could push inside you and fill you up so good, Jade. So good." I kiss her cunt again. "But if that's too fast for you, I can wait—"

Jade grabs my horns, forcing me to look up at her. Her eyes are wild, her pupils dilated with pleasure. "You're asking right NOW if we're going too fast? Are you serious?"

"Well, yeah, I don't want to rush you—"

She makes a sound of pure frustration and wriggles out from under me. "Your...timing..." she pants, even as she pushes on my shoulder and nudges me onto my back. "Is...fucking...awful..."

The moment I'm on my back, she swings her leg over my hips and then grinds her cunt down against my cock.

All the breath steals out of my body. I wasn't entirely sure what she planned on doing, but now I can see. I'm taking too long for Jade, so she's going to mount me and ride me, and kef me if that isn't the sexiest damn thing I've ever seen. Her hair is wild around her face, her tits bouncing magnificently as she works her slick cunt up and down my shaft, rubbing against the underside of my cock.

I growl with hunger as she moves, grabbing her hips and dragging her even slower up and down my length. "If you're going to torture me, we're both going to suffer."

Jade groans, planting her hands on my chest. She rocks against my length, her hips frantic as she tries to push me to move faster instead of the leisurely pace I'm forcing on her.

"Do you want my cock, Jade? Do you want me to push into that sweet little cunt of yours and fill you so full that you can't breathe? That you have to spread those hips wide to take all of me inside you?" I pin her hips, holding her still as she tries to move.

Her lips part, her eyes closed, and then she squirms, circling her hips instead of rocking them. "I want you," she pants. "But we...have to establish...a few things first."

I reach between us, parting the lips of her cunt so she sandwiches my cock with her folds, and rub against her again. She makes a wild sound, her nails digging into my chest, her hips frantically trying to work. "Ask away, love. I'm all yours." I manage to sound far more casual and in control than I feel. I'm dying at the sight of her atop me, her glorious breasts bouncing as she tries to rub herself on my cock. A male could die happy with this as the last sight he sees. She's so keffing beautiful I can't stand it. Slowly, I drag her up and down my cock again, her slick honey coating my length. I'm on the verge myself, but I can wait.

I need her to come first.

"Need...to know..." she whispers. "Can you make me...pregnant?" Each pause is punctuated with a little whimper as she rocks against me.

"No. No diseases, either. Don't need plas-film unless you want it." I lift a hand and push the head of my cock against her folds, and when she moves, I'm pretty sure it rubs against her clit. Her entire body shudders, and pre-cum drips down my length. Kef, she's gorgeous. I drink in the sight of her like this, because it's not going to last. The moment she gives me the go-ahead, she's going to be under me, and I'll be so damn deep inside her that we're both going to come fast.

But what a way to go.

"No...tentacles?" she asks, panting.

That makes me pause. "What?"

She pauses, too, looking down at me, all breathless. "You're not going to grow any tentacles or anything weird when we fuck, are you? No goofy alien shit?"

I give her an odd look. "Do humans really think we grow tentacles out of our cocks?"

"I'm just making sure. What's that finger thing?" She reaches down to my spur and runs her fingers over it. "Is it...does it do anything? Do I need to be worried?"

"It doesn't do anything, I promise. What you're riding now is exactly what you'll get if you let me kef you," I tell her. "Just my big, thick cock pushing into that tight, hot cunt of yours and filling you up. Or do you need more than that?"

"No," she breathes. "That's perfect. Let's do it."

That's all I need to plow ahead. With a growl, I haul her forward, pushing her against my chest, and then roll over. When she's under me, I spread her thighs wide and guide my cock to the entrance of her core. She's hot and wet here, slippery and inviting, and I tease the head against her entrance even as I glance up at her. "Say that you want me, Jade."

"Want...you..." Jade reaches for me, her fingers skimming along my jaw. "Want all of you."

She's going to get it then. I can deny this female nothing. I push into her wet channel, feeding my cock little by little. She feels incredibly tight, so I pull back and thrust lightly several times, until she's whimpering for more. Kef me, but she's amazing. Her snug cunt is paradise, even as I drive my way into her, and she just takes me, body warm and welcoming and giving.

Jade cries out, wriggling, when I finally seat myself deep inside her. Her hand slides between us, brushing over my spur. "Oh my god," she moans. "This...this...you said it didn't do anything!"

"It doesn't," I promise her through gritted teeth. She feels so good that I can't stop myself from driving into her again, surging deep. As I do, I glance down at our joined bodies. My spur glides through her slick folds and I watch as it rubs right next to the little bud of her clit, teasing the side of it. She moans again, and her cunt tightens around me, drawing me deeper.

Oh kef me, she likes that. "That feel good?" I whisper, fascinated. I put my thumb on the other side of her clit, propping myself up over her with one hand, and thrust into her again. Her entire body clenches, squeezing my cock. Kef yeah, that's good. "Look at that. My spur rubs right against that clit of yours. I bet you like that, huh? Does it feel like my tongue did when I licked you there?"

Slowly, I pull almost all the way out of her body and then rock back into her. Sure enough, my spur rubs the other side once more, and I'm fascinated at the sight of it. It's like I'm taking her in more ways than one. That my spur's claiming her clit and giving her pleasure even as I bury my cock in her warmth.

Jade just whimpers. Her eyes are closed, her head thrown back, but her hands are on my sides and she's digging in with those little nails as hard as she can. I drive into her once more, loving the feel of her channel clasping around me so tightly, and I begin a rhythm. Instead of deep, spearing thrusts, I move faster, pumping into her with speed, determined to make her come and come hard.

"Adiron," she pants. She arches her back as I pound into her, breasts bouncing in the most glorious fashion as I take her with ruthless determination.

I want to kiss her beautiful face as I claim her, but she's smaller than I am, and that would mean stopping and re-aligning our bodies. I don't think I could pause even if I wanted to. She feels too good and I'm far, far too close. "Come for me," I demand. "I want to feel this pretty little cunt tighten around me.

I want to know that I made you feel so keffing good, Jade. That every time you quake, it's because no one's ever made you feel like this. That I'm claiming all of you. That you're mine in every way possible. Tell me that," I growl. "Say it."

Jade's utterly lost to the pleasure, though. I feel her channel ripple around my cock, tightening as she arches her back. Her face contorts, and her legs jerk even as I pound into her. "Ad," she moans between thrusts. "Ad, Ad, Ad—"

"Close enough," I mutter, and run my finger on the opposite side of her clit again. "My Jade. My gorgeous female. You've got the juiciest keffing cunt I've ever sank into. Wanna push my whole face into it and just let you grind down on my mouth—"

She cries out. I don't know if it's my words, or that I'm taking her relentlessly, the entire bed bouncing with the force of my thrusts, but she comes. I can feel Jade's release as her body tightens under me, her cunt gripping me like a tight fist, and I lose my words. I can't think of a single thing to say, just that I need to claim this clenching, perfect body and fill it with my seed. I grip her thigh, press forward, and pound into her, growling as I do. I'm lost to everything but the sheer pleasure of being so deep inside this female.

My female.

When I come, stars spark at the edges of my vision, and it feels as if my entire body is releasing into her. I've never come so hard in my life, and still I keep driving into her, loving the sensation of her cunt dripping with my seed, our bodies sticky together. When I can't move any longer, I hunch over her, cradling her under me, and try to catch my breath. Her fluffy, frizzy nimbus of hair tickles my face and I feel Jade press kisses onto my chest, making my cock twitch.

Mine. Mine forever.

49

JADE

*A*diron is an absolute bed hog.

This comes as no surprise to me. If I've ever met someone who takes full advantage of the space given them, it's Adiron. He unapologetically hogs the covers, sprawls his limbs over every inch of surface, and basically takes all the room. I'm left scrunched up against the wall, no blankets, and I wake up early because my ass is cold and my neck aches from my contorted sleeping position. Next to me, Adiron snores. His head is tilted back, which doesn't look all that comfortable given his horns, but he's happily sleeping.

I don't know if I'm amused or irritated, and then I decide I can be both. I watch him sleep for a while, and then when the need to pee gets too urgent, I begin the process of slowly creeping out of bed while somehow not waking him up.

Doesn't work, of course. Adiron smacks his lips, turns on his side, and tucks me against his chest. "You can't sneak away," he mumbles into my hair as he presses my naked body to him. "S'not allowed."

"I have to go to the lavatory."

"Also not allowed," he murmurs, eyes closed. He gets quiet and I'm pretty sure he's drifting back off to sleep.

So I pinch his belly. Or try to. There's nothing there but muscle, so I move to his hip, and then his ass. It's all rock hard. "Well, this is unfair," I mutter, trying his belly again. Even around his navel, there's not enough to pinch. He's all washboard abs.

"Mmm, your hands are nice," he breathes into my hair. "Go lower."

"You want me to pinch your cock?"

"Is that what you're doing? I thought you were getting frisky." His hand strokes over the curve of my ass and tries to slide between my thighs. "I'll wake up for that."

Chuckling, I wiggle out of his grip and slide out of bed. He makes a disappointed sound, his tail clinging to me until I get too far away. It's silly, but I love that he's so grabby and affectionate. It proves that last night wasn't a bored fluke. That he likes me in daylight as much as he likes me late at night. That I'm not just a deep-space booty call if he wants seconds.

I take a quick shower while I'm in the bathroom, freshening up. Muscles that I didn't know I had are sore this morning, which leaves me blushing. Between the piercing on his cock that rubbed me inside in just the right spot and the spur that rubbed me on the outside in just the right spot? I've never come so hard. It makes me want to crawl back into bed with him and fool around all day long.

After all, I'm being responsible by being here with the sleepers, right? No one says I have to be a total martyr. I can have some fun.

I step out of the shower, intent on having that fun, but to my disappointment, the bed is empty. Across the hall, I can hear

Adiron's personal shower going. Just as well. He wouldn't have been able to squeeze into mine with me. I'm a little sad he wasn't waiting in bed, but I suppose it's for the best.

I dress and go out to make breakfast. I prepare an extra-big batch of noodles, because I suspect Adiron is going to be hungry, and eat a few bites while I wait for him to turn up. When he doesn't, I put the food back in the warmer and go looking for him.

I find him down another one of the side halls, a large piece of the molded metal wall tossed onto the floor. He's on hands and knees, his front half hidden inside the wall itself. I watch as his tail flicks, and then he cusses. "Everything okay?" I ask, a little worried. He said last night we were fine, but what if he lied just to make me feel better?

Adiron emerges, his hair wet and messy between his horns. He grins up at me, all boyish enthusiasm. "I had an idea while I was in the shower."

"About what?"

"Well," he says, turning to sit on his ass. He puts aside the circuit board thing he's holding and indicates I should come closer. I do, and he immediately nuzzles between my thighs, big hands rubbing my ass. "First I thought about grabbing you and licking your cunt again."

I squeak, holding onto his horns for balance. "Adiron!"

"Right. I know what you're thinking, focus." He presses a kiss to the fabric over my pussy, gives a little sigh, and then turns back to the panel. "Then I was thinking, keeping this whole ship powered up and cycling all the air and water is a big drain on resources. What if we locked down most of it and kept just one hall—or even one or two rooms—with life support and full power? We could potentially keep this old girl running for months longer."

"Will that matter if we end up being sucked into the ice field?"

"One problem at a time," he says with a grin. "Maybe if we have enough time, we can overwrite some of the programs that keep us locked out and figure out how to turn on part of the engines."

I blink in surprise. "You're just full of ideas this morning, aren't you?"

"I slept great," he admits, hugging my hips and beaming up at me. "Do you know how long it's been since I slept? Really slept?"

I play with his damp hair, smoothing it back from his face. "Judging by your excitement, I'd say a while?"

"Years," he agrees. "But I figured out the cure for insomnia." He looks up at me and winks. "It's between your thighs."

I bite back a laugh. He did warn me that he had a bit of a one-track mind. "I made you breakfast. It's not between my thighs, but maybe you'll want to eat it anyhow."

"You made food for me?" Adiron looks absurdly pleased. He lets go of me and jumps to his feet.

"Well, sure. You take care of me, I'll take care of you. It's not that hard."

Adiron pulls himself up to his full height and immediately crushes me against him, my face pressed to his pectorals. His tail tickles at my backside. "And did I take care of you? Last night?"

"Are you fishing for compliments?"

"Absolutely."

I arch an eyebrow at him. "I think you know the answer to that, considering I was crying out your name."

"You were, weren't you?" He gets a dreamy look on his face. "Good times. Good times."

I snort and pry my way out of his grip. I take his tail in hand and tug on it. "Come on. Let's go eat so you can get back to whatever mad science you're doing here."

He makes a short, coughing sound and covers my hand.

"You, uh, don't want to pull on my tail like that unless you want to head back to bed."

I drop the thing as if it's on fire and then burst into giggles at the odd look on Adiron's face. "Noted."

Instead of hurrying to the mess hall, though, he takes my hand in his and rubs his thumb across the back of it, his expression changing to something more thoughtful. "I should have asked you, maybe, before I got started with all this stuff. Are you okay with re-wiring a few things on this ship to make sure we stay powered up? I don't want a repeat of last night."

"I don't either," I tell him softly. It's sweet that he's so determined to make everything work just right for me. Well, not JUST for me. I'm sure he likes to breathe, too. Except I know that if it was up to him, he would have left this ship behind already. He'd have climbed into an escape pod and followed his brothers out into space. It's because I won't leave that he's here with me. "And you're welcome to do whatever you like to the ship as long as it doesn't endanger anyone on board."

"What about the ship's passenger?" he asks in a playful voice. "Can I do whatever I like to her, too?"

I eye him as he lifts a finger to the fastener of my ill-fitting jumpsuit. "Is all you think about sex?"

"It's absolutely on the top five list."

"And let me guess, you just won't say where on the list?" I tease back.

Adiron laughs.

50

ADIRON

The power fizzles again a short time after we eat. It comes on again in a heartbeat, with a low, ominous pop.

Jade blinks up at the ceiling. "Well, that's not good."

"It's fine," I lie. "I'll take a look at things after this." I point at her bowl. "You going to eat all that?"

She clutches her bowl and holds it against her chest, which is the cutest thing ever. It puts me in a good mood, even when we head out together to the maintenance rooms, where the computer's hardware is located. I get to work...and try not to show my concerns.

The more I dig into the ship's hardware, the more I'm shocked the damn thing's still running at all.

This is not good. Not good at all.

The ship we had before the *Little Sister* was an older model. We used to joke that the *Vanora* was held together by spit, crusted-on axel grease, and determination. She also died while in the middle of a very tricky piracy run and nearly cost Kaspar his head. We ended up letting the *Vanora* rot at a station impound and traded away our savings for the *Little Sister,* instead.

Looking at the controls for the *Buoyant Star,* I see things that remind me of those days, of tapping panels in the hopes that it would turn on a broken component, of constantly switching out chips to see if this one would cause the system to magically light up. Of midnight surges in power only for it to fail when most needed. We laughed about those days, but when push came to shove, the *Vanora* was a disaster and we dumped her.

We don't have that choice with the *Buoyant Star.* Jade won't leave the sleepers behind and I absolutely won't leave her. So I need to make this hunk of junk work.

I whistle cheerfully as I pry a wire out of a gunk-covered socket and glance over at Jade. I have her cleaning filters with a damp towel, removing loose particles and judging the state of them. Even from here, I can tell they've more than reached the end of their life. They smell moldy and the white filters are a stark gray, but they're what we've got. Luckily Jade hasn't noticed my apprehension. I keep whistling, and all the while, I'm trying to think of answers.

I lied to her when I said the ship was fine. The more I try to do routine maintenance, the more I'm convinced that this old gal is only still operating out of sheer luck. Luck can sometimes work in your favor—the *Star* might drift on as she is for another year or two, or she might shit the bed tomorrow. There's no way of knowing, but I don't like those odds.

So I made up some bullshit lie about how we're going to shut it all down except for a room or two. That we're saving power. Truth is, I'm going to salvage decent parts from what I can, and I doubt we have more than enough to keep only a room or two going. But what Jade doesn't know won't hurt her, so I keep on whistling a cheerful tune.

We can last a month, I tell myself. We'll pull a few wires from here and there, ensure that the life support systems are running in top shape for at least one part of the ship, and we wait out Kaspar and Mathiras's return. Heck, they might even be back sooner. Luckier things have happened.

We work on through the morning in companionable quiet. Jade occasionally asks me a question, but for the most part, I'm left alone with my own thoughts, which is always dangerous. I'm pretty sure she's thinking about last night—also known as the greatest night of my life—but I worry that she's quiet because she has regrets.

Then, the wire I'm working on pulling out snaps in half, and I have new regrets. "Uh oh."

Jade's immediately at my side. "What's uh oh? What's wrong?"

"It's nothing."

I put a few wires back into place, return the circuit board I'm working on, and get to my feet. The moment I do, Jade is right there, frowning up at me, the dusty rag in her hand. "Do not lie to me, mister. I can read you like a damn book and something's wrong."

"It's not EXTREMELY wrong," I hedge. "Just inconvenient. There was a wire I needed and it snapped." I don't point out that the wire is one that's pretty crucial for the temperature control of the ship. "But there's more of them to be found on the ship. No big deal." I pause, then wonder if there's any way to slide this in all casual like, then decide, kef it. "Quick question —which of the people in the pods do you like the least?"

She stares at me like I'm insane. "What do you mean, which people do I like the least?"

I hold up the broken wire. "There's bunches of these on the stasis pods. So if I cannibalize a few of them, we'll be good. Just point out which people look the least like they need to be saved, and I'll get to work."

"You are not doing that," she hisses at me.

"You're right. I can't get in that room." I hold the wire out to her. "Can you get them for me?"

"No, Adiron!" She smacks my chest, all indignant, and I have to admit, she looks sexy when she's angry. When she moves, her breasts jiggle, and I think about how they bounced last night when I was deep inside her...and now I want to have sex again. "We are not sabotaging other people's chances of survival to ensure our own."

"Sometimes you have to put yourself first." Jade's not going to last very long as a corsair if she doesn't.

"I thought you said this was an optional change? I don't want to do it."

"That's the thing...it might not be so optional. Some of these components are worse than I thought." I give her a bright smile to take the sting out of my words. "The good news is that if we get a few more of the conduction wires, we should have enough heat to power our quarters until the rescue arrives." I hold the wires up again. "We just have to get them."

She looks at me as if I've grown another head. "And you'd just steal them from helpless, sleeping people?"

"Well, no. I would look for helpless, sleeping criminals. Or Threshians. Those I wouldn't feel too bad stealing from. Were there any that weren't human?"

Jade crosses her arms under that magnificent chest of hers, a mutinous look on her face. "You mean like Helen?"

Mmm, good point. "Obviously I wouldn't take out a qura'aki. I'm not THAT dumb."

"First of all," Jade says in a tone that brooks no argument. "You are not dumb. And second of all, we are not slaughtering people just to suit our own needs." She lifts her chin, indicating the broken wiring in my hand. "That isn't available anywhere else?"

She's magnificent when she's angry, and I love the sight of it. I want to bask in her fury and worship at her feet—or between her thighs—but I can tell she doesn't want to hear that right now. So I do my best to answer. "Well, there are lots of these wires. It's just that most of them are broken or look like they're about to fry. This ship's on an older sort of engine, and it tends to require a lot of maintenance, which hasn't been done in years. I'm afraid that these power fluctuations are going to keep happening, and if they go down again, I'm concerned that they're going to take a critical system with them that we need. We're better off holing up in a room or two where we know everything's working efficiently versus running the entire ship half-ass and hoping for the best."

Jade considers this. She studies me. "Do you think it's serious enough that we need to take action like that?"

I sigh. "I was hoping that wasn't the case, but I've looked at twenty-one of these wires today." I hold the one in my hand up again. "Thirteen are only working because a component melted around them. Four are on the verge of breaking. We need a full seven to run the climate control panel."

Her jaw clenches. She looks up at me, and then back at the wire I'm holding. "Are you lying to me?"

"I really wanted to, but then I thought you'd never have sex with me again, and I'd really really like that to happen again." I give her my most charming smile.

Her mouth twitches and I know I'm winning her over. "We're not killing anyone," she says softly. "I'm not doing that. Can't we just cannibalize the pods we came in? Those of us that were woken up?"

I look at her in surprise. "They're still here on the ship?"

She nods.

"Yeah, we can do that." When a relieved smile crosses her

face, I press my luck. "And then we can have sex again? It's been hours since I licked that glorious cunt of yours and I'd sure like to refresh my memory."

"Is this what I have to look forward to for the next month?" she asks in an amused tone, even as her hand goes to my belt.

"Honestly? Yeah."

Jade just laughs, and I'm glad she doesn't hate me. Also glad because I'm pretty sure laughter means I will absolutely get to feast on that glorious cunt of hers after all.

51

JADE

*J*ust because I'm protecting the sleepers doesn't mean they don't creep me out.

Walking through the cargo bay reminds me of walking through a morgue. Not that I've done a lot of that, of course. It's just that if I had, this is what it'd feel like. Passing container after container of sleeping people with waxy-looking skin, chests unmoving, eyes closed. There's so damn many of them, too. It's just row after row of bodies. Of people, stolen from their homes and dragged out to god-knows-where for a horrible fate.

It's one reason we've been so reluctant to leave the *Buoyant Star* behind. We had a taste of that horrible fate. We know what it's like when you wake up.

Adiron is with me, though. I passed through the cargo bay door with no issues, and he accompanied me. Of course, he immediately pried open the door panel and started ripping out wires, and now the thing hangs open permanently. I tell myself that it's fine. That Adiron's destructiveness comes from a good place. The next time these sleepers wake up, I want them to be in a much better, safer place.

I wander through the rows, not peering at the faces that stare out from the windowed pods. I tried to look at most of them, once. The sight of all those human faces—young and female—was far too upsetting. There's a mixture, of course. There's the occasional male slave, and a few that are from other planets, but the overwhelming majority are human females. I have an idea of what they're going to be used for.

Adiron doesn't share my reluctance, though. He wanders through the hold, rubbing a bit of condensation off each window and peering inside. He stares at each one with a little "hmph" and then goes on to the next. He does this for a while, offering a little bit of commentary as he walks.

"Praxiian," he says about one. "Probably a gladiator."

"Brown skin," he says about another. "Like you. Pretty."

"Pregnant," he says about yet another pod. He pauses over another and then turns back to one he just passed. "I thought humans didn't do cloning?"

"We don't," I tell him, edging to his side. I automatically reach for his belt, as if holding onto him will somehow fix the sense of unease I feel when looking at the sleepers. He tucks me close against him, his tail looping around my waist in an alien semi-hug. "Why do you ask?"

He points to a pod. "This one has the same face as that one." He points at the one behind him. "Do you think they're cloning the humans they capture?"

His question sends terror rocketing through me. Is it possible? Could something like that have happened while I was asleep? Is there another Jade somewhere out there having a miserable time in space? It's a horrible concept, and one that's never occurred to me. I peer at the window of the pod Adiron points at and study the sleeping woman's face. She's got red hair and a light dusting of freckles, big eyebrows and a small nose. I go to look at the other one...and breathe a sigh of relief. While they look similar, this one's face is rounder, the eyebrows less pronounced, her freckles less abundant. "They're sisters, I think. This one's not as freckled as that one."

Adiron leans over, studying the girls, and then gives me a sheepish look. "This is the part where you chastise me for thinking all humans look alike, right?"

I shake my head. "I'm too relieved to even give you a hard time. And I'm sure I'd probably run into the same scenario with your people. Alien features can be tricky."

"Especially humans," he points out, and taps my nose. "You all have such small faces and big, sad eyes."

I bat his hand away. "Very funny. We do not."

"You do too."

Hands on hips, I give him an irritated look. "Is that why you fell in love with me at first sight, then? Because I looked like every other human you've seen?"

"No, because you're much fiercer and your eyes aren't sad, just full of smarts." Adiron puts his hands to his chest. "And you have great big—"

I smack him lightly.

He just laughs. When he notices I'm not laughing with him, he takes my hand and tugs me close, pulling me against his chest. His big hand cups my face. "What's wrong, love?"

I shrug, and then because I'm weak, slide my arms around his waist and press my cheek to his chest. Being held by Adiron makes everything just a little bit better. "I don't like being in here. It's creepy and it makes me wonder what they did to me when I was asleep."

The big alien strokes my jaw. "You're with me now. I won't let anything happen to you ever again. I promise."

It seems like an awfully big promise to make, but I'll take it. I snuggle against his chest, letting him pet me for a few moments. "Let's just hurry up and get what we need, all right? You can come stare at them another time."

"Of course." He bends down and presses a kiss atop my head, right into my springy hair. "Where are the empty pods at?"

I take his hand. "Come on. I'll show you."

I lead him through the maze of coffin-like pods. I can tell that Adiron really wants to peek at all of them, his natural curiosity getting the better of him. It's because of me that he doesn't wander, and I appreciate that. He stays close to my side, as if he thinks I'll need the moral support.

I gesture at the open coffins. They're at the far end of the bay, scattered into a heap. "Voilà."

"Perfect." He doesn't head right for them, though. Instead, he puts a hand on the back of my neck in an oddly possessive gesture and rubs it lightly. "If you want to go, you can. I know these bother you and it might take me a little time to get the components I need."

I love that he asks, almost as much as I love the heavy hand on my neck. It's like after last night, he's decided to claim ownership of me, and I am absolutely not upset about it in the slightest. In fact, I rather like it. The next month stretches out ahead of us with endless possibility. Him on top. Me on top. In the shower. Me on my knees. Me on the table. Me splayed out on the captain's station on the bridge again.

Endless. Possibilities.

So I reach to his side and give his tail a teasing little stroke, because I know it makes him all riled up. "I'll be all right," I promise him. "Just work as fast as you can, please."

"After that tail pull? You bet I will." He growls low in his throat, picks me up, plants a hot, fervent kiss on my lips, and then sets me atop the nearest stasis pod. "You sit here. I'll handle things."

"Right on someone's face?" I joke, wriggling a little. It's

disturbing to me that I'm sitting atop a coffin that someone's asleep in. I know it's not really a coffin. I know they're not really asleep...but I can't shake the feeling that whoever's in there is going to be highly aware of my ass on their property and not approve.

Adiron just grins at me, all boyish charm. "I'm sure she won't mind."

As he walks away, I peer at the window between my thighs and shudder. "I think it's a he. A really ugly he, too."

That gets Adiron's attention. He immediately changes course, heading back to me, and leans over to peer at the window. I obligingly spread my thighs as widely as possible so he can see what's underneath, and it occurs to me that there's a sexy pun or two to be had here. I look up at him, ready to crack a joke, and the look on his face makes me pause. "What's wrong?" I ask.

He draws up a little, giving me an odd glance. "You've... never felt the need to open these, right?"

"No, never. I thought it was kinder to let them sleep. Why?"

He taps on the stasis pod I'm perched on. "Because this one? This one is a problem. A big, keffing problem."

52

ADIRON

E very time I turn around, this keffing ship is giving us a new, unpleasant surprise.

Jade looks up at me with those wide, gorgeous eyes, no idea that she's seated atop the nastiest, most brutal killer I've ever seen.

Here I've been joking about opening the pods or killing the inhabitants to ensure our survival, but I wasn't truly serious. Now, though, after seeing Crulden the Ruiner, I want to space every keffing pod in this hold and forget we ever stepped foot in here.

I pull my mate off the pod and tuck her behind me. "Don't sit on that one."

"What is it?" She asks. "What's the problem?"

I point at the pod. "Under no circumstances are you to ever, ever EVER open that one, all right? I don't care if you open all the other ones in this hold..." I pause. "Well no, actually, I do care. If there's one gladiator in this mix, there's bound to be others. In fact, we're not opening any of these. Ever again. We'd be doing the universe a favor if we just spaced every single non-human here—"

Jade grabs my hand and strokes it. "Slow down. We're not spacing anyone. Why are you panicking? Breathe, all right? Just breathe." Her fingers brush over my skin in a calming motion. "I'm right here. Let's go sit down AWAY from the pods and talk."

I let her lead me to the far side of the cargo bay, and when she indicates I should sit on an empty crate, I do, and immediately tug her into my lap. She doesn't protest, just looks up at me with that concerned expression. Jade reaches up and brushes my hair off my forehead, watching me and waiting for an explanation.

"That alien in that pod is bad news. Very bad news." I hold her close, latching my tail around her just in case she tries to slip out of my grasp. "I know you think everyone deserves a chance, but Crulden the Ruiner absolutely does not. If we want to do the galaxy a favor, we'll shove that pod out the cargo bay doors and forget it was ever here."

Her small dark brows furrow together. "Is he like...Hitler? What alien race is he?"

"I don't know who Hitler is, but that male in that pod is a splice. He's not any specific race but a creature born in a lab, made from all the worst bits of a bunch of races so they could make a killing machine. He's a gladiator. Kind of. He got banned for being too brutal for the vid audiences...and that should tell you everything you need to know about him." I don't want to tell her that I've seen a few vids and had to turn them off myself. Of Crulden eviscerating his opponents and feasting on the pieces. Of him breaking through to the next match and killing those gladiators and their handlers, too, before his team could get him under control. Of him doing terrible, terrible things to his "prizes" that he won, and that those prizes were usually small, fragile females.

Kind of like the one in my lap right now.

I remember hearing the news that Crulden the Ruiner had been banned from even the most uncouth of gladiator arenas. He was impossible to control, and so destructive that other slave owners complained he was destroying their stock. He disappeared off the circuit five years ago or so, and I thought he'd been quietly put down by his owner.

Turns out he was sold and tossed into stasis.

I will die before I let her open up that particular stasis pod.

"Never go near it again," I tell Jade urgently. "Do you hear me? I don't care how safe you feel with me. That safety is a lie. The moment someone touches that pod, you get out of the room. You get off the keffing station and you head to the farthest galaxy you can find, all right? You do not want to be anywhere near that thing when it awakens." I cup her face. "And if you're wise, you'll let me space it right now." I think of her and the humans, sitting innocently on this ship for three long years with this monster in the hold. She's keffing lucky no one got curious and decided to wake it up.

The fact that the other pirates took other slaves and not this one speaks volumes. Crulden would be worth a fortune in the right hands, but he'd need a lot of handlers. A LOT of them, and expendable ones to boot.

It occurs to me that this ship might not have been abandoned for the wrong reasons...but for the right ones. Like say, trying to cover up the family's slave trade. And trying to dump slaves that will garner too much attention. Suddenly Straik's retreat looks less churlish and far more sinister.

Jade caresses my face, trying to ease some of the stress weighing me down. "Look, we won't go anywhere near it, all right?" Her voice is soft and soothing. "I have no desire to wake any of the sleepers up because we don't have the food to spare. We'll let him and all the others keep on sleeping, and when we get somewhere safe, we make sure he's handled appropriately. It's going to be fine."

"Right. Sure." I hold her closer. Maybe after she's asleep tonight, I'll sneak in here and—

"And you're not going to do anything to that stasis pod when I'm sleeping," Jade says calmly, stroking my hair off my brow. "You're going to leave it alone, because it's not our responsibility to determine who lives and who dies. Our responsibility is just to get these people to safety. It's not our place to determine their fates."

It's like she can read my mind. "I wouldn't do that," I lie.

She laughs, the sound light and sweet. "Oh yes you would. You're a terrible liar, Adiron. I can see it in your face. We need to focus on the ship, remember? Two rooms with climate control and no others? And then we'll have our cozy nest and we won't have to worry about this pod or any others." She runs her fingers over my face in a way that makes my cock twitch, and I love the soothing, gentle sounds of her reasonable words. "Even if he woke up somehow, there'd be no environment, right? So the best thing we can do to protect ourselves is to do what we originally planned and get those wires."

I lean in and kiss her brow. "You're so reasonable. Have I told you how sexy that is?"

"I'm almost positive you have, yes." She tilts her head up and smiles at me. "Now, let's get this done so we can go, all right?"

I nod, forming a plan in my mind. I get the wires needed. Check the other pods to ensure that no other monstrous splices or gut-churning criminals are hidden amongst the sleepers.

Then I barricade the door to the cargo bay. Just in case.

Then turn off the climate control to most of the ship except for the end of the hall. We can seal off a portion of the living area, the room closest to the kitchen quarters, and dwell there.

Then barricade the closed-off portions of the ship. Again, just in case.

Then...take my woman to bed and kef the daylights out of her. Because that's how every day needs to end from now on. A nice, solid afternoon of work, followed by sweaty, toe-curling matings that will make her forget everything but my name.

Gonna be a busy day, but I'm sure I can squeeze it all in. I kiss Jade again, then set her down and hop to my feet. Time to get to work.

53

JADE

I don't like how worried Adiron gets about the sleeper. He makes sure to check all the other pods, and when he doesn't find another that concerns him, I can see the relief move through his body. For happy, carefree Adiron to be so bothered, it must be bad.

I give him space to work through his mood. I remain close because he seems to relax more if I'm near, but I'm quiet so he can focus. Adiron works tirelessly, extricating tiny wires from complex-looking systems, and when two of them break, he swears a blue streak. After hours pass, though, he has enough to satisfy him, and we head back to the main living area of the ship.

I say nothing as he barricades the cargo bay. He forces the doors shut again, then drags a metal panel off of the wall and hammers it into the doorway, forcing it into the space even as the metal creaks and groans in protest. He picks up another tool, and when it lights up with fire, I realize it's a blowtorch.

Adiron solders the door, a look of grim determination on his face. I've never seen him like this. Now I'm the one that's worried.

We close down area after area in the ship and I watch as Ruth's quarters are closed up, then my own. I've taken everything personal out of them, stacking them neatly in Alice and Helen's shared room, which has been elected to be our new sleeping quarters. It's the largest room, with two beds because Helen doesn't like to be by herself. It's also got the largest connected lavatory, and is only a short jaunt to the mess hall. I tidy things up in the room as Adiron replaces wires out in the hallway and then solders more of the doors shut. I get that we're making ourselves a small, protected bubble, but I can't help but worry that we're sealing ourselves in.

One problem at a time, just like Adiron always tells me. I need to stop borrowing trouble.

So I keep a bright smile on my face and maneuver the two single beds together into one large one, and spread the blankets over it. There's no sense in playing coy or pretending like we're not going to fuck like bunnies every single night that we're together. Why deprive myself? We might never leave this ship, so why not spend every minute I can in sheer bliss with a big, handsome man who loves to go down on me?

I wonder if anyone's ever returned the favor and gone down on him?

The moment the idea hits me, I'm in love with it. Adiron's certainly been a giving lover so far, and I like the thought of going down on him and easing some of that tension that's just rippling through him today. He needs a distraction. I need a distraction.

Sounds perfect to me.

So I think about how I can set the scene as he works in the hallway. More noodles, of course. He's going to be hungry after all that work. Then I can persuade him to take a nice, hot shower. Then I can innocently suggest that I dry him off, and then start the seducing. I dig through the small amount of clothing I have to call my own and pull out my ridiculous-looking dress again. He liked this, because he liked my cleavage. Once the bedroom is all set, I head into the lavatory and primp a little, because I want to look nice for him. I fluff and tease my natural hair until it puffs prettily around my face and frames it. I lick my finger and shape my eyebrows as best I can, and bite my lips so they flush and plump up. I look sexy, I decide. Sexy and womanly and ready for a fucking.

Or a dick-sucking. Knowing Adiron, one will probably follow the other, and I'm totally good with that.

I study myself in the mirror, trying to decide if there's more I can do to sex up my appearance. It's been a long time since I had a boyfriend. I was going through a dry spell back on Earth long before I got snatched up by aliens, and I feel rusty and out of practice on getting ready for a date...even if it's just a blowjob date.

An idea hits me.

I lift my skirt and study my bush. I keep things neatly trimmed, but I've never given it much thought. Adiron is completely bare, though, and I wonder if he'd like it more if I was bare, too? It might be a nice surprise for him, something to make him suck in a breath and get all distracted. Something that makes him lose his control.

The more I think about it, the more I like it. I fidget through the grooming tools in neat little slots next to the mirror, find one that will do the trick, and get to work.

IT'S BEEN a long time since I went completely bare, and I forgot how it feels.

Everything feels sensitive. When I sit down, I can feel my

folds brushing against each other and it turns me on. I cross my legs, squirming a little, as I wait for Adiron to join me for dinner. It's more noodles, but food isn't my primary focus right now. Instead, I'm impatient as I wait for Adiron to return. He's taking his sweet time working on the control system in the hall. I've checked on him a half-dozen times in the last hour only to find him on his back, chest deep into a panel full of wires and hard at work.

"Done?" I ask lightly, feeling awfully bare and incredibly frisky. Other than my dress, I'm not wearing a stitch, and it feels twice as exposed as it ever did.

"Just cleaning up a few things." He picks up a few bits of shredded wire, taps a button on the wall, and the panel pings open for trash disposal. He dumps the discards there and I notice his hands are covered in smears of grease and there's a swipe on his cheek, too. "We should be good to go, now," Adiron says. "We're sealed in here, the climate controls are purring, and the air filters won't have to work as hard since we're just focusing in on this small area."

"That's great," I say brightly, even though I'm a little disturbed by the whole "sealed in" comment. "So we just need to hang tight until your brothers return, right?"

He nods and then sniffs the air. "That dinner?"

"I made noodles. Hungry?"

"Famished." Adiron moves to my side instead of heading into the mess hall. He leans down, careful not to touch me with his dirty hands, and offers his face for a kiss. I lean in and peck him on the mouth, and his expression brightens a little. "Sorry if I've been a little mentally absent today. I'm not trying to neglect you."

"Don't apologize," I tell him. "I know you're not." I cup his face in my hands and press another kiss to his mouth, my lips lingering on his. "You're trying to keep us safe. I'm not going to complain."

"The good news is that it's all done, and we can spend the next month in bed." He gives me a teasing look. "Unless you want to kef up against a wall or something."

I roll my eyes and tap his cheek with my hand, pretending to be annoyed. "You always think about sex, don't you? Go and shower. I'll keep dinner warm for you."

Dinner...and I plan on having him for dessert.

54

ADIRON

I can't help but notice how keffing sexy Jade looks as we eat our noodles. She eats hers delicately, her full lips giving me all kinds of ideas. Her glorious cleavage practically spills out of her dress, taunting me. She's stunning...and all I can think about is that keffing gladiator in a pod far too close to here.

I can't stop thinking about how casually they talked about opening the pods and freeing others. How they might have innocently freed him, thinking they were doing the right thing. How when we boarded this ship, we might have found Crulden the Ruiner standing over the broken, destroyed bodies of the human females—

I squeeze my eyes shut and take a big mouthful of food, determined to get that image out of my head. Happy thoughts, I tell myself, and think about Jade's nipples instead. How they're this lovely, warm dark brown that just invites touching, and how they tighten into these tight little puckers with prominent tips the moment I brush her skin. I wonder if she's ever fallen out of that low-necked top of hers. If her nipples ever just "oops" busted out while she was eating.

Kinda wish that'd happen right now.

"Are you okay?" Jade asks, giving me a curious glance.

"Yeah. Why?" She doesn't need to know that I'm that worried about Crulden...or whatever else could be in the hold. For all I know, those pregnant females are pregnant with splices themselves, and then we're going to have a whole mess of them to deal with. For all I know, there's a hidden compartment somewhere on this ship with a few more splices tucked away...

Kef me. I didn't even look for hidden compartments.

Jade pokes me with her eating sticks. "Your expression keeps changing while you eat. I can't decide if you're upset about something or turned on. What's the deal?"

"Just, uh, thinking."

"About?"

"...stuff?"

She gives me an exasperated look, pushing her bowl aside. Jade leans forward on the table, her arms resting on the surface, and it plumps her gorgeous tits nicely, distracting me all over again. "Adiron, we've talked about what a terrible liar you are. I know you're lying. You're upset about that darn gladiator, aren't you?"

"I'm getting less upset with you sitting like that," I admit. "I do like looking at those tits of yours."

I expect her to get all shy—or to hit me with those eating sticks—but she just straightens a bit more, smiles, and her breasts give the most enticing little quiver. It's like they know it's about to be their turn. As soon as I'm done eating, I'm going to lay Jade on this table and feast on her. My sac tightens and I lift my bowl to my face, eating as fast as I can.

She's what I need to distract myself from the situation, I decide. A month of me and Jade, learning each other. Maybe by the time I empty myself inside her inviting body a dozen (or three dozen) times, I'll forget all about what's in the hold.

It's not that I mind danger. It's never bothered me before. But Jade's safety has never been on the line in the past. I've got her to think about now, and I know that if that splice was freed, he'd just try to kill me. What worries me is that he wouldn't try to kill Jade. At least, not right away. And that just wrecks me.

Tonight, I think I'll sleep with my weapon within reach. And when my brothers send back a message, I have to figure out a way to let them know the problem we have on board. Part of me wants to catch up with Straik and dump Crulden the Ruiner onto his nice, pretty ship...but Dopekh and the other clones were good guys. They don't deserve that shit.

A small wooden stick taps on the back of my hand. Jade. "I've lost you again," she teases. "Come back, Adiron."

I swallow the last of my noodles and wipe my face on my sleeve. "Just thinking...and finishing dinner. You did a great job on the noodles."

She arches a brow at my compliment. "Which part did you like best?" she teases. "The part where I added water, or the part where I put them in the bowl?"

I laugh, because she's got a point. Noodles don't require much skill to prepare. "Just take the compliment, love."

Maybe it's because I'm leering at those fantastic breasts of hers that it takes me a moment to realize she's getting to her feet. Jade rises from the table, crosses the distance between us, and then turns my chair so I'm no longer facing the table, but her instead.

"Is it time for dessert?" I ask, making the most tired joke in the entire universe.

She moves onto my lap, lifting one leg and sliding it over my hip before her arms go around my neck and then she straddles me. "I have a better idea," Jade says in a light, soft voice.

"I don't know if 'better' is a thing. My idea was pretty keffing amazing."

Her smile is full of promise. "Oh, trust me. I think you'll like what I've got in mind."

"Does it involve your breasts?" I reach between us to touch her.

She flicks my hand away. "Maybe if you play your cards right. I thought it'd involve my mouth first, though."

Kissing, then? I'm down for kissing. And when she leans forward and lightly presses her mouth to mine, I know I've guessed correctly. Pleased with myself, I kiss her back, loving the warmth of her smaller body against mine, the taste of her on my lips. My beautiful, sexy mate. She nips on my lower lip and then sucks on it, and I groan, my hands sliding to squeeze that plump ass of hers.

"Mmm," Jade purrs. "Your lips taste good."

"All of me does," I joke automatically.

"Do you, now?" She lifts a hand and moves it to my collar. "I wouldn't mind finding out."

I blink, absorbing that. "Oh?"

She nods, a sultry little smile curving those gorgeous lips. "In fact, I thought I might taste all of you. Unless you feel that violates some hygiene law of yours."

Does she mean...my mouth goes dry when she rocks her hips against me, dragging her cunt against my cock, and her hands manually ease the auto-fastener down my chest. Yes, I realize. She absolutely means that.

"Violate away," I murmur. "I'm all yours."

55

ADIRON

*J*ade is all confidence as she leans in and kisses me again, deliberately brushing her breasts against my chest. She peels back the front of my uniform, then runs her hands up my bared skin. "See, I was thinking about you and me all day today," she whispers. "You were hard at work, and I was thinking dirty, dirty thoughts."

I groan. "I'd love to hear some of those thoughts. Or all of them. Actually, yeah, all of them sounds better. Hit me with it."

She smiles, the look full of promise. "Actually, I thought I might show you what I had in mind."

"I'm equally good with showing and telling." I run my knuckles lightly along the curve of her cheek. "If you want to dirty talk, I'm good with that."

"I think you'll like what I have in mind—"

"I know I will."

Her fingers graze my lips, and Jade gives me an amused look. "Do you ever stop talking?"

"When my mouth is on your cunt, yes. Then I'm licking. Actually, if you want me to shut up, I think that's the new requirement. You have to sit on my face—"

She pinches my lips shut with her fingers. Not hard, just enough to silence me. I bite back a chuckle, because I love this sassy side of her. Confident and playful Jade? Hell, yeah. I give her a goofy grin of approval as she finishes undoing my tunic and then rocks her hips over mine. "I'm going to get up now," she tells me. "You don't get to move, though."

I nod. "I'll stay right here."

"And be quiet?" She arches a brow, the smile on her lips telling me that she's teasing.

"Would I really be *me* if I was quiet?"

"Excellent point." She leans in and presses a kiss to the base of my neck, her tongue lightly skating over my flesh. "How about you just sit there and keep your hands on your legs, then?"

I don't like this turn of events. Not touch Jade? She might as well tell me to stop breathing. Tell a starving man not to eat the banquet in front of him. "I can't put my hands on you? With these amazing breasts so close nearby, just begging to be touched? This is cruel and unusual punishment."

She turns slowly, grinding that plush, perfect ass against my cock as she does, and then gets to her feet. I let out a very un-corsair-like sound of protest as she does. Jade only gives me a sweet look, moving forward and putting her hands on my thighs. "Hands down, remember?"

"Cruel female."

"The cruelest," she agrees with a little toss of her hair. "Now be quiet, because you're distracting me." She moves down to my stomach, pressing a kiss there, and then moves lower again.

And I suddenly figure out where this is heading. Sweet. Keffing. Stars. Above. "Jade," I groan. "You magnificent creature."

She kisses up to the waist of my trou and then looks up at me. "You're supposed to be quiet, remember?"

"Quiet. Naturally." I can't help but tease one of those tiny straps down her shoulder, though. They barely look like enough to hold her breasts up, and sure enough, when the strap slides down her arm, her nipple practically spills out of the dress. "Well, well. Look what treasure I've uncovered."

I reach for her and she calmly puts my hand back on my leg. "You can touch me once I'm done with you."

Just another part of her teasing game, I suppose. I sigh mournfully, eyeing that pleasant little nipple. It's all puckered and tight and just waiting to be tasted. "I'm going to be doing so much keffing touching. Just you wait."

Jade quickly undoes the clasp on my belt and hits the button that makes the belt slither back into the buckle. It makes a *snik* noise, and then she tosses it aside. Next goes the auto-fastener over my groin, and she gives me a sly little look as she reaches for it. "Lots of touching, hmm?"

"So much," I breathe, distracted by how near she is to my cock. "So keffing much."

"It sounds like you want me to stop?" Her fingers trail up and down my cock in the lightest of touches. She outlines my length under my trou, where I'm straining against the material, and considers me with that same playful smile on her lips. "It'd be a shame to finish when I'm just getting started."

"Oh?" I croak.

"Mmmhmm." Jade flicks at the auto-fastener and it slides down, and my cock practically springs free from my trou. She looks up at me. "No underwear?"

"Nah. I prefer to travel the universe free-balling. Makes me less uptight," I joke. My fingers clutch at the legs of my trou as she carefully peels the fabric away from my hips, revealing my entire length and my sac. "You know who wears underclothes?

Straik. Probably tight ones, too. Might explain why he's always in such a sour mood. He—"

"Adiron," Jade purrs, leaning in. "I'm about to put your cock in my mouth. The last thing I want to hear about is Straik and his underwear."

"Right," I say, dazed. "Sorry. Please continue."

Her gaze settles on the double piercing on the head of my cock. "Was this for anyone in particular?"

"You."

She looks up at me and her mouth twitches. "You didn't know I existed until a few days ago."

"Does it matter? I was just waiting for you to come into my life." I reach out and stroke her soft cheek, because I can't resist touching her again. "Most mesakkah get a piercing for their eventual mate. Doesn't matter that I just met mine. Everything below the belt is all yours."

She chuckles, leaning into my touch. "And above the belt?"

"All yours, too...but a lot less fun."

Jade shakes her head, her smile sweet and amused. "That's where you're wrong, love. I like all of you. Not just your *admittedly* impressive cock. I like your personality, and your smile." She leans forward and pokes the center of my chest. "I like this, too."

"My pectorals?"

"Your heart, you goof." She flicks me with her fingertip. "Now, can I please blow you properly, or are you going to continue to interrupt me?"

Now I'm confused. I draw my hands over my cock, shielding it. "You're going to hit me? There?" I knew humans were a little wild, but I don't know if I'd be into dick-smacking. It doesn't sound fun, no matter how much I try to imagine it.

Her brows furrow, then smooth as a realization hits her. "No, Adiron," she says softly. I can hear the amusement in her voice, but she keeps things so, so gentle and low, as if she's coaxing me into a languid state. "When I say I'm going to blow you, it means I'm going to take you into my mouth and love every inch of your big, thick cock with my tongue. Humans call it a blow job."

Oh.

"Thank kef, because I am really not into the hitting."

56

ADIRON

*M*an, I've never been so glad in my keffing life that humans will put absolutely everything into their mouths. It's a weird thing to be thankful for, but I knew (thanks to my sister Zoey) that they didn't have a lot of the prejudices mesakkah families (and especially those from older houses on Homeworld) have. To them, a mouth is just another tool to be used. You eat with it, you talk and sing with it, and occasionally you lick your lover's cock from sac to tip.

Kinda like what Jade is doing to me right now.

I watch in utter fascination as her pink tongue glides up and down my length. I can't stop staring. Even if the ship crashed around us and every single one of those stasis pods opened, I'd still be utterly caught up in the sight of the tip of Jade's tongue darting over the ridges on my cock, the deep blue of my shaft garishly bright against her pink mouth and brown skin.

It feels like paradise.

A lot of things feel good. That first bite of food after a long, hard day. Sinking into your bed. A hot shower. Touching the female you adore. Letting her squeeze your horns between her thighs.

But this? This might go to the top of the list. Jade uses just the tip of her tongue on me, and it's ticklish and flirty and wet, and I'm never, ever going to keffing forget this sight for as long as I live. As I stare down at her in fascinated disbelief, she traces a vein along the underside of my cock. "You enjoy this?"

"Of course I do," she murmurs, her voice all sultry and gorgeous. Her fingers curl around the base, and I love how small they are compared to my size. I don't even mind that wiggly extra finger she has. I just want her to keep touching me. "You liked going down on me, didn't you?"

Before I can answer, her mouth closes over the tip of my cock and I practically come off the chair. My hips jerk, determined to shuttle into her mouth, and it takes all of my strength to remain where I am and not plow my cock into her face. Can't be rude, I remind myself. Not when she's being so generous with that tongue and those lips.

Kef me, those lips. They enclose my cock, right down to the thick crown around the head. Her tongue rubs against the underside and she sucks on me like she would one of those hard candies on a stick that are so popular with human children in vids. Then she moans as if she adores the taste of me and works her mouth deeper.

I can't stop staring. I've never seen anything so damned incredible in my life.

Then she sucks me hard, as hard as one of the ship's vacuums, and the breath hisses between my clenched teeth. I sag back in the chair, holding onto the damned thing for dear life, because I can't come just yet. Not yet, not when she's being so keffing good to me. I keep my eyes squeezed tightly shut.

Her mouth leaves me with an audible pop, and then her

glorious fingers are massaging my balls. "Should I stop?" she asks, all breathless. "If you're not enjoying yourself—"

"Female," I growl, near-frantic at the thought of her stopping. "Do not be cruel to a male who adores you."

Jade giggles, the sound slightly gleeful, and her fingers continue to work my balls. Her breath fans hot over the head of my cock again, and then she licks another wet, teasing stripe over the head. "I have to admit, these piercings are a little troubling. Normally I'd take you so deep that you'd be fucking my throat—"

I groan at the thought, nearly undone.

"—but those piercings might scrape up my mouth, so all I can do is a lot of licking and teasing. I hope that's okay." When I open my eyes, she presses her lips to the underside of my cock, watching me, and then speaks again. "And sucking on the head, of course."

It's fascinating to watch her talk with my cockhead brushing against her lips. I can't resist pushing for more. I take my cock in hand and guide it toward her lips, pushing it between them and watching as she eagerly takes me into her mouth once more, working her tongue against my skin. Kef me. She grips me tight around the base of my cock and starts pumping, using my foreskin as she works me. Her other hand continues to tease and caress my balls, and her mouth sucks and sucks and sucks on my cock until I'm groaning like a male in agony. I twitch every time she pumps me, doing my best to stay still and failing miserably. All the while, her hot mouth slicks my length and works the tip of me like I'm the best thing she's ever tasted. She makes little noises of pleasure, too, and when I pick up the scent of her arousal perfuming the air? It's all over for me.

With my hand on her head, I come inside that glorious, hot, sucking mouth of hers. I flood her tongue with my seed, and the moment I do so, I grimace inwardly as I pull out. I love it when Jade comes on my tongue, but she's probably going to spit out my seed, horrified. I should have asked first. I should have checked to see if she wanted it.

Before I can apologize, this glorious, filthy female of mine looks up at me and swallows hard. My milky load coats her lips and there's dribbles escaping her mouth and painting her skin, but she swallows and then uses her fingers to daintily clean her face up, licking them as if I'm a treat that she's given herself. Then she leans over and cleans me with her tongue.

I just stare in utter awe, watching as she bends over me and drags that masterpiece of a tongue over my now-too-sensitive cock. "Did I mention I'm in love with you?" I pant. "Madly in love with you?"

She licks her lips one last time and then gives me a sultry smile that makes my cock twitch. "Oh, I know."

"Just...thought I'd bring it up again," I wheeze. "If I wasn't before, I'd definitely be in love now."

Jade chuckles and gets to her feet, a soft look in her eyes. "I'm glad you enjoyed that."

"Enjoyed" seems like too small of a word. Her mouth has turned my world upside down. I've been remade on her tongue. I've become a creature of bliss...and of hyperbole. And when Jade climbs into my lap and cuddles against me, I'm a male of utter contentment. I kiss her face a dozen times, languid and blissed. "You're amazing. But then again, you probably know that."

She makes a pleased little sound in her throat and tucks her head under my chin, pressing her chest against mine. Her legs straddle me, bare skin pressing up against my temporarily sated cock. I rub her back, my hands moving up and down her sweet body. She's all soft curves, this female of mine. "I'm just glad you enjoyed it," she says, voice low and breathless. "You seemed like you had a tough day and I wanted to make it better for you, since you're always making me feel better."

I don't deserve her. I squeeze her ass, loving the way her supple skin bounces under my grip. I wonder if she'd let me spank her. At the thought, my cock—exhausted soldier that it is —stirs to life once more. "You are the most generous of females, Jade."

Her laughter is sweet. She runs a hand over my bare chest, her fingers pausing over my nipples. "I'm not entirely selfless, Adiron. I'm hoping you'll be up for another round soon, and maybe we can both come this time." She draws a circle over my nipple with her fingers, making my skin prickle ever so slightly. Not that I'm sensitive there, but it tells me that Jade's still needy, and I'm always attuned to that.

"Are you all wet and aching?" I ask, unable to resist.

She lets out a little sigh. "Oh, very."

"Maybe I can ease your pain," I tell her, feeling smug and in control. I could work Jade with my tongue, I think. Get her cunt all slick and hot and tasty, and then when my cock is ready for more, I can claim her for hours and hours. Kef me, but that sounds amazing. I slide my hand under her skirt and between our bodies, seeking out her cunt.

Jade wriggles in anticipation.

At first, I don't realize what I'm touching. She's hot and wet here, but...smooth. The wiry, tight curls that framed her cunt are...gone. "Jade?"

"I shaved," she breathes. "For you. Nice and smooth. Surprise."

57

JADE

The look on Adiron's face is worth everything. I love the sheer astonishment that crosses over him, followed by greediness. He rubs his fingers over my folds, and I whimper, rocking against his hand.

"I want to see," he tells me.

I'm breathless as he tumbles me back onto the bed. Giddy with anticipation, but breathless. "Don't you need to rest?"

"Kef no. I need to get an up-close and personal look at this sweet cunt." Adiron pushes my skirt up to my waist, and when I part my legs so he can get a good look, he groans. "You did this for me?"

"I wanted to surprise you."

He lowers his big head, and I reach out and touch his horns as he nuzzles at my newly bared skin. "Your little tuft was so cute. I'm going to miss it."

His response isn't what I thought it would be. Most men are

excited when a woman goes bare for him, because they instinctively dislike pubic hair, I think. "You don't like it?"

"Oh, I like it." Adiron licks me, his tongue swirling over smooth flesh. "But I liked it the old way, too. I don't want you to change for me. I like you in all your human-ness, extra fingers and random tufts of hair and all."

"Wow. Extra fingers and random hair. So flattering."

He chuckles, and his breath huffs against my sensitive skin. "It wasn't meant to be an insult, love. You're different, because you're not the same species. It doesn't make your differences bad. I like them, because I like you. I wouldn't change a single thing about you." Adiron kisses my mound, right above my clit. "Except maybe that fifth toe of yours, because it looks deformed—"

I giggle. He's got three big toes to my five, and he's never understood why I've got several small ones in varying sizes. "I guess this means you won't suck on my toes?"

"Oh, I'll suck on them." He lifts his head and grins up at me. "If that's what turns you on, I'll lick them all day long. But I will question your tastes, considering you have these delicious breasts just waiting to be nibbled on, and this juicy, sweet cunt that's just begging to be licked."

I suck in a breath, hot arousal fanning through me.

He slides down my body. "But if you want toe play—"

"Wait, wait," I protest, grabbing at his horns. "I was joking."

Adiron presses another hot, open-mouthed kiss to my newly shaved mound. "Then tell me where you want my mouth."

"Lower," I whimper.

He does as I command, his tongue delving between my drenched folds and lapping at my skin. I let out a shuddering breath. His tongue moves unerringly toward my clit, and then he begins to lick and suck, even as he presses a finger into my core. This man is not playing fair, I realize, as his big hand folds my leg back and presses my knee practically to my shoulder. I'm spread wide open for him as he makes love to my pussy with his mouth and fingers. I cling to his horns, rocking my hips against his face, and I'm lost in the moment. My body is already primed and ready, and it doesn't take long before that orgasm starts to build, and my whimpers grow louder and my movements more urgent.

I'm almost there...and then he stops.

"You son of a bitch," I pant as he lifts his head and grins up at me. I plant my hand on his brow and try to push him back down, but he only chuckles. "That's not playing fair."

"I'm a corsair," he tells me as he moves over me. "I rarely play fair." He gives me a kiss, tasting of my arousal, and then locks a hand on my hip. A moment later, I feel the head of him pressing at the entrance to my body. Adiron's voice sinks to a low, husky note. "I want to feel you come around me, love. Can you do that for me?"

I moan, because just hearing him ask that does wild things to my insides.

He pushes deep, and I'm so wet and ready that he glides in without the slightest resistance. My body makes a slick sound as it clasps him, and he sighs with pleasure. "You were made for me, Jade. Look at how eager this sweet little cunt is to take me. Your body's just greedy, isn't it? It can't wait to be filled up with my seed."

Whimpering, I reach for him, my hands fluttering over his chest. "Adiron," I pant. "Please."

"I have you, love." He leans forward, covering me, and then begins to pump into me. Not slow and gentle. There's no languid buildup of speed here. This time, he's taking me hard and fast, my tits shaking with every rapid-fire thrust...and I love it. There's no time to let my body adjust to his invasion, no time to let my orgasm mosey on through my body before heading to the finish line. This is absolutely a claiming, and every bit of me lights up in response. I moan his name as he whispers more dirty things to me, every rough stroke of his cock into my body accompanied by a tease of his spur over my clit. Every time he sinks deep, there are more filthy promises, and it's so good and naughty that it makes me utterly wild. My channel tightens around him, rippling as he drives into me, and when he changes our angle slightly, tucking my hips under him a bit more, that piercing of his rubs against a sensitive spot inside me.

My hands scrabble against his skin, and I dig my nails in. I feel like I'm flying apart as he thrusts deep, each time the piercing hitting that perfect, perfect spot that makes every-thing in my body flare. He circles his hips, and as he does, his spur does this glorious little dance over my clit, and...I come. I come so hard and so brightly I can feel my entire body tighten up, my pussy clenching around him. I can feel the rush of fluid as everything inside me crashes and explodes into brilliance. And as I'm lost in sensation, Adiron keeps driving into me. Just when I think my body is done, he twitches inside me with the force of his own release, eliciting another delicious aftershock as he bathes my insides with his seed.

He collapses next to me, rolling onto the bed and panting, and I stare up at the ceiling in a state of near-catatonic bliss. Lord have mercy, that was amazing. "So," I manage, sucking in deep breaths. "What...what's the plan for tomorrow?"

Adiron pulls me against him, snuggling up against my breasts. They push into his face and he gives a happy sigh of contentment. "Noodles and sex."

I chuckle, playing with his hair. "And the day after?"

"Noodles and sex."

"Is that going to be the plan every day for the next month?" I ask, amused.

The big alien lifts his head and our eyes meet. He grins at me. "You have a better idea?"

I pretend to consider. "No," I say after a moment, and hold him closer. "I really, really don't. Noodles and sex sounds pretty good to me."

58

Six Weeks Later

JADE

𝓘'm off noodles.

It's finally happened. After years of eating the same shit, day in and day out, my body is finally rejecting our food source. I'd rolled out of bed, dodging Adiron's sprawled limbs, and padded to the kitchen to make breakfast. It's more noodles, of course. Noodles three times a day, in a few different flavors. But the moment I smell the cooking noodles, my stomach churns. I barely make it to the sink before I vomit the contents of my stomach. I puke a few times, then dry heave, and collapse onto the floor. I lean against the cabinet, feeling awful...but not surprised.

The scent bothered me yesterday. The texture, too. I sucked it up and ate anyhow, because there are no other options, and when I couldn't stomach any more, I pushed my bowl over to Adiron, who gleefully ate the rest. I was hoping it was a one-time situation, but it looks like not. Thankfully, we've got plenty of hot tea, so I get to my feet, make myself a cup, and hold my breath as I pour my noodles into Adiron's bowl.

Adiron pads into the kitchen a few minutes later and heads immediately for me. He presses a kiss to the top of my head, his tail curling around my shoulders. "Morning, love. How'd you sleep?"

"Good." I lean back against his thighs. "You?"

"Like a baby." He rubs his hands up and down over my arms, then palms my breasts. He's always touchy-feely in the mornings, and I lean back against him, enjoying the sensation of his hands on my body. "Kef me, you're beautiful," he says. "How am I so lucky?"

I suck in a breath as he teases my sensitive nipples through my clothing. "I made you breakfast."

"Hmm, breakfast or tits. Breakfast or tits." He pretends to consider, even as he massages my breasts in circular motions.

"Breakfast," I say firmly, pushing his hands away. "The tits are a little sensitive this morning."

Adiron plants one last kiss atop my head and then moves across the table to where the bowl is steaming and waiting for him. The moment he sits down, I put my feet in his lap, and he curls his tail around my ankle. It's a familiar routine for us. We like to keep touching, and it feels cozy this way. I sip my tea, relieved that my stomach seems to have settled a bit more. I watch as he eats a big bite, then glances over at me. "You already eat?" he asks.

I nod. He'll just worry if I tell him I puked, so I don't say anything at all. My stomach will just have to suck it up and realize that noodles are on the menu, whether I like it or not. I take another sip of tea and then tilt my head toward the wall unit. "I checked the comm. Nothing this morning."

He grunts, nodding. "Any day now. Just be patient."

"Patience is my middle name."

"Is it?" He takes another big bite. "Because I seem to recall someone whining last night how I wouldn't let her come—"

I kick him under the table. Not hard, just enough to make him laugh with amusement. Six weeks into our time together, and Adiron hasn't changed in the slightest. I wondered if he'd calm down once we settled in together, if the jokes would be fewer, if the sex would drop off once all the excitement and newness wore away.

I should have known better.

Adiron is the same big goof, day in and day out. He runs his mouth, pretends to be dumb, and yet manages to be clever and thoughtful and kind, and full of boundless energy. The sex hasn't slowed down at all, either. I'm sure some of it is because there's very little to do all day long, but Adiron is just as giving in bed now as he was weeks ago. He loves to make me come at least once before he's inside me, and he can't resist touching me all the time. We have sex at least twice a day. Not to just pass the time, but to learn each other. To talk and connect. His declarations of love are a daily thing, and I admit, I adore hearing them.

I'm starting to think that Adiron really did fall in love with me instantly, even if it defies logic. I've been fond of him from the get-go, of course. And the sex is amazing. I'm finding it increasingly hard to imagine my life without him in it in some way, so I think I must be in love...but I worry that our cozy little bubble has warped things. That once we're out of this situation and back to "normal" (whatever that may be), that things will change. That Adiron won't be all that interested in a plump black human woman who wears responsibility like a cloak. If his love for me ends as quickly as it began, it won't be all that surprising, will it?

I'm prepared for his infatuation to end, and I'm trying not to let my heart get caught up in the process. It might already be too late, though. Just thinking about what happens to us when the others return makes my chest tighten painfully.

I finish my tea and set the cup down, watching him as he polishes off the noodles. Now that my stomach is empty of everything but tea, it feels a little better. Maybe it was a bad batch of food. Who knows. "So what's the plan for today?" I ask brightly. "More work on the ship's controls?"

Adiron makes a face. "Might as well. I won't be satisfied if I don't give it everything I have, you know?"

I understand. Ever since we locked ourselves down into this small portion of the ship, things have been quiet. The power flickered once more, but Adiron changed out a few more wires and we've been cruising ever since. He's been going up to the bridge occasionally, suiting up to protect himself from the intense cold and lack of air, and heading over to the bridge to search for parts. The tricky thing is that he doesn't want to destroy the ship's actual control system in case Straik returns and we need to pilot the *Star* out of here. So Adiron's been tinkering with things, but I'm pretty sure it's a futile effort. He wants to try, though, and I can't blame him. It beats drifting without even making a single attempt to save ourselves.

He gets up to check the control panel on the wall. It was initially just supposed to be a communication port between rooms in the ship, but Adiron's rigged it to feed into the ship's status updates so we can at least know what's going on without venturing out to the bridge constantly. I get up with him, and when he gets to the panel and taps a few buttons, I rest my cheek on his arm, watching. This is another part of our routine, as comfortable as it is uneventful.

"Messages?" I ask, just because it never hurts to check again.

Adiron taps a button. "Nothing." He leans over and plants a kiss atop my head. "Remember, don't panic. It just means they're not in range yet."

"I'm not panicking." I slide my arm around his waist. He's

explained to me a half-dozen times that they have to get to the *Little Sister*, refuel and then make their way back. "And the ice field?"

"Still a month out from drifting to the danger zone. We'll handle things before we get there, I promise." He rubs my back, comforting me. "I won't let you freeze."

"I know." I believe him, too. If anyone can figure something out between now and then, it's my big, determined Adiron.

He pushes away from the panel, sits down on a nearby seat, and draws me in for another kiss—this one on the mouth. He rubs his nose against mine in a playful manner. "Okay with you if I work on my project in here? I can wheel the cart in and spread out on this table. I need the space."

His "work" always makes a mess, but it's fine. I don't mind cleaning up after him—it gives me something to do instead of just stare at the ceiling. "Go ahead, babe."

Adiron grins at me. "You're welcome to lend a hand, you know."

I snort. "We both know where you want my hands, and it's not anywhere near your tools."

He draws me in closer, his gaze locked on my breasts. "I mean, I like to think of my cock as a tool—"

Something electronic chirps.

We both freeze, staring at each other. "Is that..." I ask.

"A ship," Adiron says. "Just came on the radar." His face lights up in the biggest grin and he tugs me into his lap and puts his hands all over me. "I told you my brothers were on their way."

59

ADIRON

J'm wrong. The moment I set Jade down and triumphantly hit the comm buttons, I know it's not my brothers. The "communication" that the *Buoyant Star* receives (if you can call it a communication) is nothing more than a ping sent to see if the ship receives it. That wouldn't be my brothers. They know we're here.

I keep smiling when Jade gives me a vaguely worried look, and punch a few more buttons. A visual of the incoming ship appears on the comm monitors, and I swear to myself. That's not the *Little Sister*. Nor is it Lord Straik's *The Darkened Eye*. It's a flash cruiser, designed for speed and stealth...and a favorite of pirates with a lot of credits to burn.

It sends another ping, and the system chirps at me.

"Shouldn't we answer?" Jade asks, looking at me. "If that's your brothers?"

"It's not them," I admit after a moment. "I don't recognize that ship at all."

"How..." She pauses. "How did they know we're here, then?"

It's an excellent question. The odds of someone finding the *Buoyant Star* without specific coordinates are extremely, extremely slim. Jade and her companions had a handful of visitors over the last three years, and only after they were sending out a distress signal to lure in pirates with supplies. This strikes me as highly coincidental. Either we've left a signal on somewhere, or someone's given away our location.

If I had a credit on me, I'd suspect it was Lord Straik. I know my brothers wouldn't sell me out...so it has to be the lord. But at the same time, it doesn't make sense. He acted like he was ashamed to find out his family was smuggling humans. Why would he turn around and give that information to pirates? He wouldn't.

Unless...he was forced to. I rub my jaw as the ping chimes again. This is definitely a problem.

I look over at Jade. Jade, who looks up at me with those big, beautiful eyes, as if she's trusting me to fix this problem. As if I can reassure her that everything's going to be all right. Jade, who makes my world better with a laugh, whose smile makes my heart feel as if it's coming out of my chest. There is nothing I wouldn't do for this female, and being with her in the last six weeks has only emphasized that feeling. It's easily been the happiest six weeks of my life. I want to wake up with her wild, kinky hair in my mouth and her tits plastered against my chest every morning for the rest of my days.

And I'm not going to risk her for anything.

"Do you love me, Jade?" I ask.

Her eyes narrow as she looks over at me. "This is an odd time for a declaration."

She knows me all too well. "Just answer. Yes or no?"

"You know the answer is yes."

"Fantastic." I gesture at the wall. "I'm going to pull that panel off and I want you to hide behind it until that ship is gone."

Jade stares at me. "Do...what?"

"It's a pirate ship. Probably not friendly. I don't want them getting anywhere near you, so I'm going to need you to hide." I'm already racing out of the room, heading for my blaster. I'll give her my weapon, so she can protect herself. If she's hidden, this ship has a lot of janky re-wiring now thanks to my efforts. Maybe they won't notice another bio-signature. I can play it off as something else.

At least, that's the hope.

As long as Jade is safe, I can take anything these pirates dish out.

I snatch up my weapon from the hook on the wall and head back toward the kitchen. Jade meets me on the way there, her eyes wide and frantic. "Adiron, what if you're wrong? What if they're friendly? What if it's one of your brothers?"

"One of my brothers would have sent more than a ping. This is someone that's testing the waters to see what bites." I reach out and touch her cheek. "It'll be all right, love. I won't let anyone harm you." I'll die first.

I put my blaster in her hand. She gives it a horrified glance. "Adi, no."

"Yes," I say firmly, and steer her toward the wall. "There's a fusion component hidden behind the food processor. Stick as close to that as you can. I'm hoping it'll hide your bio-signature. I don't want you to come out until I give you the signal."

I half-expect Jade to protest more, but she's smart and cool in a pinch, my girl. She nods and takes the blaster, pulling it free from its holster and priming it before hefting it, and then turning it off again. "What's the signal, then?"

Gotta be something they won't think to use in normal conversation. I consider for a few moments, "I'll work out a way to bring up my list of five favorite things."

Jade nods. She moves forward impulsively, grabs the front of my tunic, and tugs me down toward her. Her mouth is on mine, fierce and desperate, and she kisses me so hard that her lips will likely be bruised in the morning. She pulls back, just a little, her gaze meeting mine. "I love you more than anything," she tells me.

I smooth her wild, puffy hair. I adore this female. "I'm going to keep you safe," I tell her again. Maybe if I keep saying it, I'll believe it. "Don't you worry about a thing."

She pulls back, takes a deep breath, and then nods. "You want a signal word for me to shoot them?"

Kef, I love her ruthless streak. "If we have too many signal words, we might get them all mixed up. How about if I say 'shoot' then you pick off the most dangerous-looking one and we go from there?"

Jade nods. "I can do that."

"And if it's a Threshian crew, kill me and then turn the blaster on yourself," I say. "You don't want them taking you alive."

She stares at me. "You're...serious?"

I nod once. "Just trust me on that. I don't think it'll be a Threshian crew but...yeah." I kiss her one more time and then move to the wall. I study it, looking for a good place to rip it open, and then grab one of the flat, strong metal sticks that serve as eating utensils, and then wedge it into the wall. I use it to pop up one corner of the wall, along the baseboard, and then shove my hand under there, dragging the entire thing up along the seams as I do. My hands get a little ripped up and bloody as I work, but I can deal with that later. "Quick. Hide." I gesture to Jade. "We don't have much time."

As if the ship's aware of the situation, it chimes with an alert. "Unfamiliar vessel initiating ship-to-ship docking sequence," the computer intones. "Please advise."

Jade crouches and slides into the hollow behind the wall. There's a mass of tubes and near-empty bags from the food supplies, but she sticks close to the fusion generator like I told her, blaster clutched tight in hand. I replace the panel, trying to remain calm as the ship recites the alert once more. I use the flat of my palm to smack the metal panel back into the housing, then wipe the blood away. There's a vent near the bottom, and I lean in close. "All right in there, love?"

"I'm good and I can see out," Jade whispers. "I love you. Stay safe for me, all right?"

I plan on it. There's no way I'm leaving my woman alone to face these bastards.

60

JADE

I clutch the blaster in sweaty hands, peering through the grate as the ship's hull groans and I can hear the distant hum of what sounds like the same tool that Adiron used to seal the doors. I'm nervous and worried, and my stomach churns all over again. I bite my lip so hard that I taste blood, but at least I don't puke. Puking in the wall? In this tight space that I might have to be in for god knows how long? Not a good idea. Luckily, the nausea ebbs.

As the ship sends out a variety of alerts—all of them bad sounding—Adiron hums to himself. It's a jaunty little tune, all light and cheery, and as I crane my neck to try and see through the grate, I catch the scent of noodles. He's making himself food. The chair scrapes and then I hear him sit down. It's a hell of a time to eat, but as the little tune continues, my heart fills with affection.

Adiron always has a strategy to his actions, and I know what this is. This is both an effort to calm me and to disarm whoever shows up. He wants to make them think he's stupid, and sitting calmly and eating while his ship is being invaded will definitely put that thought in their heads. I know he's not stupid, though. He hides behind it like a shield. He uses that to his advantage, because the less the enemy thinks of him, the more room it gives him to outmaneuver them. I want to tell him I have him all figured out, but I remain silent and send thoughts of love from afar.

The door hisses open and every nerve in my body screams to attention.

A gruff alien voice barks out a few syllables. Don't move, the translator implant in my head says, and I realize how jarring it is to hear the Homeworld dialect. He's speaking mesakkah, and Adiron always speaks English around me so I don't have to listen to the translation. It's just another way that he's thoughtful and kind.

I peer through the grate, and I see big, muscular legs and twitching blue tails.

I also see the remnants of the door on the floor, and one of the strangers is holding a blaster to Adiron's head.

My heart stops.

And what is Adiron doing? He's got his mouth full of noodles, his cheeks puffed out with them. One long one dangles from his lips. He slurps it up and eyes the intruders. "You the rescue party?"

They look a little confused. The one with the blaster to his head hesitates, then pushes it against Adiron's brow again. "Who are you? What are you doing on this ship?"

"I'm Adiron." He stirs his food, unconcerned that his life is in danger. I want to shoot both of them, but Adiron hasn't signaled me, and he doesn't look worried. I have to take that as a good sign. "As for what I'm doing here?" He continues, "I thought it was pretty obvious. I'm stranded. My ride took off without me."

"What ship were you with?" the other asks.

"*The Darkened Eye*, captained by Lord Straik sa'Rin. Real pain in the ass. I was working on board and he got a burr under his tail. Left me here on this piece of junk. That was about six weeks ago." He tells them just enough that it all sounds incredibly legit—because it is. He's just omitting the parts about us humans or the fact that he chose to stay behind with me while his brothers jettisoned in the escape pods. He gives the men a bright look. "Say. You guys got anything better to eat than noodles? That's all this ship has."

"You the only one here?"

"One and only." He wiggles his fingers at them. "Hand's gotten a real workout, too. Nothing to do here but daydream about cantina girls, if you catch my drift."

"Disgusting," mutters the other.

The first one lowers his weapon. "We're going to check this ship for others. What's your family name again? We'll let the captain know you're here and she can decide what to do with you."

"Va Sithai," Adiron says, and goes back to eating his noodles. "You can check the records of *The Darkened Eye*, too, and you'll see she was here in this quadrant a few weeks ago. I'm telling you the truth." He takes another big bite and speaks out of the side of his mouth. "Tell your captain I'm happy to crew for decent food and a ride back to the nearest station."

The two men confer, whispering, and I can't make out what they're saying. I can barely see their faces, the vent preventing me from watching their expressions. I can see Adiron, though. He shovels his noodles into his mouth with grim determination and never looks over at me once. I have to give him credit—for a man that is an awful liar, he's holding his shit together really well right now.

Meanwhile, I'm sweating a blue streak here in the wall. It's not just that it's stuffy. It's that I'm absolutely terrified. My hands are so slippery Adiron's blaster could fall from my grip at any minute.

One of the men leaves, and the other casually walks toward Adiron, his hand on the weapon at his waist. "You know what this ship is?" he asks, voice all casual.

Adiron lifts his bowl to his lips. "Keffing death trap is what it is. I've had to rejig half the control panels just to keep the air flowing. You planning on towing her to port?"

"Depends on what the captain says," the man replies, voice cool. "She'll let us know her plans soon enough."

Footsteps echo on the floors, and I see Adiron's tail twitch.

"Captain," the soldier says, his body turning toward the door. A long, lean pair of legs and another blue tail enter the room. It's a woman, and judging by the whipcord strong-but-slim build and the tail, it's another mesakkah. I can't see her face, though.

At the table, Adiron starts to choke on his food.

"Thought you'd be surprised to see me," the woman purrs. "Imagine finding my favorite va Sithai in the ass-crack of the universe."

"Shaalyn," Adiron coughs, his expression stunned.

61

ADIRON

*W*ell, if this isn't my worst nightmare, I'm not sure what is.

I stare at my old lover, unable to believe my eyes. Shaalyn vos Nimai is as beautiful as ever, her long, smooth ponytail high between her horns and flowing down her shoulders. Her ears are studded with hoops, just as I remember, and she's got a tiny one on her septum that glitters when she smiles. She doesn't look one bit different, despite the fact that it's been eight years since I saw her. Those bright eyes still sparkle with intelligence, her body is as lean and strong as ever, and her expression is just as hard and ruthless as the last time I saw her, when she had her knife in my gut and cooed an apology even as she left me for dead.

Funny how I used to find that ruthless nature of hers so exciting once. I loved that she was a bossy female who knew what she wanted and would step on anyone to get it. Now, though, I can't help but compare her to Jade, who puts the needs of others ahead of her, and who leads simply because someone has to, and she feels the weight of responsibility. Who cares genuinely for everyone and wants all of those she's in charge of to have a fair shake, even Crulden the Ruiner.

Shaalyn is nothing compared to Jade. Nothing at all.

"Hey there," I manage to choke out. "Crazy how we keep running into each other after you tried to murder me."

A smile curves her mouth, and she looks genuinely delighted to see me. "Holding grudges, darling? You really shouldn't. You know it wasn't personal."

The sad thing is, I know she's right. Shaalyn has always been all about herself. Even when I was madly in love with her and helping her rob others blind, I thought she didn't give a shit about anyone except me. Turns out, I was mostly right. She didn't give a shit about anyone, INCLUDING me. Ah well. That's what happens when you think with your cock. "Doesn't matter if it was personal or not. Can't say we left on good terms after you betrayed me, knifed me, and stole my ship."

She tuts, moving forward and brushing her long, graceful fingers over my cheek. "You would have done the same to me if you were in a pinch."

"No, I wouldn't have." At the time, I truly thought myself in love with her. I'd have done anything for her. Now, of course, I see that she was just using my enthusiastic obedience as another tool.

Shaalyn shrugs. "Then you're a fool. Speaking of fools..." She gestures at my surroundings. "What are you doing out here, darling?"

I pull away from her touch, though it might be smarter to let her think I still have a measure of affection for her. It takes everything I have not to look over at Jade's hiding spot. I can't give away her location. Even if she manages to shoot one or two of Shaalyn's crew, there's more than she can safely handle. I can't risk her getting hurt. Time to bluff my way out of things. "On this ship? I could ask the same of you."

She leans over me, her tail swishing. I'm not surprised to see she's got a few rings on the tip of it. Shaalyn always did love a gaudy bit of jewelry. No wonder she's always keffing broke. "I'm not in the mood for games, darling. Tell me what I need to know, or my boys might have to pry it out of you."

I glance around the room. Six pirates other than Shaalyn, now. All mesakkah, all heavily armed. All younger than me and probably all in love with her fierce, dangerous ways and desperate to impress her. I have no doubt they'd get creative with torture in order to squeeze information out of me. Lucky for both of us that I excel at running my mouth. "Went out exploring. Ran into a bit of trouble with our ride, and so my brothers left me to hold things down while they regroup." I shrug, trying to seem casual. "They'll be back any moment now."

It's a bluff, of course. Yes, my brothers will be coming back, but I have no idea when. It might be another week. It might be three.

Shaalyn taps a finger under my chin. "Aw. That's sweet. You think they're coming back. Darling, how do you think I got here?"

My gut clenches. It's the answer I fear the most, but also the one that makes the most sense. But I have a role to play, and I'm determined to keep on playing it. I smile brightly. "How do I think you got here? Intelligent flying and sharp skills? But I guess not. Those haven't been your forte. You're best at stealing other people's toys and claiming them for yourself."

She slaps my cheek. Not enough to make my head turn, just enough to let me know she doesn't like my little dig. "We intercepted your brother's escape pod, you idiot. He didn't want to say anything, either, but when his little human was threatened, he sang like an avian." Shaalyn's fingers dig into my skin, her touch turning cruel. "They're dead now."

I won't believe it. I can't. Instead, I try to focus on what Shaalyn said. Escape pod. My brother with a human. It must have been Kaspar. Must have. And if they intercepted the escape pod, Kaspar didn't have to tell them anything. Any decent pirate worth their credits would just space the occupants and download the flight route from the pod, follow it back to the source. Kaspar would never say a thing. "You're full of shit."

"Am I? He told me that you have an entire hold full of human slaves, just waiting to be sold." Her mouth curves prettily and she taps my chin again. "And he told me you stayed here with one to keep you company. Slumming a little since I left you, darling?"

"Actually, the slumming was when I was with you—"
CRACK.

Stars flash in front of my eyes as the side of my cheek explodes in pain. Dimly, I realize one of Shaalyn's goons used the butt of his blaster on my face. Guess he didn't like that comment about her. I tense, waiting, because I'm afraid that Jade's going to blow her cover if they hurt me. As long as she's in that wall, she's safe. They can't hurt her if they can't find her.

Shaalyn frowns at the soldier to my side. "Darling, don't hurt him before he tells us what we want."

"There's no human here," I lie, rubbing my throbbing jaw. "Just take the ones in the hold and leave me here. I won't stop you." It's a bluff, of course. I can't stop them either way, but it never hurts to throw the idea out there.

"I want all the humans," Shaalyn says softly. "Including the one you're hiding. I don't believe in leaving a credit behind. You know that."

I do. Shaalyn is as cheap as she is keffing ruthless. I glance up at her, her lovely features ice cold. They do nothing for me now. All I can think about is Jade, and how I need to keep her safe. How can I fix this? If I grab Shaalyn, can I kill her before the others kill me? Probably not, but I'm willing to take that risk, as long as it keeps Jade safe. The problem is, if they attack me, I can't be certain that she'll stay hidden. She'll want to help me, and then we'll both be keffed.

"There's no human," I say again. "Other than the ones in the hold."

Shaalyn sighs heavily. "Darling, you are nothing if not utterly predictable. Tell me where you're hiding her or we'll start flushing the air out of each room. I don't know a lot about humans, but I do know they need air."

I say nothing. It's an empty threat. Shaalyn is many things —stingy, amoral, selfish—but she's not stupid. She knows this ship is falling apart. She's probably seen all my re-routing efforts and the fact that a lot of the life-support systems have been re-wired and tinkered with. She can't access the controls without hard-rebooting the computer's control system, and she knows if she does that, she runs the risk of it dying on her entirely.

And Shaalyn won't leave a credit on the table. She wants Jade alive, because she's no doubt hoping that Jade has access to the systems and can get her a way in, so she can tow the *Buoyant Star* back to port to strip her of every last credit's worth. She needs Jade alive.

It's me that's expendable.

"If you value that human's life," Shaalyn says softly, "you'll speak up now."

I say nothing. Inwardly, I hope Jade trusts me and remains silent where she is. Please stay put, Jade. We're both safe as long as you do. Shaalyn's going to keep me alive and torture me until I give up Jade (which won't happen), and Jade's safe as long as Shaalyn thinks she's got the answers she needs.

Long, agonizing moments slide past. The room is silent.

Jade doesn't get out of her hiding space, and I let out the breath I'm holding in relief.

Shaalyn pouts. "Always have to do things the hard way, don't you? All right." She turns toward one of her men and puts her hand out. The pirate automatically pulls his blaster from the holster at his hip, turns it, and offers it, handle-first, to Shaalyn. She studies it for a moment, then flicks the switch, powering it on...and holds it up to my brow. "I didn't want to do this, darling, but I have no choice. If you don't produce that human before I count to five, I'm going to have to take drastic measures. And this time? I'll make sure you're dead."

The cool metal of the blaster presses to the plating on my brow. I ignore it. It's a bluff. Instead, I get ready to grin at Shaalyn, a joke rising on my lips.

A hand hammers on the wall behind me. "Wait," Jade cries. "Don't hurt him! I'm here!"

Ah, kef.

62

JADE

I can't do it.

When they threaten Adiron's life, I can't stay silent any longer. I pound on the panel, and a few moments later, a big blue alien hauls me out. I stumble forward, and then I'm dragged in front of the woman.

"My goodness. That little trick works every time, doesn't it?" The female chuckles, the sound low and lovely and somehow menacing.

Shaalyn.

I can't believe I'm looking at Adiron's old lover. When he mentioned her name, I think he was just as surprised as me. I didn't know that she was a pirate, though. For some reason, I'd just thought she was a shitty, murdering thief. Of course it makes sense that she's a pirate—she stole his ship once, after all. But to find her here? It's the worst kind of luck. I stare at the woman who held Adiron's heart before me. She's...not what I expected. Her name is a soft-sounding thing, and I know I'm certainly not badass, so I thought Adiron's tastes would go more towards...daintiness? But Shaalyn is anything but.

She reminds me of a viper. A dangerous, slithery snake that's both beautiful and utterly deadly. Shaalyn has a high, sleek ponytail, ringed piercings, and a loose-flowing one-piece jumpsuit that manages to look feminine and elegant on her while still broadcasting an air of authority. She has no weapon at her waist. Doesn't need one with all the men around her packing heat. She's got the same proud, strong ridges on her face that all the mesakkah do, but I get the impression that she's older than the others. There's an unyielding hardness in her lovely eyes, a bitter history to the curve of her mouth. She's tall and lean, though, and surrounded by all these looming, muscular mesakkah, it's impossible to not feel short and dumpy and very, very human.

"Isn't she precious?" Shaalyn coos, reaching out to finger a lock of my natural curls.

"Don't you keffing touch her," Adiron growls. He jumps to his feet, only to have two more blasters shoved in his face by the pirates.

"Touch her?" The female mesakkah tsks, glancing over at him. "If you mean harm her, I don't plan on it, darling. Humans are far too valuable to be bruised up. We'll take her on board and get her all straightened out, so she can be sold for top credits." Her smile is all sugary sweetness. "You know that I love a good auction." She turns her gaze on me and talks very slowly, as if I'm an idiot. "We'll take good care of you, little one."

"Go fuck yourself," I tell her.

The female corsair's eyes widen in surprise. "I see that you've taught her your manners, Adi." She flicks her fingers at the pirate holding me by the shoulders. "Go take her back to med-bay. Run a scan over her and make sure she doesn't have parasites or diseases or something." Shaalyn's mouth purses in distaste at the thought. "You never know what these creatures carry."

I look over at Adiron as I'm dragged away. I want to apologize to him for busting out, but I couldn't let him be threatened. I didn't know they didn't plan on hurting him. I don't regret my actions, because I'd do it again to save him. I'm not entirely stupid, either. When the room filled up with the horned pirates and Adiron started talking in that speedy, too-casual way of his, I knew we were fucked. I undid the front of my tunic and shoved the barrel of the blaster between my tits, laying the handle flat under one breast. I'm wearing a breast-band, and my tits are so tightly bound and heavy that they snugly hold the gun in place. I've held pencils in my enormous cleavage before as a joke. I've held a beer there at festivals.

And now, it seems, I'm hiding a space gun.

It's not the best way to hold it, of course. If Adiron knew the blaster was pointing at my face, he'd probably have a damn heart attack. It's another gamble, of course. The way Shaalyn talked to me, I'm hoping no one thinks to search me for a weapon. Like Adiron, I need to play it stupid and innocent. So as I'm hauled away, I say a silent little prayer that Adiron will be all right, and then I throw myself into acting.

"Where are you taking me?" I whine. "I'm scared."

The man sighs like it's a huge inconvenience to take care of me. All the while, he half-drags me forward, his steps much bigger than mine, his hand biting into my arm so hard I know I'm going to have a wreath of bruises there tomorrow. "Just be quiet. No one's going to hurt you."

Somehow I doubt that. They might not hurt me—much— but I know Adiron isn't safe with them. After all, his lover is their captain and she stabbed him. Repeatedly. Plus, I know from experience that no good things happen to humans in the hands of aliens. Most aliens, anyhow. Just because Adiron is the shining difference in the universe doesn't mean the rest get a pass. I think about my first captors and how they treated me. To them, I was an oddity that they could fuck, slightly unintelligent, and definitely unhygienic.

All of these are things I can use to my advantage.

The alien drags me across the ship-to-ship connection—the flimsy, ice-cold enclosed tube that connects the two ships together. It feels dangerous, that tube, so I don't try anything then. Not when a wrong move could rip the tunnel's sealed walls and send me out into the vacuum of space. The blaster nestled in my sweaty cleavage feels like it's starting to slip, though, and I need to somehow hide it.

"Where are we going?" I whine, doing my best to sound like a sulky, petulant child as he leads me onto the other ship. "I don't like it here."

Sure enough, he starts talking to me like I'm incompetent. "We're going to take good care of you," he says in that tone of voice adults reserve for children. "We'll take you to med-bay and then feed you, and then we'll put you in a nice, safe cage."

"I'm scared," I whine again. It's the truth, of course, but it also sells my idiocy. All the while, I look around, trying to make note of my surroundings. This ship doesn't look at all like *The Darkened Eye* or the *Star*. The tunnel-like halls feel tighter, more narrow, the lighting darker and ominous. We pass something that smells vaguely like noodles—probably a mess hall—and there's another door farther down with another female alien leaning against it, her arms crossed. She has a crude eye patch over one side of her face.

She looks irked, too. "What the kef is that?" the newcomer snarls as she stares at me.

"Merchandise," says the other. "I'm taking it to med-bay to see if it has parasites. You never know with humans."

"I had a human once," the female muses as she turns back into the room. "Unclean little shits. Give it a good scrub."

Fuck you, too, I think as the male hauls me along after him.

If he scrubs me, he'll find the blaster hidden in my breast-band. "I have to urinate," I say, desperate. "Right now."

"It can wait," the male says.

"No," I cry. "Right now! Or I'm going to go everywhere!"

The alien growls in frustration and takes a sharp right turn into a side-hall. Before I can say anything again, he slaps a hand on a door panel and it slides open. "If you keffing shit everywhere, I'm going to make you clean it up," he snarls at me.

I don't have to feign my whimper, and when he makes a disgusted sound and slaps the door panel again, I watch as the door whizzes shut. He must figure I'm safe here on the ship. That I'm helpless and stupid.

Well thank god for that. Quickly, I fish the sweaty blaster out of the underside of my breast-band and look for a place to hide it.

63

JADE

"*D*id you know that you're pregnant?" The male holding the med-scanner glances up from it to look at me.

"What?" I'm seated on the table in the med-bay, wearing a plas-film little gown as he scans my mostly naked body. I should feel vulnerable and afraid, but I'm too worried over Adiron in Shaalyn's clutches to give myself much thought.

"Pregnant. You." When I continue to stare at him, he talks slower. "There's a baby growing inside your belly."

I blink, stunned. I touch my stomach. Here I thought I was sick of noodles and my breasts hurt because we were too vigorous in bed. Instead...I'm pregnant? "How is that possible?"

The male pirate sighs, as if utterly beleaguered by my questions. "When a male puts his penis inside of a female and ejaculates, his sperm can fertilize an egg inside of her."

I know that part, I want to snap at him. I press my lips together firmly, so I don't lose my shit. "I don't understand how

I can be pregnant," I say, choosing my words carefully. "I'm not mesakkah. I thought humans and mesakkah weren't compatible."

"They're not, usually." He shrugs, tapping away on his device as if it's far more important than answering my questions.

I reach out and put a hand over the damned thing, getting his attention. I ignore the cross look he gives me. "So...how?"

He tilts his head. "How did you end up on that ship?"

I lick my lips, thinking hard. "I...I don't know. I was stolen from my planet. Woke up in a stasis pod."

He pries my fingers off his device. "That'll do it, then. It's common among some slavers to give merchandise fertility treatments. They shoot you full of hormones and put you to sleep. Your new owner can decide if he wants to breed you or not. Kinda a bonus for reluctant buyers, you know?"

Oh my god. I think back to the other humans in the stasis pods. How there were a few pregnant ones. How, when our captors first woke us up, they were very, very careful to always use plas-film...

Oh my god.

It never occurred to me that this could happen. Now it's not just me and Adiron in danger. It's this baby. Shit...I don't even know if Adiron wants a baby. Kinda late to ask, though.

My captor turns back to the device in his hands, frowning. "Not sure if Shaalyn's going to want me to take it out of you, though. She didn't say."

"Leave it in for now," I blurt.

He looks up at me. "What?"

"More leverage," I say. "It's Adiron's. He's going to be very protective of it."

The pirate grunts. "Good point. I suppose we can always get rid of it later if we have to."

I want to scream at how casual he is. I want to wrap my

arms around my waist and race out the door, but I know I have to play this cool. I have to be just as stupid as they think I am, so they don't suspect anything. Then, when their guards are down, I can go retrieve the blaster I have hidden away underneath one of the sinks in the lavatory, and do some damage.

For now, though, I have to be a dummy. "So," I say brightly. "Will my next owner have a neat ship like this one?"

He shrugs. "Dunno."

I want to ask how many people are on here, but that might be too obvious. "Will I get a room of my own?"

The pirate snorts. "Doubtful. But if you're good, you might get to sleep at the foot of someone's bed."

I make a positive noise in my throat, even though I want to choke a bitch. Sleep at the foot of the bed like a dog, huh? For a moment, I let the fantasy of shooting this man in the nads play out in my mind. Then, I get back to work. "What about Adiron? What's going to happen to him?" I phrase it as cool as I can, even though I'm anxious as fuck inside.

To my relief, he just shrugs. "Boss has some history with him, so I imagine she'll toy with him for a while. Once she's tired of him, then she'll likely space him unless he joins the crew."

I let out a terrified whimper. My Adiron.

The pirate just pats my shoulder, then wipes his hand on his pants leg. "Don't worry. I'm sure the captain will keep you nice and safe. She's got an eye for things that make her credits."

I say nothing to that. Of course he thinks I'm worried about my own hide. I'm worried about Adiron, though. If something happens to him...I don't know what I'll do. I hug my arms to my chest as the alien continues to scan me with his device, and I try to be calm. Emphasis on "try." My thoughts are whirling, though. Kaspar and Alice are dead, according to Shaalyn and her crew...but Adiron didn't act worried. I have to have faith in him. If he doesn't think they're dead, then they're not dead. He hasn't steered me wrong so far. I take a deep, calming breath.

We just need to worry about our own asses.

"All right," the pirate says, and puts the medical device away. "Looks like everything's a clear scan. You're good to go into stasis."

I make a sound of protest in my throat. "Stasis? I don't want to go into stasis."

He snorts and taps a command onto the wall. "Well, we're sure not feeding and entertaining you for the next few months. Stasis makes more sense than a cage, especially with you pregnant."

As if my worst nightmares are coming true, a slender stasis pod slides out of the wall. He initiates another sequence, and then the door panel to the stasis pod opens, showing a lightly cushioned bed for the occupant. The knot in my throat is growing bigger and bigger. I can't go into stasis, because then I can't help Adiron escape. I can't go into stasis...because I'll lose all control of myself. What if I wake up two years from now? Ten? What if I wake up to find out Adiron's been killed? What if I wake up and they've taken my baby?

What if I wake up pregnant with someone else's baby, like the girls in the cargo bay back on the *Star*?

Panic floods through me, and when the alien reaches for my hand, I jerk away.

"Don't make this hard," he growls. "You—"

"Enough for now," a new, cool voice interrupts. We both turn, and Shaalyn is in the doorway, looking as elegant and put-together and nail-hard as ever. Her eyes narrow as she focuses on me. "I'd like to talk to Adiron's little plaything before you put her in cold storage," she says.

I wonder how much trouble I'd get into if I claw her eyes out?

64

JADE

*M*y skin prickles with fear as Shaalyn saunters toward me. How is it that one person can manage to look so completely menacing and yet sultry all at once? She eyes me up and down, considering me, and I can practically hear the dollar signs in her head. I'd forgotten what that look feels like—the one where you're regarded as a prize bit of livestock instead of an actual person—and I remain still as she circles around me. I glance out the door, but I don't see Adiron behind her.

I don't know if that's a good or a bad thing.

"The female is pregnant," the male pirate tells Shaalyn. "I was going to put her in stasis, unless you have a different preference?"

"Stasis is fine," Shaalyn replies coolly. "I just came to get a second look at her. My old lover is quite enamored, it seems. Won't stop asking about her." A flash of annoyance crosses her lovely features. "I wanted another look at her charms."

"Shall I leave, then?" the male pirate asks.

She turns and stares at him.

"Right. Leaving." He nods. "I'll take care of what's left once you've finished with her."

What's...left? My stomach drops.

Shaalyn just chuckles, though she doesn't move a finger as the male alien hastily exits the room. She eyes me, all amusement. "He thinks I mean to destroy you just to get revenge on my lover." She shakes her head, long ponytail swaying, as if this is foolishness. "As if I'd ever let so many credits go to waste."

She slinks forward, regarding me.

I say nothing, waiting for her to bring up Adiron. Waiting for her to bring up the baby. I'm not entirely sure how I feel about being pregnant, given that all of five minutes have passed, but I do know one thing.

If she tries to take this baby out of me, I will absolutely cut a bitch.

But for now, I have to remember my "stupid" act. I have to remember this is a woman who talks slowly in front of me because she thinks I'm too dumb to understand big words. So I keep my gaze unfocused and as helpless as possible. Calm, I remind myself. Focused. Wait for the right moment to retrieve your gun and then you can go apeshit on these assholes.

"Where's Adiron?" I ask, since that seems safe enough...and I have to know. If she's hurt him...

Shaalyn circles around me, pinching the fat of my arm and then squeezing my flank, as if I'm nothing but meat. I've suffered worse indignities, so I do my best to ignore it, especially when she touches my hair again. After a moment, though, she responds. "He's been taken to my hold until I decide what to do with him."

A prisoner, then. Okay. I feel some of the tension easing out of me. I can work with that. "Why? What did he do wrong?"

"Oh, my darling. You humans ARE simple, aren't you? I

swear, I don't see the appeal in keffing one, but there are all kinds of deviants in this galaxy." She gives a delicate little shudder, her tail swishing. "Let's just say he and I are at odds with what we want in the universe."

"And what's that?" She seems chatty enough that it seems like an okay thing to ask. Of all the things I expected Adiron's murderous ex-lover to be, chatty was not one of them.

"He wants adventure and fun. Adiron wants nothing more than to make his friends happy, a warm place to lay his head at night, and a warm cunt to fuck when he wants to fuck." Shaalyn shrugs delicately. "I want credits. It's very simple, really. Wealth is power, and I like wealth. You wouldn't understand."

I like Adiron's version of the world better than hers. I think she's wrong about him, too. It wouldn't surprise me if she underestimated him, given that she's still talking to me like she would a simpleton—or worse, a dog. "Adiron is nice," I say, trying to emphasize that yes, I am dumb, and please don't think about me too hard. "You should be nice to him."

"What a sweet little thing you are," she coos, touching my hair again. I want to slap her hand away, but I don't dare. "You're going to make someone very happy, you know, and bring me lots of credits." She taps her lip with a long finger, thinking. "You were one of the slaves in the pods, were you?"

I nod, going along with her questioning for now. "They got me out early. Wanted company."

"Were you the only one?" She pets my arm, stroking me in a mockery of Adiron's gentle touches. She...really does think I'm like a dog, doesn't she?

I decide to press it even further, moving to cuddle up against her. I want to punch her a billion times, but if I pretend to be dog-like, she'll let her guard down, won't she? So I snuggle against her, even though it feels like snuggling with a snake, and she enfolds her arms around me, humming with approval. Bitch. I force myself to smile, so I don't sound like the seething hatred I feel when I answer her. "Only one what?"

She pats my back. "Human, darling. Were you the only one woken up?"

She...knows this answer, doesn't she? If she ran into Kaspar and Alice—and killed them—she knows a lot more than she's pretending. It's a test, slyly inserted into a casual conversation. I try to think of the right answer to tell her. Do I lie and say it was just me and Alice? What if she's in contact with Straik and he's found Ruth? What would Alice have told her? I consider this for a moment. I don't think Alice would have told her anything. She would have protected Helen, and she wouldn't have said anything about me on the ship...except that Shaalyn knew I was there.

Unless that was a lucky guess.

Fuck. I...don't know what to do. "Two," I finally say. "Me and Alice. She's the blonde one that was with Kaspar."

"Mmm." She keeps rubbing my back, and I don't know if that's the right answer or not.

Desperately, I look around the room, wondering if there's something I can grab to use as a weapon. I'm in Shaalyn's arms...if I can find a knife, I can get revenge for Adiron. I never thought I was the type to murder someone in cold blood, but I like this idea far too much. I have to defend myself, I reason. The tablet-like med-scanner is in its compartment on the control panel, and it looks heavy enough that I might be able to do some damage if I use it on Shaalyn's head...maybe. Then again, maybe not. Adiron's plated brow is hard as rock, and she's got the same one, and the metal-covered horns. It wouldn't be like knocking out a human. I need something stabby.

I need my gun back.

"And where is the oldest va Sithai brother, hmm?" Shaalyn asks, interrupting my murderous thoughts.

"Who?" I blurt out.

"Mathiras va Sithai? He's the oldest one of the brothers, and the smartest. Where's he off to?" Her voice is calm and sweet.

"I don't know," I answer honestly, and then gloss it up with a lie. "I never saw him." I can't tell if Shaalyn buys my lie or not, so I decide to gloss it up with a little more acting. "I'm hungry. Do you have something other than noodles?" I make my voice as whiny as possible.

I'm not hungry, actually. But if I can leave this med-bay, I can get back to my gun and...what, hide it under my paper gown? I don't know. But Adiron's on this ship, and I need to stay awake to be with him. Better yet, I need to get the gun to him.

Shaalyn makes the clucking noise with her tongue again, as if I'm a naughty child. "Would you like fruit then, my darling? Something sweet?"

I lift my head, nodding.

She strokes my hair again. "Or perhaps a cake of some kind?"

"Yes, please." Preferably one with a file in it, so I can break Adiron out of his prison.

The long-fingered hand tightens on my hair, and suddenly my head is wrenched back, pain slamming through my body. I gasp in shock, staring at the menacing woman that looms over me. "Then you shouldn't have lied, should you? Do you think I'm stupid?" She pulls on my hair tighter, so painfully that I can feel strands of hair ripping out of my scalp. "Tell me the truth, you little shit. Where. Is. Mathiras?"

My eyes flood with tears of pain, but a different sensation courses through my body. Adrenaline. At least I don't have to pretend to like this bitch any longer. With all of my strength, I pull my hand back and punch Shaalyn right in that proud blue nose of hers.

Blood sprays everywhere. She shrieks.

I do, too. I'm pretty sure I've broken my hand. I'm also pretty sure she's going to kill me now.

Worth it.

65

ADIRON

I twiddle my thumbs as I lean against the wall of my prison cell, my tail flicking patterns into the dust on the tile floors. I can't help but compare Lord Straik's prison cell —the one with the gentle scents and shiny new walls—to Shaalyn's pit. There's crusted, dried blood on the plas-film bedding, the lavatory's little more than a hole cut into a panel, and I'm pretty sure it's overflowing. There's three cells down here in the dank, cold brig of Shaalyn's ship, and I'm pretty sure whoever was in cell number three died two days ago.

Then again, that smell might just be the overflowing lavatory.

Up above, I hear the sound of booted feet running back and forth, and I can't help but hope all that hubbub is Jade giving them utter hell. I worry about her—I wouldn't be a mesakkah male if I didn't worry about my mate—but I know she can take care of herself. I just want to hover over her while she does. Protectively. But she survived for years on her own without me.

She'll get through this, too. Shaalyn won't want to kill her. The moment Jade crawled out of that wall (taking all my hopes with her) I could practically see credits flashing in Shaalyn's eyes.

There's nothing that Shaalyn likes more than easy credits.

Right now, I'm guessing they've found the pods in the cargo bay and are trying to figure out the best way to extract them. I blew the door controls open, so it's not like they can't get in there. Getting in there isn't the problem at all. It's getting them out of the *Star* and back to civilized shipping lanes. Shaalyn's little cruiser is speedy, but it's not built to haul large cargo. She's more of a cut-and-run sort, a rob-them-and-leave-no-one-alive type. But the *Buoyant Star* is going to scream of credits—stripping that big ship would ensure a small fortune all on its own —and the ship and the cargo?

Shaalyn's going to want it all.

Which is a good thing for me. It means I've got some time to figure out how to get out of this hold, reunite with my female, and save the day. It's not going to be easy. I have no weapon. No plan. No allies. Jade's been separated from me. I'm outnumbered at least seven to one.

I've had worse odds, though.

I can figure something out, though. I just need an opportunity. As long as I don't give up (and I won't), something will present itself. Luck's great and all, but a lot of the time, it's less about luck and more about leaving yourself open to whatever falls into your lap. And when luck fails you, you make your own keffing luck.

I've been trying to make my own for the last few hours. There's no food or water down here. The plas-film is the type that won't tear no matter how much I fuss with it, so I can't turn it into a rope or a garrote. I could always fling shit—literal shit from the lavatory—onto my jailers in the hope that they'd come into my cell and pick a fight, but with my luck, they'd just gas me.

Or beat the stuffing out of me again. I rub the lump on the back of my head, wincing. I'm kind of glad Jade can't see me right now. She'd panic, because one of my eyes is swollen shut and my lip feels as big and inflated as Mathiras's ego. My knuckles are bloody and bruised and I'm pretty sure one of my fingers is broken, but at least I gave Shaalyn's crew a little work before they overpowered me.

I shouldn't be surprised that she's surrounded herself with young greenhorns. She always did love males who couldn't say no to her. It's a tick in the advantage box for me, though. They might be ruthless and amoral, but Shaalyn wants me alive...at least until she can torture me to death on her own. That means they'll do what she wants, so I need to use that. Add in the fact that her crew looks like they're all too young to have served in the Threshian Wars—and the fact that they hit about as hard as a drunken ooli—and it shouldn't be hard to take them down.

Just waiting on that advantage, and then I can get to work.

I get up and pace my cell again. There's no guards down here, which means they're utterly confident that I can't get out. Never a good sign. I'm not deterred, though. I tell myself they're just avoiding the smell and anyone creative enough can get free. I saunter over to the door and run a hand over the smooth metal walls, looking for a crack in the molding. When I find one, I wedge my fingernails in and try to pry it up. If I'm lucky, there'll be a few wires on this side and I might be able to splice something together.

Two broken fingernails and a removed panel later, I have to conclude that I'm not that lucky. I should have known the control wiring wouldn't be accessible from this side, but it was worth a shot. I pry at other panels, just to see what I can find, because I've got nothing to do but sit here and worry. Worry that they've done something terrible to Jade. Worry that one of Shaalyn's crew is "entertaining" himself with my human female. Worry that some keffing idiot's opened up Crulden the Ruiner's stasis pod—

A door down the hall opens up with a rush of compressed air, and I hastily shove the panel I'm working on back onto the wall. There are two others laying on my cot, so I carefully sit on top of them and lean back, crossing my arms and hoping I look casual enough that no one notices.

The slot in the door opens and a bowl is shoved through. Noodles.

"You got anything better than that?" I ask, not getting up. I'll take it, of course. A liquid is useful, because I might be able to short-circuit something with it. I just can't seem too eager. I think of Jade, again. Poor love—if they serve her noodles, she's really going to lose her shit. They've not sat well in her stomach for the last few days. She pretends like she's fine, but I notice.

I notice everything about her.

"You really complaining?" asks a slightly gruff, feminine voice. I can see nothing but a pair of blue-skinned hands through the meal slot, and the pirate drums impatient fingers on the surface. "Really? You should be thanking Shaalyn for feeding you."

I'm a little surprised that Shaalyn's got a female crew member. I thought she liked them young, muscled, and male. Guess she's branching out. "Speaking of your captain, where is she? I didn't expect her to let me sit down here, unmolested. I thought for sure she'd show up to start her torture games."

The pirate leans down, and I get a glimpse of shaggy hair in front of her face and a big eye patch. And a smell. Kef me, that smell's almost worse than the one two cells down. I discreetly put a hand to my nose and make a mental note not to eat the noodles the pirate's currently hovering over as she stares at me through the meal slot. "Shaalyn's been delayed."

"Great. Go away, then." If Shaalyn's delayed, I have a chance to do more rooting around.

The female snorts. "You really are dense, aren't you, Adiron?"

I frown, getting to my feet. The way the female says my name sounds familiar. I pace over to the meal slot and peer through, meeting the one-eyed gaze of the other. Kinda ugly and dirty looking, with a mop of nasty hair...but vaguely, vaguely familiar? "Who are you?"

The female flips the patch up and gives me an utterly exasperated look. "And here I thought this disguise wouldn't be enough. Turns out males really are dumb creatures." The voice modulates, growing more feminine, less ragged. "You really do only see what you want to."

I stare in surprise—and delight—at the female. "Bethiah! What are you doing here?"

Bethiah glares at me through the slot and flips the eye patch back down over her perfectly good eye. "Trying to rob this female of her ship, of course. You just had to show up and kef everything up, didn't you, you big fool."

I bite back a laugh of delight.

The universe has just given me the advantage I needed.

66

ADIRON

"Don't call me Bethiah," the female pirate hisses through the meal slot. "I'm Vathi on this ship."

I lean against the door. "What the kef are you doing here, Vathi?"

She snorts. "Didn't I just tell you?"

Yeah, but... "I'm gonna need a bit more context."

"Okay, well, I had an incident with my own ship—"

"Incident?"

She shrugs. "The original owner might have stolen it back. Whatever. Then, I'm on Haal Ui Station, drowning my sorrows in a vat of ooli brew, when this female just saunters in with a ship full of idiots." Bethiah-slash-Vathi shoves her face down into the food slot, next to my noodles. "I mean, if you staff with just greenhorns, you're just asking to be robbed, aren't you? So it's not really a bad thing. It's me teaching them a well-deserved lesson. Do you know how easy it was to get a job on this ship? It's pathetic, really."

I can guess. Shaalyn has a few weak spots, and most of them involve money. "Let me guess, you offered to work for cheap?"

"For free! An internship! I said I wanted the experience! And they bought it!" She shakes her head, incredulous. "They turned me down at first, but unfortunately for them, one of their crew had SUCH an unfortunate accident while on station. Really, such terrible timing." A wicked smile curves her lips. "They're so lucky I was there."

"The luckiest," I say dryly. Bethiah is my friend Jerrok's cousin and...I'm not entirely convinced she's not half-mad. Chaos seems to follow her, a lot of it entirely of her own making. "You killed him, didn't you?"

She shrugs. "If you're trying to make me feel guilty, I don't. He was not an upstanding sort. Do you want details?"

I shake my head and make a rolling gesture with my finger. "Just get on with it. How are you taking over this ship?"

"Well, my original plan was a much slower sort of takeover involving lots of mind-games. But that was before you showed up." She props up her chin on her hand, peering at me through the slot. "You're kinking my plans. Now I have to rethink things."

"Or we could work together," I propose. "Partners." Sure, partnering with Bethiah will be like partnering with a black hole—unstable and completely dangerous—but I'll take those chances.

"Mmm. I work best alone." She scrutinizes me. "Let's say I entertained thoughts of your partnership, though. What sort of split were you considering?"

I shake my head. "I don't want anything Shaalyn has. I just want to get out of here alive with Jade."

Bethiah rolls her eyes. "So you want to keep the human female? They fetch a fair amount of credits, you know. That's not exactly 'nothing.'"

"She's a person," I growl. "You're not allowed to sell her." I can see right now that I can't trust Bethiah any more than I can trust Shaalyn. The moment Jade's safe, I can't rely on Bethiah's assistance any longer. There are the people in the stasis pods to consider, too, but I'll take things one crisis at a time.

Right now, I'm focused on Jade. She's the only thing that matters, because if I lose her, I have nothing.

"Touchy, touchy," Bethiah says. "I guess that's an acceptable split...for now."

I don't miss the grudging tone in her voice. Until everything's settled, I'll be sleeping with one eye open and a blaster at my side. "So what's the plan?"

"Take over this ship," Bethiah says immediately. "Tow that derelict hulk to Jerrok's asteroid so he can strip it. Profit."

It's not the worst plan. Jerrok won't betray his cousin or me. His asteroid base is remote and secluded and the ships will need to be stripped of their identities before they're taken anywhere. And...Jerrok's sympathetic to humans. At least, I think he is. If anyone can make him sympathetic to a human's plight, it'll be our soft-eyed little Sophie. She's the gentlest little thing.

Poor Sophie. I hope she hasn't given up on me and my brothers.

My brothers...

I lean in toward Bethiah, confronting the piece of news I didn't want to think about. "Is what Shaalyn said about Kaspar true? Is he alive?"

She shrugs. "Ish?"

I scowl. "How can you be 'ish'? It's either a 'yes' or a 'no.'"

Bethiah gives an exaggerated shrug. "Okay, so technically it's a yes."

I breathe a sigh of relief.

"But!" she continues. "He might be dead now." When I give her a blank stare, she glances around the hall to make sure no one's listening and then leans in again. "We intercepted his pod.

He was in there with the yellow-haired human. Kinda cozy if you ask me, but I suppose you didn't. Anyhow. We pulled in their pod but ran into a problem. The human had a sickness, and so we couldn't extract him from the pod in case it was contagious. We kept the pod in our bay overnight. I think Shaalyn wanted to keep him until their health could be cleared, because you know she's never met an opportunity she didn't like."

She's right. I don't know how I ever missed this before. Shaalyn has always been greedy and all about herself. I was just too dazzled by her to think it was a problem...until she turned on me, of course. Jade's nothing like her, and I couldn't be more thankful. "What happened, then?"

A ruthless little smile curls Bethiah's mouth. "There was an accident in cargo bay. They must have broken out somehow. Took down a perfectly attractive, completely inexperienced greenhorn, too. Such a shame that sort of thing keeps happening."

I breathe a sigh of relief. Bethiah had a hand in that, too, then. "Thank you."

"Like I said, though, the human was sick." She shrugs. "Don't know what happened after that, but it's Kaspar. He'll turn up somewhere, probably with the authorities from three different planets chasing his tail."

Truer words never spoken. "How do we play this, then?"

Her smile grows even more dangerous. "As brutally as we want."

67

ADIRON

I've got Bethiah on my side, and I almost feel bad for Shaalyn.

Almost.

"So when do we do this?" I ask Bethiah, leaning against the door. The noodles she brought are congealing slowly, as our conversation goes on for longer than anticipated, but I don't care. More important things are afoot. "Tonight, when everyone's sleeping? Tomorrow?"

She shakes her head and looks around again. "Our window of opportunity is right now, if you're ready to do this."

"Right now?" I echo, surprised. So fast? "Why right now? Not that I'm not ready, just curious."

Bethiah smirks, then straightens and types an access code into the control panel of the door. A moment later, it slides into the wall, sending the bowl of noodles tumbling to the filthy floor of my cell. "Poor, poor Shaalyn is nursing a busted nose and wounded pride."

Busted nose? Wounded pride? "Jade?" I ask.

"Jade. Your little human's a fierce one."

Kef yes, she is. I grin. "That's my girl. Where is she?" My heart thumps as I glance over at the next cell, but it's empty, of course. I knew it was, but...there's only so many places to hold someone on a cruiser like this. I turn back to Bethiah, a horrible feeling clenching in my gut. "Shaalyn didn't..."

Bethiah shakes her head, tapping away at the panel to the elevator off this floor. After a moment's frustration, she sighs and pulls out her blaster, then shoots the panel. A curl of smoke rises from it, an alert chirping. She ignores it and glances over at me. "Your human is safe, because she's worth a lot of credits. Shaalyn would have killed her otherwise. Instead, she just put her in stasis. Cold."

"Cold?" I shudder. Being sent into stasis cold is brutal. It's only happened to me once, when there was no time to administer the drugs to slowly ease me under. It's an awful feeling, of being closed in and trapped in the pod while your veins are fed liquid ice that feels as if it's freezing you bit by bit. You're awake while your limbs stop responding, and your brain is the last to go under. I know of weathered soldiers who don't bat an eye at the worst war has to offer, but panic at the sight of a stasis pod.

And she did that to my Jade? My soft, funny, loves-to-be-in-control Jade? "She did it to get back at me," I growl. "Keffing Shaalyn."

"Don't take all the credit," Bethiah says drily. "I'm pretty sure the fist to the nose had something to do with it, too."

Right. Doesn't matter. If I get my hands on Shaalyn...well, I'm going to see if Jade wants to kill her first. "Where's her pod at? Med-bay?"

Bethiah nods once, handing me a blaster. "No time to go play tongue-games with your human right now. We need to move. She left a blaster in the lavatory, you know."

I frown to myself, trying to follow Bethiah's line of conversation. "I want to see Jade and make sure she's all right. I won't wake her up yet." I want things to be completely safe before she opens those beautiful eyes again, just because I need her to know I can take care of her. That I've got her back. That I'll always look out for her. "And uh...who left a blaster in the lavatory?"

My partner glares at me. "Pay attention! This is no time to moon over a human!"

I want to shake her with frustration. "I'm not mooning. But I'm also not doing this without knowing if she's safe or not." She's the most important thing in the universe to me, and I need to make sure she's all right. How Jade's been treated is going to determine whether or not Shaalyn dies fast or dies slow.

"Does it matter if she's safe or not? She's a human. She can't help us in this fight. Did you not hear the part where I said she left a keffing blaster in the lavatory? It fell onto the floor when I was taking a shit." Bethiah makes a face. "She's lucky I'm the one that found it."

My Jade snuck a blaster on board the ship? I know she didn't have it with her when she came out of the wall and Shaalyn took her captive. I thought she'd dropped it or left it behind. Instead, she smuggled it in somehow. My pride for my female raises a few notches. She's so smart and clever. I grin. "Atta girl."

Bethiah just rolls her eyes as if I'm an idiot. "Just...come on."

"Med-bay first," I insist stubbornly. "Then we kick everyone's asses."

68

ADIRON

*O*ur plans to kick everyone's ass aren't going as, well, planned.

Since the elevator won't respond thanks to an impatient Bethiah shooting the controls, we take an emergency access ladder hidden away in one of the walls and climb up. Once we get on the main floor of the ship, though, we run into one of Shaalyn's greenhorns. He's sprawled on the floor, his blaster gone, a pool of blood cooling around him.

I nudge him with my toe, but he's dead. "You do this?" I ask Bethiah.

"No." She frowns down at him. "Come on. Let's just get to med-bay."

We head there and find another dead body in the hall. So much for kicking asses. Turns out the asses have already been kicked. I pat the dead male down anyhow, but he's very much dead and there's no weapon. "Another mutiny?"

"Shaalyn's idiots? Not likely." Bethiah snorts. "I'm starting to think she's onto us, though."

"Well, you DID shoot the control panel." A subtle partner, she's not. "They'd have to be unconscious not to notice something's up."

Bethiah just gives me an exasperated look. "Just come on already. The sooner we take over this ship, the sooner it's mine." Her expression turns toothy, and then she races down the hall, her blaster out.

Kef me. And I thought *I* was the dumb one. Maybe pairing up with Bethiah isn't the best idea, but too late to turn back now.

We find two more bodies along the way to the med-bay. "How many does that leave?"

"Two and Shaalyn," Bethiah replies, standing outside the med-bay doors. She peers in and then indicates it's clear. "Go lick your human or whatever it is they do with their mouths, and then let's go take Shaalyn down, all right?"

"It's called kissing," I tell her. I shove my blaster into the waist of my pants and head for the stasis pod that's lit up, the window fogged with the chill inside it. I run my hand over the glass, and I see Jade inside. She's unconscious, her full lips with a blue tinge to them. Her clothes are gone and she's naked, her hair a halo around her face. She's calm looking, though, and whole. Thank kef. I feel like I can breathe again. I stare down at her. She's so beautiful that my heart hurts just looking at her. "I'm going to take care of this," I whisper. "You can count on me."

I touch the glass one more time and force myself to turn away from her. I want to pry her out of there, but I can't. It takes time to recover from stasis, and I can't risk her being hurt. Shaalyn's not going to play fair, and me and Bethiah are used to space battles and backstabbing pirates. We can handle ourselves.

And if we can't...I don't want Jade to face the consequences.

"I'm ready," I growl as I storm out of the med-bay. Seeing my mate—because Jade is absolutely, positively MINE—laying there in stasis has flipped a switch in my head. Gone is carefree Adiron. In his place is an angry, protective male out to get revenge for his mate. Shaalyn's going to wish she never touched one single curl on Jade's head.

"Yay!" Bethiah cries, bounding after me. "Let's go take my ship!"

We storm through the halls, heading for the bridge. I'm not entirely surprised to find that when we get there, the doors are sealed, the control panel shot out, and yet another dead male on the floor in front of us. She's cannibalizing her own crew to save her hide. It's a foul move, but one I'm not entirely surprised to see. Of course Shaalyn cares only about Shaalyn. She can always find more idiot males to dance to her tune. If nothing else, she's good at convincing a male that she's in love with him.

Been there. Done that. Got a gut full of stab wounds to show for it.

I turn to Bethiah and gesture at the bridge doors. "Don't suppose you know how to get this open?"

She shrugs, a bright smile on her face. "Shoot it until something opens?"

I'm never going to give my brothers shit again for groaning at one of my bad ideas. I stare at her.

She shrugs again. "Space her?"

I shake my head. "The bridge is locked down tight. She has access to all the controls there. We can't space her. If we try to force our way in, she could destroy all the controls and leave us stranded here. We need a plan."

Bethiah taps her blaster on her chin. "Want to try negotiating?"

"With *her*? Are you serious?"

"Oh, I'm sorry. I didn't realize you were swimming with so

many other ideas?" Bethiah hisses at me. "Why are you being such a grump? I thought that was Mathiras."

Am I like Mathiras? I guess when it comes to Jade and her safety, I'm turning into a boring stodge, just like my brother. I'm not even mad about it, either. I just need to make sure Jade is safe, and if Bethiah doesn't like my plans, too bad. "You do realize negotiating with Shaalyn is pointless? She's just going to lie to you to save her skin."

"So? Like I'm going to keep my end of the bargain?" Bethiah looks at me as if I'm insane. "I'll say whatever we need as long as we get her ass out of the bridge so we can take control."

I don't have any better ideas, so I gesture for Bethiah to do her best.

She steps up and taps a communication request onto the panel.

Waits.

Glances over at me.

Waits a bit longer.

"Initiating vacuum sequence," the ship chirps helpfully. "Airlocks will be opened in ten minutes. Please secure all loose equipment."

Bethiah and I exchange a look of horror.

Shaalyn isn't going to negotiate. She's going to expel us from the ship itself.

69

ADIRON

I race to the door panels, but the controls are a bright red, the alert flashing over the screen. Not only are they locked down, but the sequence can't be changed.

I'm glad Jade's still in stasis. She'll be fine. I'm just sad I won't be there when she wakes up. I look over at Bethiah. "Any last words?"

"This is some bullshit," she grumbles, shoving past me and pounding on the panel as if that will somehow activate it. She hammers at it, and then lets out an incoherent cry of rage. "I am not going to be bested!"

She's taking this rather poorly. I watch her have a tantrum for a moment longer, and then I turn and head down the hall to med-bay.

"Where are you going?" Bethiah asks me.

"Gonna go spend my last few minutes with my mate," I tell her. Really, we've walked into a boneheaded trap. The moment Shaalyn suspected things were turning on her, she secured herself in the room with all the controls. If Bethiah was half as clever as she thought, she'd have locked down the ship herself before starting her mutiny.

Nothing to be done about it now, though. It was an attempt, and not all attempts are successful. I'm just sad I won't get to see Jade smile again. To hear that soft, reluctant laugh of hers when I do something ridiculous and unexpected. My chest squeezes painfully. We should have had more time together. It's unfair to only be given a little over a month with the female I love, only to lose her. I'm not normally one to mope about fate, but all I can think about is Jade. Jade waking up and I'm not there. Jade feeling like I abandoned her, when it's the furthest thing from the truth.

I'm going to spend the last of my time draped over her stasis pod, gazing down into her beautiful, sleeping face. I want her to be the last thing I see before the vacuum of space sucks me out of the ship. I want—

I pause as I head down the hall toward med-bay.

Turn around.

Head back to the window I just passed.

There's a ship there. A very familiar-looking ship. As I watch, it extends the ship-to-ship docking mechanism, like a long, thin finger, even as the *Jabberwock* pulls up alongside Shaalyn's ship.

"Nine minutes until airlocks are opened," the ship says helpfully. "Please secure all loose equipment." It pauses for a moment and then continues in the same expressionless voice, "Unfamiliar vessel initiating ship-to-ship docking sequence. Please advise."

I shove my face against the glass, wondering if my sister can see the delight on my face from her ship. Probably not. Talk about a rescue in the nick of time. I race back down the hall, nearly collide with Bethiah, who giggles and does a happy little dance and then rushes right next to me as we head for the portal. The ship-to-ship dock extends painfully slowly and then pauses right before it can connect, and my heart skips a painful beat.

"*Jabberwock* hailing the *Decision Maker*," comes Zoey's voice over the intercom, and it's like a breath of fresh air. My little sister sounds so strong and in control, and I could not be prouder. "You have ten minutes to accept our docking sequence, or we will take drastic action."

Uh oh.

"Uh." Bethiah looks over at me. "This is going to be an incredibly ironic death, isn't it?"

"I sure hope not." I try to send positive brainwaves to Zoey— as if that'll do shit. Move faster, I tell her silently. We're about to be splattered on your windshield.

Another tense minute ticks past, and it feels like I have rocks in my stomach as I stare at the *Jabberwock's* docking connection, still frozen in place.

Come on, runt, I tell her. Come on. All the while, I wait for the next tick of the countdown to my death.

There's an unearthly cry of rage that comes from the bridge, so loud we can hear it through the walls.

"System override," the ship says, and Bethiah grabs my arm. "Vacuum sequence cancelled. Accepting ship-to-ship connection."

"I did not accept this!" Shaalyn cries angrily over the intercom. "You are not allowed on board! This is a hostile takeover!"

My sister's voice comes in, strong and proud. "As opposed to, what, a polite and friendly takeover? Better hold on, because you're not gonna like what else we do, either, bitch."

I race to the control panel, trying to send my sister a message, but I'm still locked out. I hammer a hand against the wall in frustration and begin to pace, watching as the dock slowly, slowly creeps toward Shaalyn's ship and eventually latches on with a whoosh of air and a chorus of messages announcing the connection. A million thoughts are racing through my mind—how did Zoey know we were here? Is Shaalyn going to retaliate somehow? Did Kaspar or Mathiras somehow contact the *Jabberwock* and let them know about the fact that I remained behind on the *Star*?

More importantly, will Zoey like Jade? Will Jade like Zoey? I want them to get along. They're the two most important females in my life, and the thought of them not liking each other makes my palms all sweaty.

Or...that could just be the near-death experience.

I glance over at Bethiah. Her ratty hair is disheveled, held back by her patch that's now resting against her horns like a headband instead of on her face. The look on her face is all smiles, though. "Never thought I'd be so glad to see that idiot Kivian," she tells me. "You think he'll let me have this ship? Since I practically took it anyhow?"

I shrug. "Can't hurt to ask nicely. And maybe don't call him an idiot."

She puts on a sweet smile. "He's a clever, clever male...and I love his outfits."

I snort at that. Impatience bubbles through me as I glance toward the bridge. My weapon's still at the ready, but I doubt Shaalyn's going to come out. She's probably destroying as much equipment as she can now that the *Jabberwock* has hacked into her systems and taken over. I stare out into space at the *Jabberwock* and see a couple of figures heading down through the ship-to-ship connection. I want it to be my sister... but at the same time, it's far too dangerous for her to be the first one to board an enemy vessel. If it is her, I'm going to give her a stern talking-to...right after I hug the living kef out of her.

Impatiently, Bethiah and I wait for the doors to open. There's a hiss and the faint metallic smell of space. Then, two big males charge in, blasters held high. Before I can even blink, the smaller soldier—Alyvos—has one pointed at my forehead. Tarekh pins down Bethiah with his.

I put my hands up in the universal sign of surrender. "Okay, maybe I'm not as glad to see you two as I thought, if that's the welcome we're going to get," I joke.

Alyvos lowers his gun a fraction and stares at me in surprise. "Adiron? What the kef are you doing here?"

"Surprise," I say, grinning.

70

ADIRON

"This is my ship," Shaalyn snarls as Tarekh drags her into the hold and places her in the middle cell. He throws the last surviving greenhorn in with her, a male that looks more confused than indignant.

"Don't care if it's your ship," Tarekh says easily. "Not sure what part of 'We're robbing you' that you don't understand." He slams the door shut and leans against it, grinning up at me. "You sure you don't want her dead?"

In the cell, Shaalyn makes an indignant noise.

"I want to ask my female if she'd rather do the honors," I tell him. Upstairs, I can hear booted feet as the rest of the *Jabber-wock's* crew takes over the hijacked ship. Bethiah's up there with them, but I came with Tarekh, because I had to make sure that Shaalyn was locked up behind bars and safely put away. When she is, then I can relax.

"Your female?" Tarekh echoes, a surprised look on his face.

He puts his blaster away and crosses his arms over his chest. "You and Bethiah...?"

I make a choked sound. "No. Not Bethiah. Mine is Jade. She—"

There's a happy little cry and before I can fully turn around, Zoey's flying down the ladder. She flings herself at me, all arms and legs, and I snatch her out of midair in the biggest hug possible.

"What the fuuuuck, Adi?" she cries, even as she squeezes my neck. "What are you doing here?"

"Hello, runt," I say happily, hugging my sister tight. "Glad to see they're taking care of you."

"I can't believe you're here," she sobs. I pat Zoey awkwardly, giving Tarekh a look. Zoey doesn't cry much. She's a tough little nugget, just like we raised her. I'm not sure if she wants Tarekh to see her weeping, so I carry her a short distance away, reluctant to let her go. Holding her in my arms like this reminds me of when she was just the littlest scrap, all attitude and spindly legs as she tried to learn how to be a proper corsair. It makes me long for those old times, just for a moment, when life was easier, and the four of us gave the universe hell while in the *Little Sister*.

Now the ship's missing and my brothers are, too. But I have Jade...and I have my sister, Zoey. It's something, at least.

She composes herself, sniffling, and wipes her face on my tunic. Then, she smacks my shoulder. "Put me down. I'm not a baby."

"Are you sure? You're just the littlest runt," I say, using my baby voice. "Who's a widdle bitty human? You are! Yes you are!"

Zoey scowls. In the next moment, she licks her finger and shoves it in my ear.

"Argh!" I set her down, rubbing my ear and laughing. "I guess I deserve that."

"You absolutely do," Zoey says smugly, and then flings

herself into my arms again for another hug. "Are Mathiras and Kaspar here?"

My spirits plummet. "You haven't seen them?"

"They're not with you?" She gives me a worried look. "We found the *Little Sister* a while back, empty and in Slatran space, of all places. No sign of any of you."

"We had to split up back on the *Buoyant Star*," I explain. "It's a long story and one I should tell you later. How did you know I was here if you didn't run into Kaspar or Mathiras?"

"We didn't," Zoey exclaims. She pokes my chest and glances over at Tarekh, who's still leaning against the prison cell and probably will be until we decide what to do with the two in there. "We were out searching for you guys, and then we intercepted a distress signal from Shaalyn. Said she had a mutiny, and I figured it'd be a good time to score some easy credits and teach that bitch a lesson." Her lip curls. "Please, please tell me you didn't get back together with her."

I'm stung. "You really think I'm that dense?"

Zoey purses her lips.

Tarekh coughs.

"Sometimes, you, ah, don't make good choices," Zoey tells me. "That's all I'm saying."

"I love Jade," I say, still mildly offended at the thought of preferring Shaalyn to the most perfect creature in the universe. "She's kind, and strong, and loving, and always wants to do the right thing, even if it's inconvenient for her. She thinks of others first. She's keffing gorgeous, and she has this wonderful laugh and this amazing hair and the softest keffing skin and the most beautiful eyes. She's smart, too. So smart. And..." I shake my head. "I can't believe you thought for a moment that I'd prefer Shaalyn to her."

Zoey just gives me an utterly blank look. "Who the kef is Jade?"

I scratch at my chin. "I didn't mention Jade yet? She's my mate."

"Your mate?" my sister yelps, her eyes wide. "When the fuck did this happen?" She puts her wrist close to her face and activates a personal comm. "Sentorr, my idiot brother's gone and mated someone without telling me!"

"Does he have to check in with you first, love?" Sentorr's starchy voice is calm and easy and ever-so-slightly amused, as if he finds everything his mate does just cute as could be.

"Of course not! But I'd like to be told...and you're not helping!"

"Love you," is all he says.

"Love you, too," my sister barks at her wrist and then kills the connection. She turns her focus back to glaring at me. "You could have said something to me!"

"I'm saying something now? This is kinda the first chance I had."

My sister just scowls at me. She continues to scowl at me as if I'm somehow to blame as I steer her through the ship. All around us, it's chaos. It's a familiar chaos, though. It's the chaos that comes with the takeover of a craft. Alyvos moves through the ship, dragging bodies toward the airlock so they can be disposed of. Cat, Tarekh's tiny human female, is busy disabling panels so no one can do additional overrides or try to take the ship back over. As we walk past her, she jerks out a handful of wires and gives us a toothy grin. Somewhere in the distance, I can hear what sounds like Kivian arguing with Bethiah on the bridge while Kivian's mate Fran tosses valuables into a lockbox as she raids the storerooms. They're efficient, these pirates.

As my sister complains about how I've gone and got myself mated behind her back, I make it to med-bay. Jade's stasis pod is still untouched, thank kef, and I move toward it and put a hand on the surface protectively. "This is my mate," I tell my sister. "Isn't she beautiful?"

Zoey's expression softens and she peers at the female inside. "A human?"

"Well...yeah." I frown at her. "You thought she was mesakkah?"

Zoey flings her hands up. "We're surrounded by mesakkah constantly! Why wouldn't I think that?"

Excellent point. I activate the controls on the stasis pod, and the top peels back, letting out a puff of frigid air. Jade's bare skin looks slightly frosty, and I shrug off my tunic, because she's going to be cold. "I dunno. She's just so perfect that it never occurred to me that you thought she'd be anything else. She's just...Jade." I hover protectively over the pod, watching my mate's face carefully. I want to be the first thing she sees when she opens her eyes. "I wouldn't want her to be anything other than what she is. I hope you like her."

Zoey just sighs. "You big romantic dummy. Of course I'm going to like her. If you love her, I'm sure she's amazing."

"So amazing," I agree. I scan Jade's face. Is that a flutter of her lashes?

As I watch, Jade sucks in a deep breath, the same gasping, terrified sound everyone makes when they're coming out of stasis. It's like being interrupted out of a long, intense nightmare when you come out of stasis, and I'm sure she'll be disoriented. Her eyes open a crack, and she looks up at me with confused eyes, her pupils enormous.

My beautiful mate lifts one small fist...and promptly socks me in the nose.

71

JADE

*T*he last thing I remember is Shaalyn's face smirking down at me as the cold rips through my veins. Then, nothing but ice and darkness.

When my lungs fill with burning air again and I wake up, I'm terrified and confused. My eyes are unfocused, and my entire body hurts. It feels as if I've been flash-frozen and then left out to thaw, and it's painful. A blue face looms in close again, and instinct kicks in.

I punch.

My hand explodes in pain and I bite back a whimper, even as the blue face falls back. Then, there's a low, familiar groan. It's the sound I've heard dozens of times before, usually in bed, though.

"Adiron?" I whisper, desperately squinting at my surroundings. "Where are you?"

"How is it all those tiny wiggly fingers can pack such a hit?" my big alien asks, his voice jovial despite the fact that it sounds like he's pinching his nose. His tone is muffled, but a moment later when the big, blurry blue face leans in again, I can just make out his familiar grin.

Oh. Oh. "Adi. I'm sorry." I reach up and touch his face, and he covers my hand with his. He's so damn warm and my fingers feel like ice. "I thought—"

"I know. It's okay. You're safe now. Can you sit up?"

When I nod, he puts a hand to the base of my neck and helps me sit. It takes a moment, but I realize I'm still in med-bay, still naked with dozens of tubes attached to my skin, and still in the hated, hated stasis pod. A whimper escapes me as bad memories flood back. "I want to get out of this thing."

"I've got you," Adiron says gently. He helps me yank the tubes off, each one leaving behind a little prick of pain as it exits my skin. Then, his big warm hands are on my back and he lifts me out of the stasis pod and into his arms. In the next moment, I'm curled against warm, familiar chest and he drapes fabric around me. "Did they hurt you?" Adiron asks, the protectiveness back in his voice.

I swallow hard. I want to whine that they did, that after I punched Shaalyn she had her goons hold me down and shove me into the stasis pod, kicking and screaming. That it was awful and traumatizing, because I could feel my body dying as the chemicals spread through my veins to put me to sleep. That she just smirked down at me as if it gave her great pleasure to fuck me over. But I'm alive, and I've woken up in Adiron's arms, so I can live with this. I can be fragile later, in private. "I'll be all right. Where's that bitch?" I peer around the room. "We're still on her ship. Where is she? I'm going to kill her."

"She's imprisoned," Adiron tells me, adjusting the blanket around me as a cocoon. "We've taken over the ship."

I shake my head, tucking myself against his chest. "I...I don't understand. How?"

"Let's just say that the stars aligned in our favor." He presses a gentle kiss to my forehead. "If you're done punching things, I'd like to introduce you to my sister."

"Your...sister? Zoey?" My brain must be fried from stasis because none of what he says makes sense. "She was on the ship somewhere?"

"Er...no. We've been rescued."

"We have?" I rub my eyes, but my fingers are so cold and my eyes so blurry that I feel like a popsicle. A popsicle with a brain still frozen.

"Maybe we should get her something to eat," says another voice. It's human, and female, though she speaks with the same sharp accent in English that Adiron does. His sister. I peer around, but my eyes feel like bricks of ice and I can't see farther than a few feet.

"Food's a good idea," Adiron says, pressing another kiss to my forehead. He cradles me against his chest and shifts his weight, getting to his feet. "Stasis on an empty belly can be hard. She'll perk up once she has something in her."

The woman who must be Zoey groans. "Must. Resist. So. Many. Filthy. Puns."

Adiron just chuckles.

I press my face closer to his neck, breathing in his scent as the world bobs around me. My stomach isn't doing so hot, but then again, what part of me *is* right now? Some water and something cracker-like will settle my gut and perk me up.

Zoey speaks again. "You know what she needs? A big bowl of piping hot noodles."

Noodles. Just the word brings to mind a bowl of the hated things, and their scent, and my stomach rebels. My mouth fills with saliva and a cold sweat breaks out over my skin.

"Uhhh," Adiron says as the knot in my throat grows enormous.

I tap on his chest, bile rising. My guy must know what's up, because he sets me down a split second before I puke everywhere.

"We're gonna have to find something other than noodles," Adiron says, good-humored. "Jade, love, let me know when it's all out. I've got you." He holds my hair back and pets my shoulder as I get sick everywhere.

It's ridiculous, to be so sick over nothing at all. I tell myself it's the stasis and an empty stomach. I tell myself it's nerves and the gently swaying movement of the ship. I'm lying to myself, of course. I know exactly what it is. It's a baby. Our baby. And I don't know how Adiron is going to feel about that.

He's a pirate. I'm not exactly sure "dad" is high on his list of career choices. Even if it is...how can I mention it? His brothers are still missing. He needs to go after them. I'm just not sure what that means for me.

It also means that I can't go back to the *Star*, either. Lost in space is no place for a baby.

Maybe it's the stomach ache talking, or the stasis drugs, but I've traded one crisis for another. Sure, Adiron loves me when we're by ourselves and snuggled in bed. But how does a baby fit into his life?

Or is he going to ask me to get rid of it?

72

JADE

To my everlasting relief, this ship has foods other than noodles. I nibble on a protein bar and drink a cup of hot tea, curled up in Adiron's lap as he strokes my hair and the cleaning bots whirr in action behind us.

The crew of the *Jabberwock*—whom it seems showed up and hijacked the pirates, of all things—are busy in action, stripping the ship, overriding systems, and arguing with someone named Bethiah, who wants the ship and doesn't like that they're taking everything.

"Bethiah's a friend," Adiron murmurs into my ear when I ask. "An absolute lunatic, but a friend."

I'm still having a hard time digesting everything that went on while I was in stasis. Though I wasn't "under" for longer than a few hours, a lot has happened. After the pirates took Adiron captive, he schemed with Bethiah to turn on the crew, but it seems that Shaalyn was onto them, double-crossed her men and killed them before she could be taken, hid on the bridge, and then the *Jabberwock* showed up.

It's a hell of a lot of coincidence, but Adiron and the others seem to take it in stride. Of course the *Jabberwock* was nearby— Zoey has been looking for Adiron and his brothers. Of course Bethiah was on the ship and offered to help Adiron. It seems that space pirates are a lawless, hijacking lot who are unsurprised by constant double-crossing.

And I'm pregnant with a space pirate's baby. So, you know, no pressure or anything.

I keep the news about the baby silent, though. There's so much other information flying around that stepping forward and blurting that I'm carrying Adiron's baby seems like bad timing.

Adiron and I sit together on the bridge. He's found a seat big enough for the two of us to sit, me with my legs over his lap and a little tray in mine, so I can have my tea and crackers. I'm still wearing nothing but his shirt, but no one seems to notice my nudity...or the fact that I'm human. They're too busy. I listen in as Zoey talks up a storm to Adiron. She's not what I expected his sister to look like when he said she was human. I don't know why, but for some reason I pictured Zoey with impish features and red hair. Kinda like Pippi Longstocking or some shit, the ultimate sisterly vibe. Zoey is nothing like that, of course. She's a little short, even for a human, and top-heavy. She's white, with flat brown hair and an average face, but when she smiles, it's that naughty smirk similar to Adiron's and it's obvious that they've grown up together.

She also cusses a blue streak, which I would expect any pirate to do, really.

Adiron won't leave my side, so Zoey leans against a nav panel that an overdressed someone named Kivian is working on. She tells Adiron that they found the brothers' ship at someplace called V'tarr Station, and it had been found abandoned.

Adiron, in turn, tells Zoey all about meeting up with Lord Straik and teaming up together to hunt down the *Buoyant Star*. "Really, no one should have picked up the *Little Sister*, considering we left her floating in the middle of nowhere with no distress signal. We figured we'd just swing by and hop in once we were done."

Zoey just rolls her eyes. "You fucking idiots lost your keffing brains when I left, didn't you?" She crosses her arms over her chest. "Lucky for you guys, the *Little Sister's* safe. Jerrok and Sophie took her back to his station, and he's going to give her a quick tune-up while we were out hunting for you."

"And no sign of Mathiras or Kaspar?" Adiron asks again. He's already asked more than once, but I know how it feels to not want to accept what you're hearing.

"Not a goddamn peep," Zoey says, frowning. "I'm sure they're out here somewhere. We just have to find them. Think like them. If you were Kaspar, what would you do?"

"Run head-first into danger?" Adiron smirks, even as he rubs one of my feet absently.

"Exacta-mundo." Zoey says. "Plus, if Shaalyn really did rendezvous with his escape pod like she said, we'll have coordinates in the ship's logs. We'll find them and go from there. It's as good a place to start as any."

"And Straik?" Adiron asks.

"Haven't looked for him." Zoey shrugs. "Haven't bothered. One messy bitch at a time."

Adiron glances over at me. He squeezes my ankle, as if he knows what I'm thinking. "We need to find him, too. He's got one of Jade's people on board his ship. She's going to need rescuing."

"Like I said, one crisis at a time." Zoey looks disgruntled. "Surely he can wait for a while? What's his connection to all this shit other than he's got a human on board?"

"It's not just that. We've got to get our hands on the *Star* again before he does. If he turns around and goes back, I worry what's going to happen with the ship."

Kivian pauses and leans over the control panel in front of him. His sleeves look like they have more fabric on each arm than I do on my entire body, and all of it shimmers. "Can I just say it's damned odd that he'd spend all that time hunting for his family's ship, then turn around and leave in the middle of the night? Seems strange and unlike him." He shakes his head. "Rumor has it that he's fairly ruthless. What is it that's got him tucking his tail?"

Zoey tilts her head. "Who cares about him? I want to know what was on the *Star*." Her eyes glitter with excitement. "Silks? Weapons?"

"Oh, kef." Adiron grimaces. "Speaking of problems..."

73

JADE

"*H*umans?" Zoey swallows, pale.

"A whole kef-ton of them," Adiron agrees. "We think Straik was just as shocked as we were, and that's why he ran. Didn't like finding out his precious family was into dirty business." His big hand plays over my foot, rubbing the underside and then tweaking my little toe. It's a silent call-out to me, that little touch, because he's always joking about how our "extra" toes and fingers are weird. He's trying to distract me.

It's sweet, and it makes me love him all the more.

"What do we do?" Zoey asks, glancing over at Kivian.

Kivian doesn't even hesitate. "My brother lives on a farm planet that shelters humans. They'll be safe from slavery there. They'll get a plot of land, a home, and they can be free. We just have to get them there."

Adiron looks over at me, and I realize that if I object, he'll support me. It's a good feeling. "I suppose Earth is out of the question?" I ask, because I have to. It doesn't come up at all, so I suspect it's not an option, but I still have to ask.

The hand on my feet tenses, ever so slightly.

"There's nothing left to go back to," Zoey blurts out, her expression hard. "Earth had an 'event' a few years back and the world as we know it is gone. Unfortunately, mesakkah space is all there is for us."

"Oh," I say softly. So much death. All of humanity...gone? I can't process it. Maybe it'll sink in later, but for now it doesn't register. Absently, I wonder what it was that finally killed my planet—nuclear bombs? Global warming? I guess it doesn't matter, but it makes me sad. I'm three years gone from life on Earth, but those in the pods aren't aware of what's happened. "Farm planet it is, then."

"It's the best, I think," Zoey says.

"Some of the stasis pods house gladiators," Adiron says, a warning in his breath. "One or two dangerous ones particularly. Crulden the Ruiner's in there."

Zoey looks nonplussed, but Kivian's eyes widen.

"If that's the case, then there's bound to be a bounty or two for their safe return." Kivian shrugs. "We can return them to pay for fuel costs, or turn them over to the authorities to be properly imprisoned."

"Imprisoned?" I ask. "Why?"

"They're killers." Kivian and Adiron exchange a glance. "Killers that are usually pumped full of chemicals and trained to kill whatever's in front of them...so they're rewarded with a nubile female slave. You can't mix them in with the normal population."

Oof. Okay. I have to remember that this end of the universe has different rules to what's acceptable in their society. How ironic that a kiss is considered revolting, but they don't blink an eye at a gladiator tearing his enemy apart. "All right. When do we take the humans to this planet, then?"

"Once we get this ship coded over to Bethiah—"

Bethiah pops her head up from behind a panel and grins wickedly. "I'm glad we came to an agreement on that."

Zoey rolls her eyes. "More like no one wanted to hear you screeching all the way back to Jerrok's asteroid."

"Effective, isn't it?" Bethiah seems unbothered. "Speaking of my ship—I think I'll call her *The Sore Loser*. You know, after her original owner. What are you planning on doing with Shaalyn?"

"What, you mean we can't leave her in your hold?" Zoey looks over at Bethiah.

"Only if you want me to accidentally 'oops' space her." Bethiah shrugs. "I can make it happen. No one needs to know."

"I think she needs to be given to Jade," Adiron says.

Wait, what? "Why me?" I squawk, alarmed.

"Well, you can't let her go," Bethiah says in a helpful way. "She'll run her mouth and come after you—and your cargo of humans—the moment you let her go."

"You just want her taken care of so she doesn't come after your ship," Zoey mutters, but she looks over at her brother. "Whatever you want to do, I'm fine with."

Adiron just looks over at me.

I stare back, my mind blank. How am I supposed to know what to do with Shaalyn? I mean, I punched her and I enjoyed it. Now that everyone's safe, though, I don't know that I can deem myself her executioner. I shake my head. "I can't."

"She wouldn't think twice about killing you," Zoey says, a hard expression on her face. "Or selling you."

"I'm not saying I like her," I retort. "Or that I want to be best buddies. I just don't want to kill her. Just because she's evil doesn't mean I need to stoop to her level." Is that a flash of disappointment in Adiron's eyes? I feel guilty that I can't be as casual about someone's death as they are. Maybe I'd feel different if Shaalyn had a gun in her hands and I had to rely on instinct. Right now, though—she's neutralized.

"So you'd rather her come after you the moment we dump her somewhere?" Zoey's expression remains hard. "Because that's exactly what's going to happen unless you silence her somehow."

"Does that have to mean death?" I ask, frowning.

Bethiah brightens. "I'll cut her tongue out. Silence, just like you wanted."

"She's got hands," Kivian points out. "She can type."

"I'll get rid of them, too." Bethiah doesn't seem too bothered by this thought.

I press my hands to my face, because now I'm envisioning a handless, tongueless Shaalyn and it's not doing wonders for my stomach. "Mutilation isn't the answer, either." It's clear that we can't let her go, though. This is like when we were back on the *Star*, confronted with pirates we had to get rid of, somehow. "When we were on our ship, we were boarded by pirates a few times. We'd pretend to be helpless, gas them until they were unconscious, and then toss them into an escape pod from their ship. The gas we used wiped their memories for the prior period and so they didn't know how to get back to our ship— we'd turn off our distress signal for months on end, and no one ever came back around. Can't we do something like that?"

"Drug her, strip the pod of any sort of communication equipment, and launch her into deep space?" Zoey nods slowly. "I don't hate it. It'd be easier to just rid the universe of her entirely, but we can do it this way, too."

I look over at Adiron, and for once, his expression is impossible to read. Is he disappointed I don't have the stones to hang with them? That I'm showing too much conscience to be a pirate? Zoey doesn't seem disturbed at the thought of killing Shaalyn, but just like I can't abandon all those sleeping people to their fates, I can't cold-bloodedly murder a woman just because she's an awful bitch.

But Adiron nods. He rubs my foot again, touching my little toe. "We'll do as Jade wants."

74

JADE

*T*he *Jabberwock* is a much bigger ship than Shaalyn's (now Bethiah's), but it's still far smaller than the *Star*. We're shown on board, and I meet everyone. They have eight people on board—four men and four women. Fran is Kivian's wife, utterly beautiful and absolutely gracious. She acts as a hostess as she leads me around the ship, showing me the mess hall, the lavatories, and which parts are off limits for guests. There's a spacious rec-room that the crew loves to use, and when we get in there, I meet Alyvos and Iris. Iris wears a strange blinder over her eyes, and I can tell immediately that her vision is impaired. It's in the way she holds her head, the way she scans the room before settling on someone's location. But she's an absolute sweetheart. She's all smiles as she gets up and hands a baby to Fran.

A baby, of all things.

"This is my daughter," Fran says, pressing a kiss to the top of the baby's head, right between a pair of nubby horns just starting to sprout. "Her name is Jasmine, and if you tell me that she looks like me and not her father, I'll love you forever."

I drink in the sight of the infant, who's all wriggling arms and legs. She's blue skinned and...she really doesn't look like Fran. Maybe in the eyes, but the rest of her seems to be her father. "Um..."

Iris just chuckles. "Don't worry. Everyone comes to the same conclusion."

I smile, and when Fran holds the baby out to me, I take her. Jasmine's like any human baby, really. She's bigger, and she's got blue skin and horns. She's got a tail. But the bright eyes that look up at me are the same as the ones on Earth. The toothless mouth and drool on her chin are universal, as are the flailing fists as she stares up at me and makes gurgling noises of happiness. She's...adorable. Maybe my maternal instinct is kicking in, or maybe Jasmine is utterly gorgeous, but I've never seen such an appealing baby, and I'm filled with longing, excitement, and a hint of dread.

Just because Kivian wants a baby doesn't mean Adiron does.

"I could eat her up with a spoon," I tell Fran, snuggling Jasmine against my cheek. "She's adorable."

"She is, isn't she?" Fran adjusts the charming little outfit on her daughter—it's little more than a pale purple sac with sleeves, but it's got ruffles all over the hem and great big puffs on the arms...and I realize Kivian's dressed almost exactly like his daughter. My heart squeezes all over again. He's clearly a proud dad. "Where's Adiron?"

Before Fran can answer, someone speaks up behind her. "He's helping Tarekh handle Shaalyn's pod."

I turn and look over at Zoey. Her expression is neutral, but I can tell she's not happy with me. Fran clears her throat, takes the baby from my arms, and goes to sit with Iris. "Any time you want to come give Jasmine a snuggle, you're welcome," Fran tells me. "Since you're here, Zoey, why don't you show Jade to her quarters?"

I almost feel like I'm being set up. My skin prickles, but I keep a smile on my face. Zoey is Adiron's sister. I don't think she'd do anything to hurt him. The affection between them is too great. Even though I've just met Zoey today, it's obvious to me in the way they grin at each other, the way they tease, and the way Zoey seems so relieved to have found him. And I'm much safer here on the *Jabberwock* than I am on Shaalyn's ship, especially with that Bethiah person at the helm. She seems... not all there.

A ship with babies and a bunch of human women can't be bad, especially if they came to rescue Adiron. I'm just...worrying. There's so many things up in the air right now—the fates of my friends, the people in the stasis pods, the baby inside me —that I can't seem to turn around without running headlong into another crisis.

I just want to curl up in bed with Adiron and have everything be okay for just a day or two.

I wave goodbye to the others and follow Zoey through the ship. She's pleasant enough, pausing to tease Cat—big Tarekh's diminutive mate—a little before leading me onward. We get to a door and she opens it, then gestures I should go inside. I do... and I'm not entirely surprised to see that the room looks very similar to the one I left behind on the *Star*. Double bed, neutral plas-sheets and no pillow, a wall panel with buttons all over it, and the door to a lavatory. In the corner, there's a small table attached to the wall and a couple of chairs for sitting. Zoey pulls a slim paperback out of her pocket and sets it on the table. "Housewarming present. We tend to swap books, just FYI. If you ever run across anything—and you will—save them. We meet up every other month or so and do a big book swap with some of the Earth women we know."

"Thank you," I tell her sincerely. "I haven't read a book in over three years. I'm going to enjoy every page."

She purses her lips and nods, hesitating in the doorway.

Time to get it all out in the open. "You don't like me, do you?"

Zoey opens her mouth, and then closes it with a snap. "I don't know you," she confesses. "But if Adiron is in love with you, then I'm sure we'll get along. He's been lonely for a long time and I've never seen him so happy. I think you're good for him..." She pauses and trails off.

"But?" I ask, because I know there's a "but" in there somewhere. My stomach is tight with nerves.

She drums her fingers on her crossed arms and then sighs. "It's not you specifically. It's that..." She pauses and then rushes on. "You're still thinking like a human."

I tilt my head, confused. "I am human."

"Yes, and you've seen what this end of the universe does to humans, right? If we're not lapdogs, we're chewed up and spit out." She paces for a moment, frowning. "You're thinking that life is good and fair and things are just and that bad guys always get their due. You think it's not your place to be executioner, right?" She shakes her head. "And that's going to fuck you up, in the end."

I blink in surprise. I can't believe Adiron's human sister is telling me I'm not bloodthirsty enough. "You think I should have told them to kill Shaalyn?"

She pauses, clasping her hands under her chin. "I think you're not thinking far enough ahead. What if she comes back for revenge? What if she decides that Adiron has wronged her and makes it her mission in life to fuck him—and his mate—over? That's my point. You think like a human—but these people don't. You have to think like them if you're going to survive." Her expression grows firm. "Or you're going to die and take my brother down with you."

I stare at her in shock.

"I'm telling you this as a friend," Zoey says softly. "No one would be happier than me to see you and Adi happy and growing old together. But I've been out here in space for over ten years now. I have seen the good, the bad, and the ugly. I've adapted. And I think you should do the same." She moves forward and puts a hand on my shoulder. "You chose to spare Shaalyn because you didn't want to be the one with blood on your hands. That she deserves a fair shake, yes?"

Wordlessly, I nod.

"Did they tell you that Shaalyn murdered her crew?" When I gasp, Zoey ruthlessly goes on. "Bethiah was serving on her ship, right? And she turned on her to try and take control. Shaalyn couldn't be sure who else was on her side, so she went through the ship and slaughtered her own men in order to save her own hide. That's the kind of person you're dealing with. That's the kind of person you sent off in an escape pod because you couldn't get your hands dirty. I'm not telling you this to be cruel. I'm telling you that if the tables were turned, she would absolutely take every chance she had to claw her way ahead, and you need to realize that." She pats my arm. "Kindness is an admirable trait, but only back on Earth."

She turns and leaves me alone in the room with my thoughts.

75

ADIRON

I'm itching to get back to Jade. Everyone on the *Jabberwock* is great, and I love seeing my sister and her mate Sentorr, but it's been far too many hours since I held my mate, and I need her desperately. I want to bury my face against her soft, dark skin and just breathe in her scent. I want to hold her curves against my body and just...lie there for a week, wrapped around her. Yeah, that sounds good.

Eventually, Shaalyn and her sole remaining greenhorn are dispatched into the pod. Her shrieks of anger are the last things I hear as the pod is sealed, and then she's the universe's problem. I watch as the pod drifts away, on a slow trajectory into nothing at all.

Bethiah comes to my side. "You think I should have 'oops' programmed her to fly right into the ice field?"

I shake my head. "Jade wants her to have a fair shake, so she will." My female has a heart as soft and ample as her bottom, and I love that about her. "Speaking of, I'm going to go find my female. Good flying to you." I clap a hand on Bethiah's slim shoulder. "Where are you headed?"

"Someplace quiet where I can give this girl a new face." She strokes the ship's wall panel.

"To Jerrok's, then?"

A strange expression crosses her face. "Not for a while."

"Something happen?"

"Nope. Just, ah, I had a prisoner the last time I visited Jerrok, and said prisoner might have gotten away." She gives me an impish look. "Once I give this lady a new face, I might go hunting for that prisoner. I don't want him to think I forgot him."

Er, okay then. "Good hunting, then."

When I get to our quarters on the *Jabberwock*, I find Jade laying on the bed, a distant look on her face. She looks...sad? The sight of that guts me. "Jade, love. What's wrong?"

"I'm fucking everything up."

I have no idea what she's talking about, but she looks so miserable that my heart hurts. I move to the bed and slide over to the other side of her, spooning her smaller body with my bigger one. My tail wraps around her leg and I slide my arm around her. She pushes back against me, tucking herself even closer, and I press a kiss to the side of her face. How many times did we curl up like this on the *Star*, doing nothing at all? We'd talk for hours. We'd share stories. We'd kiss. We may not be on the *Star* anymore, but as far as I'm concerned, nothing's changed. I brush her hair back from her face with gentle fingers. "Why do you think you're fucking everything up?"

She takes a deep, shuddering breath. "None of this would have happened if I'd stayed in the wall like you told me to. I messed up, and I just keep on messing up."

I pause. "I mean...if you had stayed in the wall, it might have worked out differently, but it might not. And you didn't know Shaalyn like I do. You didn't realize she was bluffing. But it's over and done with. She's in the pod now, drifting out to who knows where and probably yelling at her last remaining crew member." I shake my head at the thought, because I can't blame those males. I once fell madly in love with the female that I thought Shaalyn was. Ruthless, yes, but fun-loving and exciting. Turns out she's just ruthless and self-serving. Those dead crew-members she slaughtered to save herself? That could have been me, and I'm glad that I had my brothers to pull me free from her influence. "I'm not mad about Shaalyn, though. It all ended well, so there's nothing to worry about."

"Did it end well, though?" Jade sounds morose. "I couldn't let them threaten you, so I gave up my own safety and our chances at outwitting them. And then when it came time to dispose of her, here I go insisting that you should let her go. Your sister told me I have too soft of a heart and that I keep thinking like a human, and it's going to end up causing us problems in the future. And I think...maybe she's right."

I bite back a groan. Zoey means well, but my sister's just as protective of us as we are of her. "No, Jade. There's nothing wrong with your soft heart. My sister thinks that because she grew up with a bunch of pirates that the only way to thrive is to be as rough and tumble as the rest of us. Yet she mated a male that's practically her opposite, because she fell in love with him. Just because she thinks you need to be tougher doesn't mean that I do."

She sinks into my arms. "I love you, Adiron. I just don't want you to feel like you're trapped or stuck with me—"

"Stuck with you?" I repeat, incredulous. "There's nothing I love more than being 'stuck' with you." I press a kiss to the side of her face, and when that garners a hint of a smile, I keep kissing her. I press fervent kisses against her cheek and her hair, until she's squirming and chuckling at my attention. "I would love nothing more than to be stuck with you for the rest of my days." I kiss her ear and then give it a gentle nip with my teeth. "Stuck in bed with a sexy, gorgeous female. It's SUCH a hardship."

A smile curves her mouth, and I feel a little better at the sight of it. I kiss her again, just because I love kissing her, and my cock stirs in my trou. Right now Jade needs comfort and affection, but of course, my body doesn't know that. My dick thinks it's playtime. I don't act on it just yet, though. I just keep holding and kissing Jade, because she seems to need it. Her hands are on the arm I have wrapped around her, and it almost feels as if she's clinging to me for dear life.

"Does that ease your mind?" I ask her between kisses. "That I like that soft, bleeding heart of yours? I think it's good to have a different perspective. A gentler one. Sometimes a ship full of males needs it."

She turns her head, and this time, I kiss her lips. Jade gazes up at me, but her eyes still look troubled. "What happens now?" she asks.

"We get to the *Star* and use the *Jabberwock* to haul it to my friend Jerrok's. He's the one I told you about that lives on an asteroid. He's the one we left Sophie with. We'll pick her up, too. She's probably more than ready to leave. And there's the carinoux, though I'm not sure what we're going to do with that thing. Find a buyer, I guess."

"What about you and me?" Jade asks softly. "And what about my friends? And your brothers?"

"We'll hunt for them, too. They're bound to show up some-where." I can't resist nipping her ear again, because it usually leads towards sex, and my mind is absolutely focused on sex right now. I've solved Jade's worries, and now my cock can get some attention, hopefully. "And then you and I go gallivanting around the universe."

She looks up at me. "Is that what we're going to do?"

"Did...you have a better idea?"

"I don't know," she admits. She presses her mouth to my bicep. "Do pirates need a bleeding heart human with them?"

"This one does," I reassure her, and flick my tail over the apex of her thighs, testing the waters. And when Jade turns over and slides her arms around my neck, I kiss her fully on the mouth, dragging her leg up around my hips. It's been hours since we've mated, and I need her just as much as she needs me.

76

JADE

I wake up the next morning with Adiron wrapped around me and a view of the *Buoyant Star* in the window. I sit up and stare out at it. Sometime while I slept and fooled around with Adiron in bed, we returned to the *Star*, hitched it up, and are now tugging it behind the *Jabberwock*. I can see delicate metal cords tying the ships together, though that seems dangerous to me. These people know how to operate their ships better than I do, though, so I try not to worry too much. I vaguely remember something about my space teachings back in school, about how an object in motion will remain in motion until something else acts against it, so I suppose it's less "hauling" and more "leading."

Just seeing the *Star* there makes me feel a little better, though. There's no danger of an ice field. There's no worry about being a sitting duck, all alone in unfamiliar space.

Now if we can just find Adiron's brothers and Alice, Helen

and Ruth, I'll be thrilled. I'll be able to finally relax a little. Hopefully.

I glance down at Adiron in the bed. He's got all the blankets wrapped around him, because of course he does, and his big body takes up most of the bed. He slept for most of the night with me clutched against his chest, though, so I don't mind if he's a bit of a bed hog. After yesterday, I'm just thrilled to have him in my bed at all.

I shiver, thinking about how it felt to go into stasis. How painful it was as the cold crept through my body. It was like being forced to watch your body slowly turning to ice, and just thinking about it makes me cold. I lie down in bed again, and Adiron immediately reaches for me, dragging me against his big body.

Next to him in bed might be my favorite place in the universe, I muse. He—

My stomach lurches, and my mouth fills with saliva. This time, my body isn't waiting for a bowl-full of noodles to get sick.

I bolt from the bed and slam into the lavatory, then puke my guts up.

"Jade?" Adiron's sleepy voice drifts through the cabin. "Love?"

"Just...just a minute." I manage between retching. "I'm...fine."

"You don't sound fine." Footsteps echo in the room and then the lavatory door opens. In the next moment, a hand is on the small of my back. "You don't look fine, either. What did you eat?"

"Nothing," I manage, gasping. I feel a little better now that my stomach is empty, and I wipe my mouth and manage a wan smile as I look over at my mate. "It's okay, really."

The look on Adiron's face is one of worry. "You have been sick repeatedly. Is this a human thing? Zoey was never sick like this unless she ate something bad." He rubs my back, eyes wide. "Is this the sickness that Alice had, do you think? Shaalyn said that they wouldn't let Alice and Kaspar on their ship because Alice was sick."

I shake my head. "I don't think so. It's fine. I just need to eat something." And tell him about the baby. That's the obvious solution—tell him that I'm sick because I'm pregnant. But I can't make the words come out of my mouth. I'm afraid he won't be excited. That whatever tenuous happiness we have right now will disappear into thin air the moment there's a baby in the mix.

Adiron doesn't look convinced. "More crackers?"

I shrug and get up from the floor...and then immediately go down again as another wave of nausea hits me.

"I'll get you some food," Adiron tells me, and leaves.

By the time he returns, I'm dressed and cleaned up and feel like myself again. My stomach growls, and when he shows up with a hard protein bar and a tumbler of water, I give him a grateful smile. "It's passed," I say. "But I appreciate the food."

"It's not noodles," he tells me, setting the food down on the tiny table and then guiding me over to it as if I'm feeble. "I made sure it wasn't noodles."

"Really, I'm fine," I protest.

"Should I talk to Kivian and Fran? Get you some medicine?" he asks. It's clear he doesn't believe my protestations.

I shake my head and take a hearty bite of the protein bar to prove that I'm fine. Adiron doesn't believe me, and keeps watching me with a worried expression, even after I finish eating and drinking. I reach over and take his hand, inter-locking our fingers. "What's the plan for today? Do we just hang out in here?"

"I'm supposed to help Tarekh and Alyvos go over the systems over on the *Buoyant Star* to see what we can get running, but I'm going to tell them you're sick. I can do it some other time—"

I interrupt him and squeeze his hand. "You can go. Really. I promise you the sickness has passed." When he hesitates again, I continue, my expression full of smiles. "I'll see if Fran and the others need some help. I'm sure they can give me something to do. It'll be nice to stay busy after years of idleness."

Adiron rubs his jaw with his other hand, looking as if he doesn't quite believe me. After a few moments, though, he sighs. "Are you sure?"

"Positive."

"And you'll tell me if you start to feel sick again? You'll have the others send me a comm?"

I nod.

He doesn't seem happy, but eventually, Adiron agrees and we leave our room, then part after sharing a few kisses with the promise of more tonight. He casts me a worried look over his shoulder as he heads toward the maintenance rooms, and I keep my expression bright and chipper until he's gone. Then, I head for the rec room and peer in, looking for others.

Fran's inside, seated on a couch, the baby on a blanket on the floor. She's got a book in her hand and one eye on Jasmine, and she looks as beautiful and put together as usual. Her hair is sleek and glossy, and her clothes are subdued (at least compared to Kivian's) but fit her gorgeous body like a glove. She looks up when I approach and sets her book down carefully. "I was wondering when you'd come to talk."

"Me?" I ask, curious.

She just gives me a knowing look. "Adiron came into the mess this morning all frantic. He needed a protein bar for you because you were sick. Told us you were off noodles, too." She licks her lips and eyes me. "Same thing happened when I was pregnant with this one. Does he know?"

Busted.

77

JADE

$\mathcal{J}$ move to sit next to Fran, the weight of my secret pressing on me. She knows I'm pregnant. And if she's figured it out, it won't take long before the entire ship knows. Not that I really care about what anyone thinks other than Adiron...but I need to be the one to tell him. "I haven't said anything yet," I admit. "There hasn't been much time. I just found out when we got captured. I didn't even think it was possible."

"The mesakkah are interesting," Fran says, her voice mild. "Some of the things they do seem strange and antiquated to me, but their technology is leagues ahead of anything Earth has, and their medical expertise is incredible. Babies between two different species are easily handled, as long as you've got the money to pay for the doctor."

"Doctor?"

"Right." She grimaces. "Your path was different than mine, I'm guessing, if the pregnancy was a surprise to you. Kivian and

I saved up for fertility shots. You pay a doctor that's familiar with treating humans, he stuffs you full of hormones and medical treatments, and it makes you pregnant. I'm guessing they did something similar to you while you were sleeping?"

"They must have." I shake my head. "I don't remember any of it."

"Well...I'm not going to tell you what to do with your own body." Fran picks up a metal ring with a few clanky bits on it and shakes it in front of Jasmine's face. The baby's arms and legs flail and she bounces on her stomach, trying to get to the "keys." "But if you need to intervene, we have a med-bay on the ship that can take care of it."

It's that simple, I guess. Just push a button and all your problems are solved. Adiron never needs to know.

I swallow hard, because everything about that feels wrong to me, and yet...it's a simple solution, isn't it? "I just don't know if it's safe to bring up a baby. I don't have a home. I don't have a dollar to my name. I'm completely dependent on Adiron and you guys. That frightens me."

"I understand." Fran's voice is full of sympathy. She shakes the keys again, and Jasmine makes a gurgle of excitement, her little legs dancing.

I don't know if she does understand. She seems so calm. So at ease. "Do you live somewhere else? Are you just visiting?"

Fran smiles. "No, I live here all the time. I think Kivian would die if he had to leave me and Jas behind. I might, too. We're not good at being apart."

I'm a little afraid of offending her, but fuck it. "Do you think it's wise to have a baby on a pirate ship? That it's safe? Because it doesn't seem safe to me."

"You'd think that, wouldn't you?" Fran seems unruffled by my words. She leans over and picks up Jasmine. The baby has drool all down her chin, but the look she gives her mother is adoring, and Fran is rewarded with a bright, happy smile full of gums and slobber. "But being here on a ship with people that love and care about me is safer than anywhere else in this universe. It's not a nice place for humans." She gives me a wry smile as she bounces her daughter on her knee.

Not a nice place for humans is kinda an understatement. "I know it's not safe. I just..."

"Have a hard time reconciling this lifestyle to one back on Earth?" She gives me a knowing look. "You'll get there. And really, who's to say we were any safer back on Earth? Someone could drive their car through your living room or your plane could crash and you'd be just as dead. I'm happy with Kivian. Jasmine's happy. We have a crew full of people that help out when we need a break." She lifts the baby and kisses one fat, pale blue cheek and then holds her out to me. "Time to stop thinking about what you've been told is the right answer, and adapt to life out here." Fran shrugs. "If you don't want children, it's a different conversation entirely but...that's not what you were asking, is it?"

It's not. Because as worried as I am, I do want children. Maybe my biological clock is ticking, but the thought of having Adiron's baby fills me with such joy and such utter terror. I've always wanted a family...I just never thought I'd have it with an alien. In space.

But like Fran said, maybe it's time to stop thinking like I'm back on Earth. It's the same thing Zoey said, too. "I'm worried Adiron doesn't want kids," I confess, even as I take Jasmine in my arms and settle her on my lap.

"Have you asked him?" Fran studies me.

"Of course not," I joke. "I'm busy being a big scaredy cat."

Fran laughs. "If there's one thing I know, it's that a human that manages to live on their own for three years on an abandoned ship is anything but a scaredy cat."

"Heard about that, did you?" I murmur, studying Jasmine. The baby stuffs one little fist into her mouth and stares up at me with fascinated eyes. God, she really is cute. Large, but cute. Adiron's baby would be large, too. A guy that big would never have a tiny child. I wonder if our baby would have my hair or my skin, or if it'd look just like Adi. The thought makes me melt inside. A big, fat baby with his naughty grin and easygoing sense of humor. "I guess...I'm just telling myself that I need a moment for things to be calm and quiet. For it to be safe."

Fran's look is sympathetic. "You might be waiting a while."

Boy, don't I know that. I could be waiting years again. After all, Ruth's gone god-knows-where, Alice is lost in space—literally—and there's been no sign of Helen at all. My little family is scattered to the four corners, and all I've got is Adiron.

I've put my trust in him, but at the same time, I'm terrified. I like being in control, and ever since Shaalyn arrived to turn our world upside down, things have been anything but in control.

"Waiting a while for what?" a familiar voice asks from the doorway.

My stomach clenches. I turn and give Adiron a bright smile. "Didn't see you there."

He grins and saunters into the room. "I haven't transferred over to the *Star* yet. I wanted to see if Jade wanted to come with me. Thought you might like to visit your stomping grounds to see what's being changed." He moves to my side and strokes my hair, then holds a finger out for Jasmine to grab. "Looks like you're having fun without me, though."

I look up at him, a little surprised. I don't know why I am. He's always so thoughtful. It's me that never quite seems to believe someone like him exists. Someone so perfect for me. Wordlessly, I gesture at the baby. "Want to hold her?"

It's a test, of course. Fran casts me a knowing glance, but I say nothing.

"Aw, I'd love to." Adiron scoops Jasmine up from my lap and swings her into the air. He gives her a little toss that makes my heart stop, but Fran only smiles. "Have you missed your Uncle

Adi, Jasmine? Have you?" His voice takes on a silly note, and he makes a ridiculous face as he nuzzles her belly. "You want me to teach you to be a mean old pirate just like Zoey? I bet you do."

Jasmine squeals with laughter, her little legs kicking. She giggles, the sound sweet and full of joy, and it's clear she's played this game with Adiron before.

I feel a little silly at giving him a test. Of course he likes kids. He's incredibly close with Zoey, who they've raised since she was small. Of course he likes babies. Judging from the way he's acting with Jasmine—all kissy faces and silly voices—I've been worrying over nothing. "I'll come with you over to the *Star*," I agree.

Once we're over there, I'll confess my secret.

78

ADIRON

*J*ade seems to be in a better mood as we take one of the escape pods and zoom over to the *Star*. She wants to know why we don't do the ship-to-ship walkway, and I explain that the angle of the ship we're towing makes it easier, cost-wise, to just take a pod there and back. As we fly the escape pod into the *Star's* receiving bay, I glance over at my mate. She's not sick, and her eyes seem bright. It's a good thing, but I still can't help but worry. I don't like that everything upsets her stomach lately, and I need to see if there's something I can do to help.

"How long until we get the *Star* back to your friend's place?" Jade asks, curious as I settle the pod gently in the bay.

"Couple of weeks," I say. "I imagine there's more direct, faster routes, but we're going to try and stay off the main shipping lanes. Less questions."

"And then how long at your friend's?" She looks over at me. "Jerrok?"

"Just long enough to get the *Sister* up and running. Jerrok's not a big fan of company...and he's probably still mad at me for leaving Sophie and the carinoux on his doorstep for as long as we have." I grimace at the thought, because I can only imagine how pissed he was when he found out about the carinoux that we neglected to mention. I hope it hasn't torn up his entire station. "Sophie will be joining us after that, I imagine."

She looks at me thoughtfully. "I hope she doesn't feel I'm taking her place."

"Sophie?" I make a choking sound even as I power down the pod. "How are you taking her place?"

Jade shrugs. "She might feel threatened if another human shows up with you."

"I doubt that. Sophie's the mildest little thing. You won't have to worry." I hope Jade isn't threatened by Sophie, though. Sophie's pretty enough, as humans go, but I've never felt anything for her other than sympathy and responsibility. She's a good kid...whereas I feel completely and utterly different about Jade. The feelings I have for this female are decidedly not brotherly. "It's going to be fine," I say again. "Are you worried?"

She considers for a moment. "No, I don't think so. Just thinking aloud."

A horrible thought occurs to me. Jade's been acting a little odd since we got onto the *Jabberwock,* and I initially attributed it to all the changes, but a new worry's making itself known. "You...do want to go with me, right? If you don't, I'll under-stand." I practically choke on the word. "I'll take you somewhere safe if that's what you'd like—"

"Adi," Jade says softly. She takes my hand in hers and rubs her thumb over my palm. We probably should be getting out of the pod to go and help with the others, but I don't want to leave until we get everything straightened out between us. "I love you. Of course I want to go with you. I don't know why you'd think otherwise."

I shrug. "I'm not great at reading people. I think my past relationship with Shaalyn shows that." I give her a wry smile. "But you just seem a little distant in the last day or two and it's worrying me."

"I'm fine. I promise."

"I don't think you are." I clasp her hand between mine and rub it. "Like I said, I'm not good at reading people, but I know you. "You've been worried about something...and with the sickness..."

Kef me. A horrible thought crosses my mind.

I study Jade's face, looking for answers. What does a human look like when they're sick? Do they look haggard? Circles under the eyes? Because Jade has both. I thought it was because of what we've been through, but now I'm wondering. "Are you dying?" I choke out.

If she's dying, she's going to take me with her. I can't imagine a life without a happy, healthy, smiling Jade.

Her eyes go wide and her mouth drops open. She squeezes my hand, shaking her head. "Adiron, I'm not dying—"

"You wouldn't tell me if you were," I point out. "You don't like it when I worry—"

"Adi—"

My mind is racing. If she's sick, we can fix this. There are doctors out there that know about treating humans. "Change of plans," I say abruptly. "We have the *Jabberwock* abandon the *Buoyant Star*. We can get to Jerrok's asteroid a lot faster that way, and once we get the *Sister*, we can find a doctor—"

"Adiron," Jade says softly. She reaches out and touches my chin, directing my gaze to hers. "I'm not dying."

"Jade—"

"I'm pregnant."

I blink. "You're what?"

"Pregnant." The worried look crosses her face again. It's the same expression she's worn for the last day—the slightly pinched, slightly distant, stressed expression. "I think they did something to me when I was sleeping. Modified something. At any rate, I'm pregnant, and you're the father, and we're going to have a baby."

I stare at her. "You're not...dying?"

"No." Her expression is grave. "I found out when they did a medical scan on me before they put me into stasis, back on Shaalyn's ship. I'm pregnant, and that's why I'm sick. I wasn't sure how you'd feel about being a father, and so I've sat on the news, but I figured it was time to tell you—"

Before she can finish, I reach over and haul her out of her seat, tugging her into my lap. She sprawls against me, her arms going around my neck, her thighs straddling mine, a confused expression on her face. I look up at her...and then I crush her against me in a tight, relieved hug. I bury my face against her neck and hold her tight.

My mate. My keffing beautiful, perfect mate.

"Adi?" Jade asks. "Your horns are in my face..."

I swing my head wide, so I don't jab her in the face. I don't let go of her, though. I don't think I'll ever let go. I keep her tight on my lap, running my hands up and down her body. She's pregnant. My mate is pregnant with my baby. I stare down at her belly. It's always been rounded, which I love. I know it's too early to see evidence of our child, but I look anyhow. Just because. "Jade."

"If you ask me how it happened, I'm going to be very disappointed," she teases, her voice falsely light. There's a hint of nervousness on her face. "I'm not sure how you feel about being a father, but...I don't think I want to get rid of it."

Startled, I meet her eyes again. "No. Don't get rid of it." I put my hand to her stomach. "Please."

"Then you...you're happy?" She looks as if she desperately

needs reassurance. "Tell me what you're thinking. It's not something we've ever talked about and I know it's a big change..." Her voice trails off and she looks ready to cry. "I just don't want to mess up what we have."

It's moments like this that I wish I had a smooth tongue like Mathiras. I wish I'm not the dumb one. I wish I could think of beautiful, reassuring things to say that would make the worry ease off of her face. That I could tell her that I'm utterly flummoxed, but in the best way. That I'm amazed that we've made a child between us. And that child will be incredible. It'll have her smarts (hopefully) and my...well, it'd probably be better if the baby was mostly Jade. She's smart and strong and proud and brave. We're going to have a family. A few years from now, I'll be able to hold my son or daughter in my arms. I'll be able to raise him or her just as we raised Zoey, and just as my father raised us.

It'll be a new person to look after, a new bruise in my heart. Already my chest aches with the thought, and I'm both terrified and elated and I want nothing more than to hold that child RIGHT NOW...even though I know I'm not ready. But I don't know how to sum all those things up. I don't know how to tell Jade how overwhelmed this makes me, or how much bigger my emotions feel at this moment. How I don't think I've ever been so happy, and yet it feels like more than that.

A thousand times more.

But I can't think of anything, and she's looking at me with worried eyes, so I come up with something. "Yay!"

She blinks. Recoils a bit. Smacks my chest. "Yay? That's all I get? Are you fucking serious, Adiron?"

"I'm not good with words," I tell her, my voice stupidly husky with emotion.

She crosses her arms over her chest.

I put my hand between us, touching her stomach. "I just..."

Kef me, there must be a breeze in here. My eyes are watering. "I'm good. I am. I just can't think of the right words that you'd want to hear."

Jade's expression softens. She reaches up and brushes a bit of dampness off my face. "Just tell me that you love me."

"I love you," I manage hoarsely around the keffing knot in my keffing throat. "So much."

"Are you happy?" Her voice is soft.

I nod.

A tiny smile curves her mouth. "I'm a little terrified. Happy, but terrified. How are we going to raise a baby in space?"

I touch her stomach again. I can't stop touching it. I wonder how long it'll be before I'll be able to feel the little guy—or girl—in there. "We'll make room on the *Little Sister*. You're not leaving my side."

"I just...after what happened with Shaalyn, I worry it won't be safe." She bites her lip. "But I don't want to force you to give up your dreams."

"My dreams?" I repeat dumbly. Does she not get it? "Jade, you are my dream. A family is my dream." I rub my knuckles lightly over her stomach. "Corsairing is just a way to make credits. If it becomes dangerous or if you start to hate it, we can do something else."

"Are you sure?"

"A thousand times sure," I tell her. "Who knows, maybe we'll set up on Risda like Kivian's brother. They seem happy enough."

A little smile curves her mouth. "What about your brothers?"

That's definitely a question. It's always been just the three of us—and Zoey. We took in Sophie, of course, not because we needed another crew member, but just because she was lost and afraid and she just seemed desperate to have a job of some kind. After years of Zoey on the ship, it was odd to have no female presence. Jade and I—and a baby—would definitely change the dynamic. I can't do stupid shit anymore just for fun. I've got a family to think about. "When we find them again, we'll work something out. They won't mind more crew."

Even if they do, Jade and the baby come first. They won't, though. I know my brothers. They know how miserable I've been since the Shaalyn incident. They'll be thrilled that I'm happy...and something tells me Kaspar and Mathiras might be tangled up with her friends.

That's a future worry, though, and I'm a male that likes to live in the present. So I press a kiss to Jade's plush mouth...and then kiss her again, because there's nothing better than kissing my female. I bury my hands in her hair when she lets out a soft little sigh, and I deepen the kiss.

Jade chuckles against my lips, trying to pull back. "Won't someone see us?"

"Don't care," I say, capturing her mouth again. I slick my tongue against hers and put my hands on her hips. I lift her up, just a little, and then drag her cunt against the length of my cock. "No one will look."

She moans, rocking her hips against mine, creating more friction between us. "Adi...we shouldn't."

"Yes we should." I tug on her jumper. "You think it doesn't turn me on to know that you're carrying my baby? That I put my child inside this gorgeous body of yours?"

I hear Jade suck in a breath, followed by a whimper. Her hands go on my face, and then she's kissing me even harder while she lifts her hips up so I can undo the fasteners on her trou.

My gorgeous, hungry mate. Kef, I love this female. I growl against her pretty mouth, even as I tear at her clothing. The fasteners come apart, and I shove at the material between us, until it pools between her thighs. When I touch her cunt, she's hot and slippery, and she rocks against my fingers with a moan.

"No one's going to look," I promise her between kisses. With one hand, I undo my own trou, and my other hand plays along the folds of her cunt, searching for her favorite spots. I slide a finger into her heat, using my thumb to tease her clit. She practically sits on my hand in her eagerness, panting my name against my mouth. "If they do look," I whisper, "all they'll see is you bouncing on my cock. They'll see that I'm giving it to you so hard. That I'm so deep inside you. No one's ever claimed you so hard, have they, Jade?"

"Never," she pants against my mouth. Her hands are greedy as I free my cock, and she strokes me before guiding me toward her body. I hiss when the head of my cock nudges against her entrance, and I can't wait any longer. I grab her hips and thrust up into her, slamming her down onto my length. She moans again, wrapping her arms around my neck, her mouth hungry on mine.

"You want everyone to see me claiming you?" I ask between pumps of my cock into the tight clasp of her sheath. "You want everyone to know that I own this body? That you're my mate and this is my cunt? That my seed goes here?" I nip at her lower lip. "That my seed got you pregnant?"

I love the whimper she makes.

No one's out here, of course. If they could see into the pod, I'd drag Jade to the back and kef the daylights out of her properly. As it is, the engine of the pod is on the bottom, so the windows are far too high for anyone to see in. We can see below, but no one can see us. Which is a shame, because the sight of my glorious mate riding my cock, panting with need, is the best sight ever.

"Mine," I tell her, lifting her up and rocking her back down onto my cock. "You're mine, aren't you?"

"Yours," she breathes. Her breath hitches, her cunt tightening around me, and I know she's close. "Yours, Adi."

"Gonna come for me?" I drag my hand from her hip to the front of her body, teasing the little clit that's poking out from her folds. "Gonna squeeze me so tight it's like you're milking my cock? Because you need it?"

Jade cries out, her body shuddering over mine, and then I feel it—the clamp and squeeze of her cunt as it ripples with her release. She comes hard and fast, our bodies slapping together and making lewd, wet sounds. I love it. Love her. I tell her that, over and over again as I drive into her, seeking out my own release. Doesn't take long—she feels far too good—and I bury my face against her neck and bite at her soft skin when I come, filling her with a fresh round of seed.

For some reason, it gives me animalistic pleasure, and I growl through my climax, latching an arm around her waist and holding her tight against me as I fill her cunt with my release. Jade clings to me, her fingers in my hair as she murmurs my name over and over again.

When I can breathe, I relax back in my seat and let out a heavy sigh. "You're amazing."

"You're just saying that because you nutted," Jade teases, leaning forward to press a little kiss to my mouth. She likes cuddling after sex, small touches that draw the pleasure out for longer, and I'm happy to oblige.

I play with the globes of her glorious ass, fascinated by her lack of tail and the bounce her cheeks have. She really does have an amazing body. "Well, yeah. But it's true. If I didn't think you were amazing, would I have gotten you pregnant?"

She snorts, tucking her head against my neck and then snuggling close. Her movements make her body twitch on my cock, reminding me that I'm seated deep inside her still and our bodies are messy. We'll have to do a bit of cleaning up before we get out of the pod...and I'll need to air it out to get rid of the sex smell.

"I hope no one was filming that," Jade tells me as I rub circles on her ass with my hands. "Do these things have cameras?"

"I kinda hope they were filming it," I admit. "I'd love a copy."

She smacks my chest. "Very funny."

I was serious, but I just shrug. A vid of Jade in all her splendor, riding my cock? What's not to love?

Her hand traces a pattern on my chest, and as she starts petting me, I realize she's getting all pensive again. "Are you sure you're happy, Adi?" Jade asks in a soft voice. "About the baby?"

"I really am," I say, and I mean it. "I'm keffing delighted. Being a father is on my list of five favorite things."

Jade lifts her head to look me in the eye. She's grinning as she does. "But let me guess, you won't say where on the list it is?"

This time, I absolutely will. I give my lovely mate a serious look. "Being a father is number two on my list of favorite things, right below being your mate. Because you're the best thing that's ever happened to me, Jade. Nothing will ever change that. I love you. I love every moment we're together, and I can't imagine waking up a day without you by my side. I want to grow old and gray with you, with a dozen children that look just like you." I give her a rueful look. "And we can hope none of them inherit my smarts."

She lets out a soft little cry, and then her arms are around my neck and we're kissing again. "Stop that. You're smart. You're brilliant and clever and I love you, too," she says between kisses, and her hips rock against mine. "I love you. I love you. I love you. And our kids would be lucky if they were as smart as their father. So lucky." She licks at my parted lips, all intensity. "Just like I'm lucky to have you."

Jade rubs her body against mine, the tips of her nipples dragging across my chest. Our kissing grows more intense, and she's in no hurry to leave her spot on my lap. If anything, her movements become more obvious, her body rocking down against mine. My cock realizes it might be getting lucky again and starts to pay attention once more. I kiss my mate harder and run my hand lightly over the controls, making sure that the pod is locked.

The world outside can just wait.

EPILOGUE

Weeks Later

ADIRON

I always thought not much changed in the universe. That we race around in crazy circles for this or that, but nothing ever truly changes. As we disembark on Jerrok's station, though, I can't help but notice that things are very different.

Jerrok's clean, for starters.

It shouldn't be a big deal, of course. Everyone bathes. For the last several years, though, every time I'd visited Jerrok, he seemed to have a new layer of filth on his skin, his clothing equally dirty, his hair long and stringy. He didn't care about being clean, he said. Why did it matter when he never saw anyone? Who wanted to look at him anyhow?

But when the *Jabberwock* arrives, Jerrok greets us with a smile, and he's wearing clean clothing. His skin glows a brighter blue than I've ever seen, and his long hair is carefully braided between his horns, tucked out of the way. And he's holding hands with Sophie.

So...I guess that happened.

Sophie looks good, at least. Her cheeks are pink and she smiles shyly at the crew of the *Jabberwock* as they visit and chatter and work on refueling the ship. They won't stay long. The *Buoyant Star* is floating in space, tethered and hidden behind a nearby asteroid, and Jerrok has plans to put a neutralizer on the ship that will disguise it from any readings. We've sent a comm out to Lord sa'Rin on Risda III informing him of our findings, but it'll take some time for him to get back to us.

In the meantime, Jade and I will stay here. Once we figure out what to do with the *Star*—and the *Little Sister*, who's also docked here, is ready to go—we'll head out and look for my brothers. We'll be out of Jerrok's hair soon enough...but something tells me that he'll mind less than he normally does. He seems almost like a different person. If it weren't for the prosthetics and the mismatched eyes (and the surly attitude) I'd think he'd been replaced by a clone of himself.

The station is busy as the *Jabberwock* pays Jerrok for new fuel cells. Tarekh and Alyvos install them while my sister Zoey and Tarekh's mate Cat spend time with Sophie, talking about books and seeds. She takes them to see the terrarium, and I squeeze Jade's hand as they head inside. "You sure you don't want to go?"

"Positive," Jade says, and leans against my shoulder. She hasn't left my side, and I have to admit, I don't mind at all. I never get tired of Jade's company, and I like having her next to me. There's nothing for us to do except wait; the crew of the *Jabberwock* has everything under control and the *Star* is in limbo. So I sit down on a bench in the cargo bay, tug Jade into my lap, and we watch everyone work. She slides an arm over my shoulders and presses a kiss to my ear. "Did you know that Sophie and Jerrok were together?"

"The last time I saw Jerrok, he smelled like a trash scow. Looked like one, too." I shake my head. "Maybe Sophie feels sorry for him."

Jade pinches my earlobe. "Or maybe she realized he was sad and lonely and they fell in love? And now that he's not depressed and full of despair he's taking care of himself again?"

"Or that," I say easily. I'm not going to argue with my mate. She's the smart one.

Eventually, the hustle and bustle dies down, and the crew of the *Jabberwock* return to their ship. We say our goodbyes and Zoey hugs me for so long and so hard I feel that keffing breeze making my eyes water again. "I'm going to comm the *Sister* every day," she tells me, a stubborn note in her voice.

"I won't get it every day. If we're farther apart, there might be a delay."

"Then you get two messages at once," she tells me, thumping her fist into my gut. "You'd better comm me back."

"I will, I will. Jeez. Sentorr, come get your mate," I call out. "She's all cranky."

My sister's stiff-necked mate moves to her side and puts a comforting hand on the back of her neck. It's amazing to watch her melt against him, given that he's not what I would have picked for her at all. Sentorr was military, just like me, but he still acts like he's serving. His hair is short and immaculately groomed, and his collar is so high and tight, his ship uniform so crisp I have images of him sending it through the cleaner every morning. Zoey, who's always been a little wild, adores him, though. She wraps her arms around his waist and tucks herself against his larger, lean frame. "She's allowed to worry about you," Sentorr says in that slightly disapproving, crisp voice of his. "She thinks you don't look after yourselves for some reason."

"Uh, because they don't?" Zoey retorts.

"Look who's talking," I send back. "I'm not the one that

stayed up for three days straight once trying to chart out a more efficient fuel run between three stations."

Zoey only snorts.

Sentorr strokes her neck, and the gentle movement of his thumb against her skin almost makes me feel like I'm seeing something I shouldn't. "I take care of Zoey. I make certain she gets enough sleep. Don't worry about her."

My sister smiles and then flings herself out of her mate's grasp to envelop Jade in a bone-squeezing hug. "And you're going to take care of my dumbass brother, right?"

Jade hugs her back, grinning. "First of all, he's not dumb. And second of all, yes."

I grin at the sight. They're not the best of friends yet, Zoey and Jade. They're both incredibly stubborn and each one is protective of me. But as we spent time on the *Jabberwock*, Jade relaxed around my sister, and I think Zoey's come to like Jade and her ready defense of me. The moment someone implies that I'm dumb (even if it's me), Jade leaps to my defense.

I love it.

Zoey finishes hugging Jade and moves back to give me another hug. I embrace her again. "Comm me the moment you hear something about Mathiras or Kaspar, yeah?"

"Of course." Then my sister pops a wet finger in my ear and I bellow in outrage. I walked right into that one. I mock-vow revenge as they head back onto the *Jabberwock*, but truth is, I let my sister get away with everything, because she's just the littlest runt of our clan, and she's family.

I feel a lonely pang as the *Jabberwock* takes off, leaving us behind. It's always hard to see my sister go. Jade squeezes my hand, and I hold her tightly. "Dunno how there's a breeze in this damn cargo bay."

"So strange," Jade agrees with a murmur, wiping the wetness from my cheeks. "You'll see her again, love."

"Of course I will," I grumble. "Let's go annoy our host for a bit."

It's funny, because while the *Jabberwock* was here, Jerrok was on edge. He always is when there's a ship visiting, he's told me before, and I don't take it personally. After the *Jabberwock* leaves, however, it's Sophie who seems to be on edge. She's a little anxious as she shows us around the newly cleaned-up station.

"These rooms were filled with junk," she says as she indicates the rec room they've set up. "We're working on making things a little more homey and comfortable."

"It's lovely," Jade says warmly. She points at the shelving. "Is that a VHS tape?"

"Yes!" Sophie declares, laughing. "It's *Planes, Trains, and Automobiles.* I can't watch it, of course, but I remember the movie from when I was young and seeing it makes me smile. Jerrok's saving all the human stuff he can find for me." She glances over at the male, gives another nervous laugh, and then gestures that we should follow her. "Come on. I'll show you where you'll be sleeping."

Jade squeezes my hand, but I'm not sure what she means by it. Probably telling me to shut up, so I do.

Jerrok says nothing, just files out after us.

Sophie's anxious as she heads down the hall to another room and hesitates with her hand over the door panel. "Sleipnir's in here, but he won't hurt you. Just don't make any sudden moves and don't act threateningly toward me." She thinks for a moment, and then adds, "Or Jerrok."

"Threateningly?" I ask, baffled. To Sophie?

Jade just squeezes my hand again.

Sophie gives us a nervous smile and then opens the door. She crouches low, murmuring soft words, and then the beast lumbers out into the hall, moving past her. I'd forgotten how terrifying the carinoux is. He's all teeth and enormous, menacing body as he prowls toward us. "He's been very protective lately," Sophie says in a soft voice. "But we think he's adjusting to being on the station and so he's more comfortable. He won't attack unless he feels we're in danger."

I don't so much as twitch my tail as the big animal circles around me. Jade remains still, too, and my protective instincts go through the roof when it nudges its big head against her hand. But Jade just laughs. "Is it okay to pet him?"

Sophie nods, smiling. "He loves women. It's just men he's a little uncertain around."

Jade drops to her knees, releasing my hand, and it takes everything I have not to snatch her back as she rubs the deadly creature's opalescent skin. "He's beautiful. Reminds me of a cross between a lion and a dragon. What's your name, pretty boy?"

The thing licks her face, and I twitch, feeling the need to protect my mate.

"He's Sleipnir," Sophie says. Her gaze slides toward me. "And I know you don't want to hear this, Adiron, but we've decided we're keeping him."

"We?" I ask.

Jerrok moves to Sophie's side. He doesn't touch her, but it's obvious they've got... something going on between them. "I can pay you some of what he's worth, " Jerrok tells me. "And I'm hoping we can arrange payments for the rest. Sophie's very attached to him and I think it's a good idea for her to have another protector."

"I'm still stuck on the 'we' part," I admit.

Sophie and Jerrok exchange a look. Her hand steals into his. "I haven't said anything yet because I didn't want to spring it on you, but..." She takes a deep breath. "I'm staying with Jerrok. Here. Permanently."

JADE

I'm not entirely sure if Adiron is thrilled about Sophie staying. He says he's happy for her. He gives her bear hug after bear hug, until the cat-creature starts to growl at him and even Jerrok is casting annoyed glances in Adiron's direction. For all that, though, I know how my big guy's mind works. He sees Sophie as another little sister that's leaving the nest, and it's going to eat at him. He won't let her know that, because he wants her to be happy, but Adi's got a soft heart when it comes to human women, and I make a mental note to distract the hell out of him later.

Me, I'm just surprised that all three brothers were around Sophie and no one made a move on her. She might be one of the most beautiful women I've ever seen. Her hair is long and thick, dark and tumbling, and she's got perfect bone structure and lips that would make anyone jealous. Her voice is husky and sexy, and I can't help but feel slightly frumpy and fat standing next to her. Sophie could have been a model back on Earth, or an actress. She's stunning.

She's also a little...fragile. Sophie reminds me a bit of a wounded bird that's just learning how to fly again. Her smiles are slow to come, and she hovers near Jerrok as if constantly seeking protection. In a way, I do understand why Adi and the others viewed her as a sister—there's something about Sophie that makes you want to protect her from the universe. She makes me think she would crumple under pressure.

I guess we're different in that way.

Jerrok's a little more alarming to look at. He's one of the brutal, muscular mesakkah, but he's also scarred all over. There's a network of white scars all over his face, and his eyes are mismatched, one with a red center that tells me it's cybernetic. He moves oddly, too, and one of his legs looks like an oversized, clumsily put-together limb. It doesn't take me long to realize it's cybernetic, as well. At one point, something starts humming loudly. He slaps his leg, and then the humming stops. So yeah, that tells me not everything there is natural.

But the way he looks at Sophie...it's beautiful. He gazes at her with a hungry sort of adoration, as if he can't believe this angel is his. He serves her food and hovers over her protectively as we ready for dinner, and when she rewards him with a shy smile, I swear the man looks as if he's in utter bliss. They're sweet together, and it makes me happy that they've found each other.

I'm quiet through dinner. It's noodles, but I don't complain and choke them down as best I can. Sophie and Jerrok talk with Adiron about his brothers and possible places for them to go. They talk about the *Little Sister* and the improvements Jerrok made on the ship while they've been waiting for someone to return for her. They talk about how the ship was taken from V'tarrian space and how Sophie found the message in the mirror—and was attacked. I just listen quietly, my hand on Adiron's leg in quiet support. He doesn't like hearing about Sophie and Jerrok in danger, I realize, and I suspect they're considered family to him, just as much as Kivian and Fran, or even crazy Bethiah.

Hearing about their adventures and the ordeals they've been through should make me worried. After all, I've got a baby to think about. Oddly enough, though, I'm calm. I trust Adiron to keep us safe. I've had weeks to see how he is around babies, and his excitement is sincere. He told everyone on the *Jabber-wock*—multiple times—that we're having a baby. He'd insisted we watch Jasmine for Kivian and Fran multiple nights so we can "practice" for when our baby arrives. And he'd been obsessively protective, hovering over me the moment he thought I might not feel well. He even carried around a stash of protein bars, ready to offer me one at a moment's notice if my stomach rebels. It's sweetly adorable, and I love him for it.

I've also seen how the crew handled Fran's baby. No one resented her or their captain for having a child. Instead, the little one is treated as an integral part of the crew—just one that doesn't contribute. Fran spent a lot of time watching the baby, but I've seen Kivian walking around the ship with his daughter strapped to his chest, and I've seen Iris playing with her. Cat and Zoey were less eager around the baby, but they helped Fran with her tasks around the ship when her hands were too full. Everyone pitched in, because they're a community.

It's lovely to see, and the way Adiron reacts—as if this is totally and completely normal—makes me think it's how it would be on the *Little Sister*, too. That his brothers would easily pick up any slack if we needed to focus on our child. I'm no longer filled with worry about having a baby in space. I'm just... excited for the future.

I haven't been excited for the future in a long, long time.

After dinner, I help Sophie clean the dishes while Jerrok goes over the things he's done to the *Little Sister*. He's changed out all the filters and done some additional small improvements to fusion cores and reactors and things I don't even know about. Sophie and I exchange books, and we talk a little about home as she shows me the plant-filled terrarium and the carinoux plays fetch with what looks like a fat metal pipe.

I'm glad when it's time for bed, however, because I want to spend some time with Adiron, picking his brain before we drift off to sleep. We finally part ways, and then Adiron leads me to our quarters. The bed's a good size, and I sit on the edge of it. "Thank goodness for this or I'd have nowhere to sleep," I tease.

"You could always sleep on top of my chest," Adiron says, as if that's a perfectly sensible sort of thing. He kneels in front of me and picks up my foot, undoing the auto-fastens on my shoes. I've nagged him about his fussing before—I'm perfectly capable of pulling off my own shoes—but he likes to take care of me. The moment my shoes are put aside, he moves forward and slides between my thighs, still on his knees. His hand goes to my belly. "Have you felt anything yet?"

"I'm only two months along," I say, laughing. "According to Fran, I have around another fourteen to go."

Adiron just grins up at me. "Are you telling me I'm impatient?"

"Yes!"

He leans forward, talking to my belly. "Don't you listen to your mother. She's got the wrong idea about me. I'm the most patient male on this side of the universe."

I chuckle, smoothing a black lock back from his face. It always falls over his brow, giving him a devilish sort of look. Very piratey, I decide. I like it. I tease the hair back behind his horns, only to watch it fall forward again. "Are you okay with everything?" I ask, running my fingers along the side of his face. I touch his jaw and trace my way along to his chin, just because I love touching him. "With Sophie staying and the cat and all?"

He shrugs. "Sophie's just seemed so lost ever since I met her. This is the first time I've seen her face and felt like she was happy. And I want her to be happy. Jerrok, too. I don't think I'd seen him smile since the war and I've seen him smile twice today. He's actually clean." Adiron lays his head in my lap, and even though one of his horns digs into my thighs, I don't mind it. I play with his hair, stroking his face and his head as he hugs my legs. "The loss of the carinoux hurts the pocket a little, but I'm fine with it staying with Jerrok and Sophie. Better than it being in a cage."

He makes it all sound so reasonable. "And yet you're sad to see them go, aren't you?" I ask softly.

"Me?" he scoffs.

"Yes, you." I run my fingers along his jaw. "You're losing a sister again, aren't you?"

He's quiet for a long moment. "I know it's not the same..."

I stroke his cheek. "You don't have to make excuses to me, Adi. I understand." My heart aches with love for him. I wish I could make this better. I know he wants Sophie to be happy, and his friend, too, but it's hard when you realize you're probably not going to see that person much anymore because they're choosing a different path. "Talk to me. Get it all out so it doesn't fester."

Adiron lifts his head, rubbing his mouth against my palm. He looks a little sad. Defeated. "It's just that everyone's scattered. There's no sign of Kaspar and Mathiras, and I can't help but worry. I know they can take care of themselves. Just pile that on top of the runt leaving and now this about Sophie...it feels like a lot." He kisses my hand. "I'll be fine tomorrow, but tonight I'm a little mopey."

"I understand. And we're going to find your brothers. And my friends." I give him a fierce look, as if sheer determination can will something into being. "We just haven't had a chance to look yet."

"One crisis at a time," he agrees. "You know what makes me happy, though?"

"What?"

His hand goes to my stomach. "My baby."

I snort-giggle. "'Your' baby?"

"Well, yeah." Adiron gives me a lazy, playful smile. "I had the hard job, after all. You're just sitting there and letting it grow. Me, I had to work to get it in there."

"I had no idea you were so delusional." I give a mock-shake of my head. "So sad, all those noodles have finally gone to your brain."

"It's true," he tells me. "My brain is full of noodles. Not even the good ones." His hands slide to my waist and he tilts his head thoughtfully. "Do you think they're salty noodles or the sweet ones?"

I roll my eyes, amused at this line of questioning. "I think you're more like the noodle scraps at the bottom of the container. All fucked up and impossible to get onto your sticks."

To my surprise, a sad expression crosses his face. "When Zoey was little, those were her favorite parts of the noodles. She'd make us cut hers up so she could use a spoon that she had, because she didn't want to use sticks. So we cut her noodles into all kinds of bits."

Well hell, I just reminded him of his sister again. "You know what you need?" I say, wiggling against his hands as they curve around to my ass.

"What's that?"

"A massage."

He looks intrigued. "A...sexy massage?"

"Would I give you any other kind?" I ask playfully.

Lust flares in his eyes, and my pussy clenches in response to the look he gives me. God, he's sexy. I love it when he looks at me as if he wants to devour me whole. My pulse pounds, and it feels as if it's centered between my thighs as he gets to his feet. Then he's looming over me, seven feet of strong, blue muscle. I'm pretty much staring level with his cock as I sit on the edge of the bed, and it's a tall bed.

"Where do you want me?" Adiron asks, voice all husky. I can tell he's completely forgotten about his sadness, and that makes me glad. If nothing else, I can provide a distraction. Really, it's a joy to do so. I don't think I'll ever get tired of touching Adiron. He's just so...delicious.

I'm so stinking lucky.

I put my hands on his belt and tug him forward, just a little. "Are there any parts of you that need a particular massage?" I ask in a flirty tone, peeking up at him through my lashes. "Any-thing...stiff?"

He groans, hips edging toward me. "Here and there."

"Hmm. Looks like more 'here' than 'there.'" I run my hand

over the bulge of his crotch, where his cock is thrusting against the fabric of his trou. The material is tented around him, but he's growing so hard that it's probably going to be painful very shortly. That's all right—I don't plan on keeping him clothed for that long. "Especially right here," I purr. "So very, very stiff. I bet you're just aching, aren't you?"

Behind him, his tail thrashes, flicking back and forth in the way it does when he's turned on. "Definitely could use a good rubbing," he breathes.

"We'll have to take care of that, won't we?" I lean forward, my gaze on him, and lick the length of him through the fabric. Adiron lets out a choked groan, his hand stealing to my hair. I don't let up, nuzzling against his thick shaft and using my lips on him. It doesn't matter that there's a layer of clothing between us. I can tell that he loves this. I do, too.

I love making him feel good. I love hearing his sexy groans. I love seeing him lose control.

I press another kiss to the outline of his cock, and as I do, I reach behind him. I wrap my hand around the base of his tail and squeeze. From what I can tell, it feels a little bit like when my ears or neck are played with. Not quite as sensitive as his dick, but still pleasurable to manipulate. I rub my mouth against his spur through the material of his trou, pumping the base of his tail with my other hand.

"Jade," he pants. His hand tightens in my hair, as if he wants to direct my head. "My filthy, beautiful Jade."

"I'm just trying to help." I keep my tone playful. "I thought you wanted a massage. I just didn't say I'd use my hands." And I rub my face against the tent of fabric below his belt.

Adiron growls low, the sound a mix of frustration and need. "So keffing naughty. Be careful or I'm going to spank that slippery little cunt of yours."

This time, I'm the one that sucks in a breath. "Don't distract me," I breathe, squeezing around the base of his tail again. I rub my nose against the piercing on the tip of his shaft, evident through the material. I tongue it, too, and then try and fit my mouth over the head of his cock. It's really the cruelest tease, but I'm having so much fun.

He fists my hair and then reaches for his belt, for the fasteners that I've deliberately "forgotten" all about. With one quick motion, he flicks at the auto-fastener and before the belt can slither into its casing, he's shoving his trou down and then his big, thick, glorious cock is in my face. The head of him is so deep a blue it's practically purple, and as I watch, a bead of pre-cum glides down the rounded crown. "Take it," Adiron rasps. "Take it in your mouth, love."

My pussy clenches hard again. He's being so bossy, and it's turning me on like wild. I love that his hand is forceful in my hair, pressing me toward his cock. As if I need more encouragement. I drag my parted lips over the ridges along his shaft, teasing and lightly sucking. I deliberately avoid the head of him just because I know it's the most sensitive. I do give his tail another squeeze, though, and then slide my other hand up to toy with his spur. Weeks of trial and error have taught me that it's not all that sensitive, but sometimes when I rub him on the underside, it sends a shiver up his spine. I do that tonight, milking the base of his tail as I do, and I'm rewarded with a shudder.

"Keffing tease," he growls. "You were all over my cockhead a moment ago. Do I need to paint an arrow on my thighs pointing to it?"

I giggle, giving him a naughty look. Adiron always makes sex fun. Even when he's trying to be firm and take control, there's still an element of teasing. "You act like it's been years since I licked your cock. I don't think it's even been a full day."

"It's been at least twelve hours," he pants. "Twelve long, arduous hours without that sweet mouth."

"Poor baby." I stick out my lower lip in a pout and then

throw him a bone. I flick my tongue out and give him the tiniest, most ridiculous little lick on the head of his cock.

"Now that's just sad," Adiron says, even though another shudder rips through him. More beads of pre-cum slide down the head, and his tail jerks wildly. "You can do better than that."

Chuckling, I give him another stingy lick. My pussy is absolutely flooded at this point, and I'm about to slide my hand into my own pants and give my body some relief.

"Oh, Jade. Jade, Jade, Jade." He pretends to be disappointed. "I'm going to have to show you how to lick properly, aren't I, baby?"

And just like that, he turns the tables on me. I suck in a breath. "Yes, please," I whisper.

"Get on your back for me, love. It's time for lessons."

I bite back a whimper as I lower myself onto the blankets. He helps me undress, undoing the auto-fasteners on my clothing. I lift my hips to help along, but my focus is entirely on my big, sexy mate. I love the way he watches me, his eyes gleaming with approval when my heavy breasts spill out of the band I use to hold everything in place. I love how he tugs my pants off and then runs his hands over my wide hips—because he loves my generous body. He loves my rounded stomach and my jiggly thighs and my oversized, un-perky breasts. He adores every bit of me and it shows in the way he looks at me, like I'm a treat he can't wait to eat up.

Nothing's a bigger turn-on than a man that finds you incredibly sexy.

I cup my own breasts as he tosses the last of my clothing aside, teasing my nipples. They're small and tight with arousal, the tips sensitive, and I wonder if he's going to go for breasts first or just head straight between my thighs. "Waiting on my lessons," I tell him, breathless. "Ready to be schooled."

Adiron groans, his hands skimming my legs from knee to thigh before he pushes them apart. He falls between my knees, kneeling next to the bed. "Shall I show you how it's done, then?"

Oh god. I manage a tiny nod, my fingers teasing my nipples.

He leans in and plants his mouth over my pussy, brushing his lips over the curls covering my mound. After the first shaving, I grew the hair back because he actually likes the way it looks. He thinks my body is fascinating, and there's no shame in the hair it grows. It's just another thing I love about him, and when I feel his tongue flick against my clit, I give up on playing with my breasts and prop up on my elbows instead, so I can watch him work my pussy.

Our eyes meet as his hands clasp my legs and his tongue dances over my clit. I shudder, breathless, as he begins a delicate lapping, each stroke of his tongue teasing the underside of my clit. It's the lightest, flickering touch, and he knows it makes me absolutely wild. I let out a little cry as he continues, his gaze locked on me, his tongue endlessly working against the bud of my clit. He doesn't change his rhythm even when I start to squirm against his mouth, or when I push my hips at his face. He just keeps on, licking and licking and licking until I'm begging for more, begging for him to fuck me hard, begging for him to fill me up.

"So close," I whimper, grabbing at his horns and working my hips frantically against him. "Please, Adi. Give me your cock. I want to come with you deep inside me."

His tongue swipes hard at my clit, earning another cry from me. He slides his big body over mine, moving on top of me on the bed. His mouth is wet with my juices, and he leans in and gives me a hard, earth-shattering kiss even as I wrap my legs around his waist. I need this. Need him.

"Tell me what you want, Jade," he murmurs between kisses. His hips roll against mine, his cock rubbing against my wet folds in a tease.

"You," I pant, desperate. "Want you deep inside me."

"You want this?" He presses the head of his cock to my entrance. "You want me to fill you up? Take you so hard that you scream my name?"

"Yes," I moan. I dig my nails into the fabric of his shirt, desperate to hold on. "Give it to me."

Adiron hauls my leg up, resting my ankle on his shoulder. "You want deep?"

Do I ever. I nod frantically, arching against his cock.

He thrusts into me with one searing push that takes my breath away. For a moment, the invasion of his cock into my body feels like too much, and then it immediately slides into the sweet ache of being filled. I close my eyes in bliss, because there's nothing quite so perfect as your lover stuffing you full of his cock. He fills all the hollow spaces inside me and somehow still leaves me hungry for more.

"Does that feel better?" He adjusts himself over me, hand on my hips. When I open my eyes, I see nothing but Adiron, my foot next to his ear, his face toward mine

I choke out a word that might be an agreement of some kind. It might just be me making noises. All I know is that his piercing is rubbing right against the perfect spot inside, and every twitch of his body makes my pussy clench in response. He changes the angle slightly, and then I'm getting his spur, too, and it's glorious. He knows just how to move over me, how to make my body sing, how to make me come so hard that I see stars and my body floods with release.

It's over too quickly. It always is. Someday, I tell myself as I float down from my orgasm. Someday we'll figure out how to last for hours. For now, though, chasing the sweetness of a quick climax is perfection, because it leaves room for so many more.

There's nothing sweeter than hearing Adiron pant my name as he finds his own release, too. Nothing better than feeling him shudder over me, his seed jetting inside my body. I love the way he tenses up and collapses over me, careful not to crush me under his weight. I run my fingers lightly over his arm, his shoulder, his neck, all the way up to his horns as he catches his breath.

"Better?" I whisper as he rolls onto his side. The slide of his cock out of my body always leaves me feeling a little bereft, as if I've lost something special. Of course, in the next moment, he pulls me against him, tucking my head against his chest, and that lonely feeling is gone just as fast as it arrived.

"You always know how to make me happy," Adiron tells me, hugging me against his chest.

I let my fingers "walk" along the planes of his pectorals, down toward his navel. "Well, I didn't get to finish my sexy massage, so I guess we'll have to pick up where we left off later."

"I agree," he says immediately. "My cock feels relaxed, but now you need to work on the rest of me."

I snort, amused, and my smile widens when he presses a kiss to my wild hair. My natural, kinky curls are probably standing on end right about now, but I'll fool with them in the morning. I dip a finger into his belly button. "So how long do you think we'll be here, since Sophie doesn't want to go with us? I know it probably changes your plans."

He rubs my shoulder, and I can tell by the silence that he's thinking. "Not really," Adiron says after a long pause. "Sophie's not a good navigator, so it's not like I could rely on her anyhow. She mostly just cleaned up after us and did odd jobs on the ship. If you don't mind pitching in to help me run things, I think we'll be fine. I can show you how to work some of the basic controls, too."

Learning how to fly the ship? "I like that idea. So, just you and me on the *Little Sister*?"

"You, me and some weaponry." His fingers dance up and down my arm. "I'll show you how to work those, too. It's gonna be a lot of learning for a while. Hope that's okay."

"You mean we won't be able to just make love all day long?" I tease.

"I didn't say that. You can sit on my cock while I show you how to work a blaster." He pauses for a moment. "Kef me, that sounds really hot."

I smack his chest. "Focus, Adi."

"Oh, I'm focused. Give me a moment and I'll be ready to go again."

This man has ridiculous stamina. I just roll my eyes—but I'm secretly pleased. I love that he can't get enough of me, because the feeling is mutual. "So where are we headed once we leave? Any ideas?"

His hand drops to my stomach. "First, we'll head to a nearby station and get some additional fuel cells and supplies. We'll load up on protein cakes and some alternatives to noodles, because I don't want you wasting away. You need to eat."

"And fruit?" I ask hopefully.

"All kinds of fruit," he agrees. "Jerrok says he's got a few contacts at Three Nebulas Station. They'll be able to help us out." He rubs my arm thoughtfully. "Once we're done there, I think we'll head back into Slatran space. An escape pod's supposed to chart a course for the nearest habitable planet or closest station, so we'll head to the *Buoyant Star's* last location and see what we can find."

It sounds reasonable. "What if we run into Shaalyn again?"

Adiron chuckles. "Well, that would be some luck, wouldn't it? It'd be your call again, though. We'd do with her as you want."

I think about what Zoey told me. How Shaalyn killed her crew to save her own ass. I think about how she stabbed Adiron in the gut and left him to die, too. I think about the baby inside me, too. I might never be as stone-cold as some of the corsairs, but Zoey was right. I do need to stop thinking like a human and expecting the laws to be fair and just.

They weren't exactly fair and just on Earth, either.

The soft heart can stay, but it can't interfere with the life I'm building out here. The next time we meet Shaalyn, I won't feel like a monster if her execution is in my hands. I'll remind myself about her stabbing Adiron.

"Once we find my brothers and your friends, well, there's just the matter of the sleepers on the *Star*. Jerrok's promised to keep them safe on the *Star* until sa'Rin comes for them."

"They'll be safe on his planet?" I ask again, though I know I've asked it a dozen times since I first heard about it.

"Absolutely. I've been there a few times myself. Humans everywhere." He chuckles. "And lots of crops. Maybe if you and me ever get tired of the corsair life, we can take our kid and head out that way."

I smile up at him. "I think I'd like that. But for now, I'm just happy with you."

He touches the tip of my nose. "Not scared of raising a baby in space anymore?"

I've seen Fran handle things for the last few weeks and while a ship isn't an ideal situation, I feel at home in one after spending the last three years in confined halls. And if I learn how to operate one, so much the better. "Not at all. Especially if you're going to teach me how to fly."

"I will teach you anything and everything you want, Jade." Adiron taps the tip of my nose again. "Just as long as you love me."

I slide my hand lower, to where his messy, half-hard cock rests on his thigh. "You couldn't get rid of me if you tried. Haven't you heard? We humans are a clingy, filthy lot."

His eyes flare with interest. "How filthy?"

I lick his nipple and give his stirring cock a squeeze. "The filthiest."

Adiron gives a sigh of pleasure. "My favorite."

Mine, too.

AUTHOR'S NOTE

Hello there!

Whew, what a year this has been! 2020 has definitely been one for the books....and we call it the black moment. ;) That's the moment in plotting a romance where everything hits the fan and everything is terrible and it seems as if nothing will work out for the hero and heroine. So yeah. 2020. It needs a collective punt out the door.

This is a series I've meant to do for a long time. Those of you that have followed me on Facebook for a while know that I have PLANS! GREAT PLANS! And not all those plans come to fruition because my eyes are too big for my plate. I've wanted to write about Adiron, Kaspar and Mathiras ever since they showed up in Zoey's book (Deceiving the Corsair). I also had an idea for a ship 'abandoned' in space but a few humans were left behind on it and they lured pirates to their doom, just like space sirens.

(Sidenote: I totally should have called this Space Sirens. Hello, missed opportunity.)

The two ideas collided and I couldn't wait to get started on the Corsair Brothers...except I'm already writing a jillion things. Sigh. So it got pushed. And pushed. Every January I make my tentative schedule for the year and wiggle things around as we go, and Corsairs always got wiggled off because there were dragons to write, or Icehome books, or what have you.

BUT! With the pandemic raging, I started doing serials. I know how brutal it is to wake up and see nothing but terrible shit everywhere you click, so I wanted to keep the serials going. I like the idea of having something shiny and fun to look forward to on the 'net every day. I threw up a poll and asked people what story they wanted for the serial after WHEN SHE BELONGS and Corsairs won!

Thus, I was finally able to start the books. :)

You'll notice at this point not everything was wrapped up. Is Shaalyn gone for good? Where's Kaspar? Where's Mathiras? What happens with Straik? How *did* all those humans get there? Since this will be a series that's very closely tied together, I'll be answering them throughout the books. By the time we hit the end of book 4, all questions will be answered, but I might dance around them for a while first. :)

Adiron was truly fun to write. It's so nice to have a hero that doesn't take himself (or anything else) too seriously but is still head over heels for his heroine. He's a simple man with simple pleasures, but still gets shit done and wrecks things if his woman is in danger.

I did get a little flack from people who didn't like Jade nearly as much as Adiron. Some readers thought Jade was too boring, too responsible, or that Adiron needed someone more fun. I feel that a relationship works best when both parties bring something special out of their partner. In my opinion, Jade works well with Adiron *because* she's thoughtful and serious and responsible. She doesn't try to change him, either, just offers another perspective. Likewise, Adiron loves that Jade cares about others and pulls him back from making foolish decisions. He needs that gentle guidance or he'll go around the universe half-cocked. I thought they were well-matched, personally. Adiron makes Jade feel a little reckless at times, and Jade helps Adiron remember to have a damn plan.

(Also, let's be real. A heroine as fun-loving and careless as Adiron would be a recipe for disaster paired with him. It would make you crazy to read it. Think of 300 pages of Adiron paired with say, Bethiah. You get the idea.)

I had several people disappointed that I didn't show Sophie's reunion with Adiron and Jade on the serial itself. I didn't say anything on Facebook but the truth is, I'd already written the epilogue of them together! I hope it answers any burning questions you had. :)

Kaspar and Alice will be up next. What will it be like to read about a daredevil alien paired with a neurotic sidekick heroine? WE'LL ALL FIND OUT TOGETHER!

I'll be starting this serial mid-January. If you want to follow along, I'll be posting daily chapters on Facebook. If Facebook isn't your thing, I'll also be posting the chapters daily on my website, so you can follow along there!

Stay safe and let's get 2021 here already!

<3

Ruby

WANT MORE TO READ?

All of my books are in Kindle Unlimited, so borrow to your heart's content! Here are my suggestions if you're looking for more to binge on.

Want to read the other Corsair books? Start with:
The Corsair's Captive

...or just Zoey's book?
Deceiving the Corsair

Or maybe you're in the mood for the first serial? An epic slow burn with some sweetness and a cat-alien gladiator hero?
When She Purrs

Or maybe Sophie's book (and the second slow-burn, extra long serial) in which she meets a junker named Jerrok?
When She Belongs

Enjoy!

Made in the USA
Coppell, TX
15 October 2023

22912671R00249